For the first time in one volume, Signet Regency Romance is proud to present a brand-new romance sure to become an instant classic with a title that already is one.

Praise for Melinda McRae's Regency Romances

The Defiant Miss Foster

"Melinda McRae's *The Defiant Miss Foster* is delightful from beginning to end, and the unconventional heroine and caring hero are sure to warm any Regency fan's heart." —Karen Harbaugh

A Highly Respectable Widow

"Ms. McRae delves into her complex hero with the delicacy of a butterfly and the impeccable strength of a master storyteller. These vibrantly alive lovers will linger in your minds and hearts for a long time to come." —*Romantic Times*

The Defiant Miss Foster

and

A Highly Respectable Widow

Melinda McRae

A SIGNET BOOK

SIGNET
Published by New American Library, a division of
Penguin Group (USA) Inc., 375 Hudson Street,
New York, New York 10014, U.S.A.
Penguin Books Ltd, 80 Strand,
London WC2R 0RL, England
Penguin Books Australia Ltd, 250 Camberwell Road,
Camberwell, Victoria 3124, Australia
Penguin Books Canada Ltd, 10 Alcorn Avenue,
Toronto, Ontario, Canada M4V 3B2
Penguin Books (N.Z.) Ltd, Cnr Rosedale and Airborne Roads,
Albany, Auckland 1310, New Zealand

Penguin Books Ltd, Registered Offices:
80 Strand, London WC2R 0RL, England

Published by Signet, an imprint of New American Library, a division of Penguin
Group (USA) Inc. *A Highly Respectable Widow* was originally published by Signet in January 1992.

First Printing, August 2003
10 9 8 7 6 5 4 3 2 1

To all my wonderful coworkers at FCN and SON.
And, of course, Liz, Jena, Megan, Sharon,
Elizabeth, and Jen,
without whom writing would be impossible.

The Defiant
Miss Foster

Chapter One

London, 1817

"**W**hat do you mean, no one has seen to the welfare of these children for the past seven years?" Valentine Debenham, late of His Majesty's 20th Light Dragoons, and fifth Baron Newkirk, stared aghast at his man of business.

The thin law clerk cleared his throat. "Apparently it slipped your father's mind before his death . . ."

"Along with a hundred other matters," Val mumbled under his breath. The estate had been in a shambles when Val returned from the Continent after Napoleon had finally been vanquished. But this gross neglect on the part of his father was beyond understanding.

"Has there been any contact whatsoever with these children?" he asked. "Do you even know if they are still alive?"

"The quarterly allowances have been paid out regularly," the clerk replied.

"To whom?" Val demanded. "Did no one ever think to ask?"

"As long as there were no irregularities with the funds . . ." The man fell silent under Val's baleful glance. "I will assign someone to make inquiries. . . ."

Val rose to his considerable height, all the better to intimidate the man. "I shall investigate the matter myself. And you can tell Mr. Jenkins that if this is how he intends to manage the rest of my affairs, I shall transfer my business to another firm."

"Oh, I am certain that won't be necessary." The clerk smiled uneasily as he sidled out of the room.

Val walked to the window and stared out, oblivious to the bustling London street below.

Damn his father. Of all the irresponsible, mismanaged actions that had marked his sorry existence, this was by far the worst. Neglecting the welfare of a family of innocent children. It was beyond all belief. But then, his father had never taken any responsibility seriously while he lived. Why should it be any different after his death?

And now, instead of finally having the freedom to lead a carefree existence, Val found himself obligated to journey to Gloucester to investigate the fate of his unknown wards. And to try to rectify the ill effects of years of neglect.

If it were even possible.

Val shook his head. What did he know about raising children? Soldiers he could deal with. But children? He didn't even know their ages or sex. How could he make provisions for them when he knew so little?

Yet he had led soldiers through the mud, rain and heat of Spain, the fields of France, and the hedgerows of Belgium. Managing the affairs of a group of children could not possibly be that difficult.

Three days later, Val left his well-sprung coach, driver, and valet at the inn in Wickworth, and rode on alone to Kingsford Manor, to make the first acquaintance of his wards. If the situation was an unmitigated disaster, the fewer who knew of it, the better.

After twice riding down the wrong lane, Val finally guided his horse along the drive of what he hoped was his destination. Judging from the appearance of the neglected grounds, he was in the right place. Large ruts that would endanger the wheels of the sturdiest carriage pocked the drive, overgrown shrubbery warred with unmowed lawn, and as he neared the house, he saw several boarded-up windows in the old Jacobean structure.

Pray that all the children were alive and well. The eldest boy, he'd learned, was twenty and no doubt had cared for his siblings all these years. Val must beg his forgiveness. Even if their dismal situation was not Val's fault, he was legally their guardian—had been for seven long years, even if he had not known of it—and the blame for their unfortunate condition would be laid at his feet. He vowed to rectify the situation as soon as humanly possible.

Fearing the lack of stabling suitable even for a hired horse, Val looped the reins through a bush and left his mount chomping contentedly at the knee-high grass. Brushing the fine road dust from his coat, Val crossed the weed-strewn drive and started up the stairs.

"Halt!" A childish voice hailed from behind him. "Who goes there?"

Val turned and looked around, but he did not see anyone.

"I am seeking the children of Gerald Foster," he announced.

"Why do you want them?" the unseen child demanded.

"Is this the Foster house?"

Val thought he heard a whispered exchange, coming from his left. There, by that overgrown forest of rhododendrons. Their untrimmed branches were tall enough and thick enough to conceal an entire regiment.

"Is this the Foster residence?" he asked again.

"Maybe," came the reply. "Who are you?"

"I am Valentine Debenham. Guardian to the Foster children."

"Guardian? We—I mean—they don't have a guardian."

Val smiled with relief. He had arrived at his proper destination. "Oh, I assure you that they do. And unless I am mistaken, I am speaking with one of my wards at this moment. Come out and show yourself."

He heard whispered consultations—there were clearly two of them hiding in the bushes.

"Come out," he said. "I will not hurt you."

A loud rustling sounded and the branches bent and swayed, then a young boy of about eight or nine crawled out from under the boughs and gingerly edged toward him. His grimy face and tattered, mud-splattered breeches spoke of the neglect Val feared.

"How do I know you're who you say you are?" the tow-headed boy demanded with wary eyes.

"Why would anyone pretend to be who they are not?" Val asked, feeling a growing exasperation at the young man's doubts. He was here to help them, after all, and they should be welcoming him with open arms. "Now, let's go inside and find the rest of your family."

He turned back toward the house and found himself staring into the barrel of a shotgun.

Gingerly, Val lifted his hands, palms up, without taking his eyes from the young boy who held him at gunpoint. The lad couldn't be more than a few years older than the other boy, and although his hair was darker, the resemblance between the two was obvious. Brothers.

"I mean no one any harm," Val said.

"We will have to see about that," the older lad said, gesturing toward the house with the gun. "You can answer our questions inside."

"Really, there is no need for this." Val forced a smile. "There has been a bit of confusion, and I did not know that I was your guardian, but I assure you that all has changed. You will have an adult to look after you from now on."

"Inside," the lad with the gun repeated.

Val shrugged. Once he sat down with the older brother and explained the situation to him, there'd be no more of this nonsense. He started up the stairs, the two boys following closely behind.

"Is your eldest brother here?" Val asked. Surely, he'd be more reasonable than these children. But they did not answer.

The entry hall was dim and empty of any furnishings. A sharp odor of wet dog assailed his nostrils. They escorted him into what he supposed was the drawing room. Dust covered every surface, the window hangings were torn and faded, the furniture old and patched. Val felt a stab of guilt at these obvious signs of neglect.

"Sit down," the armed boy ordered, pointing to a chair by the window.

Val complied. He did not truly feel he was in danger, but it would not do to antagonize his captors, either. Not while they were armed.

"What is your name?" he asked, hoping to assuage the youngster's apprehensions.

The boy continued to eye him with suspicion, but did not answer.

"Really, this is growing absurd," Val said. "Run along like a good lad and get your older brother. I will explain matters to him."

"Now, Eddie," the armed boy said.

A rope dropped over Val's chest, trapping his arms and pinning him against the chair.

"What the devil!" Val pulled and strained at his bonds, but the surprise attack had given his captor enough time to secure the knots and Val was truly a prisoner. He'd eluded the best soldiers France had to offer, yet here he was, imprisoned by two grubby urchins.

"Tie him good," the gun-wielding boy urged his brother. "We don't want him to escape."

From the corner of his eye, Val caught a glimpse of the first boy he'd encountered.

"Eddie? Is that your name? Untie me now, and we can both forget about this unfortunate episode."

Eddie glanced at his brother, then shook his head.

Val glared at the older boy. "Tell him to release me at once!"

"We'll leave that decision up to Nicky," he said. "He should be back in a few hours."

A few hours? They planned to keep him here trussed up like a goose for that long? Val's gaze narrowed with his growing anger. "If you do not free me this minute, I assure you, I will—"

"We'll take turns standing guard outside," the armed lad said to his brother as they headed for the door. "I'll take the first watch. Go find Sam and have him keep a lookout for Nicky."

"Stop!" Val yelled. "Both of you come back here right now!"

The door shut behind them, leaving Val alone.

He struggled against his bonds, but the knots were expertly tied and did not give an inch. *Trapped!*

The situation would have been laughable if it were not so emblematic of his own failure—however inadvertent— to provide the family with proper guidance. Well-raised children would never have done such a thing.

There was nothing to do but wait until "Nicky" came back and straightened this mess out. Once he was free, however, Val vowed to take steps to make certain that those hellions never practiced their crimes on unsuspecting visitors again.

"Really, Kat, how can you think that Jacobson's animal is anything more than a knock-kneed plow horse?"

Katherine Foster glared at her older brother, astride the bay horse beside her. "How many times have I told you, Nick, you have to look them in the eye. *That* is where you can see their true nature. He might not be pretty, but I wager he'll sail over a fence like a bird."

"Hmpph." Nicholas Foster shook his head. "I think you've got it wrong this time."

She flashed him a smug smile. "We shall see. I intend to buy him."

"You're making a mistake," he warned.

"Tell me that again after the first hunt next fall." She dug in her heels, and her mount took off down the road. The element of surprise would allow her to beat Nicky this time.

Still, it was nearly a dead heat when they pulled up in front of the stables.

"I nearly had you," Nick shouted.

"Nearly is not close enough." Kat gave her mount a congratulatory pat on the neck before they started walking their heated horses toward the front of the house.

"Nicky! Kat! Come quick!"

She swiveled about to see Sam, one of the ten-year-old twins, come running out from behind the house.

"What new disaster have you tumbled into now?" Nick grumbled as he quickly dismounted. "Can't leave you alone for even an hour without—"

"We've captured a prisoner," Sam gasped. "He's in the drawing room now. Tom and Eddie are guarding him."

Nick arched a brow. "A prisoner? Don't tell me you've tied up the vicar again."

"He says he's our guardian," Sam announced. "But we don't have one, do we? So we know he's lying. That's why we tied him up."

Kat exchanged a surprised glance with Nick. "Guardian?" she whispered uneasily and swung a leg over her horse and slid to the ground.

Nick tossed his reins to Sam. "Walk the horses while we go investigate," he said. "And don't you dare put them into their stalls until they're completely cooled down."

"But I want to see what you do with the fellow!"

"Then you shall have to wait until we finish walking the horses," Kat said.

She watched as Sam's transparent emotions flitted across his face. He wasn't often allowed to take charge of their horses, but the lure of a mysterious visitor was compelling.

"Don't decide anything until I'm done," he said at last with a warning look as he took the reins from her.

"Wouldn't think of it," Nick replied briskly and made a sweeping gesture toward the house. "Lead on, sister, dear. Let's find out why this poor, unfortunate man has crossed our path."

Thomas, Sam's twin, stood sentry outside the drawing room, looking fiercely vigilant with his shouldered shotgun.

"The prisoner is inside," he reported.

"Dare I ask why he was taken prisoner?" Nick asked.

"He was nosing around outside," Thomas replied. "Gave us this cock-and-bull story about being our guardian. We thought it best that he be detained until you could question him."

"Good thinking, soldier." Nick ruffled his hair.

"He's been a most unruly prisoner, sir."

"We'll soon see to that," Nicky said. "Now, run outside and help Sam with the horses."

"But . . ." Thomas's enthusiasm faded.

"Are you protesting an order, soldier?" Nick demanded with feigned sternness.

"No, sir." Thomas swallowed hard, then handed Kat the shotgun and dashed down the hall.

"Why would anyone come here and claim to be our guardian?" Kat asked as she reached for the door latch.

"Mark my words," Nicky said. "He's a troublemaker, up to no good. We'll soon send him on his way."

It seemed an interminable time until Val finally heard new voices in the hall. Had "Nicky" arrived at last? He hoped so; it was damned uncomfortable being tied up.

The drawing room door swung inward, and his spirits lifted as two young bucks sauntered into the room.

"So you're the bothersome prisoner." The taller man stepped forward and carefully scrutinized Val. "My brothers tell me you've been feeding them some taradiddle about being our guardian. What kind of a low-life beast are you, to scare small children like that?"

"I—am—your—guardian." Val spat out the words. "Now, get me out of this damned chair."

The other, slighter man stepped closer. "I don't know, Nick," he said. "He doesn't look very trustworthy to me."

"I am completely trustworthy," Val protested. "I am the Baron Newkirk."

"Do you have any documentation to prove your tale?" the one named Nick demanded.

"Well, no," Val said. He'd expected to be welcomed with open arms by the hapless children. Who would have thought he needed to justify himself to them?

"I see." The two men exchanged looks.

"What do you think we should do?" the shorter one asked.

"Untie me," Val said in the voice that had successfully urged countless soldiers into the heart of the maelstrom.

"I want some proof that you are who you say you are," the slight man insisted.

"How can I prove anything when I'm fastened to this blasted chair?" Val demanded, his temper growing shorter. "Let me go and I shall prove who I am."

That blasted brat Eddie ran back into the room. "Don't listen to him, Nicky, it's a trick! He already said he doesn't have any papers."

"Well?" Nick demanded. "Explain yourself!"

"My carriage, my coachman, and my valet are waiting at the Crimson Goose in Wickworth," Val said. "I rode here alone so as not to cause undue alarm." He looked at them grimly. "Obviously an error on my part. My men will vouch for me—and the purpose of my mission."

"I could ride to Wickworth and investigate," the slighter brother suggested.

Nicky pulled up a chair facing Val. "Tell me your story—the whole of it."

Val took a deep breath. "My father—the late Baron Newkirk—was apparently appointed your guardian many years ago. And while this is no defense of his actions, I can only say that he neglected all his affairs as industriously as he neglected yours."

He glanced at the two older brothers, whose expressions remained impassive.

"Upon my father's demise, the guardianship came to me, but I had no idea of this, as he left no indication that such an obligation ever existed. My man of business only revealed the matter three days ago. I am here to apologize for what has transpired over the years, and to set about making matters right as quickly as I can."

Nick regarded him thoughtfully for a moment, then rose from his chair. "Untie him, Eddie. I think we need to listen to his story."

With obvious reluctance, the little brat began working at the knots that held Val prisoner. Once his hands were free, he rubbed his cramped wrists, seeking to restore feeling to his numbed fingers.

When he felt his legs would once again support him, Val rose, took two steps across the floor and grabbed Eddie by the collar.

"I intend to have a word with you," he growled.

"Tom told me to do it!" Eddie cried. "I wouldn't have touched you otherwise, honest!"

"The mark of a true man is taking his punishment and not making excuses," Val said.

"Then you'll have to punish me, too, sir." The slight lad who'd accompanied Nick stepped forward.

"And me." The lad who'd first pointed the gun at him came in from the hall and hastened to his brother's side. "I helped guard you."

"Well, I did not have a damn thing to do with this escapade, and I am not going to take any blame whatsoever," Nick drawled. "Do what you will with them. Bed without supper. Scullery duty. Mucking out the stables."

"We have to do that already," Eddie mumbled.

Reason soon tempered Val's anger, and he released his hold on the squirming boy. The lad scurried over to the others and hid himself behind Nick. Val clasped his hands behind his back and stared back at them.

During his years in the military, he'd dealt with all kinds of men—scared young boys, cynical battle-veterans, and even hardened criminals. Men who came from backgrounds as diverse as their appearances. But the military had given them one thing in common—discipline and order.

It was the one thing every member of this household appeared to lack. And it was his duty as guardian to provide it.

"Why don't you all introduce yourselves," he said. "It's time we got to know one another."

"I'm Eddie," the smallest announced, peering cautiously from behind his brother. "But you knew that already."

"I'm Sam," confessed the one who'd first held him at bay with the shotgun.

"Thomas." Another boy, identical in size and appearance to Sam, stepped forward. Twins, Val realized.

"Would you like to try that again?" Nick demanded, glaring at the two.

"Thomas," said the shotgun-toting one—or had that been the other one? Val's head was starting to swim in confusion.

Nick grabbed each twin by a shoulder. "This is Sam," he said, shaking the one on his left. "And the one who captured you is Thomas."

"Identical?" Val asked with dismay.

The slight brother nodded. "No one *outside* the family can tell them apart."

Val looked to the older siblings. "And you two are?"

"Nicholas Foster." The taller young man executed an elegant bow and turned to the last, remaining brother.

"I'm Kat."

Val looked at him in puzzlement. "Kat?"

"It's short for Katherine," Eddie announced.

Katherine? Val stared in disbelief, but as he peered closer, he noticed the soft line of the jaw, the delicate earlobes peeking out from beneath the short cropped curls, the saucy tilt to the nose and realized, to his horror, that the booted, breeched, and jacketed person who stood before him, smelling strongly of horse, was a female.

Chapter Two

Kat felt herself reddening under the tall, dark-haired baron's intense scrutiny. His brown eyes assessed her with arrogant disdain. She lifted her chin and glared back at him with growing dislike.

"Please tell me that you only wear those clothes around the estate," he said, his displeasure evident.

"These are my riding clothes," Kat replied. "I was riding."

"I expect you to dress appropriately for dinner," he said, and his gaze spanned the group. "That goes for all of you. You do dine together in this house, don't you?"

Nick laughed. "Of course we do."

"Good." The baron regarded them each in turn. "I intend to take the time between now and dinner to speak with each one of you, individually, to discuss my plans for your future."

His plans? Kat opened her mouth to protest, but Nick delivered a well-placed elbow in her side that kept her silent.

Well, she would not remain silent for long. Thomas and Eddie may have gone a bit far tying the man to a chair, but she was not going to allow this stranger to suddenly appear and make plans for *her* family. They had survived just fine without anyone's help for years, and they had no need of it now.

Newkirk turned his stern gaze on Eddie. "Since you're the youngest, I shall start with you."

Eddie tossed a pleading glance at his older siblings. "Don't leave me alone with him, Nicky. He doesn't like me."

"Can you blame him, brat?" Nicky playfully tousled Eddie's mop of dirty blond hair, then winked at the baron. "Don't be too hard on him."

"I won't," Newkirk promised.

Nick pulled Kat into the hall before she could offer up a protest. Sam and Thomas came trooping behind them. The moment they were in the hall, with the drawing room door closed behind them, Nick grabbed them both by their collars.

"You two run along to the kitchen and tell Cookie that there will be one more for dinner. And stay out of trouble until then!"

"Race you!" Sam cried and dashed across the floor, Thomas at his heels.

"Do you think it wise to leave Eddie alone with that man?" Kat asked, glancing toward the drawing room. "I don't trust him."

"Eddie's old enough to take responsibility for his actions," Nicky replied. "You can't mother him forever, you know."

"He's only eight!" Kat protested.

"And high time he learned to fight his own battles."

Kat looped her arm in Nick's and pulled him out the front door.

"What are we going to do about the baron?" Kat sat down on the top step, resting her chin on one palm.

"I don't know that there's much that we can do."

Nick's indifferent shrug only increased Kat's irritation.

"How can he suddenly decide to interfere in our lives?" she demanded. "It's simply not fair."

"Well, I, for one, am not so certain that this is a bad thing. He may only be a baron, but he can offer an entrée into society that we never had before."

"Society—poo! What do you or I care for that?"

"We'll have access to a better pool of horseflesh, for one," he reminded her.

"I doubt he's much of a horseman," she sniffed.

"He may have friends who are. Just think of it, Kat, we could go to Tattersalls, watch the races at Newmarket and Ascot. Maybe even hunt with the Quorn."

"*You* could hunt with the Quorn. Even I know they would not permit me to ride."

"There are other big hunts—surely some of them allow women." He looked thoughtful. "I wonder if he has a house in London."

"The baron?" She snorted derisively. "He probably lives in the country and grows prize mangel-wurzels."

Nick laughed. "If mangel-wurzels are his passion, then I don't think you have much to worry about. He can plant the whole back field in them; it won't bother us."

Despite Nick's optimism, Kat felt her spirits sinking. "I have a bad feeling about him."

"Nonsense. You're worrying over nothing. Now that he knows we're alive and well, he'll go back to his own affairs. He'll send us a Christmas letter every year, and that will be the end of it."

Kat did not find Nick's words at all reassuring. There was something about this man—those dark, perceptive eyes that had assessed her with such dismay, his arrogant assurance that they would fall in with his plans for them. She knew he was going to disrupt their lives.

Well, if it came to that, he'd soon find out that the Foster family was made of sterner stuff. Once he realized that they had no need of him in their lives, he'd go away and leave them in peace again.

"Dress appropriately for dinner," indeed!

Val shook his head in amazement as the last of the three younger boys scampered off. That had been far easier than he had feared. He'd expected some opposition from the brats, but they seemed delighted with his plans for them.

Well, Samuel and Thomas had been excited. Eddie was a mite displeased at learning he was not going to be joining his brothers. But at eight, he was too young to start life in the Royal Navy. St. Giles School would suit him far better. And he was young enough that the discipline there would eventually overcome the lapses of his haphazard upbringing.

Val felt a twinge of dismay that the two older ones had not picked his first choice for them—the military. But even Val had to admit that to a young lad, sailing the open seas sounded far more exciting than banging the drum on a drilling field. The navy in peacetime looked far more enticing than the army.

He thought they would do well, the both of them, once they subjected themselves to the discipline of the naval training school. And discipline they would have; he'd made no bones about it. But it had not dampened their enthusiasm in the least. For them, the navy spelled adventure and they were willing to put up with any discomfort to achieve that.

Val tilted back in his chair before remembering the worn state of everything in the house. The thing would probably collapse under him. Planting all four legs firmly on the floor again, he awaited the arrival of the eldest Foster, Nicholas.

His situation would be more difficult. There was the outside chance that the lad would want to go to university, but Val doubted it would be possible. The poor fellow probably had little Latin or Greek, and without those languages, it was pointless to send him to school. That eliminated the clergy as well, although Val felt it an unlikely choice.

Without a university education, medicine was not possible, either, although there was surgery. Val did not hold the prejudices of many of his class, who regarded surgeons as lesser beings than doctors. He had seen them save too many lives on the Peninsula to doubt their medical skills. But most surgeons learned thorough apprenticeships, and Nick was rather old for that.

Well, Val thought as the door opened, he'd try the easy option first.

"You wanted to see me?" Nick asked.

"Indeed," Val replied. "Please, sit."

Nick sank into the faded-green upholstered chair facing Val, regarding him with a look that held not a trace of apprehension, only rapt curiosity.

"I have dealt satisfactorily with your brothers," Val announced.

"So I hear," Nick drawled. "I warn you, my sister is not going to be pleased with you for sending them away."

"I am doing what I think is best for all of you," Val said.

"So what do you propose to do with me?" Nick asked bluntly.

"Unless you are hiding the soul of a scholar under that devil-may-care exterior—" Nick grinned—"I intended to propose something a little more active. How would you like a commission in a military unit?"

Nick sat up a little straighter. "What regiment do you suggest, sir?"

Val sighed. He knew he was going to have to call in some favors for this one. But it was the least he could do to make up for the years of neglect.

"I think one of the Guards regiments might be possible."

"The Guards?" Nick shot out of seat. "You can get me a commission in the Guards?"

"It is highly likely," Val said, motioning for him to sit down again. "I take it my suggestion meets with your approval?"

"Approval?" Nick exhaled. "I can't think of anything I want more."

"Good. I cannot promise that it will happen immediately—it depends on the state of openings right now—but it shouldn't take too long to find you a spot."

Nick was on his feet again, pumping Val's hand. "Oh, thank you, sir. You cannot know what this means to me."

"Show your gratitude by behaving yourself properly," Val said gruffly, embarrassed by the lad's enthusiasm. The Guards, after all, were not *real* soldiers. Peacocks who strutted their stuff in London. Just the thing to appeal to a naive boy from the country.

"I will make you proud," Nick promised.

"Good. Now, there is one more matter with which I need to consult you."

Nick regarded him impatiently, his mind clearly more focused on the gilt and braid of a Guard's uniform than the fate of his family. "Yes?"

"It concerns your sister," Val said. "I was not told there was a young lady in the family. Obviously, I need to make arrangements for her future as well. Are there any suitable young men in the area whom she—"

Nick laughed aloud. "Kat? Married to one of those louts?"

"Then we shall have to cast a wider net," Val sighed. "I suppose I must take her to London and find her a husband. I wonder if my sister will . . ."

He stopped and stared at Nick, who was making strangled noises.

"You have a comment?" Val asked.

"Don't you think you should discuss your plans with Kat first?" Nick asked.

"What is there to discuss? She shall have a wide range of suitors to chose from in London. With a decent dowry . . ."

"You don't know Kat very well and . . ."

"I will have a chat with her after dinner," Val said. "I'm sure she will be thrilled at the chance to go to town. Now—we had both best hurry, or we will not have time to dress for dinner."

Nick's smile faded. "I wish you the best of luck, sir." He ducked out of the room.

Val shook his head, dismissing Nicholas Foster's misgivings. The girl might be a bit surprised when he first announced his plan, but she would soon warm to the news. After all, what young lady would not wish for a Season in London? Even one as unusual as this one. With his sister Sophie's help, he'd soon have her married off.

He beamed with self-congratulation. He had done a masterful job of sorting out this mess; his job was nearly complete. Being a guardian was not such a difficult task after all.

Kat stood before her wardrobe, her eyes roving over the dresses hanging there. The sprigged muslin would be suitable for dinner *en famille*. But she had no intention of letting that tyrant of a baron dictate to *her*.

She grabbed a linen shirt and the pegged trousers she'd pilfered from Nick. She intended to follow the man's instructions to the letter and dress "appropriately" for dinner. Appropriate for a man, that is.

After searching up and down for a clean cravat, she finally found one that only had a small spot. Clever knotting would easily disguise that defect. With deft hands, she manipulated the length of cloth into an artful design, and with a last look in the pier glass, felt she made a dashing picture. Kat slipped on what had once been Nick's best jacket, with only a few frayed threads on the cuff, stepped into the hall, and headed for her brother's room.

He came out the door before she reached it. He stopped suddenly and gave her a skeptical look.

"Is that what you're wearing to dinner?" he asked.

"Yes," she replied.

"I don't think that's what Newkirk had in mind," Nick mumbled.

"It's too late to change now." She started toward the stairs. "Besides, they say trousers are all the thing and perfectly acceptable these days, even for dinner."

Nick shook his head.

"Well?" She looked at him anxiously. "What did the ogre have to say? What dastardly fate has he planned out for you?"

Nick's eyes brightened. "You won't believe it, Kat! He's going to get me a commission in the Guards."

She frowned. "You're right, I don't believe it. Why would he do something like that? He doesn't even know us."

"He is our guardian," Nick reminded her. "And a right bang-up one, too."

"He didn't waste any time winning you over," she said, feeling a surge of irritation at her brother's enthusiasm. "We shall see how matters stand a few months from now, when you're still waiting for that commission."

"I don't think Newkirk is the type to promise anything he can't deliver," Nick said.

"I would not rely on anything that man said."

Kat pulled open the door and stepped into the drawing room. Sam and Thomas were already there and ran toward her.

"Kat! Kat! Guess what? We're going to be sailors!" The two beamed with equal delight.

"Sailors, hmm?" She grinned at the idea of their latest mad plan. "And how do you hope to accomplish that without any body of water within miles of here?"

"It's Newkirk. He's going to send us to the naval school in Portsmouth."

Kat stared at them, disbelieving what she'd heard. "He is going to what?"

"The naval academy at Portsmouth," a deep voice behind her repeated. "Just the place to straighten out those two scalawags."

Kat whirled about to face Newkirk. "You can't send them away!"

His eyes widened as he took in the sight of her, slowly perusing her from head to toe. Then his gaze narrowed in growing anger. "I thought I asked you to dress for dinner."

"I did," she retorted.

"I hardly find trousers and jacket *appropriate* garb for a young lady of your station. Go upstairs and change immediately."

"I will do no such thing," Kat replied. "This is what I am accustomed to wearing. My brothers have no objections to these clothes."

"I do." Newkirk's voice was icy. "It may come as an unfortunate shock to you, young lady, but outside of what must be the very small circle of your local acquaintances, women who dress in men's clothing are regarded as trollops."

Heat flashed to Kat's face and she balled up her fists in pure rage at the stinging insult. How dare this . . . this *interloper* say such a thing to her.

"Would you care to . . . repeat that?" she demanded.

"He called you a trollop," Eddie said helpfully, then looked around. "What's a trollop?"

"A young woman who does not behave as she ought," Newkirk said.

"Do you stand by those words, sir?" Kat asked.

Newkirk gave a slight nod of his head.

"Then I demand satisfaction," she replied. "You cannot insult me with impunity."

"Oh, for God's sake, quit acting like a hotheaded jackanapes." He gave a disgusted sigh. "You're a female and it's time you started looking—and acting—like one."

Nick took a step forward. "I do think you owe my sister an apology," he said, his voice low and tight.

Newkirk glanced at him, and then back to Kat. "I will apologize to your sister—when she appears before me dressed properly as a lady."

"I will do no such thing," Kat said. "Did you bring pistols with you, or should you care to borrow a set of ours?"

"Don't talk nonsense." Newkirk gave her a dark look. "No one is going to be shooting off any pistols."

"Do you refuse my challenge?" Kat demanded.

"Of course I do," Newkirk snapped. "I cannot duel with a female."

"Then accept mine." Nick took another step toward him.

Newkirk flung up his hands. "Are all the members of this household mad? I'm your guardian—you cannot challenge me."

"I can, and did," Nick said. "Do you accept, or do you concede your honor?"

"This is ridiculous," Newkirk said, his fury apparent in the tightness of his voice. "Pistols it is. At dawn, I suppose?"

"Right now is good enough," Kat said. "Sam, get the pistols from the gun room." She glanced coolly at Newkirk. "Would you like Thomas to be your second? He's quite skilled at loading."

"I can load my own pistol, thank you very much," Newkirk said curtly.

Sam returned with four guns, which he lay on the table, along with powder and balls.

"You may choose first," Nick said to Newkirk.

"Oh, thank you for your hospitality," he said sourly and grabbed one of the pistols.

Kat watched as he expertly loaded it. He had not been protesting out of lack of skill. *Good.* It would make matters more interesting.

Nick quickly loaded a second pistol.

"Where do you want this farce to take place?" Newkirk demanded.

"The lawn out front is best," Nick said. "The ground is fairly level."

"Then let's get this over with. Our dinner, no doubt, is growing cold." Newkirk marched out of the room.

Newkirk was furious at how these striplings had backed him into a corner. When those brats tied him to the chair, Val had not thought his life could possibly get worse. Now, because of the obstinacy of these hell-spawned children, he had to endure this charade of a duel. He could concede, of course. But something told him that if he did, he'd never gain their respect. Once on the dueling field, he would delope and that would be the end of it.

Dueling with one of his own wards. He'd never heard of such nonsense. And he hoped that no one else learned of his folly—he'd be the laughing stock of the entire country.

"Take your spots, gentlemen," Sam said with the casual aplomb of one who managed duels on a daily basis. For all Val knew, he did. The family was probably the bane of the entire county.

"Pace off ten steps, turn, and then shoot at will," the little commander explained.

"Will honor be satisfied with a delope?" Val asked.

Sam nodded. "We observe the official rules here."

"Fine." Val hastily paced off his ten steps, and turned sideways to present a narrow target to his opponent. Not that it mattered; he and Nick would both shoot into the air and the matter would be over with.

He looked at his opponent and found himself staring at that blasted girl.

"Oh, this is ridiculous," he said, and carelessly fired his pistol into the air. "Are you happy now?"

As if in a dream, Val saw the flare of flame and powder, heard the crack of the pistol, and felt a sharp sting on his left buttock. His hand went to the sting; he pulled it away. It was streaked with red.

"She shot me!" he exclaimed, staring at his bloodstained hand with growing realization. "The bitch shot me!"

Chapter Three

*K*at turned to share a grin of triumph with Nick, but her brother was staring at her, his face ashen. He grabbed the still-smoking gun from her hand.

"What have you done?" he demanded.

Kat glanced back at the baron, who regarded her with an expression of disbelief.

"Get into the house, now!" Nick hissed. "I'll try to salvage something from this mess." He gave her a none-too-gentle swat on the rear and pushed her toward the steps.

With one last disdainful glare at Newkirk, Kat stalked off to the house.

That would teach him to insult *her*.

She fixed herself a tray of food from the dining room and carried it upstairs. No telling how long it would be before the others sat down to eat and she was hungry. Besides, Newkirk would no doubt be moaning and groaning about his "terrible" wound, when she'd barely nicked him. Just enough to teach him a lesson.

At least she wouldn't have to worry about him breaking her family apart now. He'd be eager to wash his hands of the lot of them, and they could go back to the way things had been this morning, before the high-and-mighty Baron Newkirk had intruded on their lives.

The thought of his imminent departure cheered her so much that she ate her dinner with great relish and was just finishing the last bite of custard tart when a knock sounded on the door.

"Come in," she said.

Sam, Eddie, and Thomas tumbled into the room.

"Boy, are you in trouble!" Sam chortled.

"The baron's really mad," Eddie said. "He's still yelling at Nicky in the drawing room, and you can hear him clear to the top of the stairs."

"I think it would do the man good to vent a little spleen," Kat said, with supreme indifference. "He has far too much of it."

"But if he gets too mad, he won't let us go to the navy school," Thomas protested. "I want to be a sailor!"

"Me, too," Sam added.

"Nonsense," Kat replied. "Fosters were not meant to be sailors."

"Does this mean I won't be going away to school, either?" Eddie asked with a hopeful expression.

"Away to school?" Kat stared at him, appalled. "He was going to send you away to school?"

Eddie nodded solemnly and looked as if he would cry.

Kat held out her arms and pulled him close. "Of course you are not going to be sent away to school. You will stay here with me and Sam and Thomas and Nicky, just like you always have."

"Promise?" he asked, looking up at her with a hint of tears in his eyes.

"I promise." She planted a kiss on his forehead. "Now, run back downstairs, you three, and see what else you can find out. Try to learn when Newkirk will be leaving."

"Not any time soon, if he intends to ride his horse," Sam said with a snicker.

"That was prime shooting," Thomas added, admiration shining in his eyes.

"Why, thank you," Kat replied. "Now, go!"

She was tempted to follow them downstairs and listen to the tirade coming from the drawing room, but she knew Nick would give her a full report later. And she admitted it probably would be smart of her to keep out of Newkirk's sight for a time. The entire incident was his own fault, of course, but men were so reluctant to acknowledge their failings. There was no need to lord it over him. She could be a gracious victor.

The minutes crawled by, and to her growing unease, neither Nick or the others appeared at her door. Surely, the baron's tirade had worn itself out by now. If she did not receive any news soon, she intended to go downstairs and find out what was going on.

Kat had given one last, impatient look at the clock and rose to her feet, heading for the door, when Nick finally appeared.

"It's about time," she exclaimed. "I was beginning to think the baron had tied *you* to a chair." Then she noticed the grim look on his face. "Nicky, what's wrong?"

"You have to get out of here—now," he said.

"What? Why?"

"He's planning to lay charges against you with the magistrate."

She stared at him in disbelief. "He's what? Is the man mad?"

"Furious is the adjective I would use to describe him." Nick shook his head. "You went too far this time, Kat."

"Nonsense. His nose is merely out of joint because I bested him."

"Be that as it may, we need to leave. Now. I've got Sam hitching the horses to the gig. Pack as many clothes as you can—I don't know how long you're going to have to stay away."

"Where are you taking me?"

"To a friend's," he said. "Once I have you safely settled, I'll come back and try to reason with the man."

"Why don't we reason with him now?" she demanded. "His threats don't frighten me—Petersham won't charge me with anything."

"Petersham isn't the magistrate anymore, in case you've forgotten. Ives has the task, and you know how he holds you in antipathy after you led the hunt through his kitchen garden last fall."

"Oh, that's right." She sighed. "I suppose I must resign myself to exile. A poor stranger, cut off from family and friends, left to shift for herself in a cold, cruel world."

"Lay off, Kat. This is truly serious. We can only hope that if you go away for a time, Newkirk will be willing to forget the whole matter."

"What about the boys?" she asked. "If you go with me, he'll ship all three of them off to the navy before you return."

"I think they'll be safe for a few days. Newkirk is not in a position to do much right now."

"I don't know." Kat felt uneasy at the thought of leaving her brothers alone with that man. "Maybe we should all leave."

"There isn't room for all of us in the gig," Nick said. "Now, hurry! Pack a bag so we can be gone. I want to be well away from here by morning."

"Ha! The man probably sleeps until noon."

"Don't count on it. Just get ready—fast! Go down the back stairs and meet me in the kitchen when you're ready."

Kat was already throwing clothes into a portmanteau when he shut the door behind him.

What was the matter with that horrid Newkirk? He wanted to break up her family, had roundly insulted her, and now threatened to drag her before the law for merely defending her family and her honor.

Circumstances called for a temporary retreat, but if the baron thought that she was going to stand quietly by while he ruined her life, he was sadly mistaken. Kat vowed to not rest until he was out of their lives for good.

*   *   *

"Well?" Val glanced up as Nick reentered the drawing room. "Were you able to persuade her?"

"She was packing as I left," he said, then grinned. "I told her you were planning to call the magistrate."

"That is not such a bad idea." Val took a step and winced at the pain the movement caused.

"I know her actions were inexcusable," Nick said hastily. "And I must accept part of the blame for giving her the gun, but believe me, I had no idea . . . Kat has always been a bit hotheaded and—"

"Do not worry. I don't intend to lay the matter before anyone. Fine picture it would make if I had to admit my own ward shot me in a duel," Val said.

"I'm certain she will wish to apologize when she has thought matters through."

"She can send me a letter." Val winced, the throbbing in his rear growing stronger every minute. "You will send someone for my valet?"

"Thomas," Nick replied. "He could find his way to Wickworth in the dark."

"I don't care how easily he gets there—I just want to make certain he brings my man back." Val limped over to the desk. "Now, here is my sister's direction. I'll post a letter first thing tomorrow, and with luck, it will arrive before you do."

"You are certain that she will not object to having a stranger thrust upon her?" Nick regarded him doubtfully.

"Of course not." Val handed him a leather wallet. "Here is money for your journey."

Nick drew himself stiffly upright. "I am able to pay for our expenses."

"More than likely you are," Val said. "But take this anyway. I will bill the estate if it will make you feel any better."

Nick took the proffered money.

"You are not going to alter your plans regarding . . . my brothers?" he asked anxiously.

"What you really mean is am I still willing to get you a commission?" Val snorted. "Of course I am. You cannot help that your sister is an ill-mannered brat. In fact, I intended to suggest that you continue on to London after you deposit her at Sophie's. I'll send a letter to my staff—you can stay at the town house." He shifted his weight to ease his growing discomfort. "No telling how long it will be until I can travel comfortably."

"You want me to stay in London?" Nick's eyes widened in amazement.

"Only if you promise to behave yourself." Val realized belatedly that turning a young country lad loose in London without supervision was not perhaps the best of ideas. He'd send another letter to one of his army cronies and ask him to take Nick in tow.

"Oh, that I will." Nick regarded him eagerly. "Do you keep a stable in town?"

"You'll find a suitable mount for riding," Val replied.

"That's wonderful!" The young man stared at him, as if unable to believe his luck.

"I suggest you get back to your sister," Val said. "It would not do for her to find us together—it might arouse her suspicions."

Nick swallowed hard, as if he suddenly remembered the part he still had to play in this upcoming drama. Val thought that having to face his sister's wrath when she discovered she had been tricked into leaving the house would more than make up for Nick's part in the duel.

"I will deliver her safely to your sister's home," Nick said.

Val nodded his dismissal and the lad slipped out. At least now he could be sure they would travel with speed—the sooner Nick freed himself from his sister, the sooner he would arrive in London.

He almost wished he could be there to see the scene when the girl learned she'd been duped. He did not envy her brother one bit. Val had to hope that Sophie would be witness to it all and would send him a blow-by-blow account by letter.

Because he was stuck here in this godforsaken place until his injury healed enough for him to travel. Which presupposed that his valet—who had acquired a great deal of medical knowledge while on the Peninsula—would eventually arrive to treat him. Val himself knew enough about medicine, but it was damned difficult to tend to your own posterior.

It occurred to him, in a lowering thought, that she had shot him with great care and deliberation in a spot calculated to cause minimum damage but maximum discomfort. If he wasn't in such pain, he could almost admire her skill.

Val wondered if there was any brandy in the house he could use to ease the pain of his injury.

"Now, Thomas, I am putting you in charge while I am gone." Kat stood with her brothers in the kitchen. She turned to Sam and Eddie. "I expect you two to listen to him."

"Why can't I be in charge?" Sam asked.

"Because Thomas is the older." She pretended not to see the triumphant sneer Thomas gave his brother.

"When are you coming back?" Sam asked.

"As soon as I can," Kat promised.

"Why can't we go with you?" Eddie demanded.

"Because there is not room in the gig," Kat explained. "Do not worry, Nicky will be back in no time."

"But I want you to stay." Eddie looked about to break into tears again.

"I will be back as soon as Newkirk is gone," Kat said. "Now, promise me that you will stay out of his sight as much as possible until Nick returns."

"I bet we could tie him up again now that he's wounded," Sam said.

"That is why Thomas is in charge," Kat replied dryly. "He has sense enough not to try. You are to do absolutely nothing to that man, do you hear me?" She scanned their faces, and they all nodded their reluctant agreements.

"We need to be gone," Nick said, dancing from foot to foot. "Time's a wasting."

"Give me a hug and kiss," Kat said, holding her arms out to her brothers.

Eddie stepped into her embrace. She gave him a fierce hug, kissed him on the cheek, then released him. "Sam?"

"I'm too big for kisses," he said scornfully.

"Samuel Foster! Come here this instant and give me a kiss or I'll . . ."

He reluctantly complied. Kat made her farewells to Thomas, then slipped out of the house to where Nick waited beside the gig. In the dark, she dashed tears from her cheeks, hoping her brother would not see.

"I am worried about the boys while you are away," she said as she scrambled into the seat.

"Nothing is going to happen to them."

"Nothing except Newkirk."

"Newkirk, no doubt, is flat on his stomach, thanks to your shooting," Nick replied acidly. "There is not much he can do to them from that position."

"But what if he sends them away while we are gone?"

"They will be fine," he repeated.

"What if he carries out his threat and goes to Ives?" she asked. "I might never be able to come home again!"

"Should have thought of that before you shot Newkirk," Nick said. "You've had some harebrained plans in your life, but that one takes the cake."

"He needed to know with whom he was dealing," she said. "He will not dare to insult me again."

"No, since now he can throw you in jail instead. You really need to learn to think before you act, Kat. You're not a child any longer. You are going to have to start thinking like an adult."

"Hmmph." Kat crossed her arms over her chest and deliberately looked off into the night.

She felt like she was being sucked into a nightmare from which there was no awakening. This morning, she and Nick had been riding and laughing together without a care; now her family was threatened with dispersement, she was fleeing from the law, and there was no end to their troubles in sight.

All because some stupid man had decided that he knew what was best for her and her family. How typical of a male, to walk in with such an attitude of arrogance, to think that he knew what was best for everyone. She hoped his wound festered and rotted.

Then she winced. She probably would be in a great deal of trouble if the baron died. She changed her wish to incorporate a full recovery, but not after a great deal of lingering, excruciating pain.

"How much farther do you think we have to go?" Kat demanded of Nick as the gig bounced down the country lane. She was hot, tired, dusty, and thoroughly tired of riding in a carriage, even if it was an open gig. They had driven straight through the first night, then stopped for breakfast and a nap before journeying on. Last night they'd slept at an inn, but that had done little to refresh her. Now, as the second afternoon wore on, Kat wondered if they were ever going to reach their destination.

"It shouldn't be too much longer," Nick said. "The inn-keeper said it wasn't above fifteen miles."

"Are you certain this friend of yours will welcome us? He can't be that good of a friend if I've never heard of him."

"I don't tell you *everything*," Nick said. "You should be able to stay a few days, at least."

"What if he isn't there? I wish you'd let me stay with the Phillipses."

"Too close to home," Nick said. "We can't make it too easy for you to be found."

"I'd have been better off hiding in the attic," Kat said. "No one would ever find me amid that jumble."

Nick gave a short laugh.

The afternoon shadows were lengthening when he reined in the team in front of two brick gateposts.

"I think this is the place," he said.

"Then drive on," Kat said. "I am resigned to my exile here."

"It shouldn't be as bad as all that," he said. "Once Newkirk has had time to think matters over, I'm sure he will relent and you can return home."

"You must promise to write me every day." Kat grabbed her brother's elbow. "I want to know everything the boys are doing."

"There are not enough hours in the day to put all *that* to paper."

She gently punched his arm. "You know what I mean. And make certain that Thomas and Sam include Eddie in their plans. I don't want him moping about the house by himself."

"They will be fine." Nick gave her a reassuring smile.

"Newkirk will surely calm down within a week, don't you think?" She searched his face for confirmation. "I could be back home in no time!"

"It's possible," Nick replied.

Kat swiveled back in her seat, eager and apprehensive at the same time as her place of exile drew near. The tree-lined drive seemed to go on forever. Where was the house?

In answer to her question, the drive took a sharp curve

to the left, and they were presented with a splendid vista
of the estate. A sturdy country house that looked to be
twice the size of her family's home sat amid a neatly land-
scaped yard. There did not appear to be a single blade of
grass out of place. Nor any broken windows, chipped
stones, or missing roof tiles. With a start, Kat realized just
how shabby her own home had become.

Nick pulled the carriage up to the entry. Before he could
jump down, a small, dark-haired woman came rushing
down the stairs.

"Oh, you are here at last!" she cried, a broad smile on
her face. "I was hoping you would arrive today."

Kat gave her an uneasy look and followed Nick from
the gig.

"You are Nicholas, certainly," the woman said, taking
Nick's hand. Then she turned toward Kat. "And you, of
course, are Kat."

To Kat's surprise, the woman enveloped her in a welcoming hug. "I am so excited to meet you! We are going to
have such fun together."

Kat darted Nick a bemused glance. He turned away and
lifted her bag from the gig and set in on the ground.

"You are probably exhausted after such a long drive,"
the woman said, linking her arm in Kat's. "We shall have
refreshments inside."

Kat disengaged her arm. "I need to help my brother see
to the horses."

"Oh, don't bother," Nick said.

There was something about his tone of voice that suddenly made Kat uneasy.

"Tell me." The woman took Kat's arm again and leaned
close, her dark eyes wide with curiosity. "Did you really
shoot my brother?"

It took a moment for the import of her words to sink in,
then Kat's eyes widened as the realization hit her. She
whirled to face Nick. "What have you done?"

"It couldn't be helped," he said with a shrug. "You
brought this on yourself."

"Nicholas Foster, of all the underhanded, sneaky, devious things you have ever done in your life, this is the—"

"Is something amiss?" asked the woman Kat now knew
was Newkirk's sister.

"Nothing is amiss," Kat snapped, and walked toward her bag, sitting on the gravel drive by the gig. She grabbed it and made to swing it into the carriage, but Nick took it out of her hands.

"Sorry, Kat," Nick said, an apologetic smile on his face. "But it's for your own good."

"You lied to me!" she yelled. "You're in league with that . . . that monster!"

"Oh, dear," the woman said. "Has Val been up to his usual tricks again?"

Kat glared at her. "You knew all about this!"

"Val wrote and said you would be coming to stay for a while," she said, her expression growing troubled. "I gather he did not share that information with you?"

Kat shot a dark look at Nick. "No, he did not."

The woman shook her head. "How like Val. He forgets he is not in the army any longer and cannot go about ordering everyone around to his liking."

"Well, he is not going to order me around. I am leaving." Kat started to march toward the gig, but Nick grabbed her by the arm.

"You will stay here," he said.

"I most certainly will not!"

"You don't have any choice in the matter," he said.

"Sold your soul for a commission in the Guards, have you?" She felt a grim sense of pleasure at the guilty look that washed over his face.

Newkirk's sister plucked at her sleeve. "I daresay you are unhappy with my brother—and yours—but do not let that ruin matters. I would love to have you stay. We shall have an enjoyable time together."

While Kat frowned at her, Nick climbed back into the gig and swung the horses around.

"I'll never forgive you for this!" Kat yelled as he drove down the drive.

Then the true state of matters hit her. Newkirk had exiled her from the house, imprisoning her here with his sister, so he could carry out his cruel plans for her brothers. Sam, Thomas, Eddie . . . all would be sent away. Her family would be gone.

Kat sank onto the ground and burst into tears.

Chapter Four

*N*ewkirk's sister knelt beside Kat and slipped an arm about her shoulder.

"You're exhausted," she said. "No wonder, with all you have been through. Come inside and rest."

"I can't!" Kat swiped the tears from her face with the back of her hand. "I have to go back before he sends them all away."

"Sends who away?"

"My brothers! He's going to send Thomas and Sam to the navy and Eddie"—Kat choked back a sob—"he's going to send Eddie to school!"

"That does sound dreadful." Newkirk's sister gave her a sympathetic smile.

"That's why I have to get home," Kat said. "I must stop him!"

Newkirk's sister clapped a guilty hand over her mouth. "I am forgetting my manners. I haven't even introduced myself. I am Sophie Bellshaw, Val's sister, as you've guessed. And I know you are Katherine."

"Kat," Kat replied automatically. She examined Newkirk's sister more closely. She had the same dark hair and eyes as her brother, but where Newkirk's expression had seemed to be formed into a perpetual frown, Sophie's was bright and cheerful.

"I find I can never make important decisions on an empty stomach," Sophie said. "Am I right when I guess that your brother didn't bother to stop for a meal since this morning?"

Kat nodded.

"Then come inside and let me feed you. It is the least I can do after Val has caused you such distress."

"But if I don't hurry, it will be too late!" Kat protested, although the mere mention of food set her stomach growling.

Sophie glanced at the failing sun. "You can't think of leaving now! Why, it is nearly dark. Traveling at night is far too dangerous."

Kat had paid no attention to the passing of time, and when she glanced up, she saw Sophie was right. It was nearing dusk. She scoffed at the idea of danger, but she did not relish getting lost in this strange part of the country.

And Newkirk *was* still recovering from his wound. He would not be able to do much until it healed. It had taken her and Nick two days of hard driving to get here; it would take at least that long to return. Newkirk wouldn't even be out of bed before a week.

"I could wait until morning," she said with reluctance.

Sophie clapped her hands. "Good! Now we shall have the entire evening together."

"But I must leave at first light," Kat insisted.

"Is that when your brother is coming back for you?" Sophie asked.

The question hit Kat with the force of a blow. Nick had the gig and was already on his way home. How was she going to travel?

"No," Kat admitted. "He is going home."

"Then there is no hurry for you to leave, if he will be there to see to matters! You can stay here for a few days, at least."

Kat nibbled on her lower lip. After what Nick had done to her, could she trust him to keep the boys safe? He could be working hand in glove with Newkirk regarding their fate, as well.

"I cannot, really," Kat said. "I must get home as soon as possible."

"But how do you propose to travel?" Sophie asked.

Kat stared at her. "Don't you have a carriage I can use? I can drive nearly anything."

Sophie shook her head. "There's only the estate wagon, and one could walk faster than it moves."

"How about a horse, then?"

"Val keeps all his horses in London. There are the farm horses—and my mare—but she could never travel that far. She is a delicate thing."

"Then I'll just have to hire one at the nearest town."

"Did you bring any money with you?"

Kat flushed. She had not given the matter any thought—never anticipating that Nick would first trick her, then drive away without leaving any means to provide for her needs.

"I fear that Nick was carrying our purse. Could I prevail on you . . . ?"

"Val handles all the household accounts, and I only have my pin money, I'm afraid. Will that be enough to hire a coach?"

"It should be enough for a horse, at least," Kat said.

"We still have to get you to the village, and find you a mount. That will take some arrangements." Sophie leaned over and took Kat's hand. "Why don't you do this instead? Write to your brother, reassure yourself that your other brothers are safe, and have him send you the money for your return journey. Or he can even come after you himself. That is far better than you trying to travel alone. Val would be horrified if I permitted you to do such a thing."

Kat gave her any angry glare. "I am supremely indifferent to your brother's opinion."

"Of course," Sophie said hastily. "Think of me instead—I would be worried to death if I knew you were traveling by yourself, and would not be able to eat or sleep until I knew you were safe." She clutched Kat's hand. "Surely, you can wait long enough to have a proper escort? Your brother could be back here within a few days. Is that too long a time to spend in my company?"

Sophie gave her such a pleading look that Kat's resolve wavered.

She did not share Sophie's concerns about traveling. Kat knew she would easily pass for a boy; it would not be that difficult to find a mount and lodging for the one night she had to spend on the road.

But money was the issue. She needed to hire a horse, and unless she intended to travel at a crawl, she had to change mounts periodically. Add to that the cost of food and lodging, even for one night, and she could see that the undertaking was more complicated than she'd first thought.

A letter would reach home before she did. And perhaps by now Nick was having second thoughts about his role in all this. If she wrote persuasively, he might be willing to return for her. And if not, at least he could reassure her that the boys were still safe. She could then apply to their solicitor for funds and—

Her musings came up short when she realized that as their guardian, Newkirk now held the purse strings. She had to appeal to him for every penny that she wanted.

Sophie was right. Kat had to rely on Nick to make arrangements for her return.

"I will write to Nick," Kat announced, "and ask him to send me funds for the journey. If you are so concerned about my traveling alone, you can accompany me. Then it will become your brother's responsibility to get you back here."

"That sounds like a capital plan," Sophie exclaimed. "I shall write to Val and tell him I am coming."

"I don't think that is a good idea," Kat said quickly. "He's rather angry with me right now."

"Oh, that is right." Sophie looked at her eagerly. "You have not told me what happened. You actually shot him in a duel?"

Kat nodded.

"I have tea waiting inside," Sophie said. "And I can arrange to have a simple meal set out in no time. We must be comfortable while you tell the tale."

Kat sniffed again and wiped her nose on her sleeve, embarrassed by her lack of composure. Tears were a rarity for her. "You must think me a big baby."

"Not at all. I am Val's sister. I know what an overbearing tyrant he can be."

Kat thought that she just might get along fine with Newkirk's sister.

Sophie tucked her arm through Kat's, and they walked up the stairs to the front door. "I know you do not wish to be here, but please try to enjoy yourself. I promise you that this will all work out in the end. And I am so excited to have company!"

They walked into a spacious, high-ceilinged entry hall, with carpeted floors and polished woodwork that shone

with a brilliance Kat had never seen in her house. A wide
stair with a carved railing led off on the right to the
upper floors.

Kat found it warm and welcoming.

"Is this your house?" Kat asked.

Sophie laughed. "It is mine in the sense that I live here
and run it. But the estate belongs to my brother."

Kat stiffened. "Does he live here, too?"

Sophie shook her head. "He's been gone so long I don't
know that you can say he lives anywhere. Since he returned
from the Continent, he's been making his home in
London."

"Where was he?" Kat asked, curious in spite of herself.

"In the army, fighting Napoleon."

"At least he's done *one* good thing in his life," Kat muttered under her breath. "Do you have a family?" She
thought a shadow crossed over Sophie's face.

"I live here alone," she said.

"All by yourself?" Kat could not imagine such a thing.
"How dreadful!"

"Exactly," Sophie replied, her cheerful expression returning. "Which is why I am so thrilled that you have come
to visit. Please say that you will stay for a little while,
won't you?"

"I cannot promise that," Kat said. "I have to take care
of my brothers."

"Of course." Sophie led her up the stairs and down a
short hallway. "I hope you do not mind if I entertain you
here. It's my own private parlor. I prefer it to the drawing
room; it is much more the thing for a comfortable coze."

So saying, she walked into a room decorated entirely in
hues of blue and cream. A large vase of fresh flowers stood
on a side table.

Sophie spread her hands. "Isn't it lovely? I decorated
it myself."

Kat gave an indifferent shrug, then realized she was
being rude. It was not Sophie's fault that she was related
to Newkirk.

"It is lovely," she said, although privately she felt as if
she was inside of a large blue jar. The lace and ruffles that
trimmed the curtains and pillows gave the entire room a

cloying, girlish appearance. But the furniture looked comfortable, and it was certainly all quite new, unlike the worn-out furnishings at home.

Sophie sat on a settee covered in pale blue velvet and patted the seat beside her. "Sit down and tell me about your brothers. How old are they?"

Kat gingerly perched on the sofa's edge. "Sam and Thomas are both twelve. And Eddie—he's only eight. Far too young to go to school."

"I certainly agree." Sophie shook her head. "I shall have to speak with Val myself. You all live together then? What is your house like?"

"It's not very elegant but it's comfortable," Kat said. "My brothers and I like it."

"Tell me about Nicholas—he was the one who brought you here—he is the eldest?"

Kat nodded. "He is a mere year-and-a-half older than I."

Sophie let out a sigh. "It must be nice to be so close in age to your brother. Val and I are eight years apart."

"Is he married?" Kat asked.

Sophie shook her head.

"No wonder he is so indifferent to the boys," Kat said. "How old is he?"

"Eight-and-twenty," Sophie replied.

The answer surprised Kat. From his sour disposition and stern expression, she'd thought Newkirk far older. Well past thirty, at least. "You must be the same age as I," Kat said to Sophie. "Nineteen."

"Nearly—I'm past twenty. How wonderful. We could be twins!" Sophie laughed. "Except that we do not look anything alike."

"You don't greatly resemble your brother," Kat said, considering that a great compliment.

"Alas, he did get the best looks in the family."

"Newkirk?" Kat scoffed. "I did not find him handsome."

"Then you must consider me a troll!" Sophie laughed.

"Not at all," Kat said. "You are very pleasant-looking. While he . . . he is a . . ."

"Ogre?"

"Exactly," Kat said. "How did you ever abide living in the same house with him?"

"He was not here often." Sophie looked sad for a moment, then smiled. "Did you enjoy growing up with all those brothers? I think it would be a dreadful madhouse."

"Oh, it is," Kat agreed with a grin. "But an agreeable one. There is always something going on, for good or ill. We are never bored."

"You will probably find life rather dull here, then," Sophie said. "I fear I live very quietly."

Kat was already inclined to agree with her, but did not say so. After all, she did not intend to stay here long enough to grow bored.

A maidservant appeared at the door, carrying the tea tray.

"Ah, here is our tea. This will have to do until I can arrange a more substantial offering." Sophie told the maid to have a tray of bread, meats, and cheeses prepared, then turned back to Kat.

"Oh, do help yourself," Sophie said. "I do not stand on ceremony."

Kat quickly filled her plate and shoved one of the tiny, frosted tea cakes into her mouth.

"These are really good!" she said.

"Our cook does have a way with pastries," Sophie said. "Why, I would be as large as a house if I let her bake as much as I'd like."

"These would be gone in an instant at home," Kat said. "My brothers live for treats."

"That would be the case, too, if Val were here. He loves his sweets."

Kat found it difficult to imagine the baron being fond of anything—except perhaps his own importance. For a moment she wished he were here so she could stuff one of the tea cakes in his mouth and pray that he choked on it.

"What do you and your brothers do for amusement?" Sophie inquired.

"The boys generally get into trouble," Kat said with a rueful laugh. "Nick and I ride, mostly. And visit the neighbors."

Sophie surveyed her breeches and boots. "Astride, I imagine?"

Kat nodded. "Riding sidesaddle is a silly affectation. It's dangerous, for one thing. And even Queen Elizabeth rode astride, so I cannot see why I may not."

"That argument has merit," Sophie said, taking a sip of tea. "I understand that Val does not agree with you."

Kat grinned. "He thought I was a boy at first."

"No!" Sophie stared at her with amazement. "I would have liked to have seen the look on his face when he discovered you weren't."

"Imagine a thundercloud come to life," Kat replied.

Another servant entered the room, carrying a platter of more substantial food. Kat dug into the new offerings with great relish. Traveling always made her hungry.

"Aren't you going to eat anything?" she asked with a guilty twinge when she realized that Sophie was not joining her.

"I am fine," Sophie said. "I did not have such an adventurous day, and I do not need to eat to regain my strength."

"Nick always teases me about my appetite," Kat said, "but I can't help it. I get hungry!"

"There is nothing wrong with enjoying food," Sophie said.

The conversation lagged as Kat busied herself with eating.

She rather liked Newkirk's sister. Sophie was not at all like her stern-visaged brother, which drew Kat to her immediately. She seemed to recognize her brother's imperious nature, and certainly sympathized with Kat's tragedy. Kat had never had a female friend before, and she guessed that Sophie might make a tolerable companion. But there was not time for that now.

Kat would not be staying here long enough to make friends.

Val shifted his position on the pillow. He'd been sitting for far too long, but he was sick of standing or laying on his stomach. Damn that wretched girl. Why couldn't she have nicked his leg instead?

He took Sophie's newly arrived letter from the table beside him and opened the seal, hoping to read the news that her charge had arrived. Coming up with *that* plan had been a stroke of genius on his part. It removed the most bothersome aspect of this guardian business from his hands.

He squinted at the crabbed writing, trying to make out his sister's words. "Heartless beast." "Cruel monster." Obviously, the brat had arrived safely and regaled his sister with tales of his perfidy.

Val concentrated closer on his sister's cramped scrawl.

I had a terrible time keeping her from heading home on foot, if need be, but we have arrived at a compromise of a sort. She wishes her brother to send funds to pay for her return journey, on which I will accompany her. I can delay any precipitate action on her part for a number of days, but I cannot promise I can keep her here beyond a week.

Val—are you certain that you are doing the right thing regarding the younger boys? Would it be better to allow them to stay with their sister for a few more years, and avoid all this fuss? They are not soldiers to order about the battlefield, but mere children.

He tossed the letter aside. He'd thought he could rely on Sophie's good sense in this matter, but it looked as if the wool had been pulled over her eyes already by that scamp.

Sophie could think what she liked; he was not going to change his plans now. The twins were already packed and ready to leave for Portsmouth in the morning, with his valet dancing attendance on them for the journey. By the time he returned, Val judged he would be well enough to travel, and he'd personally escort that hellion Eddie to his school. Thank goodness he'd had the foresight to investigate matters before he'd come here, and knew that Eddie would be welcome at the place he'd chosen for him.

Then Val would continue on to London and try to set his life back into order again.

He groaned. He'd forgotten that Nick was already in London, no doubt making a shambles of the town house. All the more reason to get back to the city as soon as possible, where he could keep an eye on the lad until he could turn him over to a commanding officer.

Sophie, despite her protestations, would do her duty and transform Katherine Foster into a young lady who could be publicly seen and received, and would bring her to London in time for the great husband search to begin. He'd start making inquiries as soon as he returned; if he was lucky, he might have a match lined up before the girl even arrived in town. That might be to his advantage; the less time she was in the city, the less time she would have to do something outrageous to spoil her chances for a decent marriage.

Val knew the girl was not happy with the arrangements he had made for her brothers. It was obvious she was accustomed to being in charge of her siblings, and resented being relieved of her responsibilities. Yet she would benefit a great deal from his actions, for she would now have the freedom to think about her own future instead of worrying about her brothers'. When this was all over, she would thank him.

Chapter Five

"Are you certain this is how I should hold the gun?" Sophie stared doubtfully at the dueling pistol clutched in her hand. "It feels so awkward."

"That is because you are not accustomed to shooting," Kat replied. "Now, sight along the barrel until you see the mark on the tree and then squeeze the trigger."

The gun went off with a loud bang and puff of smoke. Sophie jumped back in alarm and dropped the weapon.

Kat quickly picked it up and handed it back to her. "Never drop your gun," she said. "You don't want to clog the barrel with dirt."

"Did I hit the tree?" Sophie asked hopefully, squinting at the target.

Kat shook her head. "Next time, keep your eyes open. You'll never hit anything if you don't look at your target."

"But the gun makes so much noise!"

Kat picked up one of the other loaded pistols, aimed at the mark, and sent the bullet slamming into the tree.

"You make it look so easy," Sophie complained.

"All it takes is practice," Kat replied. "If you work at it every day, you'll be shooting like a regular trooper in a few weeks."

She'd been pleased when Sophie had asked to learn how to shoot. The activity came as a welcome break from the slow pace of life at Newkirk Abbey. After five days, Kat was restless. Sophie was a pleasant enough companion, but to one accustomed to the lively antics of three young boys, life was dull in the extreme. If she didn't hear from Nick soon, Kat vowed she would walk home if she had to.

"I do wish these pistols were smaller," Sophie said, letting the long barreled gun droop toward the ground.

"You need a lady's gun," Kat said. "I doubt you will have much call for a dueling weapon."

"I like that idea." Sophie's expression brightened. "Will you help me buy one?"

"Of course. Now, let me show you how to reload again. You must learn how if you intend to have your own gun."

Sophie giggled. "Val will be so impressed when he sees my new talent."

Kat flashed her a wide grin. "He'll probably have my head, and you know it."

"No, no, I shall insist that I must know how to protect myself, living alone as I do."

"Why do you live here alone?" Kat asked. Sophie had eagerly plied Kat with questions about her family and life, but remained rather reticent about her own. "You keep telling me how wonderful London is—why don't you live there?"

"London is full of too many sad memories," Sophie said quietly.

"A broken heart?" Kat asked teasingly.

"I spent the happiest days of my life in London," Sophie said. "I lived there for six months with my husband before he was—"

"You're married?" Kat asked, stunned by her admission. Where was her husband?

"Widowed," Sophie corrected. "He was killed at Waterloo."

"How awful," Kat said. "Do you miss him dreadfully?"

Sophie gave her a wan smile. "I am growing accustomed to my solitude."

"Were you married long?"

"Less than a year." Sophie sighed then turned back to the tree. "Let's see if my aim is better this time."

Sensing Sophie did not wish to talk any more about her sorrow, Kat hastily reloaded a pistol and handed it to her. At least now she knew why Newkirk's sister lived so quietly in the country. Yet, having suffered her own loss, Sophie might be much more sympathetic to Kat's plight.

The practice session over, the guns cleaned and put away; Sophie and Kat sat in the blue parlor, sipping tea, when the maid entered with the mail.

Kat looked eagerly at Sophie. "Is there a letter from Nick?"

Sophie glanced at the two letters she held and shook her head. "Both are from Val, I'm afraid." She handed one to Kat. "This is addressed to you."

Kat took it reluctantly, afraid of the news it might contain.

"Read your letter first," she said. "I'm not sure I want to know what he has to say to me."

Sophie nodded and broke the seal. Kat watched as she scanned the letter, her apprehension growing as she saw a frown develop on Sophie's brow.

"Well?" Kat asked. "What does he say?"

"I think you should read your letter," Sophie replied.

To Kat, her words sounded ominous. She tore her letter open and began to read.

> *My dear Miss Foster,*
>
> *I am taking the liberty of writing to you in lieu of your brother, as he is no longer at Kingsford. At present, he is staying at my town house in London.*
>
> *I wish to assure you that your brothers have safely been deposited at their respective schools. I personally escorted Edward to St. Giles and can*

*report that he is settled in with his new
classmates.*

 *I should like you to stay with my sister for a
while longer. Town is a bit thin of visitors at the
moment, but when it begins to swell for the Season,
I wish the both of you to come up and participate in the entertainments.*

 *Until then, I remain your most devoted
guardian—*

            Newkirk.

Kat dropped the letter into her lap, fighting back tears.
Her worst fears had come true—Newkirk had broken up
her family. And Nick had done nothing to stop him.

Sophie lay a comforting hand on Kat's arm. "He is doing
what he feels is best for you," she said softly. "You cannot
hold that against him."

"He has no idea what is best for any of us," Kat said
heatedly. "He is only concerned for his own convenience."

"I think you should give him more credit than that,"
Sophie replied.

"Well, I intend to make his life thoroughly *inconvenient*.
He will wish he had never heard of the Foster family when
I am finished with him."

"Do you intend to shoot him again?" Sophie asked.

"I'm going to get my brothers back," Kat said. "Everyone except Nick, that is. The traitor! All Newkirk had to
do was dangle that commission in front of him, and Nick's
become his slave."

"I think it is an admirable idea to reunite your family,"
Sophie said slowly. "But how do you propose to go about
it?"

"I'll go myself and fetch them home."

Sophie frowned. "And what is to prevent Val from taking them away again?"

"He would not dare." Kat clenched her fists in
determination.

"He *is* their guardian," Sophie reminded her. "By law,
he can do what he wishes."

Kat jumped to her feet and paced the room, panic building within her. What was she going to do? She turned around and gave Sophie a despairing look. "It is not fair! We were doing just fine without him."

"I daresay you were. But now that he is involved, you must deal with him."

"No," Kat said. "He must deal with *me*. I will challenge him for the guardianship, if I have to."

Sophie shook her head. "Do you honestly think any court in the land would allow that?"

"Why not? I've been caring for them since I was twelve."

"Yes, but a single woman, asking to be put in charge of her brothers. It is highly unlikely . . . And have you thought about the legal costs? Val controls your purse strings. He could stop your suit by simply refusing to pay for it."

"I'll get the money somehow," Kat vowed. "I can't let him do this to us."

Sophie wrinkled her brow in thought. "There is one way . . ."

Kat stopped pacing and looked at her with hope. "What?"

"If you were married, your husband could assume guardianship of your brothers."

"Married?" Kat stared at her, stunned by the suggestion. "That's the last thing I want. To turn my fate over to another man? Not likely."

"A husband might be the lesser of two evils," Sophie said. "Why, if you choose the right man, you could lead him around by the nose. You'll never be able to do that with Val."

"No doubt he would disapprove of anyone I considered remotely tolerable," Kat said glumly.

"Oh, don't be too certain of that. It is what he wants for you, you know. That is why he wishes us to go London—to find you a husband."

A deep sense of foreboding crept over Kat. She'd been so worried about Newkirk's plans for her brothers she had not stopped to consider that he might have plans for her as well. "He can't force me to marry."

"No, but he can keep your brothers at school," Sophie said. "If you truly want to reunite your family, you are going to have to make a few sacrifices."

Kat eyed her with renewed suspicion. She liked Sophie, but she *was* Newkirk's sister, after all. Was she involved in Newkirk's nefarious plans? Could Kat truly trust anything she said?

"How do I know he'd agree to give up the guardianship?" Kat asked.

"You yourself said he's more concerned with his own convenience," Sophie replied.

"But marriage?" Kat frowned. It was a drastic measure.

Yet the situation was dire. She had to get her brothers back, and soon. Especially Thomas and Sam. She did not know how long they must attend school before they were sent out on a ship, but she had to retrieve them before they were, or else she might never see them again.

"How could I be certain that I could trust any man to help me?" she asked.

Sophie laughed. "My dear girl, you have a great deal to learn about men! They are eminently manageable, if you go about it in the right way."

"Will you teach me how?" Kat asked. "I dare not make a mistake—my family's future depends on it."

"I can certainly advise you," Sophie said.

Kat considered the matter. She did not have to make up her mind this moment, after all, so she could afford to listen to what Sophie had to say. After all, nothing could happen until they went to London. And by then, much could have changed.

Kat had never thought much about marriage. Oh, she'd received a few proposals, but from less-than-desirable candidates—Robbie Miller, the neighbor's son, who couldn't even sit a horse properly, or that friend of Nick's with the spotty face and clammy hands. She assumed she would marry one day—it was what women did, after all. But that time had seemed far off; she'd been far more concerned with looking after her brothers. Now she was faced with the prospect of having to make the most monumental decision of her life in a very short time. It was a rather frightening prospect.

Yet Kat had never shrunk from any challenge. She hoped to convince Newkirk to change his mind and let her brothers come home. She'd wear dresses, go to London, and act the perfect lady, all to make him think she was falling in with his plans. Yet all the time she would work to persuade him to send her and her brothers back to Kingsford.

Only if that plan failed—and Kat had no intention of letting that happen—would she seriously consider marriage as a solution to her problem. But if marriage was the only way she could keep her family together, marriage it would have to be.

Kat glanced over at Sophie again. "What did your brother have to say in your letter?"

"Only that he wished us to come to London." She wrinkled her nose. "And that I am to give you some semblance of 'polish' before I bring you to town."

Kat grinned. "Polish? What does he think, that I will ride bareback through Hyde Park, pistols in each hand?"

Sophie's face crumpled with mirth. "No, he's afraid you'll challenge the Prince of Wales to a duel."

"With that wide a target, even you couldn't miss."

They both shook with laughter.

"No, we must be serious," Sophie said. "I must properly prepare you for your entrée into society. And *ladies* do not laugh like this."

"Then we are both done for," Kat said, setting Sophie off into fresh gales of laughter.

"Oh, do stop," she said, wiping her streaming eyes. "We must have a *plan*."

"I know!" Kat said. "I will go home. *You* go to London and flush out the game. Once you've found a suitable candidate, send him to me. We won't have to even bother your brother."

"But London would be so dull without you," Sophie protested. "Besides, Val would never permit it. This way, you will be able to see your older brother."

"I'm not certain I wish to see him, after what he's done," Kat said. "But if you say I must go, I guess I must. At least with you there, it will not be too awful."

"Oh, London is wonderful. We shall have so much fun! The shopping is glorious. I can spend hours merely deciding over the color of a pair of gloves. And the theater . . . well, sometimes it's rather dull, but the activity in the pits is always amusing. And dancing." Sophie gave her an intent look. "You can dance, can't you?"

Kat shrugged. "Not very well."

"Good! That is something else I can teach you. It's not

so difficult, and if you do make a mistake, you always pretend that it is your partner who stepped wrong. A gentleman will dare not argue."

"Do you really think I shall find someone who is willing to help me get my brothers back?" Kat asked.

"You shall have to beat them off with sticks," Sophie assured her. "Val will be overjoyed at your success. Why, you could be wed and have your brothers back with you before the summer is out."

"I think you are far too optimistic," Kat said, shaking her head. If all went as *she* planned, they would be back at home by that time—and without any husband.

"We will have fun, I promise," Sophie said. "And find you a suitable husband in the process. I shall write Val and tell him we both agree to his plan."

She jumped to her feet, spilling her letter onto the floor. "Goodness, there is so much to do and so little time. I shall have to gather my fashion journals. And contact my modiste to see what she recommends." She clapped her hands in glee. "I cannot wait to get started."

Kat returned her a doubtful smile. She feared that Sophie was going to make far too elaborate plans for what would turn out to be a short stay in London. But since Sophie had been so kind to her, Kat did not want to disappoint her. She would merely have to do what she could to keep Sophie's exuberance in check.

"What do you think of this dress?" Sophie pointed to a sketch in *La Belle Assemblée*. It was the following afternoon, and they sat in Sophie's parlor, planning Kat's wardrobe for London. Fashion journals covered the table as Sophie flipped through one after another, looking for illustrations she liked.

Kat took one look at the dress and shook her head. "Too many flounces. I want something simpler."

"We could take the flounces off," Sophie said, scanning the drawing closer. "Although it would not be nearly as pretty."

"I like this one." Kat handed her a drawing of a dress more to her taste. "It's plainer."

Sophie vehemently shook her head. "That's a riding habit. Of course it is plain."

"It doesn't have to be worn for riding, does it?" Kat asked.

"Well . . ." Sophie reluctantly considered the outfit.

"And look at this coat!" Kat eagerly shoved another plate at her. "Four capes! I shall look like a regular dasher in that."

"You will look like a coachman," Sophie protested.

"Caped greatcoats are all the rage," Kat insisted. "Even Nick says so."

"For young bucks trying to cut a dash."

"But is that not what you wish me to do—'cut a dash'?"

Sophie rolled her eyes. "I want you to look less like a boy, not more. Someone will see you wearing that in Hyde Park and challenge you to a duel before they notice you're a female."

"Can I at least have the hat?" Kat pleaded, pointing to the sketch of a giant leghorn bonnet dripping with feathered plumes. "I do so like those feathers."

"You will not tolerate the tiniest flounce, but you want a hat that makes you look like a peacock nested on your head?" Sophie gave Kat an exasperated look.

Kat couldn't hold back any longer and burst out laughing.

Sophie's eyes narrowed. "You're teasing me, aren't you?"

Kat smiled and pointed to another hat—a military shako with only a small plume. "Now, I honestly like this one."

"Much better," Sophie said. "If only your hair were longer, we could make those small ringlets . . ."

"No curls," Kat said, grimacing at the thought. "I'll chop my hair off first."

"You are bound and determined to make this difficult, aren't you?" Sophie sighed. "If you wish to tie up a gentleman as soon as possible, you need to play the fashion plate to draw their attention."

"Would it not be easier to put an advert in the *Times*?" Kat asked. " 'Young lady with younger brothers looking for suitable husband to take over guardianship of same. Must be cheerful, knowledgeable of horseflesh, have a good seat, and drive to an inch. Regular hunt subscription a bonus.' "

Sophie burst into laughter. "I daresay it might work. But I do not think Val would approve."

"All the more reason to do it."

"Kat, you dare not antagonize Val too much, or he might not be willing to give up the guardianship of your brothers."

Kat made a face. Being civil, even amiable, to her guardian was going to be the hardest part of her plan.

Sophie gave her hand an encouraging squeeze. "Remember, you are doing this for your brothers."

Sighing, Kat acknowledged the truth of Sophie's words. She would walk through hot coals for Sam, Thomas, and Eddie, so she supposed that Sophie's wardrobe demands were not *too* onerous. Kat would grit her teeth and do all that was necessary to persuade Newkirk she could act the lady.

"Look at this dress," Sophie said. "If you took off all but the bottom flounce, it would not be so bad. I do like those sleeves."

"But the bonnet has no feathers."

"We can put feathers on the bonnet." Sophie glared at her with feigned annoyance. "I do not think you are taking this as seriously as you should. We must have your wardrobe all planned within the next two days if I am to get the order into the modiste in time to have it ready."

"Just tell her no flounces, dark colors, and plain lines." Kat ticked the list off on her fingers. "That should be simple enough."

"Nonsense. Now sit down again and help me choose these dress patterns!"

With a weary sigh, Kat turned back to the matter at hand. She pointed to an illustration of a plain gray dress. "I like that one."

"That's a mourning gown! You're not in mourning."

"Can't we pretend?"

Ignoring Kat's remark, Sophie handed her another print. "The style is elegant," Sophie said. "In a different color—a pale blue, perhaps?"

"Dark blue," Kat replied.

"*Pale*," Sophie said, making notes on the paper at her side. "You are a young lady in her first Season."

The maid entered with the tea tray and the mail, and Kat was overjoyed at the interruption. Sophie was intent on planning every minute detail of her wardrobe; Kat appreciated her efforts, but they were merely clothes after all—clothes that she probably would not wear often after this trip to London.

She had her own wardrobe plans. It would be nice to have a new riding coat, and a pair of breeches specially tailored for her, instead of wearing Nick's hand-me-downs. She suspected Sophie's "modiste" would never agree to make her such a thing, but Kat vowed to find a good tailor in London.

It was too bad Nick had been such a traitor, and she wanted nothing more to do with him, because he would be the perfect accomplice in such a task. Kat would just have to gain the information the best she could, and give both Sophie and Newkirk the slip.

If she had to go to London and dress like a fashion plate, Kat intended to acquire some useful clothing as well.

Val sprawled in the faded padding of the upholstered chair in his private parlor at the Goose and Grouse. His less-than-elegant surroundings could not dampen his sense of satisfaction.

All his male wards were now taken care of. Even the youngest, that rascal Eddie, had gone off to school with little fuss. Val had feared there'd be some sort of teary reluctance at the last minute, but Eddie had remained annoyingly cheerful and talked incessantly the entire journey. More than once Val had desired to stuff him in the luggage boot to gain some peace and quiet.

When they'd finally reached St. Giles, Val warned him to stay out of trouble and apply himself to his studies, although he didn't know if the child had taken those words deeply to heart. It did not matter. Unless he tied up the headmaster or set the school on fire, he'd be there for a long, long time.

Now, only the girl was left. As soon as he reached London, Val would start making inquiries about suitable candidates for her hand. As much as he wanted to get the girl wed, Val did have his standards. He did not intend to marry her off to just anyone. As her guardian, he must ensure that she was suitably provided for. While her portion was ample, it was not large enough to attract fortune hunters, so that was one worry eliminated.

No, what he needed was someone without too much town polish—someone who would not look down his nose at the country airs of Miss Foster. A man who spent most of the year in the country, engaged in sporting pursuits, would suit her perfectly.

And since she seemed so attached to her brothers, what better situation than a widower with young children? A man like that would not be so exacting—would be willing to look beyond her lack of refinement. And once she had her own brood to worry about, she would not be nagging Val constantly about her brothers.

Then, as soon as he engaged a reliable administrator to handle the business end of things, he would hardly need to devote any time at all to the welfare of his wards.

Which, of course, was what he wanted. He'd never asked to be named their guardian, after all; only his father's ineptness had led to that. Val thought he'd done an admirable job of dealing with his unexpected duties. Once the girl was married off . . .

In the far recesses of his mind, there lingered the nagging doubt that somehow, he'd made some miscalculation, and despite all his careful planning, something would go awry. But what? The boys were eagerly embarking on their new adventures, and Nick was so eager for a commission, he'd scrub the scullery if Val asked him to.

No, the only possible difficulty could come from the girl. And he trusted Sophie to take care of that matter. After all, had not Sophie once been the toast of London? Or at least, so she claimed. She knew all the minute details, the nuances of proper behavior, fashion, and style that must be observed to make the girl's trip to London a success.

Still, it might not be a bad idea to stop at the abbey on his way to town and see how Sophie was getting on. If the Foster chit was a hopeless case, better to know now before he advertised her availability.

He'd start for home in the morning, remain there long enough to reassure himself that Sophie had matters well in hand. If all looked well, he could proceed to London and prepare for the ladies' arrival.

Chapter Six

*K*at led Sophie's mare around the stable yard while waiting for her to come out of the house. The horse was a dull, placid creature that Kat would not have given a second glance to in ordinary circumstances. But since it was the only riding horse here, Kat had taken her out several times, hoping to discover the animal had some redeeming qualities.

To her dismay, the creature was hopeless. She was perfectly suited for Sophie, but Kat found it frustrating to ride a horse that considered breaking into a trot a cruel imposition. How she wished to have her own horse here. Kat had asked Sophie to write to Newkirk and ask, but so far she had heard nothing from him.

She smothered a laugh as she glimpsed Sophie slinking guiltily across the yard, peering over her shoulder as if fearing someone was watching. She was outfitted in Kat's extra pair of breeches, ready for a lesson in riding astride.

"I feel absolutely *naked* in these breeches," Sophie said with a rueful grin.

"You'll find you like them," Kat said. "They make much more sense for riding. Are you ready to start?"

Sophie nodded and Kat led the horse to the mounting block. She held Sophie's hand to steady her and explained how to step in the stirrup and then swing her leg over.

Sophie had to fumble to get her foot in the far stirrup, but otherwise mounted in good order.

"This feels so . . . odd," she said. The mare turned her head to look at her rider, as if she, too, thought it unusual to have her mistress riding astride.

"That's all there is to it," Kat said. "Walk her around the yard."

"Hold on to the bridle!" Sophie said. "What if she bolts?"

Kat snorted at *that* idea. The mare did not know the meaning of the word. But to ease Sophie's qualms, she put a hand on the bridle and walked alongside while the mare plodded around the yard.

"This reminds me of when I got my first pony," Sophie said with a laugh. "Val led me round and round the yard in circles until we were both dizzy."

"It's hard to imagine him being so agreeable," Kat said.

"You must not think him a complete ogre," Sophie said. "He was a wonderful older brother. He was always helping me with my lessons, or taking me riding."

For an instant, Kat wondered if she had judged Newkirk too harshly. Sophie was obviously fond of him. But no. He might have treated his sister kindly, but he had not extended the same courtesy to Kat and her family.

"Am I doing all right?" Sophie asked, her cheeks flushed and an eager look on her face.

"Quite well," Kat replied, turning her attention back to her task. "I'm going to let go now; you are managing fine."

Sophie gave a little shiver of nervousness, then grasped the reins more firmly and turned the mare toward the house. Kat watched her with a critical eye. Sophie sat rigidly at attention and looked as if she expected the mare to break into a wild gallop at any moment, but Kat knew she was safe. Nothing could induce that slug to move quickly.

Sophie took a few more wide circles around the yard and then reined in next to Kat.

"This is fun!" she said, her eyes gleaming with pride.

"I'll have to write and tell your brother." Kat grinned at Sophie's initial look of horror.

Sophie then broke into laughter. "You would not dare! He would skin me and roast me on a spit if he knew I was doing this."

"No, I'll be the one spitted and roasted for encouraging you," Kat said.

"I don't see how he can complain. I am showing you how to get along in London, and you are showing me how to get along in the country. It is a fair exchange!"

Kat shook her head. "I doubt he'd see it that way. Are you ready to get down?"

"I am going to ride around the house first," Sophie announced with surprising determination. "Wish me luck!"

Kat watched with amusement as the mare's fat rear end slowly disappeared around the corner of the house. She'd like to see Sophie on a *real* horse someday. Once she gained confidence, she could handle a more spirited mount.

She sat down on the mounting block to await their return.

A few minutes later she heard the sound of trotting hooves, and she jumped up. Sophie and the mare came hurriedly around the side of the house. Kat had never seen the horse move so fast.

"It's Val!" Sophie cried. "He's coming up the drive! I've got to get out of these clothes!"

Newkirk! Kat groaned aloud. What in the devil was he doing here? Had he come up with a new plan to make her life even more miserable?

"What would he do to you if he saw you dressed like this?" Kat asked as she quickly helped Sophie down.

"I do not know, and I do not care to find out," Sophie cried. "Put the mare away, and I'll try to delay him so you can change, too."

"Pooh," Kat said. "There's nothing he can do to me now that he hasn't already done."

"Hurry anyway," Sophie said. "He will want to see you, I am certain." She ran for the back door.

Kat patted the mare on the nose. "Didn't know you had it in you to go at such a pace." She took the bridle and swung up into the saddle. She had to keep Newkirk from the house long enough for Sophie to change her clothes. Unfortunately, it meant he was going to see Kat in breeches; not the best way to start out her campaign to convince him she really was an unexceptional young lady who deserved to be in charge of her brothers.

Kat tapped the horse with her heels to see if she, too, could induce some speed, but Sophie's frantic dash must have taken everything out of the mare, for she moved forward at a painfully slow walk.

"Slug," Kat muttered, and headed toward the front of the house to await Newkirk's arrival.

She heard the clatter of carriage wheels on gravel seconds before the coach came into view. It halted in front of the house, and Newkirk climbed out—wincing as he stepped down, to Kat's delight. His wound was obviously still paining him. He looked about, saw her, and she waved gaily. His face clouded as he walked closer.

"Up to your usual tricks, I see," he said. "You do realize you cannot ride like that in London."

"Don't worry, I'd be embarrassed to be seen riding this nag in public," she retorted, all conciliatory thoughts fleeing her brain at the sight of his sour expression.

"I was referring to your breeches," he said.

"Are your own horses as bad as this one?" Kat asked, ignoring his comment. "I might not wish to ride at all while I am in town."

"That sounds like an excellent idea," he said, and turning abruptly, started walking toward the house.

Kat could not resist one last jab.

"Still limping a bit, I see," she called after him.

Newkirk halted then whirled around, and Kat thought he was going to let fly with a blistering retort. But he clamped his mouth shut, turned back toward the house, and walked off without another word.

She knew she had won that round.

Kat turned the mare back toward the stable yard, put her back in the stall, then sauntered toward the house.

Of course, she had just ruined her chance to make a good impression on Newkirk. But there was something about the way he looked at her—the open disapproval in his eyes—that set her back up and kept her from speaking civilly to him.

She would have to gain firmer control over her tongue if she ever hoped to gain her brothers back. From this moment forward, Kat vowed to speak to the baron only in the politest of terms.

She found them both in Sophie's parlor, with the tea tray on the table beside the sofa, piled high with delicious cakes and sweets.

"Oh, good, Kat, you are here to join us." Sophie patted the cushions beside her. "Do have a cup of tea."

"Perhaps Miss Foster would like to change out of her riding clothes, first," Newkirk said.

"Oh, I am perfectly comfortable as I am." Kat sat down and took the teacup that Sophie quickly handed her. They shared a conspiratorial smile.

Newkirk shot Sophie a doubtful glance before turning back to Kat. "Miss Foster, I thought you were preparing yourself to come to the city."

"I have been riding," Kat said, knowing her garb was the reason for his displeasure. "What else do you expect me to wear?"

"The proper riding attire for a lady."

"I have no intention of riding sidesaddle, so there is no need to be encumbered by yards of skirts," Kat said. "I will walk rather than do that."

Newkirk shot Sophie a dark look. "I thought you said you were making progress with her."

"There is nothing wrong with Kat riding as she pleases on the estate," Sophie said, calmly sipping her tea. "She knows how to go on in London."

"That remains to be seen," Newkirk said.

"Goodness, you are in a testy mood," Sophie said. "You must be fagged from your journey."

"I think his bottom is paining him," Kat muttered under her breath.

Newkirk glared at her. "I insist that you do not refer to that unfortunate incident again, Miss Foster."

She shrugged, mentally berating herself for slipping up again. "Just making an observation, *my lord*."

Newkirk set down his teacup and rose. "I have some estate matters to deal with. We can resume our conversation at dinner. Endeavor to show me, Sophie, that you have achieved some measure of success."

The moment he was out of the room, they both burst into giggles.

"What have you done to the poor man?" Sophie asked. "I have never seen him act such a crab."

"I do bring out the worst in him," Kat admitted. She set down her cup and stood. "I will go change so I don't give him any more excuses to chastise you."

"If he is going to be this unreasonable, *I* may start wearing breeches around the house." Sophie shook her head. "I hope he is not like this for the entire length of his stay."

"Did he say how long he was going to be here?" Kat

asked. Perhaps he was only pausing overnight and would not be here long. Surely she could keep herself in check for such a short time.

"He did not say," Sophie said. "I imagine he will remain until he feels confident you are prepared to go to London."

Kat rolled her eyes. "In other words, if I behave myself, he will soon leave."

Sophie nodded.

"It will take a great deal of fun out of things," Kat said. "No riding for you, no shooting, no—"

"As long as you do not antagonize him too much, I suspect he will grow bored within a day or two and leave."

"I will forbear from reminding him of his wound," Kat said with mock glumness.

"He is sensitive about the matter," Sophie said.

"Only when he sits down," Kat replied with a wicked grin.

Sophie smothered a laugh with her hand.

Kat helped herself to a few more cakes, then said farewell to Sophie and walked toward her room.

Her resolution to be polite to Newkirk had lasted all of a few minutes. She could not allow that man to constantly provoke her or she would never get her brothers back.

Kat shuddered with frustration. At home, she was easily able to ignore her brothers' baiting remarks. She merely had to learn how to ignore Newkirk as well. She would never get anywhere with him if they continued to trade barbs.

If Kat only had herself to think of, she would do everything in her power to irritate the baron. But that would not help her brothers. And for Sophie's sake, she intended to be on her best behavior, no matter how much she wanted to respond to his prickly remarks. Kat would bite her tongue bloody if she must—her family's fate was at stake. She had to convince Newkirk she was perfectly capable of taking care of them.

Although, as she thought about it, Kat realized it would be rather amusing to disconcert Newkirk. He obviously expected the worst from her; she would give him her best and let him see just how wrong he was. The sooner he approved of her behavior, the sooner he might be willing to reconsider his plan.

Her concern for her brothers grew daily. Despite the fact that she'd written them every day, she had still not heard a word from any of them. Were they not permitted to write, for fear they could not reveal their miserable existences? Or worse, had Newkirk forbidden them to even receive her letters? Did they think she had abandoned them?

If she did not receive a letter by the end of the week, she would prevail upon Sophie to find someone to look into matters—even take her to their respective schools so she could be assured the three were all right. Who knew what sort of harsh military discipline Sam and Thomas were being subjected to, and to think of poor Eddie away from home for the first time in his life, amid total strangers . . .

For the hundredth time she cursed Newkirk and his meddling, interfering ways that had brought such disruption to her family. She would find great delight in taking her brothers back from his unfeeling clutches. If she could not persuade Newkirk to relent, she would just find herself a husband to help her. Either way, she would win.

Later that evening, Val waited impatiently in the drawing room for the ladies to join him before dinner. While he had his doubts, he was willing to give Miss Foster a chance to prove herself. He'd brought two trunks filled with her clothes, which she'd left behind in her mad flight, so he knew she had something to wear other than those damn breeches.

If she chose to dress properly. He remembered too well what had happened last time he'd asked her to dress for dinner. He rubbed his backside, still sore from the lengthy carriage ride. There'd be no more dueling; he knew better than to challenge her directly. If she rebelled again, he'd do something more practical, such as lock her in her room on a diet of bread and water until she cooperated—or starved herself to death.

Val hoped he would not need to take such stern measures. He wanted to make this easy for the both of them, and the sooner she accepted his plans for her future, the better it would be for everyone.

He stood by the far window, staring out over the lawn, thinking that he should try to spend more time here, when he heard the drawing room door open.

"Good evening, my lord."

Miss Foster. Apprehension tensing his muscles, he turned to greet her.

Had Val not seen her at Kingsford Manor with his own eyes, he would find it hard to believe that anyone could ever have mistaken her for a boy. He did not see a trace of the breeched urchin who'd faced down his pistol in the young woman who stood before him.

She wore a dress of some soft blue material, plain in line with only a modest trimming of ribbon at the sleeve and neck. But the simple, elegant lines set off a surprisingly feminine figure, and the color brought out the hue of her eyes and the roses in her cheeks. Her cropped hair was twined with ribbon, a gold locket encircled her neck, and a cashmere shawl draped her shoulders.

Val realized that if he could only control her exuberant spirits, he would have no trouble finding a husband for her. She was not an exquisite beauty, but far prettier than he could have imagined from their first meeting.

She gave him a challenging look. "Well? Do you approve? Have I passed muster?"

Val realized he had been staring.

"You look very presentable, Miss Foster." Val glanced at the clock. "And prompt. I do not think Sophie has ever been on time for anything in her life."

"Promptness is certainly an admirable virtue," she agreed.

"One I'm certain you inculcated in *all* your brothers," Val said.

A shadow crossed her face at the mention of her brothers. "Are they—were they . . . ?"

"As pestilential as ever?" He laughed. "Of course. Selkirk—my man—nearly lost the twins on the way to Portsmouth when they ran off to investigate a tinker's cart while stopped at an inn. And Edward did not stop talking during the entire journey to St. Giles."

Her expression turned wistful. "I do miss them."

"I assure you, Miss Foster, once you and Sophie are in London, you will not even have the time to think about them."

"Did you tell them that they could not write to me?" she asked bluntly.

He looked at her with surprise. "Good Lord, no. Why would I do a thing like that?"

"For spite," she said.

"If they have not written to you, I daresay it is because they are far too busy settling into their new surroundings."

Sophie came in at that moment.

"Kat is a dutiful sister and writes to them every day," she said, then stood back, giving Kat's gown a thorough scrutiny. "I do believe you are right, Kat. Simple lines do look well on you."

Kat grinned. "No flounces?"

"Well . . . maybe a very few. Only on the hem." Sophie turned to Val. "Doesn't she look lovely?"

"Very pretty," Val agreed, amused by the rosy hue of embarrassment that crept over Miss Foster's cheeks.

"Wait until we have her new dress," Sophie said. "She will be a vision of loveliness."

Val cleared his throat. "Since you are late, as usual, Sophie, dinner is waiting. Perhaps you and Miss Foster can continue your wardrobe discussion after dinner."

Sophie laughed. "Val, you should know better than to tell two women *not* to discuss clothing. Now it will be the only thing on our minds all through the meal."

He rolled his eyes in mock despair. "Heaven help me."

Sophie took his arm and motioned for Kat to take his other. She hesitated, then gingerly lay her fingers on his arm.

"Val will have to grow accustomed to squiring two ladies about town," Sophie said.

"If you think I am going to accompany you everywhere in London, you are sadly mistaken," Val told her. "You are a perfectly suitable chaperon for Miss Foster."

Sophie sighed. "Ah, Val, you know so little about how these things are managed. Of course I do not expect you to accompany us on calls. But we shall demand your escort in the evening. You are not going to slip out of your responsibilities as guardian as easy as that!"

"I agree," Miss Foster said, directing a simpering smile at him. "I would hate people to think that my guardian was neglecting me."

He gave her a suspicious look as he pulled out her chair.

He was certain that Miss Foster did not care a fig for what anyone thought of him.

Val found it difficult to sit and concentrate on either his dinner or the conversation at the table. He would have been far more comfortable with a pillow on his chair, but he was not going to give Miss Foster the satisfaction of knowing that his wound still bothered him.

He struggled to keep an eye on her without appearing too obvious, hoping to learn how well she could manage herself in a social setting. So far she had not slurped her soup, eaten her peas with a knife, or tucked her napkin into the bodice of her gown, which boded well for the future.

"Val?"

Sophie's loud tone finally captured his attention.

"Yes, Sophie?"

"I asked if any of your military friends were going to be in London for the Season."

"How should I know?"

"What exactly did you do when you were in town?" she asked with exasperation. "Did you not venture out once?"

"Of course I did," he said. "But I was not going about asking everyone their plans. I had no idea I was even going to be in the city this spring until I found out about those blasted—the Fosters. Haven't been back since."

"Do not feel that you have to make drastic changes in your life to accommodate me," Kat said acidly. "We have no need of your presence in London."

Val regarded her with mock innocence. "I thought you wanted me to display a proper guardian's concern for your welfare?"

"Perhaps you could transfer the guardianship to Sophie," Kat said. "Surely, since she is a widow, she has standing in society. Then you could be relieved of your onerous burden."

"I could only imagine how that would go," Val replied. "No, Miss Foster, I may not have asked to be your guardian, but I intend to fulfill my duties to the best of my ability. If I must escort you and my sister around London to accomplish that, I will do so."

She mumbled something under her breath, but he chose

not to hear it. They were already treading on dangerous ground.

"I, for one, cannot wait to get to town," Sophie said. "I do not know why I stayed away so long."

"To save me money?" Val teased.

"Oh, I intend to make up for that in no time. Kat and I have already been making our shopping lists. We have so many things to buy."

"You have a closet full of gowns already," he protested.

"Val, I must have an entire new wardrobe! Everything I have is two years out of style, at least. I could not possibly appear in London in anything I currently own."

"The dress you are wearing looks quite suitable."

She laughed. "Val, you are a military man. What do you know of fashion? I assure you, I would be laughed out of every drawing room in town if I wore this old thing."

He threw up his hands. "I will defer to your finer knowledge, then. Just try not to bankrupt me."

"Am I to have use of my own money for purchases?" Kat asked.

"Certainly," he said. "I assume Sophie has designed an entire wardrobe for you as well?"

"Of course," Sophie replied. "She will be most elegant when I am finished with her. The exquisites will be clinging to the front steps awaiting her appearance each morning."

"I do not know how 'exquisite' he will be, but I have every confidence that we can find you a suitable husband, Miss Foster." Newkirk gave her an encouraging smile.

"I am certain of it," she replied.

"Oh." Her alacrity surprised him. He'd expected more reluctance on her part to his plans for her, and it was a relief to learn she did not hold objections. The sooner they wrapped up the whole business, the better.

Following the meal, they retreated to the drawing room, where Sophie and Miss Foster leafed through fashion magazines, their heads close together, whispering and giggling. Val endeavored not to look as bored as he felt.

He felt like a great weight had been lifted from his shoulders this evening at seeing how well Miss Foster could behave. Sophie's optimism was in no way misplaced, and he would gladly take Miss Foster to London right now if it was not for the matter of her—and Sophie's—wardrobe.

At least he could leave for town in the morning. And as a reward, he'd leave Miss Foster a token of his appreciation for her decorous behavior.

"This dress would look lovely on you." Sophie held out a picture to Miss Foster.

The girl laughed. "I would look like a French pastry in that gown."

"Val?" Sophie called to him. "Come look at this dress. Don't you think it would be lovely on Kat?"

Val reluctantly rose and walked over to where the two women sat, and looked at the picture.

His ward was right. She would look ridiculous in that frilled concoction dripping with lace.

"I am afraid I must agree with Miss Foster," he said. "She might look like a particularly delightful pastry, but a pastry nonetheless."

He saw a hint of a smile tugging at the corners of Miss Foster's lips, and he resisted the temptation to respond with a wink. He did not think she had a dueling pistol hidden in the folds of her gown, but he did not wish to test her volatility. They had reached an uneasy truce of sorts during dinner, but he did not think it would take much to provoke an outburst from her. He preferred to retain the pleasant illusion that she was truly a modest, well-behaved young lady.

Instead, he took the fashion journal from Sophie and flipped through the pages, looking for another dress that would suit his ward. If his military comrades could see him now . . . But he suspected that being guardian to Miss Foster would put him in any number of unusual situations before he was through.

Chapter Seven

*I*n the morning, Kat awoke early, as was her custom, but she lingered beneath the covers. If she'd been at home, she would have leapt from bed, quickly dressed, and gone to the stables for a morning ride. But Sophie's gentle mare offered no temptation to rise.

She thought about last night. Her performance for Newkirk had gone well. He seemed convinced she could behave as a lady ought. And she had seen an unexpectedly, pleasant side of him. Kat saw why Sophie was so fond of her brother. He was an amiable host, a good storyteller full of amusing tales of his military experiences and adventures on the Continent.

And you could have knocked her over with a feather when he'd sat down beside them and offered opinions on her wardrobe.

Why, there had been times when she'd completely forgotten that he was the same cruel man who'd dispersed her family. Until her thoughts flashed on Eddie, or Sam, or Thomas, and she remembered that this man held all their fates in his hands.

Her task was to persuade him that she knew what was best for her brothers. Quickly. Last night had gone well. She must continue her campaign and pray that she could keep her temper in check while he was here.

Kat stretched and threw off the blankets. If she could not ride, at least she could walk before breakfast. She'd be more eager to charm Newkirk on a full stomach. She pulled on her breeches, a shirt, and coat, and hurried down the rear stairs and entered the kitchen, intending to grab a bite to eat before she went out.

She pulled up suddenly when she entered the room.

Newkirk sat at the cook's table, the remains of his breakfast spread out before him.

He looked up and Kat stared back in surprise. Sitting there, dressed casually in shirt and well-worn jacket, he looked younger, more friendly. Almost approachable.

Newkirk gave Kat a quizzical look. "I thought you were an early riser, Miss Foster. I've been up for ages."

Kat shrugged. "There is little reason to rise early here," she said.

He raised a brow. "Not even for a morning gallop?"

She snorted derisively. "On what? That mare of Sophie's does not know how to gallop."

"No, but I imagine your horse does."

"My horse?" She stared at him for a moment until the meaning of his words sank in. "My horse? My horse is here?"

He nodded.

Without another word, she dashed out the door and raced across the yard to the stable.

There he was, in the third stall. Blaze raised his head when he heard her fumble with the latch, and nickered a greeting as she pulled the door open and flung her arms around the tall chestnut's neck.

"I am so glad to see you!" She stepped back and eyed the horse with a critical eye. "Has someone been taking proper care of you?" She bent and lifted a front hoof for inspection, but it was quite clean.

"I assure you, Miss Foster, all your animals have been well cared for."

She swung around to see Newkirk leaning against the stable door, arms crossed over his chest.

Kat swallowed hard. It pained her to be beholden to him for anything—but he could not even guess how much this meant to her. "Th—thank you."

"I thought you might like to have your own mount while you are here," he said.

"Did you bring the tack as well?" Kat asked. He nodded. "Then I'm going riding."

Kat quickly saddled and bridled her horse then led him out into the yard. Newkirk was still there, and for a moment, she feared he was going to insist on riding with her, but she saw no other horse.

Then she remembered that riding was probably still not comfortable for him yet. She opened her mouth to remark on that fact, then closed it again. He *had* brought her horse, after all.

Was it his manner of apologizing for the turmoil he'd caused in her life? A peace offering of sorts? If so, it was not enough. As much as she welcomed the chance to ride her own horse, it meant nothing in the absence of her brothers. If Newkirk thought this would mollify her, he was sadly mistaken. She would not be at peace with him until her brothers were back with her.

But she was not going to deny herself the chance for the first decent ride she'd had since leaving home.

If she apologized for shooting him, no doubt Newkirk would regard her with more favor. As much as it irked Kat to swallow her pride, she realized it would be the best way to establish herself on a new, more friendly footing with Newkirk. And that was what she needed if she intended to persuade him to bring her brothers back. When she returned from her ride, she would summon up the courage to speak with him.

He had made a thoughtful gesture by bringing her horse to Sophie's; it was her turn to respond in kind. Sighing, she thought about the words she should say.

Val watched as horse and rider trotted out of the yard. She'd leaped into the saddle like a trooper, and he was certain she'd have her horse at a full gallop within minutes. The girl had spirit—whether on a horse or trading barbs with him. He almost wished he could join her, but knew the only way he'd be comfortable riding would be with a pillow strapped to his saddle.

He'd have to wait until Miss Foster had her feet firmly planted on the ground again before they could talk again. Which would have to be in London, since he intended to leave within the hour. Perhaps by then her anger would have cooled further, and he could make her realize that his actions were best for her family.

Her concern for her younger siblings was admirable, but she no longer needed to bear the weight of responsibility for them. Val knew what it felt like to feel responsible for everyone and everything around you. He intended to relieve her of that burden, and if she did not appreciate his efforts now, eventually she would.

Val firmly believed that once she arrived in London, Miss Foster would be far too busy with shopping, balls and *fêtes* to even think about her younger brothers. Sophie would see to that. And once a young gentleman caught her eye, her brothers would be the farthest thing from her mind.

No, he had her best interests at heart, even if she did not yet realize it.

It was also clear that despite her unorthodox behavior, Katherine Foster was not ignorant of the social niceties. Sophie had assured him that the girl would do quite well in London, and from what he'd seen last night, he had to agree. She was not out of place in a fine dining room, could maintain the type of light conversation so admired in society, and was pleasingly attractive when she was properly dressed. She would do fine as long as he kept her away from horses and pistols.

Reassured that his plans would succeed, Val made his final preparations before leaving for London. He still had Nicholas Foster to deal with, after all.

Knowing Sophie would not be out of bed for hours, he penned her a note, called for the carriage to be brought around, and was on the road within the hour.

Kat dallied in the stable after her ride, feeding, watering, and grooming her horse until he grew indifferent to her attentions. Finally she tore herself away and returned to the house. She had put off talking with Newkirk long enough. It was time to face him and offer her apology.

He was no longer in the kitchen, so she slipped up the rear stairs and peeked into the blue parlor to see if Sophie was up yet. Kat was eager to tell her the good news about her horse—and perhaps delay her encounter with the baron for a few more minutes.

Sophie greeted Kat with a look of amusement tinged with exasperation. "Can you believe this? Val has left already. You must have really impressed him."

Kat regarded her with dismay. "Your brother is gone?"

Sophie nodded.

Kat sank down onto a chair, feeling strangely disappointed. She'd steeled herself for the apology she intended to give, and now she was deprived of the opportunity. Newkirk seemed bent on exasperating her.

She reached over and helped herself to a muffin from Sophie's breakfast tray. "Did he say why?"

"Only that he thought you and I were making excellent progress and we are free to come to London whenever we wish."

The confirmation of Newkirk's approval should have gladdened Kat, but she felt a twinge of anxiety to know that she would soon be going to London. Everything would be so much more complicated there. Newkirk and Sophie would both be focused on finding Kat a husband, while all Kat wished to do was change Newkirk's mind, retrieve her brothers, and go home. But since Newkirk was in London, to London she must go.

"Why so downcast?" Sophie asked. "This means we can leave for town next week."

"I am not certain I am ready," Kat replied. "All these social rules are so confusing. And I don't know the first thing about dealing with men."

Sophie's eyes filled with mock seriousness. "The first thing you must learn about men is that they are as biddable as can be—if you go about it in the right way."

"Horses are biddable, too, if they're trained properly," Kat said, munching on a piece of muffin. "But I haven't seen too many men wearing curb bits."

"That is because you have to train them differently," Sophie explained. "Unlike a horse, they can't be aware that you are training them."

"How do you manage that?"

"The most important rule with men is to always let them think they are in charge."

Kat snorted. "They already think that. Look at your brother."

Sophie pointedly ignored her comment and continued. "The second thing is to make them think that you always listen to and consider their advice."

"What good does that accomplish?" Kat asked.

"And the third rule is to make certain that whenever a decision is made, the man thinks that his opinion has been the deciding one."

"That's no help at all." Kat felt disappointed. She'd

thought Sophie was going to hand her some magic formula for managing men—particularly Newkirk; instead she was just telling her what Kat already knew—that men were arrogant dictators who expected everyone else to do their bidding. "What use is it to always follow their ideas?"

"You don't," Sophie said simply. "It is your job to make them believe that you are following their wishes, when actually they are doing what you want."

"That does not sound at all easy."

"Take the matter of which rout party to attend." Sophie held out her right hand. "You wish to go to Lady Drumheller's." She extended her left. "He wants to go to Lady Bascombe's for the card play. You must cleverly convince him that he really wants to go to Lady Drumheller's."

"How do I do that?"

"There are several different tactics you may employ." Sophie smiled. "First, you can try the devious approach, by telling him that someone he wishes to see will be at your party. Or mention that a person he wishes to avoid will be at the other. This is not the best plan, for it only works once or twice."

Sophie gave her a conspiratorial smile. "The better tact is to make him want to keep you away from his party. Explain how Lady Bascombe has redecorated her saloon, and you can't wait to get ideas for your own drawing room. He will fear this will cost him money, and won't want you to go there."

Kat nodded. "I can see the logic in that. Like putting the horse over the hedge because he doesn't like the brook, even if the hedge is a bigger jump."

Sophie gave her an approving glance. "Just so."

"But it's a great difference between convincing someone to attend a party and agreeing to take on three young boys," Kat said. *Or to let their sister manage them.*

"You merely have to keep emphasizing the advantages of your option," Sophie said. "No squalling infants to disturb his sleep; eager minds waiting to soak up his pearls of wisdom; companions for hours of fishing."

Kat laughed. "The poor man . . . he will be so shocked when he meets them. They won't accept words of wisdom from anyone."

"Which he is not to know until it is too late," Sophie said.

"Still, you make it sound so easy, when I know it can't be."

Sophie gave her a pointed look. "How do you get your older brother to do what you want him to?"

"Oh, that's easy," Kat said. "I just dare him."

Sophie made a face. "That may not be the best technique for dealing with a husband."

Kat shrugged. "It works with Nick. And even with the boys—it's the only way I can get them to clean up their messes. If I tell Sam that Thomas will get something done faster, they both race to finish first."

"You have the right idea," Sophie said. "We just have to alter it a bit to fit the situation. Let's say your beau wishes to take you for a drive in the park, while you wish to attend a Venetian breakfast . . ."

"What's a Venetian breakfast?" Kat asked.

"An excuse to eat a lot of food before noon."

"I'd rather go driving," Kat said.

"Pretend!" Sophie said, her exasperation showing.

Kat thought for a moment. "I could say, 'It is kind of you to invite me for a drive, but I know you would much prefer to have a filling meal.' Men always like to eat."

Sophie nodded with encouragement. "Good, good. Now, what if he wishes to attend a boxing match on the day you wish him to escort you to the new exhibit of painting at the Royal Gallery?"

"Why, we'd both go to the mill, of course," Kat said.

"*Ladies* do not attend boxing matches, as a rule."

"I'd rather do that than look at a bunch of paintings," Kat said.

Sophie gave her a stern look. "You *want* to see those paintings."

"I'd tell him I'll go look at those silly paintings with someone else if he doesn't care to escort me," Kat said.

"Perfect!" Sophie clapped her hands. "Although you wish to phrase it most carefully. 'I should not like to keep you from your sporting events. I will ask—and then name his strongest rival—to escort me to the exhibit.' No serious suitor would permit that!"

Kat thought for a moment. "One thing I do with the boys is ask who would like to have a treat—then set out the task they must perform first. They dare not refuse, for if they do, they know one of the others will do it instead to get the reward."

"See? You understand how the game is played. Only the situation is slightly different."

"This might not be so difficult after all." Kat's spirits brightened. "I cannot wait to try your advice on your brother."

"I wish you luck—he can be a stubborn fellow." Sophie shook her head ruefully. "But there are plenty of other men who are malleable—we just have to find you the right one."

"Did you practice these sorts of tricks with your husband?" Kat asked.

"On occasion," Sophie replied. "I remember, once, before he had asked for my hand, I did so want him to be part of our party at the theater. But he was otherwise engaged, so I made a particular effort to ask a certain other man to join us instead. Richard asked for my hand the very next day."

"I'm ready to go to London now and start looking," Kat said. "Can we leave this week?"

Sophie laughed. "Dear Kat! There is still so much to do. Our clothes will not be ready. And there is still so much I have to tell you. And dancing—we must practice your dancing."

Kat frowned. Just when she thought she had everything figured out, Sophie tossed another task at her. It was a very complicated thing, going about in society.

But worth all the effort if it brought her brothers back to her.

When Val arrived in London, he was relieved to discover that Nicholas Foster had not spent his time alone indulging in drunken revelries or debauched mayhem. No, from all Val could learn, the lad had behaved himself as he ought. It made Val even more confident in recommending him for a post in one of the Guard units. While nothing official had been said, he'd been privately assured that there would be an opening within the month, and Foster's candidacy would be seriously considered—as he was willing to pay the price for an available commission.

In the morning, Val paid another visit to the Horse

Guards, to learn if any openings had developed in one of the sought-after regiments. Val still could not understand why anyone would want to be a parade soldier, but in peacetime he supposed it had a certain appeal. Strutting around London in a fancy uniform would certainly attract the eyes of the ladies. And while he thought Nicholas Foster too young to be thinking about marriage, there was always that possibility. It was Val's obligation as guardian to do what was best for his ward, and a commission in the Guards would raise young Nick's value in the eyes of many calculating mothers.

Val had already approached several of his old comrades-in-arms for leads, and so he was not overly surprised when he was told that indeed an opening had developed in the Blues, and if young Mr. Foster was willing to pay the asking price, the commission as lieutenant would be his.

As soon as Val reached home, he sent up a note to Nicholas, who had developed the deplorable town habit of staying up nearly until dawn and sleeping late. His new commanding officer would soon cure him of that indulgence.

Nick appeared in the study only a scant few moments later, cravat sloppily tied and hair sticking out every which way. Val barely repressed a shudder.

"You wanted to see me?" Nick asked eagerly.

Val nodded. "Sit down." He waited for the boy to be seated and gestured to the sideboard. "Should you like a glass of brandy?"

The young man blanched. "Not after last night."

Val poured himself a glass then turned to his ward. "Well, I am sorry to tell you that your life of high living is soon to be over."

"Have I overstepped my bounds?" Nick's face flushed with guilt.

"Not unless you've indulged in some low undertakings that I have not yet heard of," Val replied, hiding a smile. "No, I fear you are going to have to conform your activities to military regulations in the near future."

"My commission?" Nick sprang to his feet. "You found me a commission?"

"Sit down." Val pointed to the chair. "I begin to think you are a jack-in-the-box the way you jump whenever the military is mentioned. I was at the Horse Guards this morning, and there is a position available in the Blues, if that suits you."

"Oh, indeed it does," Nick replied, his eyes shining with unrestrained delight.

"Now, in my opinion, the position is vastly overpriced, considering that we are at peace and advancement is at a virtual standstill."

"That does not matter to me," Nick said. "I am content to be a lieutenant forever."

"Well, you can only hope that we find someone to go to war with again so you can improve your position," Val said. "As your guardian, I must advise you that it is not a practical investment and will cost you far more than you will ever earn. I can also see that my words matter not in the least to you."

Nick grinned. "I understand what you are saying, sir. But right now, I want a commission more than anything else in the world."

"Very well, then. I will schedule an appointment with your banker to make the necessary financial arrangements, and then we shall toddle off to the Horse Guards tomorrow to begin the torturous process of the paperwork."

"How long do you think it will take?" Nick asked.

"Oh, a fortnight or so," Val replied.

"A fortnight?" Dismay filled the lad's face. "I have to wait that long?"

"You will have plenty to accomplish in that time, believe me," Val said. "Why, just the fittings for your uniforms will occupy the better part of a week. There are horses to buy, equipment . . ."

"I cannot tell you how much this means to me," Nick said. "I will be forever grateful."

"Just see that you behave yourself for the remainder of your stay," Val said. "And, of course, once you join your regiment."

"Oh, I will," Nick promised.

"Your sister may arrive before you join the regiment. I am sure she will be glad of your company."

Nick swallowed hard. "I do not think she will care that much. She is not very happy with me."

"When I spoke to her, she readily acquiesced to my plans for her. I believe her temper has cooled."

"She knows she is coming here to find a husband?" Nick asked, surprise on his face.

"Indeed she does."

Nick shook his head. "That does not sound like Kat at all."

"I believe her to be a sensible girl, despite her hot temper," Val said. "She knows that marriage is the natural future for her."

Nick let out a whoosh of air. "I hope you are right. Kat's never indicated a desire to wed before."

"Probably because the candidates open to her at home were far too limited. In London, she will have a much wider selection to choose from. I have no doubt we will be able to find a fellow who is to her liking."

"I almost regret that I won't be here to watch this," Nick said. "If you succeed, my lord, I'll take off my hat to you."

"I do not anticipate any difficulties," Val said, annoyed by the lad's continued doubts. "She will soon realize what is best for her."

He stood, indicating the interview was over. "Tomorrow morning at ten we will go to the Horse Guards. See that you are ready—and properly dressed and groomed."

"I will be," Nick promised, and nearly danced out the door.

Val shook his head. The exuberance of youth. Had he ever been that young and foolish?

No.

Thank God.

Chapter Eight

For Kat, the next fortnight with Sophie passed in a whirl of wardrobe planning, memorizing the rules of London society, and learning how to do a few simple country-dances. Finally, Sophie pronounced her ready and they started packing for the journey to London.

Now, three days later, their traveling coach neared the city. Kat was eager for the long, tiring journey to end, yet as fields and farms gave way to houses and gardens, a shiver of apprehension danced down her back. So many things to remember, and so much depending on the success of her plan—and all had to be acted out under the intense scrutiny of her guardian.

Sophie gave her a nudge. "You might catch a glimpse of Holland House through the trees. And then we shall be at Hyde Park."

Kat peered past her but only saw trees and flowering shrubs. As they drove by the park, she moved to the other seat so as to get a better view. To her disappointment, the riding track could not be seen from the road. Perhaps she could persuade Sophie to go later today and view the horses on display.

Yet once they reached the Tyburn tollgate, she could not decide which window to look out of. She had never seen the like. Oxford Street stretched ahead of them, buildings massed on either side of the road, the street itself full of every type of carriage, men on horseback, carters with their goods.

And the people! It looked like market day in Wickworth at its busiest—yet this was only one street. She suddenly grasped the enormity of the city she was entering and found it daunting.

Something on the far side of the street caught her eye, and she lunged across the seat to peer out that window, before sliding back to her place facing Sophie.

"You will be too worn out to do anything if you keep jumping about like this," Sophie observed dryly.

"I can't help it," Kat said. "I'm excited—and nervous. So much depends on this visit! If I cannot convince your brother to relent . . ."

"Val is not against you," Sophie said. "He just needs to be convinced that your solution is the best one."

Kat shivered. "I know he expects me to do something horrible. And I will, too, if he keeps watching me like a nervous mother hen."

"Val knows what a charming young lady you are," Sophie said.

"Hah! He will always fear the worst from me."

"Well, you *did* shoot him," Sophie reminded her.

"Another thing he is not likely to forget—or forgive."

Now that she was almost in his presence again, Kat felt less confident of her ability to win over her guardian. She never should have shot him. But since she had, that unfortunate incident would forever throw a cloud over their relationship, making it all that harder for her to convince him to reunite her family.

Kat needed to beg his forgiveness and hope they could start out afresh. He had made his own gesture of conciliation when he'd brought her horse; now it was her turn to respond. But would he accept her apology?

She knew it was London that made her edgy. There were too many people, too many tall buildings. She longed to be back in the country.

But Newkirk was here in the city, so here she must stay, until she had won him over to her point of view.

Kat felt relief when they turned off the main street into a more residential section, with less vehicles and people. But everywhere she looked there were buildings, buildings, and more buildings. She regretted she had not spent more time looking at Hyde Park, for she suddenly feared she was not going to see another patch of green for ages.

Then ahead of her, the buildings parted and the street

opened onto a huge square—bigger than the village green at home, with an enormous fenced-in garden in the center.

"Is this where your brother's house is?" Kat asked with hope. It would be nice to have such greenery close by.

Sophie laughed. "Hardly. This is Grosvenor Square. He would not wish to live in such a grand location, although I should like it! We are a few streets away still."

After several more turns, Kat was thoroughly lost and could not have found her way back to the square, let alone Oxford Street, if her life depended on it. She felt a sharp relief when the carriage drew to a halt in front of a modest, narrow-fronted brick house, identical to the neighbors on either side of it.

"We are here," Sophie announced.

Kat reached for the door latch, but Sophie stayed her hand. "Let the footman assist you. Remember, *ladies* do not go leaping in and out of coaches."

Kat winced. If she'd already forgotten such a simple thing, what future disasters did that portend? Sophie had tried hard to explain all she knew about proper behavior, but Kat feared she would not remember a tenth of it. Yet if she wanted her plan to succeed, she would have to. Newkirk must be convinced of her complete suitability.

It was silly rules like these that would trip her up. Why pretend to be helpless when she was perfectly capable of getting out of a carriage by herself?

The door was opened by a black-suited man, who flipped down the steps and held out his hand. Sophie took it and, gathering her skirts, stepped down with an elegance that Kat momentarily envied. Kat knew she did not exit with nearly the same grace, but at least she had not fallen on her face. It was one thing to wander about Sophie's house in a dress; climbing in and out of carriages in one was another. It was going to take a while to grow accustomed to having all that fabric swirling about her legs, getting in the way, threatening to trip her.

Acting like a lady was no easy feat.

And inside was Newkirk, the one man she had to impress, who would be watching her every move with a critical eye. Kat squared her shoulders and lifted her chin, determined not to fail in her task. She had to show him that she could be every inch the lady he wanted her to be.

And convince him that she was more than capable of taking care of her family.

The same man who helped them down from the carriage now stood on the top step, holding the front door open. Sophie turned and beckoned for Kat to follow her.

"We do not wish to stand about on the street all day," she said, and walked into the house.

Mumbling a few last-minute words of encouragement to herself, Kat followed.

While Newkirk's country house has been comfortable, the town house could only be described as elegant. Marble floors stretched underfoot, a tall, carved hall clock stood in the entry, and an ornate chandelier hung overhead. Kat looked around hastily, noticing the expensive appointments, then hurrying to catch Sophie, who was already starting up the stairs.

She followed Sophie upward and to the left, through a set of double doors that led into what was no doubt the main drawing room, running across the front of the house. It was decorated with even more elegance than the one in the country, with green and cream walls, gilt-framed paintings and upholstered furniture. Sophie untied her bonnet and set it on a chair, and Kat realized she'd left hers in the coach.

"I should get my bonnet," she said, and started for the door.

"Someone will bring it," Sophie said. She looked eagerly about the room. "Oh, it is good to be back in London."

"It is good to have you here again, Sophie."

Kat froze at the words. Newkirk was here.

"I see you have brought our honored guest," he continued.

Kat slowly turned and watched as he sauntered into the room, examining her with what she knew was a critical eye.

She took a deep breath. She had to remember that this man held her future in his hands. It was time to continue the performance she had begun at Sophie's.

Kat knelt in a deep curtsy, holding her skirts to the side, remembering all that Sophie had taught her. "My lord, it is a pleasure to see you again."

She thought she caught a fleeting glimpse of amusement

in his eyes before he bowed low. "Miss Foster. Thank you for accompanying my sister."

Sophie put her hands on her hips and stared at her brother. "And have you no greeting for me?"

"Always." Newkirk covered the floor between them in several long strides and grasped her hands. "It is good to have you in town, Sophie."

"I think I am pleased to be here," she said. "But fagged after that journey. As I am certain Kat is. I will show her to her room and help her get settled. Will we see you at dinner tonight?"

Newkirk nodded. "I shall dine with you this evening."

"Goodness, I half expected you to drag us to a grand ball on our first night here."

"Tomorrow," he promised with a faint grin.

"You are such a tease!" Sophie exclaimed, rapping him on the arm with her glove. "You know it will be another week at least before all our clothes are ready. Goodness, there is still so much shopping to be done. I intend to start first thing tomorrow. We don't have time for balls and such right now!"

To Kat's surprise, Newkirk smiled. "Ah yes, you and your shopping. I suppose I shall have to triple the footmen's wages while you are here to make up for the trouble of having to haul all your packages."

"A good plan, Val." Sophie stood on tiptoe and kissed his cheek. "Thank you for persuading me to come."

She took Kat by the arm and led her out into the hall and up the stairs.

"See?" she said when they'd reached the landing. "That went smoothly."

Kat peered out the window of the bedroom she had been given. It looked over the tiny back garden, the existence of which had come as a surprise to her. Sophie explained that nearly every house in this section of town had a garden in back and that some of the bigger mansions held wonder-works of greenery hidden behind their stone facades.

Kat was more interested in the stabling for the horses, and Sophie promised to show her the mews around the corner on the morrow—after they went shopping.

She rose again and paced the room. Sophie might be tired from traveling, but Kat was not. In fact, she had far too much pent-up energy after being trapped in the carriage for the last three days. What she needed was a nice, refreshing walk; however, she had no wish to get lost on her first day in London.

But she could explore as far as the stables. She could easily find her way there. And she was curious to see what manner of horses Newkirk kept.

Her trunks with her still meager belongings had been brought in and unpacked by a maid clad in gray and white. Kat grabbed her cloak from the wardrobe and started down the stairs. She let herself out the front door, walked down the steps and turned to her left.

Newkirk's house was in the center of a long block of nearly identical brick houses facing each other across the cobbled street. If she had to live in London, she would rather live on a large square such as the one they had passed, where you did not have the sense of buildings and people closing in on you from all sides.

At the corner, she turned and walked until she reached a gap between the houses, wide enough to allow a carriage to pass. She entered this passageway and felt a spurt of relief when she smelled the familiar stable odors—horses, sweat, hay, and dung.

The passage opened into a wide courtyard encircled by stabling for horses and carriages. A coach similar to the one she and Sophie had ridden in was being hitched up with a team of four. In front of another stable, a groom was washing down and combing a splendid bay. Kat walked closer to give the animal a more critical examination.

"Fine piece of horseflesh there," she said conversationally.

"That 'e is," the groom replied.

"Who does he belong to?" she asked.

"Lord Dandridge."

"Is he married?"

The groom gave her an odd look. "That he is, miss."

Kat sighed. She wouldn't mind being married to a man with a horse like that. She continued along, peering inside the open stable doors. The mews was similar to an inn yard, although far less hectic and much larger. Why, there must be nearly fifty horses here, and almost as many workers. She marveled at how this was hidden away behind those towering houses, like a secret world within the city.

Most of the horses looked to be decent stock, although she spotted a few that she would not have in her own stable. Seeing these prime animals made her eager to view the display in Hyde Park. Perhaps she could persuade Sophie to go there tomorrow. If Kat could not ride, she could at least watch others doing so.

Curious to learn what type of mounts Newkirk kept for himself, Kat asked around until someone pointed her to the right stable. She marched over and called out for the groom, who came scurrying out.

"You work for Newkirk?" she asked.

The man nodded.

"Good. I am a guest of his and would like to see his stable. Does he keep many horses in town?"

The groom motioned for her to follow. "He's got his riding cattle and those for the carriage. I hear tell we're to be renting a town vehicle—must be for your convenience."

Kat wrinkled her nose. "Oh no, that's for Sophie. Which horse does his lordship favor?"

The groom indicated the stall on the right, which held a sturdy chestnut that looked to be about sixteen hands tall. Kat did not think him a particularly handsome animal, but he looked like he'd have a good deal of stamina. Of course, what good that would do in the city, she did not know. She'd like to see this one put over some fences or a ditch or two.

She looked quickly at the other horses, all superior-looking animals. Kat felt a twinge of annoyance at not discovering that the baron had spavined, bow-backed nags at his disposal. It would be only one more thing to dislike about him.

But since she might actually have to deal with these animals, she supposed it was all for the best that they were worthy creatures. She thanked the groom for his time and went back into the yard.

She guessed that toward evening, as the noble owners prepared for their entertainments, it would be a bustle of activity as horses were harnessed, carriages set to, and drivers mounted. Eddie would love to see it all.

Eddie. A deep pain throbbed within her. He was the very reason she was here in London in the first place, to find a way to bring the boys home. Instead of admiring the horses, she should be back at the house trying to cozen up to Newkirk in a last—and probably fruitless—hope that he would relent and send Eddie, Samuel, and Thomas home.

After the ladies had gone upstairs, Val returned to his study, pleased with what he had seen. Miss Foster had actually arrived by carriage and not astride that monster of a horse she insisted on riding. The look on her face when she'd curtsied to him had been priceless.

Time would tell if she could retain her newfound docility in the hectic whirl of London society. Had Sophie's training gone deep enough to endure public scrutiny? He had to trust his sister's judgment; her letters had been full of enthusiasm for her charge's eagerness to learn and participate in London society.

He'd have more chances to watch Miss Foster closely over the next few days. Sophie's insistence on lengthy shopping expeditions would delay the process of launching his ward into society until he could judge if it was truly safe.

Val already had the names of a few prospective suitors, who could be called upon in the early days to pay a visit and look her over. If he was lucky, one of them would come up to the mark quickly and he would be saved from having to worry about what Miss Katherine Foster would do in elegant London company.

But if not . . . there were plenty of activities to keep her occupied. As long as he kept her away from the high sticklers, where every word she uttered would be analyzed and discussed for days afterward, matters could not go too far awry. The theater was certainly a safe location, along with drives in the park with Sophie, morning calls on family friends and relatives, and visits to educational exhibits. Miss Foster would have ample opportunity to meet plenty of young men.

Val realized it was not all that different from planning to sell a horse—make the effort to be seen in the park, put the animal through its paces, let the word get out that he was for sale, and then wait for the offers and pick the best one.

The plan would work equally well for Sophie. Val vowed to have both of them snapped up before the end of June.

Now that she was here, it was time to discuss his plans with Miss Foster. He sent a footman in search of her, but she was not in her room. Val was not concerned until he learned that Sophie had not seen her, either.

He ordered the servants to launch a search of the entire house. If that brat had run away . . .

An hour later, Val was seething. There was no sign of his ward anywhere. Sophie was frantic with worry, his house was in an uproar, and the chit had barely arrived in London. This did not bode well for the future.

Where had that blasted girl gone? This was not the country. A young lady did not just walk out of the house and stroll about the city on her own. Hadn't Sophie warned her about that? Why, the girl could be anywhere by now—Hyde Park, Piccadilly, the river.

Wait. What was Miss Foster's passion—besides her brothers? Horses. And where were the nearest horses? The mews.

Val jumped up and raced out the front door. He should have thought of this first thing.

He found her, measuring the withers on his second-best carriage horse. Judging from the wisps of straw that clung to her skirts, she had given his stables a thorough inspection.

"Does she meet with your approval?" he asked, stepping closer.

She whirled around and greeted him with a guilty look. "I wanted to see what kind of horses you kept in town."

"And what was your conclusion?"

"That you have some decent animals." She nodded her head toward the chestnut. "Is he a hunter? Have you given him a try in the field? He looks like he'd take a fence nicely."

"Yes, and no," Val replied. "Miss Foster, I must remind you that you are in London now. You are not to wander off without telling anyone where you are going."

"Afraid I intend to run away?" she demanded with a saucy look.

"If only I could be so lucky," he muttered. "No, it is for your own safety. Young ladies do not traipse around the city unescorted."

"I did not think walking the half block to the mews would cause a commotion," she replied.

"I wished to speak with you, and when I couldn't find you, I grew concerned."

"You have found me," she said. "What did you wish to say?"

Val ran an exasperated hand through his hair. "Lord knows what it was; I have completely forgotten because I was caught up searching the house for you."

"Perhaps you wished to compliment me on my decorous greeting of you on my arrival."

Val feigned concentration. "I do not believe that was it."

"Or to say that you realize you have been mistaken in your actions and you are taking my brothers out of school and sending the lot of them back home." She regarded him with a hopeful expression.

"Ah yes, now I remember. I wished to discuss the plans for finding you a husband."

She sighed. " 'Tis a pity your amnesia was not permanent."

Val ignored her remark. "Your brother assures me that you have not formed an attachment to any young man of your acquaintance."

Miss Foster laughed. "One of Nick's friends? Hardly."

"Good. Then you will be open to suggestions."

She regarded him with open suspicion. "What, have you already chosen someone for me?"

"I have not chosen anyone," Val retorted. "This is the whole point of this discussion—I wished to get a sense of the type of man you would consider."

"Until you came into my life, I had no plans to wed, so I fear I cannot tell you what sort of man I would care to marry," she said. "I have never given it a thought."

"Then you will be willing to rely on my guidance?"

She stared at him, an incredulous look on her face. "Your guidance? What do you know of marriage? I would think Sophie a better guide than you. At least she has been married."

Val winced. She was right, of course. But Sophie was not the girl's guardian, he was. "I have enough wisdom to advise you on such a serious matter. I consider myself to be a good judge of character."

She snorted derisively. "You're hardly old enough to even be my guardian."

"Really, Miss Foster, we can go about this in two ways."

Val glowered at her, his exasperation growing. "Either you can cooperate and all will go smoothly, or you can fight me every step of the way and we can both be miserable."

Her face reflected the emotions warring within her. Val could almost put words to the debate going on in her head.

"It is rather foolish for us to be constantly at logger-heads," she said at last. "After all, we will be living in the same house."

"Exactly." Val smiled encouragingly.

"It was kind of you to bring my horse to Newkirk Abbey," she said at last. "I intended to thank you, but you already had left when I returned from my ride."

"I accept your thanks," he said.

She gazed at her toes. "And I really should apologize for shooting you. It was an unfortunate . . . incident."

"I believe that entire day was an 'unfortunate incident,' " Val said, surprised but pleased by her words. "I believe we both acted hastily."

"I am willing to listen to your opinion about my future," she said. "So long as you do not force me to marry anyone against my will."

"I would never do that," Val protested with indignation.

"Then I believe we shall manage to get along," she said, and held out her hand. "Shall we cry truce?"

Somewhat bemused by this rapid turn of events, Val shook the proffered hand. "Agreed."

She turned and looked back again at the chestnut. "I do not suppose you would let me ride . . ." Her voice trailed off and she darted him a pleading glance.

"Absolutely not," he said. "While you are in London, you will ride like a lady, or not at all."

She sighed. "That's what I thought you would say. I can tell you one qualification I shall have in a husband—he will let me ride as I please."

"I think that an excellent idea," Val said. "Now, if you would allow me to escort you back to the house. I believe I left things in an uproar, and it would be good to assure everyone that you have been discovered, safe and sound."

With one last longing look at the chestnut, Miss Foster took his arm and walked with him down the length of the mews.

"Promise me, Miss Foster," Val said as they came out

onto the street, "that in the future, you will not go out without an escort, and you will tell someone where you are going."

She made a face. "I can do that."

"It is for your own safety," he added.

"I appreciate your guardianlike concern for me."

Val ignored the sarcasm in her words.

Sophie greeted them at the door, exclaiming that she just knew Kat was fine and where had Val found her and come upstairs at once so they could make plans for the next day's shopping. With a shake of his head, Val let them go and retreated to his study.

Val told himself not to be overly concerned, things would work themselves out. He felt much better after that conversation in the mews; he judged that he and Miss Foster had achieved an understanding of sorts and surely matters would go on better than they had. He'd find a husband for both her and his sister. Then he would have taken care of all his obligations and no longer would have to worry about either of them. He could do what he pleased, when he pleased, without a single thought for anyone but himself.

What would he do then?

Travel, he thought. The ultimate expression of freedom. No plans, no itinerary; he would go where his whims took him. Not France or Spain—he'd seen enough of those two countries to last him a lifetime.

Italy might be pleasant—warm weather without the unpleasant memories of Spain. And if he grew tired of the warmth, he could go north, into Germany, or exotic Russia. And stay through the winter and see if all the tales he'd heard were true: snow from October to May, with travel possible only by sleigh, and packs of ravenous wolves prowling the byways.

It would be a welcome change from London. During all those years in Spain he'd thought of nothing but returning home; yet its appeal had quickly faded once he found himself here. Now he looked forward to leaving.

Chapter Nine

*I*n the morning, Sophie took Kat for her first shopping foray in London. After their slow-paced days at Newkirk Abbey, Kat was amazed at Sophie's energy. No shop was too small, or too crowded, to discourage her interest. Every item on display required a detailed inspection, critique, and then acceptance or rejection. And Sophie had not exaggerated when she said she could spend hours deciding on a pair of gloves. Kat traipsed along through six shops before Sophie found the exact color of stockings she was looking for.

Yet Kat reluctantly found herself drawn in by Sophie's excitement. First, it had been the hair ribbons that Sophie said brought out the color of her eyes. Then it was the fan with the carefully painted hunting scene. From the enthusiasm of the shopkeeper at the sale, Kat guessed that it was not a popular motif, but she liked it much better than the ones with silly flowers.

Then she discovered the toy shop, sandwiched between a print house and one of the countless milliners that seemed to be present on every block. Grabbing Sophie by the arm, Kat pulled her inside and inspected the wares with the critical eyes of her brothers.

They all needed whistles, and clever wooden noisemakers that popped loudly when you pushed the handle. Kat knew she would regret these purchases later, when they were all together again, but right now she could not wait to be surrounded by the noise all three of them would make. For Tom, she bought a silly cap, with pointed ends like a medieval court jester's, while for Sam, she chose a black-and-white harlequin's hat.

For Eddie, she settled on a small version of a cavalryman's shako. She looked longingly at the rolling hoops,
battledore rackets, and shuttlecocks sporting full comple-
ments of feathers, unlike the pitifully ragged ones at home,
but realized they would be too difficult to send. She would
come back later and buy those when she knew they were
coming home.

Or going to their new one, if she must marry. She had
not thought about that.

"Are you quite done?" Sophie asked as Kat waited for
the last of her purchases to be wrapped. The long-suffering
footman, who had accompanied them all across town, stood
beside her, awaiting his new burden.

"For now," Kat replied.

"Good." Sophie smiled. "I need to find some new feathers for my straw bonnet."

Kat looked at her with dismay. "I thought you were finished shopping for the day."

"Finished?" Sophie looked at her with an amused look
on her face. "My dear girl, we have barely begun."

Kat groaned inwardly. She'd had enough of shopping to
last her for weeks, yet Sophie wanted more.

It reminded Kat that despite their growing friendship, she
and Sophie were very different people. While Kat might be
curious or intrigued by the city, she would never want to
live here. Yet she could see that Sophie was perfectly at
ease amid the noise and bustle.

And what of Newkirk? Did he prefer the city as well?
Kat had not seen enough of him in either place to venture
an opinion. She hoped he was a country gentleman at heart,
for she thought that would make him more sympathetic to
her pleas.

It was half past six when the carriage finally rolled up in
front of Newkirk's house. There was barely room for their
feet in the cramped vehicle as packages spilled off the over-
crowded seat facing them.

"Take everything into the drawing room," Sophie said
to the footman. "I shall sort things out there."

Kat followed her up the stairs.

"Oh, look, mail!" Sophie exclaimed, grabbing the pile on
the round Queen Anne table inside the drawing room door.

"Val must have done his work well—these look like invitations already. And here—two letters for you."

Kat's heart leaped. "From my brothers?" she asked eagerly, snatching them from Sophie's hand.

Yes! One from the twins and the other, the writing smudged and the paper dirty and crumpled, was from Eddie.

She clasped them to her chest. "I'm going to my room," she said, and raced out into the hall and up the stairs. She wanted to be alone to savor these treats.

It was about time those rascals wrote to her. She'd sent them countless letters already, and this was their first reply. Yet all would be forgiven once she read their news.

She opened the one from the twins first and began reading. But as she read down the page, her dismay grew. They were having a wonderful time. They loved their school. They'd bested everyone with their prowess at tying knots, admitted that mathematics was not all that fun, but found geography exciting. And next month they were going to go aboard a real ship for a short sail. The letter ended with a long list of things that she absolutely had to send them.

Kat felt tears prick at her eyes. This was what she had feared most about Newkirk's plans—that once her brothers were away and involved in their new studies, they would no longer need her.

She told herself it had to happen eventually; the twins were old enough to no longer need mothering, but mere sisterly guidance. Still, she felt a sharp pang of loss knowing the spell of the navy and life at sea had already caught their imaginations. Home would forever seem tame by comparison. Even worse, they probably would no longer want to come home even if she could persuade Newkirk to let them.

Damn him.

She set their letter aside and slowly opened the one from her youngest brother, almost afraid to read it, fearing that he, too, would be enthralled with his new school and friends. If Eddie no longer needed her, what was she to do?

But his first words reassured her—and made her all the more worried. He pleaded to come home, saying he hated school, hated his classmates, hated the teachers, the food, the sleeping rooms—in short, everything.

Kat sucked in her breath. How could Newkirk have sent him to such a horrid place? It sounded more like a prison than a school. The poor child! She had to get him away from there as soon as possible. Even Newkirk would have to agree after reading this letter.

She grabbed up the missive and ran back downstairs to see if the baron was at home.

The footman directed her to the study at the rear of the house. She knocked at the door, then marched in without waiting for an answer. Newkirk sat by the tall windows overlooking the garden, a book in his hand.

"Good day, Miss Foster. Was your shopping expedition with my sister a success?"

She thrust the letter at him. "You must read this."

He took the letter and quickly scanned the contents, then handed it back to her without comment.

"See how miserable he is?" she said. "You must let me rescue him."

"I see a lad who is slightly homesick, but he doesn't appear to be in imminent danger."

"He's miserable!" she cried. "How can you allow him to suffer like that?"

"Did it ever occur to you that he might be trying to paint the most piteous picture possible to garner your sympathy—and perhaps a large box of sweets?"

Kat drew herself up stiffly. "Eddie would not fabricate such stories."

"There is very little that I *wouldn't* expect that rascal to try," Newkirk replied. "If he was truly having difficulties, I would hear from the headmaster. There have been no letters, so I think it is safe to assume that your brother is doing fine."

"I want to see for myself," Kat insisted.

"Well, you cannot," he replied. "For the moment, your concerns lay here in town."

"How can you be so cruel?" Kat demanded.

"It is far crueler to keep the lad tied to your apron strings," he said.

"He's only eight!"

"As are the rest of his schoolmates, and I doubt their mothers—or sisters—are carrying on like this."

"Don't you have any feelings at all?" She searched his

face for a trace of sympathy for her plight, but his stern expression did not melt. How could this man continue to be so . . . so unfeeling? Didn't Eddie's words move him at all? Had all those years of war hardened his heart against any of the human kindnesses?

"Treating him like an infant is not doing him any favors," Newkirk replied. "Believe me, any lad who can tie me to a chair is brave enough to handle anything."

She stamped her foot in frustration. "Why won't you listen to me?"

"Because, Miss Foster, in this matter I do not think you are right. I suggest you send a letter to your brother, filled with news of your activities and no mention of his complaints, and I am willing to wager that he will reply that he is having the time of his life."

"And if he does not?"

"We can discuss that *if* the situation arises."

"You must have had a miserable childhood," she said at last, "if you cannot feel for his suffering."

He gave her an impassive look. "As a matter of fact, I did. And that is why I know that his complaints are not serious."

She stared at him, taken aback by his answer. Then, irritated that she could not think of a quick rejoinder to his remark, she turned her back on him and stomped out of the room.

Just when she thought that Newkirk was not the ogre she had originally considered him, he showed his true colors. All his conciliatory words had been a sham. How was she ever going to persuade him to let the boys come home when Eddie's tale of woe did not move him?

Kat would write to Eddie this very minute, and if he put one single word of complaint in his reply, she would take Newkirk's carriage herself and retrieve her brother. That would teach Newkirk to ignore her concerns.

Val sighed as the door slammed shut behind her. He honestly sympathized with her worries, knew the pain she was feeling, even if it was unwarranted. If a few poorly cooked meals and a boring Latin class were the only things that troubled her brother, he was a lucky fellow.

She had to learn to let her brothers—even young

Eddie—live their own lives. It had been one thing for her to oversee their every action while they were without any adult guidance, but she was not their mother; she had done far more than any sister should have been asked to. That was ultimately his father's fault—as so many things were.

Amazingly, Val realized that he no longer felt the old hatred welling up in him at the thought of the man. If he felt anything at all, it was indifference—and resignation. The past was done and gone. All the wishful thinking in the world would not change it. He could only marvel that he had survived it all—and that Sophie had emerged unscarred. If he had done one thing right in his life, protecting her from their father's abusive behavior had been it.

And if there was a particularly hot, burning pit in hell, he knew his father was roasting in it.

All this he could not tell Miss Foster. She was suffering from the same sense of obligation that he had felt for his sister, the overwhelming urge to protect her from all the ills of the world, the fear that if she was out of his sight for even a moment, something horrible would happen. He'd guarded her carefully.

Then, as part of the world's ultimate jest, after guiding her safely into womanhood, seeing her happily wed, and thinking his mission a success, her world collapsed in a Belgium farmyard. He realized that nothing was ever under control for very long; that life would take the bends and turns that it would, and his power to influence matters was limited.

Which was why he wanted to free Miss Foster from the responsibility for her siblings. Their lives would go on as they would, no matter what she did, and she needed to loosen her hold on the reins. She had her own life to live, and it was time that she lived it.

Val had waited far too long to do the same for himself. He intended to spare her that regret, at least, even if it meant she was angry with him. What she saw as callous disregard for her brothers was really deep concern for her. Maybe someday she would realize that.

And if not, well, he had not asked for this duty, so he should not expect to be thanked for it, either.

* * *

"He is the most cruel, unfeeling, insensitive . . ."

Adjectives failed Kat as she paced angrily across Sophie's sitting room. She scowled at Sophie, seated on the sofa. "I hate him!"

"It does sound as if your brother is not happy at his school," Sophie said. "But do realize, he has only been there a short while. I remember when I first arrived at school that it took me several weeks before I was certain that I liked it."

"You were sent away to school?" Kat asked with surprise.

"You make it sound so awful," Sophie said. "It was wonderful fun. I was surrounded by other girls, learned a great many useful skills, and even enjoyed most of my education."

"Didn't you miss being at home?"

"Of course I did, but you must remember that I was alone by then. It was fun to be in the company of other girls."

"Did your parents send Val away to school, too?"

A slight shadow crossed over her face. "No, he was educated at home."

"Then why is he so eager to send everyone else off to school?"

"Perhaps because that was what he wanted for himself, and couldn't have," Sophie said.

Kat sat down. "He said . . . he said he had a miserable childhood. Is that what he meant?"

Sophie frowned. "I think you will have to ask Val exactly what he meant. Remember, we are eight years apart."

"But you must know something?" Kat pressed her.

"My father . . . my father was a difficult person," Sophie said slowly. "I know that Val held him in the greatest dislike, although I do not know all the reasons. I realize now that he kept me sheltered from a great deal of . . . unpleasantness."

Kat thought about this. It might explain why Newkirk was so intent on ordering everyone else around, if he'd battled with his father as a youth. Now that he was in charge, he wanted to have his own way in everything. Even at her, and her brothers', expense.

Well, no matter what had happened in his childhood, he had no right to make others miserable now. She intended to make sure that Eddie was happy. And taking him out of that horrid school was the first step.

A light tap sounded on Sophie's door. A maid peeked in and caught Kat's eye. "There is someone here to see you, miss."

"Me?" Kat looked at her. "Who could be here to see me?"

"Who do you think, you gudgeon?" A tall man in a blue uniform pushed past the maid and stepped into the room.

"Nick!" Kat shrieked, and raced to embrace him, all her anger forgotten at the thrill of seeing her brother again.

He lifted her into the air with a crushing hug and then set her back on her feet. "Can this really be Kat? In such a comely frock? With her face washed and her hair combed? Are you sure you are really my sister?"

Kat slugged him on the arm. "Oh, stop it. Look at you— all togged up like a toy soldier."

Nick stepped back and preened. "Isn't it a dashing rig?"

Kat scornfully examined his tailored blue jacket and the shiny gold buttons and the high-gloss polish of his tasseled Hessians, and snickered. "Is the object to frighten the enemy to death?"

Nick looked crestfallen. "You don't like it?"

"I think you look magnificent." Sophie walked over and held out her hand. "I fear we were never properly introduced when we last met. As you know, I am Sophie Bellshaw."

Nick bowed low. "It is a pleasure to see you again, Mrs. Bellshaw."

"And you," Sophie replied. "I've heard so much about you from your sister."

Nick laughed. "None of it good, I will wager."

"Of course not," Kat said. "I used to think you were a pretty swell fellow, but after seeing this costume . . ." She shook her head and looked at Sophie. "Can we order tea? Or should we take it in the drawing room?"

"You can order anything you wish and talk with your brother anywhere you want," Sophie replied. "I told you to act as if this was your own house."

"Better not tell her that," Nick said. "She'll be racing horses through the downstairs hall."

"Kat would do no such thing," Sophie replied. "She is a refined young lady."

Both Kat and her brother burst into laughter.

"This I must see," Nick said.

"You will get your chance," Sophie replied. "You may accompany us about town—that is, if your military duties will allow."

"I believe we will have ample time for play," Nick said.

"And bring all your friends," Sophie said. "We shall have the ladies swooning over your dashing uniforms."

"Or running in fright," Kat muttered. She grabbed Nick's arm and dragged him toward the door. "I'm going to take him downstairs and find out what he is *really* doing."

Nick took Sophie's hand and bowed over it. "I look forward to seeing you again."

"Don't you dare flirt with Sophie," Kat warned him when they were in the hall.

"Does she bite?"

Kat slugged him on the arm again. "She's far above your touch."

"I'm merely being polite to my guardian's sister," Nick protested.

"Precisely," Kat replied with a grin, then sobered as she remembered the important matter she had to discuss with him. "Oh, Nick, I've had the most heart-wrenching letter from Eddie. He's perfectly miserable in that horrid school that Newkirk forced him to attend. We have to get him out of there."

"Oh, you know Eddie. He always makes things sound worse than they are."

"He could very well be speaking the truth. I want to go check on him and see if he is all right, but Newkirk won't allow it."

"I agree with him. There's no sense in causing a commotion if there is no need," Nick said.

"You are as heartless as Newkirk. He's just a little boy," she cried. "He's never been away from home before, and who knows what horrible things could happen to him there."

"If Newkirk is not concerned, why should I be? He knows what's best, after all."

"I cannot believe you are acting like this!" Kat cried. "You are as horrible as he is!"

"Oh, don't look at me like that. You know you mother them far too much."

"Better too much than not at all."

Nick flung up his hands. "It is far more likely that the school will demand he leave for blowing up the headmaster's study or locking all his classmates in the cellar. You don't have to worry about him."

"Well, I do, and I thought at least you would show some concern for my feelings. But I forgot—you're working hand in glove with Newkirk."

"Because I agree with him."

"I suppose you think I should get married, too?"

"There is no reason for you not to, now that the boys are being looked after. What else are you going to do with yourself?"

They had reached the hall leading to the drawing room, but instead of turning that way, Kat headed toward the front door.

"From the moment he mentioned the word 'commission,' you have been his slave. You would agree with anything he said," she complained. "I thought you would show *some* loyalty to your family, but I guess I was wrong."

"I think Newkirk is doing a bang-up job with the boys," Nick replied. "Just because you're unhappy doesn't mean the rest of us have to be."

"Thank you so much for your visit," she said sarcastically, and pulled the door open.

"Mark my words, you'll see the wisdom of his actions before long," Nick said. "He has our best interests at heart."

"Hah!"

Nick tried to give her a kiss on the cheek, but she ducked and left him himself kissing air instead. Frowning, he brushed past her, and she shut the door none too silently behind him.

Everyone was against her. *Everyone.*

And Nick, of all people, was so eager to please Newkirk that he would agree to anything their guardian said. She could no longer rely on her brother for any manner of support.

Well, she would take matters firmly into her own hands and show him that she was not afraid to take on Newkirk. She would redouble her efforts to convince him that he was wrong and Eddie needed to come home.

And if Newkirk would not relent, she would find a man who sympathized with her cause and would agree to help her.

Chapter Ten

*K*at pointedly ignored her guardian for the next two days and devoted herself to Sophie's shopping excursions. But at last, she grew so thoroughly tired of shopping that she insisted to Sophie that they do something—anything—as long as it did not involve a shop. As she pointed out to Sophie, she was never going to meet any eligible men in a milliner's establishment. Sophie suggested a drive in the park, and Kat readily agreed. She was disappointed, though, to discover that Newkirk's coachman was assigned to drive them.

"Why does your brother insist that his coachman drive?" Kat asked as the landau pulled out from in front of the house. "I'm perfectly capable of handling a team. And I know there are women who drive their own carriages."

"Perhaps Val thought you wouldn't want to be burdened for your first drive in Hyde Park," Sophie suggested. "This way, you can enjoy your surroundings."

"Hmm." Kat had not considered that. And since she had not yet driven Newkirk's team, it was probably well that she did not take them on such a public display the first time. Not that she doubted her ability with the reins, but she did admit that the clogged London streets would be challenging even to the sharpest whip.

"I am certain he will let you drive later," Sophie said. "And if he will not, I will."

"I can teach you how as well," Kat said.

Sophie regarded her doubtfully. "I am not certain that I really want to learn."

"It's a useful skill," Kat insisted. "What if you are kidnapped by some unscrupulous fortune hunter? Stealing his carriage and driving back to town may be the only way to save yourself."

"Now, that is a *real* concern of mine," Sophie replied dryly.

Kat grinned. "You did consider it for a moment, didn't you?"

Sophie nodded and they both laughed.

It was only a short distance from Bruton Street to the park entrance at Grosvenor Gate, and soon they joined the few other carriages circling the park.

"It is light of company today," Sophie said. "Which is all to the good as I do not want anyone of importance to see me dressed like this."

She was still wearing her "old" clothes. Kat agreed with Newkirk—they looked perfectly lovely and were far grander than anything she herself owned, but Sophie kept insisting they were woefully out of style. Tomorrow, they were scheduled to visit the modiste and come away with the first of their new gowns.

Kat wore her plain green traveling dress and pelisse, since there was little else she could wear. Not that she minded in the least—Kat suspected she was going to feel uncomfortable in all her elegant new clothing. But if they helped Newkirk to consider her a proper lady . . .

"Wait until you see the park at the height of the Season," Sophie told her. "Carriages so thick you can barely squeeze past, and every handsome man in London riding alongside."

"I think I prefer it like this." Kat looked with interest as they passed the Serpentine. A flock of ducks clustered along the shore, snapping at the crusts of bread tossed in their direction by two small children. The sight instantly brought her brothers to mind.

Eddie was older than these children, but even when he was younger, Kat couldn't picture him contentedly throwing bits of bread to the birds. More likely he'd be trying to catch one in a leg snare.

That was something she could send him. She wondered if they permitted hunting on the grounds of his school—or if his school even had grounds.

That she could find out when she went to investigate the true state of his situation. She'd written him promptly two days ago and awaited his reply with a mixture of trepidation and eagerness. She did not want her brother to be unhappy, but if Eddie repeated his complaints, she would have a strong case to present to Newkirk. He'd have to allow her to take Eddie out of school then.

Sophie nudged her shoulder. "See those two soldiers? They're looking at us."

"Where?"

Kat leaned forward to stare past Sophie at the two mounted men in red uniforms. One of them tipped his shako to her, and Kat waved back with enthusiasm. Sophie collapsed into giggles.

"You're not supposed to do that," she said, pulling Kat back into her seat.

"Then why did you tell me they were looking at us?" Kat asked.

Sophie shook her head in amusement.

"You do not want the men to think you are interested," she explained. "That is part of the secret of controlling them."

"Ignoring them seems rather foolish," Kat said. "I am here trying to attract suitors, after all."

"Nevertheless, that is the way it is done." Sophie pulled the carriage rug closer around her. "It is chilly today—I do not wish to stay much longer."

Kat, who was already finding driving through the park to be a rather dull prospect, did not offer an objection.

They drove along the path paralleling Park Lane, then turned and started back toward the Serpentine. Coming toward them on foot was a young man in a grass-green coat, leading a limping horse.

"Oh, look at that poor animal," Kat said. "I wonder what is wrong."

"I suppose you wish to stop and find out," Sophie said. Kat nodded, and Sophie directed the coachman to halt.

"What has happened?" Kat inquired of the young man.

"I don't know," he said, looking frantic. "I think he's

strained a tendon. I was trotting along quite nicely when he suddenly pulled up lame."

"Let me see." Kat jumped down from the carriage and walked over to the horse. She stroked his neck and uttered a few gentle words before she knelt and ran her hand down his leg.

"Nothing feels swollen," she said. She lifted his hoof and inspected it. "Here's the problem—he's got a stone. Didn't you think to check?"

The man flushed and shook his head. Kat gave him a disgusted glare and then called to Sophie. "Hand me my reticule."

Without a word, Sophie handed the bag to the man, who in turn handed it to Kat. She fished around inside, pulled out her folding penknife, then rested the afflicted hoof against her bent knee.

"This should only take a moment," she said, and pried the stone loose. It fell onto the path, and she stood and kicked it toward the grass.

"I can't believe I didn't think of that," the man said, brushing sandy hair out of his eyes. "I was so worried it was something horrible . . . I was afraid he'd really hurt himself and my brother would've . . ."

"Swiped your brother's horse, did you?" Kat asked with a grin. The young man looked sheepish and nodded.

"Then consider yourself lucky," she said, and walked back to the carriage.

"But what is your name—and your direction?" he asked. "I would like to thank you properly."

"Kat Foster," she said, then broke into a smile. He *was* a gentleman, and looked to be respectable, if one ignored that coat and his garish plum-and-gold-striped waistcoat. "You can find me on Bruton Street, at Baron Newkirk's."

"I shall present myself promptly, once I have been assured that this fellow is all right."

"I look forward to that." Kat climbed back into the carriage and took her seat beside Sophie again. The driver started the horses, and she gave a little wave to the young man as they drove off.

Sophie held a gloved hand to her forehead. "What am I going to do with you?" she whispered.

"That poor horse." Kat shook her head. "The silly fool

didn't have sense to realize it was a simple stone. I've half a mind to tell his brother what happened when I discover his name."

"Please don't," Sophie said. "I'm sure the poor fellow has suffered enough."

Kat looked down at the dirty smudge on her dress. "I guess one is not supposed to pick hooves in the park—in a dress."

"No," Sophie replied. "And young ladies do not go about introducing themselves to total strangers."

"He asked me for my name," Kat protested. "I did not wish to be rude. And he has promised to call. See, I have made an acquaintance already! At this rate, I shall find a husband in no time."

"But you do not know anything about him! He could be a gambler or a—well, something worse."

"Oh, pooh." Kat dismissed her concerns. "He is a silly young man with horrid taste in clothing who knows nothing about horses. Perfectly harmless."

Sophie shook her head. "I only fear the tale of this exploit will probably be all over London by evening."

"Is that so dreadful?" Kat asked, suddenly worried that Newkirk would be angry if he learned of this.

"I do not know," Sophie replied with a frown. "You may garner favor with the horsing set."

"I think you are worried over nothing." Kat waved a dismissive hand. "That fellow won't dare say a word—after all, he admitted he had taken his brother's horse without permission. To talk about me is to confess his sin."

"You can hope that is true."

"Was what I did really so bad?" Kat asked.

"No," Sophie admitted. "Merely rather out of the ordinary."

"I would rather be thought of as unusual than commonplace," Kat said.

"I do not think you ever have to worry about that," Sophie replied.

Kat gave her a rueful look.

Val waited impatiently in the study for Sophie and Miss Foster to return from their drive. Not that he was worried about them—they were only going to the park, after all.

Yet every time Miss Foster left the house, he did not feel easy until she returned.

He should not worry so. Her behavior since she arrived in London had been thoroughly unexceptionable. He knew she was trying hard to act the young lady. Ever since that confrontation over Eddie, he'd sought ways to distract her from her brother's plight, which Val knew was nothing more than a slight case of homesickness. Sophie was keeping her busy shopping, but he suspected that would occupy his ward's attention for only so long. Perhaps an educational outing was called for—museum visits and the like. He quickly scanned the *Times* and found exactly what he was looking for—an exhibit of paintings at the Royal Gallery. He would escort the both of them.

Val walked into the hall when he heard the two women's voices.

"I have a surprise for you two," Val announced. "We are going to visit the Royal Gallery this afternoon."

"That sounds like a lovely plan," Sophie said, setting her bonnet on the hall table.

"And how was your drive?" he asked, glancing at Miss Foster. With her tousled short hair, and her cheeks pink from the air, she looked every bit the country miss. Youthful, healthy, innocent.

"The park was quite lean of people," Sophie complained. "No one else is in town."

"That must have been a great relief to you, since I see you were forced to go out in public in that *ancient* gown."

"Believe me, I kept it covered under the rug," Sophie said.

Val looked more closely at Miss Foster, whose dress was decidedly muddy. "And how did you find the park?"

"Oh, rather dull," she said with an airy wave of her hand. "No one of importance was there."

He saw Sophie smother a giggle. He knew then that something had transpired on their outing, but whatever it was, they were not going to tell him. Probably best that he did not know. Where Katherine Foster was concerned, blissful ignorance had its advantages.

"The gallery opens at three. I thought we should arrive about half past."

"That will be fine," Sophie said. "Come along, Kat, let's

go upstairs and change. I shall have to find something that is fit to wear in public."

Val was decidedly glad that the two of them would be going to the dressmakers tomorrow so Sophie would stop complaining. He knew she was only half serious, but he wanted her mind to be focused on finding a husband for Miss Foster, not her wardrobe.

"What do you think of Kat's new bonnet?" Sophie asked Val as the three drove toward the exhibit in Piccadilly.

He gave his ward's hat a careful examination. The chip-straw bonnet, with only a simple ribbon for decoration, framed her face. The plain style suited her far better than the feathered creation that sat on his sister's head. He was relieved that all the shopping with Sophie had not altered Miss Foster's taste in clothing. For a girl from the country, she had a good sense of what looked good on her.

"Quite stylish," he said.

His ward smiled at his praise, and Val dared to hope that her anger toward him had cooled.

Sophie laughed and turned to Miss Foster. "That is a high compliment, coming from Val. He has little eye for fashion."

"If you mean can I discern the subtle nuances between this year's style of hem trimming and last's, you are correct," Val said. "But I do have a sense of what looks attractive."

To his annoyance, Sophie barely smothered her laugh. He gave her a sharp look, and turned back to his ward.

"Do you enjoy art, Miss Foster?" Val asked.

She shrugged. "I've never really thought much about it."

"Our grandfather was a collector—as you may have guessed from all the paintings in the house," Val said.

"It really does not matter whether or not you like art," Sophie said. "The gallery is much like the park—you are going there to be seen."

"Which is not all bad," Newkirk said. "It forces philistines like Sophie to be exposed to some cultural influences."

"As if you spent all your time in Spain and France visiting museums and galleries," Sophie retorted.

"Oh, I didn't," Val admitted cheerfully.

"If no one really likes art, or music, or the opera, why does anyone bother with them?" Miss Foster asked.

Val and Sophie burst into laughter.

"Heaven forbid if we only did what we liked to do." Sophie rolled her eyes. "We would all be sitting at home, staring at bare walls and listening to ourselves talk."

"I find it foolish to waste time on something you do not enjoy," Miss Foster said.

"I agree," Val said. "But because that is the way society works, we must go along with their dictates for now. When you are married, Miss Foster, you can ignore art for the remainder of your life, if you wish."

"I don't mind paintings of horses," she said. "And hunting scenes."

"Then let us hope there are some at this exhibit," he said.

At the entrance, Val paid their admission fees and guided both ladies into the first room of the gallery. He was about as interested in art as Miss Foster professed to be, but it would be good for her to see something more than the inside of a shop, and would give her a topic of conversation at future social events.

And fortunately, since all the artists in this exhibition were dead, there was not going to be anything controversial displayed on the walls.

He dutifully followed the two women as they strolled, arm in arm, past the paintings, whispering comments to one another. For an instant, Val felt a bit put out that he was not included in their confidences. Then he realized this only demonstrated that Sophie and Miss Foster were becoming close friends, and his regret was replaced by relief.

Val also noticed the admiring glances cast the two ladies' way by the men in the room, and felt a surge of optimism that his plans for both of them would come to fruition soon.

He watched as they entered the next gallery, and he let them wander freely, deciding he would catch up with them later. Val glanced at the landscape hanging on the wall before him but found its bucolic setting hopelessly dull. Surely, there had to be something more interesting in this exhibit.

He wandered about, not seeing any paintings that appealed to him, finally entering the gallery where the women had gone. He glanced about, saw Sophie standing on the far side of the room, talking animatedly with a lady in a hideously feathered bonnet, and walked over.

"There you are, Val." Sophie linked her arm in his. "I should like to present Miss Sarah Edgecombe. Her sister and I were at Miss Dunlop's together."

Val bowed low in greeting. The girl giggled and gave him a simpering smile.

"Are you in London for the Season, Miss Edgecombe?" She nodded and Val wondered if the girl could speak.

"She says Emmeline—that is her sister—is coming to town later in the month," Sophie explained. "I do so look forward to seeing her again."

"How nice," Val muttered absently. His attention was now focused on the room, which he was scanning with growing apprehension. There was no sign of Miss Foster. "Where is she?" he demanded.

"Emmeline? Why, she is in—"

"*I meant* Miss Foster," Val said.

Sophie looked around, puzzled. "She was here a moment ago."

Val sighed. If he could not rely on Sophie to keep an eye on his ward, it was going to be a very, very long stay in London. Perhaps he should tie a rope around the chit's waist and lash the other end to his wrist. At least then she could not wander off.

He walked into the adjoining room, but a quick survey of the people showed him that Miss Foster was not there. She had better be in the next room, for it was the last one of the exhibit. His steps quickened as he moved toward the doorway.

Val's anxiety dissipated as his eyes spotted the plain straw bonnet with a blue ribbon. Thank goodness, she was here. He walked toward her, curious as to why she was staring so intently at the picture before her.

He drew up beside her and glanced at the small print hanging on the wall—a young boy reluctantly being presented to an elegantly dressed woman. He glanced sideways at Miss Foster and noticed with dismay the tracks of tears on her cheeks. He looked back at the small etching and saw the title: *A Visit to the Boarding School.*

Damn. She was obviously thinking about her brother.

"The child looks healthy and well fed," he said, hoping to reassure her.

"You *would* say that." She sniffed loudly.

He pulled a handkerchief from his pocket and silently handed it to her. She took it without a word and wiped at her face and eyes, then blew her nose.

He sighed, knowing he had to do something. It would not do to have her moping about. She'd never attract male attention if she looked miserable all the time. "Give the lad a fortnight. If he still claims to be miserable, I shall drive you down to St. Giles myself and you can inspect the situation yourself."

She stared at him. "Really?"

He nodded. "Really."

The look of sheer joy on her face told Val that for once, in her eyes, he'd done the right thing.

Well, if it kept her from cutting up the peace of the house for the next two weeks, it was well worth it. And no doubt, by the time his deadline arrived, the lad would be immersed in his new school and totally indifferent to his sister's concerns.

Then he would have to devise other ways to make Miss Foster smile.

"Sophie!" Miss Foster cried out as his sister came up beside him. "Guess what your brother has agreed to? He will take me to see Eddie in a fortnight."

"Why, Val, how decidedly . . . sweet of you," Sophie said.

"This is only if young Mr. Foster still professes to be unhappy in his new situation," Val added hastily.

"And if he is, can I bring him back to London?" Miss Foster asked.

Val winced. So confident had he been that the lad would be happy that he had not considered the alternative.

"Yes, Val, can we bring the poor child back to London?" Sophie asked. "It will be so amusing to have a young boy around the house."

He knew that Sophie was perfectly aware of the role Eddie had played in his humiliation at Kingsford Manor. He would move to France before he would allow that brat in his house.

"I daresay that he will be so firmly attached to his new

schoolmates that he will wish to remain where he is," Val said.

At least he prayed it would be so.

The first thing Kat noticed when she entered the house after returning from the exhibit was the enormous floral arrangement on the table outside the drawing room.

"Oh, who are these for?" Sophie cried. She pushed past Kat and searched for a card. She found it, took one glance at the inscription, and held it out to Kat with a look of smug satisfaction. "They're for you."

From the corner of her eye, Kat saw Newkirk watching her with open curiosity.

"Probably from Nick." Kat shrugged, and tore open the small envelope. "As if he could buy his way back into my good graces with mere flowers."

But to her surprise, they were from that sapscull in the park—the one with no sense about horses. He thanked her profusely for her assistance and begged to visit tomorrow.

"Well?" Sophie tapped her foot with impatience. "Who sent them?"

"The Honorable Harold Mortimer," Kat replied.

"Who is that?" Sophie asked.

"The young man from the park," Kat said.

"Oh! What does he say?"

"He wishes to call tomorrow."

"No callers until *after* we go to the dressmakers," Sophie said firmly.

"Now, do not be so hasty," Newkirk said. "If a young man wishes to call on Miss Foster, you should not deny him."

"Send round a note saying we will be receiving tomorrow afternoon," Sophie said, giving her brother a sharp look. "After we visit the modiste in the morning."

Kat ignored their debate. She did not care if she had to greet Mr. Mortimer in her country clothes. He was her first guest, and she intended to see him no matter what. Admittedly, he did not know much about horses, but it would please Newkirk to see her entertaining a young gentleman. And right now, pleasing Newkirk was her main ambition. She intended to make sure that when she heard from Eddie again, Newkirk was in the frame of mind that would cause him to say yes when she begged for her brother to come home.

She leaned down and took a deep breath of the flowers. Their sweet smell reminded her of the country, the overgrown tangle of garden behind her house, and a wave of homesickness washed over her. How long before she would see it again?

How long before she had her family together with her at last?

Chapter Eleven

*K*at was dressed and pacing the drawing room a full half hour before her caller was due to arrive. At Sophie's insistence, she wore one of her newly acquired gowns, a long-sleeved dress of pale yellow that was plain enough in styling to suit her.

But clothing was not the thing on her mind today. A gentleman was coming to call, and she had the opportunity to show Newkirk that she was falling in with his plans for her. Ordinarily, she wouldn't give someone like Mr. Mortimer a second thought. Anyone with so little sense about horses would not elicit much interest from her, but these were not normal times.

Sophie beamed with delight when she entered the drawing room and saw Kat.

"You look lovely," she said. "I told you that dress was perfect."

"I do rather like it," Kat confessed, running her hand over the silky fabric.

"Aren't you excited?" Sophie gracefully sank onto the settee. "Your first conquest in London! And we've barely been here a week."

"I don't consider Mr. Mortimer a conquest." Kat

grinned. "He is only coming by to pay his respects because I saved him from a thrashing by his brother. I do not think he will arrive with a marriage proposal."

"Goodness, I don't think he's intending *that* quite yet," Sophie said. "Think of him as a useful subject on whom to practice your feminine charms."

"I do need to practice my social conversation," Kat said. "I suppose I should not talk with him as I do Nick."

The footman threw open the door and announced, "There are several young men asking to pay their respects, Miss Sophie."

"Do send them in," Sophie said, giving Kat an encouraging smile.

Mr. Mortimer and two companions entered the room. Mortimer was dressed in what could only be described as an *ensemble* of yellow pleated cossack trousers, a rose-pink waistcoat, and a bottle-green coat. The effect was . . . overwhelming. Kat felt quite put in the shade, despite her new gown.

"Oh, gracious lady." He flung himself on his knees before her, clasping her hands. "I cannot thank you enough for your help yesterday. You saved me from a fate worse than death."

"How is the horse today?" Kat asked.

"Right as rain—thank goodness." He scrambled to his feet and bowed with an awkward air. "I realize that in all the fuss, I failed to properly introduce myself yesterday. I am Harold Mortimer."

"So I surmised from your card," Kat said. She nodded at Sophie. "This is Sophie, Mrs. Bellshaw. My guardian's sister."

"A pleasure to meet you, Mrs. Bellshaw," Mortimer said. "These fashionable gents are Lionel Tipton—'Tippy'—and Michael Lawrence."

The other men bowed low.

"We heard what you did for Morty here," Tippy, the taller, dark-haired one, said. "Got him out of a right fix."

"Dashedly clever for a female to think of a stone," Lawrence said. Bushy red curls sprang from his head in tousled confusion. Kat suspected he was trying for a Byronic effect, but the result merely made it appallingly apparent he needed a haircut.

"Do all three of you live in London?" Kat asked. They all shook their heads in unison.

"Somerset," Mortimer replied.

Sophie cleared her throat and looked pointedly at Kat. "Perhaps our guests would like to sit."

"Oh." Kat reddened. Another silly rule. She realized an absentminded hostess could be decidedly unpleasant to visit. "Please, be seated."

The three men each took a chair facing the ladies.

"What brings you gentlemen to town?" Sophie inquired.

"Well, Tippy was looking to buy a commission and—"

"My brother just joined the army," Kat announced. "He's in the Blues."

Tippy's eyes grew wide with admiration. "The Blues? I'd give anything to have a commission there."

Mortimer leaned forward eagerly. "I thought you might like to go for a ride in the park tomorrow, Miss . . . Miss Foster."

"Are you planning on filching your brother's horse again?" Kat asked suspiciously.

He gulped and reddened. "I do have a mount of my own."

Kat was torn. She would love to ride again. But with a sidesaddle . . . She swallowed hard. "I fear my guardian does not wish me to ride while I am in town."

"Why ever not?" Mortimer asked, his face falling.

"He does not believe it to be a ladylike activity." It was not a complete lie. He certainly did not want her riding astride. She shot a glance at Sophie, who cast her a warning look. Kat turned back to Mortimer. "But he does allow me to do most other things."

Mortimer brightened. "Perhaps I can take you for a drive, instead."

"That would be nice," Kat replied.

"Have you been in London long?" he asked.

"Barely a week," Kat said. "Which has been spent shopping, as Sophie does not believe one can go out in public before being decked out in the latest fashion."

"Then you have not had the chance to see the wonders of London yet," Tippy said eagerly. "I would be honored if I could escort you to—uh—somewhere."

"Yesterday I viewed the exhibit of paintings sponsored by the Royal Society," Kat announced.

None of the men looked impressed by that information, which Kat vowed to mention to Newkirk the next time he proposed another "educational" outing. No need to bother herself with such things in the future if the young men she met did not care.

"You should visit the Tower," Mortimer suggested.

"Too bad Vauxhall isn't open yet, or we could take you to see the fireworks," Lawrence added.

"Fireworks! Oh, I would like that," Kat said eagerly. "When does it open?"

"Not for weeks and weeks," Mortimer said, casting a frown.

"I know where I should like to go." Kat leaned forward, guessing they would go along with her plan. "Tattersall's."

All three men stared at her.

Kat felt a twinge of disappointment. Perhaps Mortimer and his friends would not be as enjoyable companions as she had hoped. "Is that wrong? Am I not permitted to go there?"

"Oh no, nothing like that," Tippy said. "I have never met a girl who wanted to go there before."

"I heard Blakeney's putting up his stable for bid next week," Lawrence said. "Might be worth taking a look at the horses ahead of time."

"We could go tomorrow," Mortimer suggested.

Tippy looked over at Sophie. "Would you care to join us, Mrs. Bellshaw?"

Sophie laughed. "Of course I would. I've never been there, either."

"What sort of horses does this Blakeney fellow have?" Kat asked, but before anyone could answer, a footman appeared in the doorway.

"Lieutenant Foster," the man announced.

Kat wrinkled her nose. What was Nick doing back here, after she'd shown him the door? Had he undergone a change of heart about Eddie's fate? Or had he come in a futile attempt to convince her that Newkirk was right?

"Looks like we were not quick enough, lads," Nick said

as he entered, accompanied by two other soldiers. "Forces have already stormed the walls."

Mortimer and his friends gaped openmouthed at Nick and his fellow soldiers, who were resplendent in their new, expertly tailored blue uniforms.

"You are not the only person I know in town," Kat said archly, while eyeing his companions with curiosity. She wondered if they had any more sense than her brother.

"So I see." Nick gave Mortimer's sartorial splendor a disdainful glance.

"You might introduce your companions," Kat said, a hint of reproach in her voice, delighted at the chance to chastise her brother. "It is the polite thing to do."

"Indeed," Nick said. "This fellow here"—he pointed to a mustachioed young man—"is Lieutenant Boone and this other"—a short blond man—"is Lieutenant Weatherell."

"Are you all in Lieutenant Foster's regiment?" Sophie asked.

"Yes, ma'am," Boone replied.

"I am Mrs. Bellshaw," Sophie replied. "My brother is guardian to the Fosters."

"And this is Mortimer, Tippy, and Lawrence," Kat said, introducing the others. "They're taking me to *Tatt's* tomorrow."

"*I* was there last week," Nick replied.

"Buy anything?" she demanded.

"There weren't any mounts up to my standards," he said. "Although I daresay *you* might have found one or two that would appeal to you."

"If you rejected them, no doubt they were superior animals," Kat said with a grin. "Perhaps I shall find myself a horse after all."

"I shall have another pot of tea brought round," Sophie said, and rang the bell for the maid.

The six young men sat down, eyeing each other warily.

Kat realized this was rather fun, having six—well five, as she could not count Nick—young men paying attention to her. She wished Newkirk was here to view her success.

"I'm hoping for a commission in the Blues, myself," Tippy said, giving Nick an ingratiating smile. "We might be comrades-in-arms soon."

*   *   *

Val could barely contain his curiosity as his sister and Miss Foster entertained their visitors in the drawing room. Was his ward acting like a proper young lady? Were these gentlemen potential suitors for her hand? Were they even suitable candidates? He was desperate to learn more.

He paced the study, trying to dampen his apprehensions. A single visit would not do much to ruin—or make—Miss Foster's reputation no matter what happened. He was more interested in these young men who were holding court in his drawing room. Where had she met them? What sort of fellows were they?

As her guardian, it was his responsibility to make sure that she did not strike up an acquaintanceship with the wrong sort of person. Perhaps he should wander into the drawing room and reassure himself that all was proper—in the guise of having a word with his sister.

He hurried up the stairs. From the hall he heard the sound of male laughter. Val found that encouraging.

Val pushed open the door and smiled with relief at the scene that met his eyes. Sophie and Miss Foster were holding court amid six young gentlemen. It took him a moment to recognize Nick Foster, togged out in his parade uniform. He'd obviously brought two fellow soldiers with him. The other three men were civilians, one of whom had a very strange notion of color and style. Val almost winced at the brightness of the lad's coat.

His ward, he noted with approval, was dressed in a simple frock of springtime yellow. She looked young, fresh, and demure. Amazing how simple clothing could create such an illusion.

Nick Foster jumped to his feet and strode across the room to greet him.

"Good day, my lord." He struck a pose obviously designed to show off his braid-bedecked uniform.

Val smothered a smile.

"How nice of you to join us, Val," Sophie said. She patted the sofa next to her. "Let me pour you a cup of tea." She gave Miss Foster a pointed look.

"This is my guardian, Baron Newkirk," Miss Foster announced. "Lieutenants Boone and Weatherell, and Mr. Mortimer, Lawrence, and Tippy."

"Tippy?" Val raised a brow.

Tippy sprang to his feet and held out his hand. "Lionel Tipton, my lord. Of the Westerborne Tiptons, from Somerset."

"He wants to join a regiment," Miss Foster explained. "I told him how kind you were and how you had helped Nick, so surely you would be willing to help Tippy as well."

Val gave her a suspicious glance, but she regarded him with wide-eyed innocence. He sighed and gave Tipton an assessing look. At least this fellow dressed in subdued colors, unlike his more flamboyant companion. "Come round on Friday at eleven and lay out your qualifications," he said at last.

"Have you two been in the army long?" Sophie asked the men who'd accompanied Nick.

"Only since last fall," Lieutenant Boone replied.

"It must be dashedly exciting," Tippy said.

"Oh, it has its moments," Lieutenant Weatherell said with a self-satisfied look.

Val smothered a smile. The lads had no idea what military life was really like, but he hoped they would never see anything more challenging than the parade ground.

Lieutenant Boone turned to Miss Foster. "How are you finding London? Your brother says this is your first visit here."

"So far I have managed to see the inside of nearly every shop, the park, and an art gallery," Kat said.

"That sounds rather dull," Boone replied. "We shall have to devise something more adventuresome for your entertainment."

Miss Foster flashed her visitor a grateful smile, and Val realized that she had led a rather tame existence since she had arrived in town. He would be well advised to remedy that situation before boredom led her into folly.

"There's the lions at the 'Change," Tippy suggested. "One of them has a cub, and they've got a little spaniel acting as nursemaid."

"I was thinking of something rather more cultivated," Boone said.

"What about the new bridge construction?" Miss Foster suggested.

"That's it!" Weatherell shot to his feet. "A boat ride on the Thames would be just the thing."

"That sounds like great fun." Miss Foster glanced to Sophie for guidance. "Would that be acceptable?"

Sophie nodded. Val felt slightly piqued that no one had bothered to consult *him*.

"Wednesdays are our light duty days," Weatherell said. "We shall go next week if the weather is decent."

"I'll take you to see the lions next week, also," Tippy said.

"And we'll go to Tatt's tomorrow," Mortimer chimed in.

Val felt he should be beaming like a proud papa. His ward was getting along so amiably with her guests that she made all his worries seem unfounded. He tried to see her through the eyes of these young men: short boyish curls framed an elfin face; her mischievous blue eyes danced with animation as she chatted. No one would ever mistake her for a boy once they saw her in a dress. Slim and leggy as she was, she still had feminine curves. The more he looked at her, the prettier he realized she was. Some astute fellow would soon recognize the prize she presented, and snap her up in an instant.

It was his job to make certain that it was the proper sort of fellow. If Miss Foster thought that this sprig of fashion was the type of man he'd approve as a husband for her, she was sadly mistaken. Even her brother's military comrades would not likely gain his approval. They were too young, still too wet behind the ears to make a suitable husband for such a volatile young lady. She needed someone who could keep her exuberance in check.

Mortimer rose to his feet. "We have stayed long enough, I am afraid." He signaled to Tippy and Lawrence. They made their bows and took their leave.

"We must go, too," Nick said. "We better make haste if we are going to make our next check."

Boone and Weatherell scrambled to their feet, made their good-byes, and followed Nick out of the room.

"Well." Miss Foster looked perturbed. "They deserted us rather quickly."

"Afternoon calls are meant to be short," Sophie explained.

"And you handled yourself exceptionally well, Miss Foster," Val said. "I predict you will have all of London at your feet within the fortnight."

She rolled her eyes at his flummery, then shook her head. "Could you believe Morty's clothing? He looked like he fell into three different paint jars."

"His costume was rather . . . colorful," Sophie admitted.

"Wherever did you meet such a fellow?" Val asked.

His sister and his ward exchanged conspiratorial glances, and his suspicions were confirmed. There was something irregular about the whole thing.

"In the park," Miss Foster replied.

Val regarded her with a stern expression. "You mean to tell me the fellow is some stranger you met in the park?" He shot a baleful glance at his sister. "I thought you were possessed of more sense."

"The boy is perfectly harmless," Sophie said. "We came to his aid in the park, and he seems quite taken with Kat. It was he who sent the flowers yesterday, which shows he has the proper sensibilities."

"Except for his clothing," Miss Foster added.

"But we still know nothing of him—or his friends." Val shook his head. "I am not certain you should be escorted anywhere by them."

"I am certain Morty is only waiting to get me alone so he can carry me off to Gretna," Miss Foster said. "He is obviously after my *vast* fortune."

"There is no need to be sarcastic," Val said.

"You brought me here to find a husband," she protested. "I have already made the acquaintance of five eligible young men, and now you are complaining."

"I only want to make certain that they are suitable escorts," Val said. He realized he was starting to sound like a guardian. But he *was* in charge of this girl.

"We will have ample opportunity to learn more about Morty and his friends in the days to come," Sophie said. Val clamped his mouth closed. There was no point in belaboring the issue. And surely, once his ward was officially out in society, she would be properly introduced to numerous young men—suitable young men—and she would forget all about this fellow.

"You are right," he said, and stood to leave. "I congratulate you on your successful first morning at home, Miss Foster."

She gave him a superior smile that had a sharp tang of

"I told you so" to it. Let her feel smug. He'd rather have her feel comfortable entertaining male callers than shrinking from shyness in the corner. However, he doubted Kat Foster knew the meaning of the word "shy."

Chapter Twelve

Kat awoke the next morning abrim with anticipation. She could not wait to step into Tattersall's hallowed grounds and see what prime horses London had to offer.

But all her plans were dashed when the maid brought her a note from Morty. He was terribly ill after eating some poorly prepared food, he wrote, and had to beg off from their planned visit.

"The rest of us could have gone without him," Kat said aloud, vexed that her day was ruined before it had barely begun.

She went in search of Sophie, Morty's disappointing note in her hand. She found Sophie in the drawing room, arranging flowers in a vase.

"The trip to Tatt's has been canceled," Kat informed her glumly.

"What happened?" Sophie asked.

"Morty ate something bad," Kat replied. "Why couldn't he have waited until tomorrow to do so?"

"I am certain he would have done so if he was able," Sophie said dryly, clipping the end of a bright yellow rose with her shears.

Kat flopped onto the sofa, not caring about the unladylike picture she presented. "Now what am I going to do?"

Newkirk walked into the drawing room, hat and gloves in hand, as if preparing to go out.

"What adventure do you ladies have planned for today?" He gave Sophie a swift kiss of greeting on the cheek.

"Absolutely nothing," Kat replied with a morose expression.

"Morty's ill," Sophie explained. "The visit to Tattersall's has been canceled."

"Ah, no wonder Miss Foster looks so downcast."

"You would be too if all your plans were ruined." Kat knew she sounded like a spoiled child denied sweets, but she could not help herself. She'd been looking forward to seeing Tatt's ever since she agreed to come to London. "I have half a mind to go there by myself."

"No need for that." Newkirk flashed her a cheerful smile. "I will escort you."

Kat regarded him with surprise. "Really? You'd go with me?"

"I intended to go sometime with your brother. We can all go together. I will send a note round and see if he can join us—say in an hour or so?"

Kat glanced at Sophie. "Do you still wish to go?"

Sophie nodded. "I should like to see this famous place."

"Splendid," Newkirk said. "I will meet you back here in an hour, then." He gave Sophie a pointed glance. "And do not wear your best dress or your satin slippers. Treat this like a trip to the barn."

Kat stared after Newkirk as he departed the drawing room, hardly believing what had just transpired. He actually offered to take her to Tatt's, when yesterday she'd had the definite feeling that he had not approved of the proposed visit.

Newkirk continued to surprise her.

But she was not altogether certain she wished to go with him. He might make her stand well away from the horses, or hurry her through the ring and insist they go someplace more "educational" afterward. She guessed she'd have a better time accompanied by Morty and his friends. Yet she was not going to stay home just because Newkirk was not her favorite escort. She could always go again if this visit was not satisfactory.

She glanced over at Sophie. "We should look for a new horse for you while we are there," she said. "One that is a bit more lively."

"I like my mare," Sophie protested, then laughed. "All

right, she is a bit slow. But that suits me fine. I am never going to be a bruising rider like you."

"Oh, how I wish I dare go riding while I am here in London," Kat said. "No one of any consequence gets up before noon—if I rode at the crack of dawn, who would ever see me?"

"If Val found out . . ." Sophie's voice trailed off.

"He would be furious," Kat admitted.

"All the more reason to find you a husband soon," Sophie said. "One who will allow you to ride as you please."

"I am more concerned with finding one who will take care of my brothers," Kat replied.

"Has anyone caught your eye?"

Kat shrugged. "I expect a letter from Eddie any day now. Once your brother accepts how unhappy he is, Eddie can come home and I won't have to look for a husband."

"You are not leaving me here alone." Sophie glared at her in mock dismay. "You will stay in London through the Season no matter what."

"I am not certain your brother will appreciate Eddie staying here," Kat replied dryly.

"I shall see that he does," Sophie insisted.

Kat shook her head. She rather thought that she and Eddie would be banished to the countryside in no time—which was fine with her. All she wanted was to be home again.

True to his promise, Newkirk reappeared at the drawing room door in an hour to announce that the landau awaited them outside. They would meet Lieutenant Foster at the hallowed doors of Tattersall's.

Kat was pleased to see Nick waiting for them at the Grosvenor Place entrance; she'd been afraid they'd have to wait for him. Lieutenant Boone was with him, and he immediately offered his hand to help Sophie from the carriage.

Disdaining her guardian's assistance, Kat jumped from the carriage and strode past him into London's famous horse market. She looked around eagerly, ignoring the stares directed at her. The crowd was a mix of elegant gentlemen, dressed much like Newkirk in breeches, boots, and tailored coats, and a rougher set dressed in less elegant garb.

Sophie leaned close and whispered in Kat's ear. "We are the only ladies here."

Kat was not surprised. The boisterous atmosphere of the sales ring was not the sort that would appeal to many ladies. No doubt when they wished to purchase a horse, they either sent a man to do it or had the horse brought to them.

But Kat was not like most ladies, and she delighted in being here, in the midst of London's premiere horse-selling site.

"The pickings look a bit thin today," Nick mused as he perused the offerings.

"Bargains are not as easily had this time of year," Lieutenant Boone admitted. "Wait until the end of the Season when everyone is trying to settle their debts."

"Still, that bay over there looks worth a second glance." Nick walked toward the horse, and the others followed.

Kat inspected the animal closely. "I don't like the slope of his withers," she said.

"No one is asking you," Nick retorted. He motioned to the groom. "Lead him around a bit."

Kat watched disdainfully as the man attempted to show off the horse's advantages—which she did not find impressive.

"You'll regret it if you buy this one," she told her brother.

"And since when have I ever gone to you for advice on which horse to buy?" he demanded.

"I fear in this case your sister is right," Newkirk said quietly.

Kat stared at him in amazement. Newkirk was defending her before Nick? Even more surprising, his statement proved he did know enough about horseflesh to make a good judgment.

Nick looked at her with a skeptical expression. "What horse do you then suggest I examine, sister dear?"

She immediately pointed to a gray standing by the first row of pillars. "That one. From here, at least, he shows promise."

They traipsed across the dirt ring to look at Kat's choice.

At first, Nick examined the horse with reluctance, but he gradually grew more enthused.

"What do you think?" he said, turning to Newkirk.

Newkirk shrugged. "Ask your sister."

Nick gave her a pained look. "What do you say?"

"I'd take him," she replied promptly. From the corner of her eye, she saw Newkirk nod his head.

A surprising swell of satisfaction swept over her at seeing Newkirk's agreement with her opinion. Not because she cared what he thought, she assured herself, but because it meant he would look upon her in a more favorable light.

"I say, remind me to take your sister along the next time I look for a horse," Lieutenant Boone said, his eyes wide with admiration. "She's a prime judge of cattle."

"Why, thank you." Kat beamed at him. She looked at Sophie. "Now, are you certain you don't wish to look for a mount?"

"I will keep to Sally, slow as she is," Sophie replied.

"Perhaps the ladies would like to wait outside in the carriage while Lieutenant Foster transacts his business," Lieutenant Boone said.

Kat turned toward Newkirk in disappointment. "Do we have to leave already?"

"You can remain as long as you wish," he said. "But I do believe Sophie would be more comfortable outside. Lieutenant Boone, if you would be so kind?"

Boone nodded and led Sophie toward the doors.

"She is not as fond of the stableyard as you are, Miss Foster," Newkirk explained.

To Kat, who had not smelled the tangy aroma of horses since her visit to the mews, the enclosure exuded a pleasurable scent. But she admitted it might be a bit overwhelming for poor Sophie, who rarely set foot in a stable.

Kat stopped to examine a sprightly black who would make a perfect mount for Sophie. She had half a mind to persuade Newkirk to purchase the animal. Kat turned about, looking for her guardian, but he had walked farther along and was looking at a long-legged chestnut.

Even while he admired the horse before him, Val did not allow Miss Foster to stray from his sight. There was nothing wrong in a lady visiting Tatt's, but it was not the sort of place for one to wander unaccompanied, either. He'd give her the illusion of freedom while keeping her under close eye.

Someone grabbed his arm.

"Newkirk! You devil. I did not realize you were in London."

Val turned and recoiled in astonishment as he recognized the man standing before him. Richard Wareham, late of His Majesty's Cavalry and one of Val's comrades during the years of war.

"Wareham! What are you doing here? Last I heard, you were still in France."

"Came home last month," Wareham said. "Nothing like an English spring to refresh one. But what are you doing here? Buying more horses?"

"I could ask the same of you," Val replied. "I am here with my sister and wards."

"Your wards?" Wareham regarded him with incredulity. "You don't have any wards."

"Believe me, it was quite a surprise to find out myself. There are five of them; four boys and a girl."

Wareham burst into laughter. "That is ripe. You, playing father to a pack of children."

Val shook his head in mock dismay. "The eldest just took up a commission in the Blues, the twins are in the navy school at Portsmouth, and the youngest at St. Giles."

"You must be getting a mount for the lucky fellow in the Blues." Wareham peered over Val's shoulder. "What have you settled on?"

To his sudden dismay, Val saw Miss Foster marching toward them with determined steps. He felt a sudden reluctance to introduce Wareham to her. The man was an excellent soldier, but his reputation with women was tainted at best. Not the sort of man whose attentions a father—or guardian—would encourage.

"Newkirk," she said as she came within hailing distance. "You have to look at this horse. It would be just perfect for Sophie."

Wareham arched a questioning brow.

"My female ward," Val explained. "And an extraordinary horsewoman."

"You must introduce me," Wareham replied.

"If you promise to behave yourself," Val blurted before he could stop himself.

"Trying to find her a husband, are you?" Wareham gave him an amused look.

"You don't have to worry," Val said, forcing a grin. "You are the last person I would permit her to wed."

Wareham laughed. "I am glad you are looking out for my interests."

Miss Foster reached him and looked expectantly at the man at his side.

"Miss Foster," Val began, "I should like you to meet one of my army comrades, Richard Wareham."

Wareham bowed and took the girl's hand, casting a reproachful glance at Val. "You did not tell me she was such a charming lass."

"And may I add he is a desperate rogue, so do not believe a word he says to you," Val said.

"I am shocked to hear that you would have a friend who is a rogue," Miss Foster said, a mischievous look in her eye. She turned to Wareham. "Either my guardian is exaggerating, or he has pulled the wool over my eyes."

"Oh, Val is as straight-laced as they come," Wareham said. "But we managed to rub along together even so."

"If you were in the army together, you must have some stories about my guardian," she said. "Perhaps you will pay a visit to the house and regale us with some of them. I am certain his sister would love to hear them, too."

Wareham glanced at Val, who emphatically shook his head.

"I would be delighted to tell you everything you wish to know, Miss Foster," Wareham said, completely ignoring Val's warning. "Do you live here in London?"

"No, I've only been in town for two weeks," she replied.

"And how do you find the city?" Wareham asked.

"I have seen little of it—except the inside of shops," Miss Foster replied.

"We shall have to take steps to remedy that." Wareham smiled. "I would be more than willing to escort you about town."

"Why, thank you," Miss Foster said. "I will look forward to it."

Val gave him a pointed glance, and Wareham grinned.

"I shall present myself at your house shortly, and we can make plans." He took her hand again. "A pleasure to meet you, my dear." He bowed and turned away, quickly crossing the room.

Miss Foster leaned toward Val. "Is he really such a rogue? He seemed very nice."

Val nodded. "He left a string of broken hearts across the Peninsula and throughout France."

"A genuine rake!" Her expression brightened. "I've never met one before."

"And you would be well advised to stay away from him."

She looked thoughtful at that information. "So I am to assume Wareham is not the sort of man I should try to attach?"

"Not at all," Val said. "He is a highly inappropriate candidate."

Val thought he saw a flash of amusement in her eyes before she lowered her gaze.

This was the last thing he needed. First those idiotic young men, now a rakehell like Wareham. He'd planned to introduce her to *eligible* gentlemen, yet she seemed to attract attention from all the wrong sorts. He'd have to drop a word to Wareham to leave her firmly alone. Val did not need her becoming the subject of gossip.

He took her elbow and steered her in the other direction. "Where is this horse you wish me to examine?"

He agreed that the mount would be suitable for a lady such as Sophie, but also reminded her that his sister had firmly insisted she did not wish to have a new mount. Kat opened her mouth to protest, then shut it again.

"Do you always save your brother from mistakes with his horses, Miss Foster?" Newkirk asked as he took her elbow and steered her toward the entrance.

"Oh no," she said cheerfully. "He never listens to me. He would have bought that first horse today if you hadn't agreed with me."

"The folly of youth," Newkirk muttered. "I know whom I shall consult when I wish to purchase a new mount."

To her surprise, Kat felt herself beaming under Newkirk's praise. "Would you please call me 'Kat'?" she asked. "After all, you are my guardian. Almost like one of the family."

" 'Kat' it is then," Newkirk said. "If you promise not to address me as 'my lord.' "

"That will be easy," Kat said with a hint of a grin.

He returned her grin. "Yes, I imagine you would prefer to call me 'ogre' or 'monster.' "

She colored. "Only when I am particularly vexed with you," she said.

"Then I shall endeavor not to vex you unnecessarily," he replied.

That evening, Val waited impatiently in the drawing room for the two ladies to join him before setting out for Lady Arlington's musicale. He felt the slightest bit of apprehension over tonight's outing—his ward's first official foray into society. He'd seen that she could carry herself with aplomb in the park, or at Tattersall's, but would she be equally at ease in the drawing room?

He heard voices in the hall and took a deep breath.

His sister looked marvelous, as usual, garbed in a dress that he knew must be the latest fashion and therefore outrageously expensive. But it was Miss Fos—Kat—who threatened to take his breath away.

If he had ever doubted her femaleness, all his questions were gone. He was amazed to discover that his ward's slim, boyish figure was capable of displaying the kind of curves that were set off by her simple pale rose-hued gown. For an instant, he wondered if a bodice cut *that* low was truly appropriate for an unmarried young lady, but he reasoned Sophie would never agree to anything unsuitable.

"Well?" Sophie asked. "What do you think?"

"You both look quite lovely," he said, "which may be your only saving grace, as once again, you are late. Hurry, we must leave at once."

Sophie giggled and turned to Kat. "Even after all this time, Val thinks he is going to change me."

"Just see that you do not teach my ward your bad habits," Val said warningly as he assisted them with their cloaks. "I find her practice of promptness admirable."

"Oh, don't listen to him, Kat," Sophie said with a wave of her hand. "Men will always wait for a lady, no matter what."

Val found he could not take his eyes off Kat Foster during the short drive to their destination. Where once he'd worried that she would never attract any male interest, he now feared she might gain far too much of it. She looked far too . . . delectable.

"Are you nervous?" he asked her as they waited behind two other carriages to disembark.

"No," she replied, then gave him an impish look. "Should I be?"

"I merely thought . . . it is your first evening out in London."

She laughed. "I think you are the one who is nervous. Afraid I'll draw my pistol and start shooting the guests?"

Val snorted. "Not at all."

Nevertheless, he intended to keep a close eye on her. She seemed to have an unerring knack for attracting the wrong sort of men.

Upon reaching Lady Arlington's, the two ladies quickly abandoned him. He stood at the rear of the drawing room, trying to appear more interested than he felt. He always forgot how much he detested musicales until he found himself at one again. He'd much rather be home. Yet tonight, he had a role to play—escort to his sister and his ward, and his own personal desires were secondary.

He looked across the room as the two women chatted amiably with their hostess. He'd noticed that more than one appreciative male glance had been cast in their direction already, although he doubted that there were many eligible men here tonight. It was too early in the Season, and not the sort of entertainment designed to attract many bachelors.

A few trilling notes on the piano announced the commencement of the musical entertainment, and the guests made their way into the adjacent room, where chairs were set up in rows for the listeners. Val lingered behind so he could take a seat near the back. He did not dislike music, but these amateur performances filled him with trepidation. He took his seat, crossed his arms over his chest, and resigned himself to a boring evening.

Unfortunately, the pianist was every bit as mediocre as he had feared. Val found himself studying the oddly colored birds that cavorted across the wallpaper on the wall beside him, wondering if such creatures really existed in nature or were merely the product of the artist's imagination.

His interest in birds exhausted by the time the second singer stepped forward, Val shifted slightly in his seat, noticing that he now had a clear view of Kat and Sophie, seated two rows ahead of him. Kat toyed idly with her fan, looking bored.

As if sensing his scrutiny, she turned her head and met his gaze. She made a moue of distaste at the high-pitched shrieking of the untalented singer, and Val barely stifled a laugh.

She's enjoying this about as much as I am, he realized and flashed her a sympathetic look and winked. She responded with a rueful smile before turning back to the performance.

Val resolved then and there that this would be the last musicale they attended this Season. There was no reason to put themselves through this sort of torture again when there were far more entertaining social amusements available.

After what seemed an interminable time, the music stopped, their hostess rose to lead the applause, and the misery was finally at an end.

During the performance, supper tables had been set up in the large drawing room, and Val escorted Sophie and Kat to a table, then brought them plates heaped with delicacies.

"I found it a rather refreshing performance," Sophie said, taking a bite of a lobster patty. She turned to Kat. "Did you like it, Kat?"

She wrinkled her nose and darted a quick glance at Val before answering. "I find it interesting that ordinary people are brave enough to stand up in front of an audience and perform."

The tactful response impressed Val. If she continued to speak in this manner, she would do just fine in society.

"Val?" Sophie looked at him questioningly.

"Oh, you know me. I'd rather listen to a stirring march from a military band."

"I think I would prefer that as well," Kat said. "Nick's regiment must have a band. We should find out when they will be playing."

"Oh, look," Sophie cried, getting out of her chair. "There is Sybilla! I have not seen her in an age." She dashed off to greet her friend.

Val looked at Kat. "Did you find the music as excruciatingly painful as I did?"

She laughed. "It was rather awful, wasn't it? I've been to amateur performances back home, but somehow I expected better in London."

"I think we shall endeavor to avoid such evenings in the future," Val said.

"Thank you." She flashed him a relieved smile before spearing a piece of fruit with her fork.

He watched her eat, amused by her enthusiastic appetite, but the sight of the curving swell of her breasts above that dratted neckline made him uncomfortable. He looked at his sister's empty chair.

"At least Sophie is enjoying herself," Val said.

"I believe she would enjoy any event as long as there was gossip to exchange," Kat replied.

"An astute observation," Val said. "You have studied my sister well."

"Sophie loves society and the attractions of the city."

"And what of you? What do you think of London so far?"

She frowned. "It is far too big, with too many people and buildings. I'd much rather be back in the country."

Val shared her opinion on the city. But her presence in London was necessary to his plans for her. "You will be back in the country eventually," he said. "Can I get you more to eat?"

She cast a rueful glance at her empty plate. "I am not supposed to eat everything, am I?"

"I do not think anyone will chide you for having a healthy appetite," Val said.

"Then I should like another tart. And perhaps a few more slices of ham." She gave him a questioning glance. "And also one of those little frosted cakes."

Val laughed and took her plate. The girl certainly appreciated her food.

He picked out the items she had requested, plus a few more he thought she might like. As he headed back to the table, he saw Sophie returning, with two guests in tow.

"Val, you remember Sybilla Parker?" Sophie clutched her friend's hand. "We were at school together, and she attended my wedding."

Val bowed to a petite blonde dressed in more frills and ruffles than even Sophie dared.

Sophie turned to the man beside her. "And this is her brother, Gerald Parker."

Val shook hands with a florid-faced man with thinning hair who looked to be in his mid-thirties.

They moved toward the table where Kat was seated. "This is my brother's ward, whom I was telling you about," Sophie said. "Miss Katherine Foster. She shares your interest in country pursuits, Mr. Parker."

Val smothered a smile as he set the plate of food in front of Kat. Was Sophie matchmaking?

"Indeed," Parker said. "What part of the country do you hail from, Miss Foster?"

"Gloucestershire."

"Good fishing thereabouts?" Parker asked.

"We have good stock in the stream that runs through the farm," she replied. "Are you a fisherman?"

Parker nodded.

"Do you prefer dry flies or worms?" Kat asked.

Val glanced at Sophie, who put up a hand to hide her smile.

"Depends on the fish," Parker replied. "I've had great luck with flies in Scotland, but a good English stream trout seems to go for the worms."

"I prefer grubs, myself," Kat said. "More meat."

Sophie made a face. "Enough about wriggly things."

"Exactly," Sybilla Parker added. She touched her brother on the arm. "Come, it is time to depart." She gave Val a simpering look. "It was a pleasure to see you again, my lord. And to meet you, Miss Foster."

"Ah yes," Parker said. "I look forward to renewing our acquaintance."

"Excellent work." Val said softly to Sophie when the two had gone.

"What does he mean?" Miss Foster asked.

"Gerald Parker has a lovely country home, a nice income—and three young children," Sophie said.

"So?"

"He's also a widower."

"Oh." Kat sat up straighter. "You think I should marry him, then?"

"Goodness, I never said any such thing," Sophie said. "I merely made introductions. It is for you to decide if you care for him."

From his ward's impassive expression, Val could not tell what she thought of that news. Parker was older than he would have liked. But a steadying influence would be good for Kat. He sat back and waited impatiently while the two ladies finished their food. The evening had been a success, but it was only the first of many, long social events to come. He wondered if he would survive them all.

"Have you ladies eaten your fill and talked long enough?" he asked at last. "We could make our departure."

Sophie shared a wry look with Miss Foster. "I should be pleased—he has lasted far longer than I thought he would. Would you be disappointed if we left?"

"Not at all," she said.

They rose and took leave of their hostess, and waited for the carriage to be brought round.

While preparing for bed, Kat thought about her first evening in London society. It surprised her to discover how little it differed from similar events at home. Oh, the guests were more elegantly dressed, the food more plentiful and unusual, but underneath, it was much the same. One put on a mask of politeness, chatted about inconsequential matters, ideally acquired a new item of gossip, and generally found the evening dull.

It had been a pleasant shock to discover that Newkirk found the whole thing as silly as she did. After all his concern about proper behavior, she would have expected him to be more interested in social events. But his remarks the other day at the art gallery and his obvious dislike for the amateurish music tonight, showed that his interest in social matters was minimal.

Unless it involved finding her a husband.

She shook her head with amusement at Sophie's blatant attempts at matchmaking. Introducing Kat to a widower with three children was a bit *too* obvious. And the man was rather old, but if he enjoyed country pursuits as much as he claimed, she might be able to overlook that. And he already had children, so a few more would not matter.

Newkirk, she knew, would accept him wholeheartedly.

Which made his friend Wareham all the more interesting. Newkirk had practically ordered her away from him, serving only to pique Kat's curiosity. A rake might prove to be an amusing companion.

And if by seeing Wareham, she managed to frighten Newkirk, all the better. If he feared she might make an inopportune match, he might be more willing to listen to reason and let her and Eddie go home.

All in all, she thought, as she climbed into bed, it had turned out to be rather a pleasant day. She'd seen Tatt's, met a genuine rake, and learned that London society was really little different from that at home.

And once again she'd learned that Newkirk could be a pleasant companion who shared many of her likes and dislikes. If only he would let her and her brothers go home, he would be the perfect guardian.

Yet it was troubling that the last thought she had before she drifted off to sleep was how he was certainly the handsomest man she had seen all evening.

Chapter Thirteen

*T*he next evening, Kat hurried the maid into dressing her for the evening at the theater with record speed, then hastened down the stairs to the drawing room. She did not intend to allow Newkirk the satisfaction of labeling her arrival "late" this time.

To her relief, he was not yet in the drawing room and

she waited impatiently beside the fireplace. Now she could look forward to seeing the expression on his face when he discovered her ready and waiting for him.

She started when the door opened and he stepped into the room. She had not heard him in the hall.

If possible, she thought he looked even more elegant—and handsome—tonight than he had the previous evening. The stark black and white of formal evening wear suited him. And his tall, broad-shouldered frame made even her feel dainty.

Kat suddenly wondered what he would look like in his military dress uniform. Did he even still have it, tucked away in a trunk somewhere? If she asked him, would he don it again, so she could see, or insist that he intended to keep it forever hidden away along with his unpleasant memories of war?

She realized he was regarding her intently.

"Do I pass inspection?" she demanded.

He nodded. "You look nice. Is that a new dress?"

"Of course it is," she said. "Why do you think Sophie's been dragging me to the dressmaker's?"

"I was teasing you," Newkirk replied. "Of course it is a new dress. Sophie would never let you out of the house with anything less. You look quite lovely."

She wrinkled her nose in protest. The dress she wore tonight was not her favorite, but Sophie had insisted that the theater demanded a showy display. "I feel like an over-dressed cream puff in a confectioner's window."

"After the gentlemen catch a glimpse of you tonight, the drawing room will be overflowing with your visitors tomorrow."

She rolled her eyes. "You sound like Sophie. I do not expect all of London to be at my feet."

"Perhaps not *all*," Newkirk admitted. "But I think you will turn a few heads tonight."

"Only from rank curiosity," she retorted. "They will want to know who accompanies you and Sophie to the theater."

"I assure you, no one will be looking at *me*," Newkirk said. He pulled out his pocket watch and checked the time. "Do you care to wager how much longer my sister will be?"

"Oh, several minutes at least," Kat replied airily. "It is

no mean feat for such an 'aged lady' to get herself ready for an evening at the theater."

"Is that what she considers herself? An 'aged lady'?" Newkirk shook his head.

Kat laughed. "That is what she said after Morty and his friends visited. She claimed they made her feel like the grand matriarch, when she could not be above a year or two older than they."

"I shall have to see that she changes that attitude," Val replied, then flashed her a grin. "Or else find you older suitors. She will never find a husband if she thinks of herself as on the shelf."

"Does she intend to remarry?" Kat asked. "She has not said so to me."

"Or to me," Newkirk said. "But it is what I wish for her."

"I will help you find someone!"

Newkirk shook his head. "Your task is to find a husband for yourself."

"I thought that was *your* responsibility, as my guardian."

Just then Sophie dashed into the room, the ends of her shawl flapping behind her.

"We shall be shockingly late if we do not leave immediately," Sophie said. "Are you two ready?"

Newkirk shared an amused glance with Kat, then followed the two women out of the room.

They arrived at the theater with only moments to spare. Kat barely caught a glimpse of the crowd in the pit and the elegantly dressed ladies in the boxes surrounding the stage, before the lights dimmed and the entertainment began.

"I'll point out people during the first interval," Sophie whispered. "The house looks to be fairly full."

"Hush!" Newkirk commanded sternly.

Sophie giggled. "We shall be the only ones paying attention," she whispered to Kat again, then fell silent.

Kat feared the theater would be as boring as the musicale Sophie had dragged them to last night. Instead of music, it would be words that offended her ears. But to her surprise, she found herself enjoying the light farce being presented on stage.

The play was rather silly, and the catcalls from the pit during the supposed "romantic" moments only made the whole exercise more ludicrous. But the actors' lines were often funny, and Kat admitted there was something to seeing a professional production, rather than the amateur theatricals she had experienced at home.

Even Newkirk, seated on her left beside Sophie, appeared to be enjoying himself. He laughed out loud at one amusing line. It was a rich, deep baritone that she instantly decided she liked. Newkirk needed to laugh more often.

Sophie was fanning herself against the heat when the curtain dropped and the lights flared, signaling the break.

"Should you ladies wish for refreshments?" Val asked.

"Please," Sophie said. "It is as hot as Hades in here."

As soon as he was gone, Sophie inched her chair closer to Kat. "Scan the boxes opposite," she said. "See the woman with the white-feathered turban? That is Lady Moncrieff—she's a dreadful tyrant and thinks she has great influence in society, but really, everyone heartily dislikes her. Now that woman two boxes over, in the lavender gown—she is one of Almack's patronesses. Be glad we are not going there, as it is dreadfully dull."

"What in London is exciting?" Kat asked. "If Almack's is dull, musical entertainments boring and the theater— well, tonight's play is rather amusing, but suppose it was Shakespeare? Something has to be fun."

Sophie regarded her with a puzzled expression.

A knock on the door diverted her attention.

"Come in," she called.

To her delight, Morty, Tippy, and Lawrence entered. Tonight, Morty was almost conservatively dressed in a maroon coat with a gold-brocade waistcoat.

"We saw everyone glancing toward this box and knew it must contain the two loveliest ladies in London," Tippy said, bowing so low his forehead nearly touched his knees.

"I see you have crawled from your sick-bed," Kat said to Morty, with a touch of asperity. "I went to Tatt's without you."

"You did?" To her satisfaction, he looked grieved.

"Oh, don't pull such a long face," Kat chided him. "I am eager to go again anytime."

"Who did you go with?" he demanded.

"Newkirk. My brother met us there. As usual, I saved him from buying the wrong mount. He simply has no eye for horseflesh."

"Perhaps you would be willing to advise me on a horse I am looking at," Tippy said.

"Bring him round and I'll take a look at him," Kat said.

"Do you know anything about guns?" Morty asked. "I need a new fowling piece."

"What do you have now?" Kat asked.

"It was my brother's, and it came from Manton's, but Lawrence here says Purdey's is better."

"We should look at both places." Kat turned to Sophie. "This is the perfect opportunity—we can seek out a pistol for you as well."

Sophie gave her a puzzled look. "A pistol?"

Kat "tsked" with exasperation. "Remember how you found Newkirk's dueling pistols too heavy? You said you'd like a lady's pistol."

"Do you shoot, Mrs. Bellshaw?" Lawrence asked.

Sophie laughed. "Very badly. Kat was trying to teach me, but I was not a very apt pupil."

"You merely need practice," Kat said.

From the corridor, as he returned with the lemonade, Val heard loud, excited voices, bursts of male and female laughter, and knew all the racket was coming from his box.

Val pulled the door open, but over the strong, debating voices, no one heard him enter. As he had feared, it was the same young sprouts from the other day.

"I say pheasant is the best," one said.

"Scottish grouse," Tippy argued.

"You're all wrong," Kat's voice was loud and clear. "It's peacock."

Val smothered a laugh.

"Peacock?" the men chorused.

"Wherever did you eat a peacock?" Sophie asked.

Kat grinned. "One wandered into our yard one day. At first we were thrilled, but that lasted for less than a week. Have you ever heard their call?"

Morty nodded. "Noisy creatures."

"Exactly so," Kat said. "Then the boys kept chasing it, so it took to sitting in the tree and screaming whenever it saw someone. I decided it was far more suited to the dinner table."

She glanced up and noticed Val at last. "Newkirk, you are just in time to solve our dilemma. Whose gun do you prefer for pheasant—Manton or Purdey?"

"Oh, Manton by far," Newkirk replied.

"No, it's Purdey," Lawrence argued.

"My father says his guns are all flash," Tippy said.

"Oh, I think I'd put Purdey up against Manton any day," Lawrence said.

Val knew it was time to step in before Kat arranged a shooting match on Hampstead Heath to prove their claims.

To Val's relief, the orchestra struck a note, indicating the end of the interval. The three men made hasty farewells and quickly took their leave. He began to fear he would have to spend his days fending off Kat's inappropriate suitors instead of finding her decent ones.

At the next intermission, Kat sent Newkirk out for cool drinks again. He had barely been gone a few minutes before someone knocked on the door.

Wareham walked in. "I thought I caught a glimpse of two lovely ladies sitting in this box." He bowed low. "I see I was right." He glanced about. "Do not tell me you two are here alone?"

"Val has gone for refreshments, as you can certainly have guessed." Sophie gestured toward the empty chair. "Do sit down."

"Is this your first visit to the theater, Miss Foster?" he asked.

Kat nodded. "It is a rather silly play, but I prefer it to something lumbering like *Henry V* or *Macbeth*."

"Oh, even those can be entertaining with the right set of players," he said. "There is nothing like having Lady Macbeth's wig fall off during the sleepwalking scene."

"Did that really happen?" Kat asked.

Wareham grinned. "I saw it myself."

"You did not call on us today," Kat chided him.

"Alas, I fear business affairs kept me away." Wareham smiled. "However, those matters have been dealt with, and I am now free. Will you be receiving tomorrow?"

Sophie nodded.

"Then I shall present myself on your doorstep," he said.

"With tales of Newkirk's foibles," Kat reminded him.

"No one is going to be telling any tales about me." Val stepped into the box, carrying tall glasses of lemonade that he handed to Kat and Sophie. He turned to Wareham. "What are you doing here? Are all the gambling hells closed tonight?"

"I am seeking to elevate my surroundings," Wareham replied, then both men laughed.

"I should love to see a gambling hell," Kat said. "Would you escort me to one, Wareham?"

He glanced at Newkirk, who emphatically shook his head.

"I do not see how I am going to have any fun at all in London," Kat complained.

"When you are married . . ." Val intoned.

" 'You can convince your husband to let you do anything you please.' " Kat frowned. "Meanwhile, I shall perish of boredom."

"It is obvious that Val has not been showing you the right attractions," Wareham said. "Tell me, what would you most like to see in London?"

"Well, I have been to Tatt's. How about Jackson's boxing parlor? Or a cockpit?"

Wareham roared with laughter. "You are a rare one," he said. "But I value my head, and I know that Val would have it if I took you to any such place. Don't you have any tamer interests?"

"I should like to see the lion cub and the dog," Kat admitted. "And Hoby's and the East India Docks and the new bridge."

"To the bridge it shall be," Wareham said. "I shall arrange an excursion." He stood. "I shall not take up more of your time. I imagine there are hordes of gentlemen milling about in the hall, waiting for their chance to enter." He bowed in farewell. "Ladies, until tomorrow."

Kat felt rather pleased with herself. She had never had so much attention paid to her in one evening. It was a new—and rather heady—experience.

She knew Newkirk would never allow her to go to any of the unsuitable places she'd mentioned to Wareham. But it had given her a thrill of satisfaction to see the look of

horror on his face when she'd asked about the gambling
hell.

She also had the decided feeling that Wareham would
not have objected in the least. Cultivating his friendship
might prove interesting, if only to annoy Newkirk. She just
might be able to convince Wareham to take her some place
he shouldn't. If she had to be in London, she ought to be
able to enjoy herself.

When they finally returned home in time to enjoy a late
supper, Newkirk was not certain whether the trip to the
theater had been successful or not.

Oh, it had been quite a success in the matter of male
attention paid to his ward. But it was the source of those
attentions that gave him reservations. It was his obligation,
after all, to make a *favorable* match for the girl. He did
not want it said that he'd been remiss in his guardianship.
But so far, her choices were not encouraging.

He would have found the antics of Morty and his fellow
striplings laughable if they had not been directed at his
ward. There was nothing wrong with the lads; in a few
more years they would probably grow into respectable
country gentry. But as for now . . . he wouldn't want to
wish them on his worst enemy's daughter. They were too
young and impetuous.

Even worse, Miss Foster—Kat—seemed delighted by
their attentions. He had only himself to blame for that—
he'd kept her under wraps while he gained confidence in
her ability to appear in society; as a result, the young men
she'd met were not exactly what he had in mind.

Then there was the problem of Wareham. Val shuddered
at the very thought of the man paying his attention to Kat.
If Mortimer was an immature youngster, Wareham was the
opposite—an experienced man of the world. The kind of
man no self-respecting guardian would want dancing attendance on his ward.

But why would Wareham, whose taste in women ran to
seasoned professionals or bored matrons, display interest
in an innocent country girl like Kat? Val shook his head.
Wareham could not be seriously interested. The man might
be a rogue, but he'd never been one for seducing genteel

young ladies. Perhaps Val was being too suspicious. Wareham was merely being polite.

But politeness would get him nowhere. If Mortimer was a ludicrous candidate for Kat's hand, Wareham was a downright dangerous one. Completely the wrong sort of man for his ward. And Val intended to make certain that Wareham was aware of that.

He would consult with Sophie in the morning and see that she accepted every invitation to parties that might present suitable, eligible gentlemen who could be introduced to Kat. Tonight's crowd at the theater showed that society was rapidly returning to the city. The Season would soon be in full display.

When he'd first decided to find a spouse for her, it had seemed a simple enough matter. Put the girl on display and see who came calling. But with growing dread, he realized it was going to be a bit more complicated than that.

Well, he'd led charges against Napoleon's cavalry, labored at sieges that brought down mighty fortresses, and kept a regiment of hotheaded cavalrymen together through some of the fiercest battles of the war. This could not be any more difficult.

He needed to lay out his plans like a military campaign— one that needed quick and decisive action to achieve its goals. By the end of the following week, he intended to see that his house was flooded with eligible suitors interested in pursuing his ward.

Meanwhile, he would scheme to keep her occupied, to make sure she did not have time to make any more unsuitable acquaintances. Even if it meant he must personally escort her to every sight in London. He vowed to find her the perfect husband.

Chapter Fourteen

$\mathcal{V}$al did not want Kat to realize that he was deliberately trying to monopolize her time, so the very next day, remembering that conversation about guns, he took her to Manton's, ostensibly to advise him on a new bird gun. When he offered to buy her one as well, she'd been delighted—and knowledgeable about what she wanted.

In the afternoon, he took her to Astley's. Val knew the famous riding emporium would appeal to his ward.

"Where do you wish to sit?" Val asked as they stood outside the ticket booth. "There are boxes that look down on the arena, or you can sit on the rail."

"Oh, the rail, of course," Kat said. "I want to be as close as possible."

Val smiled at her eagerness, glad he had brought her. He purchased their tickets, took her arm, and led her inside.

He'd never been to the famous equestrian showplace and was surprised to see that the building was arranged much like a theater, with a curtained stage at one end and three tiers of boxes along the sides. A dirt arena stood in place of the pit. The crowd, however, was not dressed in such elegant finery as those at the theater, and there were many children in the audience.

"We shall have to bring Sophie next time," Kat said. "She would like this."

"There is to be a next time?" he asked.

"Only if I enjoy myself," she answered with a saucy toss of her head.

The lights dimmed and the show began.

For the next hour, Kat sat transfixed beside him, alternat-

ing between delight, fright, and amazement at the equestrian tricks displayed before her. Val found himself equally
fascinated watching her. She demonstrated the delight of a
child as she watched a man stand on a horse's back while
it circled the arena at a gallop. She clapped loudly as horses
performed tricks and elegant dance steps. A whip-wielding
clown directing the action elicited gales of laughter. And
she held her breath while a horse circled the ring, the rider
holding Union Jacks aloft in each hand while he balanced
on one foot. They passed so close to the rail that any member of the audience could have reached out and touched
both horse and rider.

Val could not remember when he had seen anyone display such unfeigned enjoyment as Kat did at this performance. She held such an innocent and untarnished joy in
life. It was one of the things he admired about her; the
thing he did not want her ever to lose.

And, perhaps, by sharing experiences like these with her,
he could get some of that joy back for himself.

She turned toward him, her eyes dancing with delight at
all she was seeing, and his heart gave a painful lurch.

What was happening to him? Was he losing his mind?
This was the same obstreperous hoyden who had deliberately shot him within hours of making his acquaintance. A
girl he'd brought to London with the express purpose of
getting her off his hands as quickly as possible.

Yet why did that prospect seem less and less appealing
with each passing day? He found himself wanting to be in
her company, thought of her far too often when they were
not together.

And the image of her in another man's arms made his
blood run cold.

Val told himself it was because he hadn't found the right
suitor for her yet; had not found a man he felt confident
about, one who would take proper care of her. His feelings
were merely protective. When he found the proper suitor
for her, his mind would be at ease again.

Time. That was all it would take. A little more time to
find the perfect man for her.

She let out a small cry of disappointment, and he started,
until he realized the show had ended.

"Didn't you like it?" Val asked.

"It was wonderful," she whispered, her eyes wide. "I wish it hadn't ended."

Val did not hurry her to the exit, but let her remain in her seat while the rest of the audience traipsed out. He, too, felt no need to leave. He wanted to preserve her pleasure for as long as he could.

Finally, with a sigh, Kat stood and took his arm.

"We can go now," she said.

"That was an amazing display," Val said as he helped her into the carriage. "I cannot believe some of those tricks."

"I only wish I had seen it years ago," Kat said. "I would love to be able to do things like that."

"You probably would have broken your neck," Val said.

She gave him a dampening look.

"I want my brothers to see this," she said. "They will love it."

He saw how her expression turned wistful at the mention of her brothers. "School term will be over soon," Val said. "We can take all of them."

Val realized that there would be an entirely new complication to his plans if the boys were out of school before her future was settled. Once Kat was distracted by her brothers' presence, it would be even more difficult to keep her mind firmly focused on finding a husband.

He had to find one for her. To put his mind at ease.

Kat sat in the drawing room the next morning, opening the invitations that had arrived in the early mail. The names of the senders meant nothing to her, but it was something to do while she waited for Sophie to begin her day. No matter how late she had stayed out the previous evening, Kat could not sleep away the morning as Sophie did.

So she amused herself by sorting the invitations into piles according to the planned event—dinners on the end of the table, card parties in the center, and balls on the other end. In the upper corner, the picnic stack was disappointingly small. She thought those sounded the most fun.

The footman announced a guest, and to Kat's surprise, Morty walked in—alone. He looked downright funereal in a black jacket and gray waistcoat. His expression appeared equally solemn.

"Goodness, where are your friends?" Kat asked as she poured him a cup of tea.

He shrugged. "Didn't tell them I was coming."

"Then we can have a comfortable chat. Have you given any more thought to the gun situation? We could visit Manton's today."

He stared at her blankly for a moment. "I'd forgotten all about that," he confessed while he toyed with a roll of paper.

"What is that?" Kat asked.

Morty reddened and held out the roll.

Kat took the paper he handed her and unrolled it. The writing was smudged, with inkblots and fingerprints and cross outs, and she could barely read what it said. She gave him a questioning glance.

"It's a poem," he said helpfully. "For you."

"For me?" Kat stared at him in surprise. Morty was writing poetry? For her?

"Shall I read it to you?" he asked with a hopeful look.

"Please do." Kat sat back to listen.

After clearing his throat several times, Morty began to read:

There is a lady fair whom one cannot see just
    anywhere;
To find this prize you must seek her out.
On bridle path or theater box,
In drawing room or city shop
Are some of the places you might encounter the
    lady fair.
Her hair is brown, her eyes are blue
Particularly when they are looking at you.
Gracefully she glides across the floor
As she walks toward the door.
Fearing you will not see her anymore
    you follow her steps as they trip lightly across
    the carpet.
For one of her smiles anyone would walk miles.
Like Helena her light shines on all those
    who worship at her feet,
    hoping someday that they may be the ones to
    bathe in the glow of her warm countenance.

He rerolled the scroll and presented it to her with a flourish.

Kat did not know what to say. The poem was . . . appallingly bad. Even she knew that. But she suspected Morty had labored long over his work—and it had been for her. It was a sweet gesture.

"Morty, that was wonderful," she said at last. "No one has ever written poetry for me before."

"I have others," he said. "But they are not quite done. The whole process took longer than I thought it would."

"It is my understanding that writing poetry is a difficult task," Kat said. "I am very impressed. I could never do such a thing."

"It wasn't *that* difficult," he said, but she saw the look of pride on his face. "Getting the words to rhyme was the hardest part."

"I think you did a marvelous job."

Morty fixed her with an expectant look, and opened his mouth to say something, but before he could speak, Sophie came into the room.

"Goodness, you are up early, Mr. Mortimer," she said as she poured herself a cup of tea and sat down.

"I had important things to attend to," he said.

"Oh?" Sophie glanced suspiciously from Morty to Kat and back again.

"Morty wrote a poem for me," Kat explained.

"How delightful," said Sophie. "May I hear it?"

Morty dutifully read his creation again.

"That is . . . amazing," Sophie said. "I had no idea that you had such a literary bent."

"Stayed up nearly all night working on it," he said proudly. "Came home from the theater all fired to write." He gave Kat an adoring look. "Must have been inspired by my muse."

Kat felt a sinking sensation in the stomach, fearing Morty was taking this more seriously than she had first thought. Did he actually believe what he'd written? Had he formed an attachment for her? She looked at him with growing suspicion.

"Well I, for one, think it is a very sweet gesture," Sophie said. "No one ever wrote a poem for me, even my late husband."

"I can write one for you, too," Morty said, then glanced nervously at Kat. "That is, if you did not mind."

"Oh, please do," Kat said. "I should not like Sophie to feel left out."

"Have you been writing poetry long?" Sophie asked.

"This was my first effort," Morty replied, puffing out his chest.

"How impressive," Sophie said. "I could never do such a thing."

"I think it is important for a man to cultivate more than just sport," Morty said.

Voices sounded in the hall, and Nick and Lieutenant Boone were led in by the footman.

"Nick!" Kat exclaimed, eager to brag to her brother. "Guess what? Morty has written a poem for me!"

"Don't know why he should do that," Nick said. "You're no Helen of Troy."

"Beauty is not everything," Morty said. "There is spirit and outlook and—"

"Are you saying I'm not beautiful?" Kat demanded, with a look of mock dismay.

Morty gulped. "Well, I—"

"Oh, I am teasing you," Kat said. "I know I am no beauty. But you will have to focus on that when you write Sophie's poem, because she truly is."

"Yes, indeed." Lieutenant Boone cast an appreciative look at Sophie.

"Enough of your flummery, or you will have me thinking it is true," Sophie said. "Has your commanding officer been keeping you two busy?"

"Oh, endlessly," Nick said. "Drill, drill, drill."

"No doubt interspersed with eating, drinking, card playing, and riding," Kat said. "I do not feel any sympathy for you."

"What new trouble have you been up to?" Nick asked.

"I have been a perfect model of propriety," Kat replied. "I attended the theater the other night."

"She was the most popular lady there," Morty said.

"Hardly," Kat replied. "But I did have several male visitors."

"I did hear London is still rather thin of company," Nick said. "You must have been the only young lady there."

Kat cuffed him on the arm. "You are a brat, brother." Then she leaned toward him, suddenly turning serious.

"Have you heard anything from Eddie? I am getting worried; he has not yet written back! I am afraid something is terribly wrong."

"No doubt he's locked in the cellars on a diet of bread and water and isn't allowed to write," Nick said.

Kat gave him an exasperated look. "Do not even say such a thing! That's precisely the reason I think he should not be at school—they can be so cruel to their students."

"If they are punishing him, I am sure it is well deserved," Nick said. "You know Eddie."

"I am going to remind Newkirk today," Kat said. "He promised I could visit Eddie if he was still unhappy."

"I am certain that if things are truly awful, you will hear from the headmaster," Nick said. "I would not rely on anything Eddie wrote. You know how he exaggerates."

Kat frowned. Nick was such an annoyance. He was still firmly in Newkirk's camp. She turned back to Morty. "Did your parents send you to school?"

He shook his head. "Didn't want to go."

"Good for you." Kat felt relief at having found a sympathetic ear at last. "We still must schedule our visit to Manton's. Newkirk bought me a new shotgun yesterday."

"He did?" Nick regarded her with surprise. "Whatever are you going to do with that?"

"Shoot birds," Kat replied dryly. She looked back to Morty. "When would you be free to go?"

"Friday, perhaps?" he asked. "As long as I am inspired, I should like to keep writing my poetry."

"You could write a poem about pheasant shooting," Kat said. "I would like to hear that."

"You would?" Morty jumped to his feet. "I have to run home and start writing. Good day, adieu, I shall return."

As soon as he was safely out of the house, Sophie burst out laughing.

"That poor boy," she said, between giggles.

"Not much of a poet, eh?" Lieutenant Boone asked.

"Abominable," Sophie replied.

"But it was such a nice thought," Kat protested.

Nick gave her a sharp look. "Don't tell me you're fond of this fellow?"

"And if I were?" Kat glared at him. "You have nothing to say in the matter. That is between me and my guardian."

"I'd certainly speak with Newkirk if I thought you were interested in such a dolt," Nick said. "I'm not going to let you go off with the first fellow who pays you any attention."

"When I choose a man to marry, you will be the *last* to know," Kat said with a sneer. "You gave up any right to interfere with my life when you sided with Newkirk back at Kingsford."

Nick had the grace to look guilty. "I did what I thought was best."

"Hah!"

"Kat!" Sophie admonished her with a hint of sharpness. "Lieutenant Boone does not care to listen to your family squabbles."

"Oh, take no notice of me, I'm—" he began, but a look from Sophie quelled him.

"We did come here for a reason," Nick said. "I've managed to borrow a phaeton from one of the fellows. We came to take you ladies for a drive in the park this afternoon."

"So sorry, but I already have an engagement," Kat replied airily.

"With whom?" Nick demanded.

"Mr. Gerald Parker," Kat replied. "Sophie and Newkirk are coming with us, so don't ask if you can go along. There won't be room."

"Perhaps we could take you ladies to the park tomorrow afternoon, instead," Lieutenant Boone suggested.

Kat looked at Sophie. "Are we free tomorrow?"

Nick hooted. "Listen to you. You're sounding like the belle of London."

Kat gave him an arch look. "Perhaps I am."

"Well, if you are *too* busy to drive with us, perhaps Sophie will consent to come," he said.

"I should be delighted," Sophie said, and glanced at Kat. "You will come, won't you?"

"Oh, I suppose," she said reluctantly.

"Then tomorrow afternoon it is," Lieutenant Boone announced triumphantly.

"Is Newkirk at home?" Nick asked. "I wish to speak with him before I go."

"Look in the study downstairs," Sophie said.

"Ask him about Eddie," Kat called after him as he headed for the door. He dismissed her concern with a wave of his hand.

"How can he be so insufferable?" Kat asked.

Gerald Parker arrived that afternoon in a well-appointed landau. Kat immediately noticed that the two horses pulling it were not prime specimens: one was a bit too swayed in the back, while the high withers on the other bespoke a rough gait. Still, there was little point in wasting prime animals on sedate carriage rides in the city. Perhaps he kept his best horses in the country.

"Couldn't have picked a nicer day for a drive, what?" Parker asked as he helped first Sophie and then Kat into the carriage. He stood back to let Newkirk climb in and then followed. A coachman handled the reins.

"Tell us about your family, Mr. Parker," Sophie said as she settled into the well-padded seat. "You have how many boys?"

"Three," he replied. "Ten, thirteen, and fifteen."

"They are of a similar age to my brothers," Kat said. Was it possible that Parker would be her savior? "Did you bring them to London with you?"

"Good God, no," Parker replied. "They're all in school, every last one of them."

"Even the youngest?" Kat's hopes floundered. The poor child was barely older than Eddie.

"Boys need a good education, and you can't start them too soon. I hate to say it, but when their mother was alive she coddled them far too much. Boys need a bit of toughening to develop into good, strong men."

Kat bit her tongue to keep from bursting out with an angry retort. She could overlook the horses and Parker's age, but his callous disregard for his poor children . . . If they'd been alone, she'd have no qualms in telling him what she thought of his child-rearing ideas.

She glanced at Newkirk, who studiously avoided her gaze. An awkward silence ensued.

"Do you prefer London to the country?" Sophie asked at last.

"The city?" Parker shook his head emphatically. "Heav-

ens, no. Bit of a nuisance, it is. I only come here for business and . . . other matters I can't take care of at home."
He gave Kat a warm glance, which made her feel queasy.
"I'd much rather be in the country, puttering about the
estate, hunting, fishing."

Kat did not care how much he enjoyed country pursuits.
He treated his poor children cruelly, and that was all that
mattered. Parker, she realized quite clearly, would be of no
use to her in rescuing Eddie and the others.

She wished she could find some excuse to make him turn
the carriage around and take her home, but unfortunately
she was doomed to spend at least the next hour with a man
she was rapidly growing to dislike. Worse, with Sophie and
Newkirk present, she did not dare treat him to the blistering set-down she wished to bestow on him. With Parker
proving unsuitable, it was all the more critical that she keep
on Newkirk's good side.

Still, that did not mean she had to encourage him. She
would treat him with civility, nothing more.

Val sat back against the cushioned seat of Parker's carriage, an amiable smile plastered to his face, bored out of
his mind. Parker had an opinion on nearly every subject,
and he was not loath to share them with his guests, whether
it be the fate of the prisoners soon coming to trial, the
military budget, or the price of corn.

The man was a prosing bore. Val did not wish the fellow
on anyone.

Let alone his ward. Val knew she would be utterly miserable with this man. Parker would stifle her eager enthusi-
asms, and Kat would either fall into despair, or rebel in
some intolerable way. Val did not want to see the light
from those sparkling blue eyes dulled by such an insensitive
and unimaginative husband.

Kat needed a man who would keep her in hand, but
with a light touch. Heavy-handedness, he realized now with
chagrin, was not the way to deal with her. Unfortunately,
Parker was not clever enough to realize that.

Val gave a silent, inward sigh. Really, it was ridiculous
to have thought that he'd be so lucky as to find a husband
for her this soon. The Season had barely started. There

were plenty of men in London—surely one of them would be right for her. He merely needed to widen her circle of acquaintances.

Val now knew enough about his ward to have an inkling of her likes and dislikes. A sportsman with a keen eye for horses was imperative. Someone who was more comfortable in the country than in town would be best. And he should not have a fondness for either music or art, remembering her dismissal of both.

The fellow also needed a sense of humor. Val had seen enough of Kat's teasing nature to know that she enjoyed exchanging good-natured jibes. And the poor soul would have to tolerate visits from those brats she claimed as brothers.

He would have to redouble his efforts to find someone who fit his specifications. Kat deserved that much from him.

And Parker was definitely not the man.

Chapter Fifteen

After finally arriving home, in her relief at being rid of Parker, Kat almost missed spotting the letter lying on the Queen Anne table outside her room. But something made her glance down, and she saw the envelope.

A letter from Eddie!

She tore the covering off and eagerly scanned his poorly written missive. "Miserable." "Dreadful." "Unhappy." Her initial dismay was replaced by excitement. She finally had the proof she needed. Eddie was miserable and wanted to leave school. And Newkirk had promised she could rescue her brother if he still wanted to come home.

With a look of growing excitement on her face, she raced down the stairs in search of Newkirk. She found him in the study, intently reading a newspaper spread out on his desk. Kat waved the letter at him.

"Look at this!" she said. "Eddie's written and he's still unhappy. When can I go get him?"

Newkirk looked up, his expression curious. "What exactly does the rascal say?"

"That he's miserably lonely, school is terrible, and he wants to come home right this minute," she announced with a note of triumph in her voice.

"Odd." Newkirk sat back in his chair and looked at her intently. "The reports I have received say otherwise."

"What reports?"

"I wrote to the headmaster after your brother's first letter," he said.

Kat stared at him. "You did?"

Newkirk gave her an exasperated look. "Did you think I would blithely consign the child to an uncertain fate without checking? I told the headmaster of Eddie's complaints, and your concerns. He wrote back and assured me that 'young Mr. Foster' was doing quite well, was popular with the other students, and did not appear to be wasting away from hunger, as he has claimed."

"That's easy for him to write in a letter." Kat sniffed derisively. "Do you think he would dare admit to harming the children?"

"I do not think he is harming any children, including your brother," Newkirk said. "The headmaster assured me that these sorts of complaints are common among children when they are first sent off to school, or when their life has been disrupted in some other way. Frantic parents arrive at school, only to find a child who insists upon staying."

"If Eddie says he is unhappy, he is unhappy," Kat said. "And you promised I could bring him home if he still wanted to leave."

"I have a feeling that Eddie knows how to exaggerate his plight to play on his sister's sympathy."

"I do not care what you think." Kat stamped her foot with growing irritation at the man's obstinance. "I want to bring Eddie home."

"It is silly to take him out of school now when the term is set to be over in a few weeks," Newkirk said patiently. "He will be home soon enough."

"Newkirk, my brother is in distress. I have to rescue him."

"He is not suffering, and, no, you are not going to take him out of school before the end of the term."

Kat blinked back the tears that threatened to blind her. She should have known better, should have known that all of Newkirk's recent amiability was only a pretense.

He still did not care.

"If you won't let me take care of him, I will find someone who will," she said heatedly.

He cast her a skeptical look.

"I will," she cried, and stomped out of the room.

As she fled back upstairs, Kat was too angry even to cry. She had trusted Newkirk, had even allowed herself to enjoy his company, and he had betrayed her. He never intended to let her take Eddie from school; he'd merely told her that to keep her complacent.

Well, she was done with playing the dutiful ward. She'd done all that he had asked and what had it gotten her? Nothing. From now on, she was going to play her own game and find a way to free her brothers from Newkirk's clutches.

Her immediate need was for a husband who would help her rescue Eddie. It was rather lowering to think that she had such limited number of candidates to choose from, but she'd barely made an appearance in London society and had met so few men yet. Only Morty, Parker, and Wareham.

She'd discovered today that Parker would be of no help—he'd probably send Eddie to an even worse school. That left Morty and Wareham to choose from. And, yes, the Season was still young, and there were other men to meet in London, but she needed one *now*. With Eddie a prisoner at that horrid school, she did not have time to waste. She needed a husband—fast.

Morty was her best hope. He had written poetry for her; she suspected that meant he liked her more than he had admitted. He might not be her idea of the perfect husband, but if he would help rescue her brothers, it did not matter. She would even marry a prosing old bore like Gerald Parker if he was willing to take the boys out of school.

Morty it must be. She could not afford to wait to see if someone better came along. Marrying someone like Morty had some advantages—she would have no problems in bending him to her wishes. If he was rather deficient in common sense, she could think and plan for the both of them. He would eagerly follow her lead.

She'd make her proposal to him tomorrow.

"M-m-married?" Morty stammered as he sat beside Kat on the drawing room sofa the next morning.

"You like me, don't you?" she asked.

"Well, yes, but . . ."

Kat grabbed his hand. "Morty, I beg you. Rescue me from my cruel guardian."

"Newkirk?" He looked puzzled. "He seems like a nice enough fellow."

"Oh, he puts on a good show in front of people, but he is the meanest man alive." She felt a small twinge of guilt at blackening his reputation so darkly, but it was his own fault for refusing to take her to Eddie.

Morty regarded her doubtfully.

"He has broken up my family," Kat said, and it did not take any effort to bring emotion into her voice. "He forced Tom and Sam into the navy, where they are practically enslaved. Once they are sent on a ship, they can never leave."

"Really?" Morty asked. "That does not seem right."

"And Eddie! He's practically a baby, and Newkirk sent him off to some horrid school. The poor child is so miserable—he cries himself to sleep every night. I've begged Newkirk to let me go to him, but he refuses."

Morty looked troubled. "I do not like to hear that."

Sensing her imminent triumph, Kat moved in for the kill. "And he wants to marry me to some horrid man who is old enough to be my father! All so he can be rid of me and my family."

"We can't let that happen," Morty said. "Perhaps if I spoke to him . . ."

"It will not do any good," Kat said hastily. "He's vowed to marry me to the first man who asks, no matter what my wishes."

"I don't know what to do," Morty said, shaking his head.

"I won't be any bother," Kat promised. "As long as I

can keep a horse or two, I'll be happy. And you could write me as much poetry as you want."

"There is that," Morty said.

"And you could help me rescue my brothers," Kat said eagerly. She had to make certain he was willing to do that before she took this irrevocable step. "I know you'll like them; they're very useful. Eddie is great at catching rabbits, and Tom and Sam, well, they know their way around a stable. They'd care for all your horses."

Morty still looked unconvinced. "Don't know what my parents would say."

Kat stiffened. She had not even stopped to think that Morty had a family—besides his brother. This was a whole new complication.

"Why, they would admire you for helping a damsel in distress," she said with her brightest smile. "A poor orphan with no one to take care of her."

She knew she was laying it on thickly, but she suspected that was the only way Morty would agree. And now that she'd started this, she was not going to let him go until he promised to help her.

"Don't know where we'd live," he said. "I don't come into my inheritance until I'm twenty-five."

"Oh, I have enough funds." Kat dismissed his concerns with a flick of her wrist. "And I bet Newkirk would pay you a tidy sum to take me off his hands."

"We need a place to live," he said again. "Can't move in with Tippy and Lawrence."

"I have a home in the country," Kat said. "Well, it's Nick's, but he has no need of it now that he's in the army. You'd like it there—the hunting is good, the fishing excellent, and plenty of pheasants to shoot."

Morty's brow furrowed as he sat deep in thought. Then he stood and regarded her with a determined look.

"I'll do it," he said.

"Oh, thank you!" Kat leapt from her chair and flung her arms around him. "You are such a dear! I will never forget this!"

Val was surprised to receive a note from Parker that morning, requesting an appointment, and even more surprised when the man arrived and explained the nature of his visit.

"Know you're looking for someone to take the girl off your hands," Parker said the moment he sat down. "Thought I'd put in my offer before it's too late."

Val stared at him, trying to hide his dismay. "You wish to ask for Miss Foster's hand?"

Parker nodded.

Val did not know what to think—other than there was no way he would agree to such a match. Parker and Kat? The very idea was distasteful. The man was all wrong for her.

"She's a bit young, but she'll soon grow out of her flightiness," Parker said. "I know how to keep a woman under firm control."

Val gritted his teeth to keep from responding as he wished.

"Suppose you want to know more about my situation," Parker said.

Val held up a hand. "No, that's really not necessary. I fear you are right—my ward is a rather flighty young lady, and I have already decided that she is not yet ready for marriage. I intend to let her enjoy the Season, gain some polish, and wait until next year to seek a husband for her."

Parker looked disappointed. "Oh. Well, I cannot promise that I will still be available by then. Been thinking about taking a wife for some time now."

"Oh, no," Val said, "I could not expect you to adjust your plans in such a manner. Who knows if the girl will even be ready next year? Best you keep looking for a suitable partner."

Parker nodded. "Bit of a shame, though. She seemed to be a spirited miss. Likes to fish and all. Rare thing in a woman, I've found."

Val nodded agreeably. "That is true. But you might prefer to find a woman you can teach to fish, rather than take on one who is already set in her own way."

Parker absorbed that idea. "You may be right." He stood and held out his hand. "Thank you for seeing me today, your lordship. I wish you well with the girl. I'll drop you a note after the new year if I'm still unattached."

"Please do," Val said, and eagerly ushered the man out of the room.

Val let out a long sigh of relief when Parker was gone. He's spun such lies to get rid of the man! But better than telling him the truth—that Val would never consent to his marriage to Kat, and even if he did, Kat would undoubtedly refuse. Val had seen the expression on her face yesterday during that carriage ride when Parker talked about children.

He should find his ward and let her know that he'd just saved her from an unimaginable fate.

She was coming down the stairs as he started up.

"Ah, there you are," he said. "I have interesting news for you."

"Oh?" She looked at him curiously.

"You have made one conquest in London, at least," he said, wanting to tease her a bit before he broke the news.

"I have?" Her eyes widened. "Who?"

"Can't you guess?" he asked.

"I have no idea. Tell me!"

"Your favorite beau, Mr. Gerald Parker."

She looked at him with a stunned expression on her face. "Parker? Parker was here to talk about me?"

"Not to just talk," Val said, enjoying drawing this out. "He offered for your hand."

He could not decide if horror or surprise was the predominant emotion warring within her.

"And what did you say?" she asked in a whisper.

"I told him you were far too flighty to even think of marriage at this time."

"Thank God!"

Val gave her a quizzical look. "You don't mind being called flighty?"

"You can call me anything you like if it saves me from a marriage to that man. How could you even think I would consider such a thing after what he said yesterday? 'Boys need a bit of toughening,' indeed."

"I did rather think you would refuse his suit, so I decided to save you the trouble," Val said.

"I do not need any favors from *you*," she said acidly and continued past him down the stairs.

*   *   *

Shaken by Newkirk's tale of Parker's offer, Kat was even more eager for Morty to make his appearance before her guardian. At first, she'd thought that was what Val was alluding to. It had come as a great shock to learn it was Parker. She shivered at the very thought.

Kat was hard-pressed to maintain a calm facade when she joined Sophie in the drawing room. Yet a superstitious fear that if she said anything, her plan would unravel, kept Kat quiet. Even so, she found it hard to contain her excitement. Why, she might have her brothers back in no time.

Kat was so involved in mentally planning her brothers' homecoming that she completely forgot that Wareham had promised to drive her to view the almost completed Thames Bridge. His arrival at the house caught her by surprise. Spending time with Wareham, which she'd looked forward to precisely because it would irritate Newkirk, no longer mattered now that she'd enlisted Morty's aid.

Yet it would be far safer if she left the house, lest she blurt her news to Sophie. So while Sophie made polite conversation with Wareham, Kat dashed upstairs to get her coat and bonnet.

The moment she caught sight of Wareham's elegant phaeton and matched team of chestnuts, her spirits rose.

"What a beautiful team," she said as Wareham helped her onto the high-perched seat. "They look like prime goers."

"They are," he replied with a grin as he took the reins and started down the street. "I thought we could take a round or two in the park before we go to the bridge. Does that meet with your approval?"

"That would be fine," Kat said, eager to see these horses display their paces.

As they drove, her thoughts returned to the impending conversation between Morty and her guardian. She would like to be there, to make certain Morty pled his case properly. Yet Newkirk was so eager to get her off his hands that even if Morty put forward his proposal in his abominable poetry, she was certain her guardian would gladly agree to the marriage.

"You are rather quiet today," Wareham said as he smoothly guided his vehicle around two carriages stopped in the middle of the lane.

Kat gave him a guilty look. She should be attending to her escort. After all, she was in the company of a handsome man, in a bang-up carriage with a beautiful team of matched chestnuts, and they would draw the attention of everyone who saw them in the park.

"I am admiring your team," she said. She'd never driven a high-perched phaeton before, and her hands itched to take a try at the reins. Dare she ask Wareham?

She saw two men riding along the path in front of them and felt a sudden, deep longing for home, where she could ride as she pleased.

"I would rather be riding," Kat confessed, looking longingly at a sprightly bay as it galloped across the green.

"Why didn't you say so? We can ride tomorrow."

Kat sighed. "It's more complicated than that. Newkirk does not wish me to ride while I am in the city."

"Afraid you might show up the other ladies?" Wareham gave her a teasing look.

"Well . . ." Kat suddenly realized that with her future secure, there was no point in prevaricating. "At home, it was only my brothers and me. So naturally, I rode with them and . . ."

"You ride *like* them," he finished for her.

Kat eyed him with new respect for his quick understanding. "Exactly. And Newkirk does not think I should be seen riding that way in the park."

"I fear he is right," Wareham said.

Kat's spirits sank. She had misjudged him after all.

"However, there are other places you could ride where no one would ever be the wiser."

"Really?" She looked at him eagerly. "Where?"

"You are relatively safe anywhere as long as you go early in the morning," he said. "But a more deserted spot, like Hampstead Heath, would be ideal."

Kat's pulse quickened. "Do you think I dare?"

"I think you would be safe, as long as you take an escort."

Kat smiled. "And who did you have in mind?"

"I would be delighted to accompany you," he said with a sly wink.

Kat opened her mouth to say yes when she suddenly remembered Morty, and Newkirk. What if something happened, and Morty wasn't able to speak with her guardian today? If Newkirk discovered she went riding with Wareham, he would be furious. She did not dare anger him, not until her future was settled.

She shivered with frustration. It would be so glorious to go for a bruising ride! But, she promised herself, once she and Morty were married, she'd be out of Newkirk's control and she could do as she pleased. It would not be too long before that happened. She could afford to wait a little longer.

"The idea sounds wonderful," she said slowly, reluctantly. "But I fear I must refuse. I dare not upset my guardian."

Wareham raised a brow. "I thought you were made of sterner stuff, Miss Foster."

She grimaced. "Newkirk controls not only my fate, but the fate of my brothers."

Wareham shrugged. "If you chance to change your mind, you may call on me."

"Thank you," she said, then glanced at him slyly. "But I know Newkirk would not object if I drove a carriage. I would love to guide your team around the park."

Wareham tossed back his head and laughed. "Now, that sounds like the Miss Foster I know. Do you think you can handle these fellows?"

She nodded eagerly.

Wareham pulled up and handed her the reins. "Show me."

Kat gave him a wide grin, then snapped the reins and urged the horses into a swift trot.

Newkirk might keep her from riding, but handling the reins of Wareham's exquisite pair was almost as exhilarating. They were by far the sweetest team she'd ever driven.

She wondered if she could persuade Nick to buy her a pair and a phaeton as a wedding present?

Val left his study door ajar so he could hear when Kat returned to the house. He intended to talk with her the moment she arrived about the hare-brained scheme she had concocted with that idiot Mortimer.

At first he had been pleased when the fellow asked for Kat's hand. Combined with Parker's earlier offer, it showed that she was attracting male attention and it boded well for her eventually making a good marriage. Val had never seriously considered agreeing to the union—Mortimer was not at all what he had in mind for his ward.

Yet there was something just a little havey-cavey about the situation. Mortimer had displayed more relief than disappointment when Val had tactfully declined the offer, which made Val wonder just whose plan this had been.

He suspected Kat had a hand in this, especially after her fury yesterday. What had she said? "I'll find someone who will help me." Val suspected the hapless Mortimer had been her first choice.

His alertness was rewarded when he heard the front door open and light footsteps treading across the hall. He was out of his chair and at the door in an instant, ready to intercept his ward.

"Kat?" he called.

She was already halfway up the stairs and peered down at him, her bonnet dangling from her arm.

"I should like to speak with you," he said, and turned back to the study before he could see how she regarded his summons.

He thought about resuming his seat and putting her in the chair facing him across the desk, but decided he would rather adopt a more superior position for the upcoming conversation. He stepped before the mantel, arms crossed over his chest.

"What is it?" She halted in the doorway.

Kat wore a gown he had not seen before—a shade of misty, sea foam green that brought out the blue in her eyes and the roses in her cheeks. She presented a fetching picture. No wonder she'd been able to convince poor Mortimer to go along with her plans.

"Please, sit," he said, gesturing toward the chair. He waited until she complied. She regarded him with a calm expression, but he could tell from the way her fingers toyed with her bonnet ribbons that she was anything but calm.

"I had a caller this afternoon," he began.

"Oh?" She regarded him with a look of pure innocence.

"Your friend, Mr. Mortimer." He noticed a trace of relief cross her eyes.

"Morty paid you a visit?" She laughed lightly. "How interesting. What did you two find to talk about?"

Val shook his head at her attempted charade. "Oh, cut line, Kat. You know exactly why he was here."

"I do?"

"He came to ask my permission for your hand in marriage."

"Morty?"

Val's eyes narrowed. She *looked* surprised. But if matters were as he suspected, it was feigned.

He made a dismissive gesture. "I turned him down, of course."

She half rose out of her seat. "You what?"

"Indeed." Val was pleased to see he'd finally gained a reaction from her. "As your guardian, it is my duty to make the most advantageous match I can. And I fear he is not it."

"But . . . but . . ." she sputtered. "What's wrong with Morty?"

"Oh, nothing that about ten years won't fix. Right now, he is far too young to be considering marriage."

"He is the same age I am, and you want me to get married."

"Women are far more ready for marriage at that age," Val said.

"How can you make a pronouncement like this without even consulting me?" she demanded. "Don't my wishes have any part in this?"

"You thanked me for rejecting Parker for you," he said.

"That was different."

"If I thought you truly desired to marry this fellow, I would have consulted you," Val continued. "But I think you have no more wish to marry him than he wishes to marry you."

"How can you say such a thing?"

Her look of righteous indignation almost made Val laugh.

"The relieved expression on his face when I told him 'no' said it all," Val replied. "Tell me, Kat, was this your idea? Did you put him up to it?"

She swallowed, guilt written all over her face. "We . . . discussed the matter. He was willing."

"Did you offer threats? Or bribes?"

"Neither," she replied. "Morty likes me. He didn't object."

"But the idea was yours?" He wanted her confirmation, to make him easy in his mind that he had done the right thing, that she did not have tender feelings for this fellow.

"I might have mentioned that you were encouraging me to wed another . . ."

"And Mortimer jumped up and volunteered himself?"

"Um—yes."

"Kat, if I for one minute thought that the lad had any deep affection for you, and you for him, I might be willing to reconsider the matter. But I fear this is just a scheme on your part to free yourself from my guardianship."

"How could you even suggest such a thing?" She managed to look indignant and guilty at the same time.

"Matters would be different if Mr. Mortimer was the type of man who would guide you properly through life." Val clasped his hands behind his back. "But as I know you would wrap him around your little finger and induce him to allow you to do each and every thing you pleased, I cannot in good faith, as your guardian, allow such a thing."

"What does it matter what I do once I'm married?" she demanded. "You won't have to worry about me anymore."

"I want what is best for you, Kat," he said. "And having a young man who will bow to your every wish and command is not my idea of a good husband for you."

"No doubt you want someone like Parker, who will keep me in my proper place?"

"No, I told you I do not think Parker is a suitable candidate, either," he admitted. "I think that you have not yet met the right man."

"Morty cares for me," she said. "He writes me poetry."

"I know," Val said. "He showed me. That alone should convince you that he is not the man for you."

She stood abruptly. "I think you are a horrible person, and you do not care one whit for what will make *me* happy." She strode toward the door, then turned. "And, in the future, if you receive any more offers for my hand, I would appreciate it if you would consult with me before summarily dismissing them."

"I am willing to do that," he said.

"Hmmph." She gave a derisive sniff and exited into the corridor, shutting the door none too gently behind her.

Val let out a deep breath of relief. She at least had confirmed his belief that she had put Mortimer up to this scheme. She was upset with him right now, but she would soon see the wisdom of his actions on her behalf. In her heart of hearts, she knew Mortimer was a bad choice.

Val must redouble his efforts to find a suitable match for her. No more young lads or widowed squires. Someone with the experience to handle a high-spirited girl without dampening the very nature that made her so delightful. Someone who would appreciate the same qualities he did in her, who would see past the country upbringing and to the budding woman who lay beneath.

Somewhere in London there had to be such a man.

Fury filled Kat as she fled up the stairs. She thought she'd concocted the perfect plan to reunite her family—and with a word, Newkirk had dismissed it. Now what was she to do?

It had been a mistake to put so much trust in Morty. The fellow was not the brightest, and she should have prepared him better for his interview with Newkirk. But how could she have known that her guardian would suddenly become particular, when all his efforts had been directed at getting her married? She'd thought he would have jumped at Morty's offer.

She would just have to find someone more suitable—and sensible. A man with some years on him. One who would not be cowed by Newkirk's scowling visage, but not a bore like Parker. Someone more dashing, who would be fun to live with. Someone like . . . Wareham.

Kat clapped her hands in delight. He was perfect! Newkirk could not cavil about his age or maturity. And Wareham would certainly not wilt under any of Newkirk's paltry arguments. He'd stand firm in the face of any opposition.

But how was she going to persuade Wareham to help her? Convincing Morty was one thing, Wareham quite another. He was a man of the world, and if Newkirk was to be believed, had plenty of experience with women. Why would he even consider marrying an innocent young girl like her when he could have any woman he wanted?

She would have to make him an offer he'd find irresistible. But what? What incentive could she offer to lure him into marriage? From a male perspective, Wareham already had everything he needed—the freedom to do as he pleased, a bevy of women vying for his attentions. His rakish reputation did little to diminish his appeal. Countless women would beg to be his wife.

That was it! The one thing Kat could offer that another woman would not—the promise that he would not have to give up his rakish ways. The complete freedom to live his life as he pleased. She had no desire to play doting wife to him; all she wanted was to live quietly in the country with her brothers. Wareham could remain in London and do as he wished. As a married man, he would be safe from matchmaking schemers, and he could carry on as many dalliances as he wished.

All she had to do was convince him that this was in his best interest.

Kat hastily scribbled a note to Wareham, telling him she had changed her mind about riding, and asking if they could go tomorrow. If he was agreeable, he needed to provide her with a mount; not a "lady's horse" but an animal with spirit. She would meet him at the end of the street in the morning at a time he chose.

Sealing the note, she rang for the maid and told her to send it immediately with a footman to Wareham's lodgings, and to wait for a reply.

Newkirk might have won the first battle, but the war was not over. Wareham would make a far more formidable candidate for her hand.

If she could persuade him to cooperate. It would be nothing like persuading Morty—that had been simple as could be. Wareham would present more of a challenge. But nothing ventured, nothing gained. And if he did agree to help her, she'd have her brothers back.

Chapter Sixteen

*W*areham agreed to meet her the following morning, so Kat made a pact with one of the kitchen girls, for a shilling and a pair of stockings, to wake her at the appointed time. In the dim, predawn light, Kat quickly scrambled into her riding clothes—which she'd hidden at the back of her wardrobe the day she'd arrived in London—and crept down the back stairs. She slipped into the garden and through the narrow passageway to the mews, then hurried away from the stables toward the street.

She rounded the corner and there was Wareham, waiting as promised on the corner. He was astride a powerful bay that filled her with envy, but then she caught sight of the well-muscled roan prancing beside him and smiled broadly.

Wareham quickly dismounted and strode forward to welcome her. He took her hand and brought it to his lips.

"A woman who is early," he exclaimed. "I did not think there was such a creature."

"We are not all ninnies," she said, flashing him a smile before patting the roan on the nose. She took a good look at the mount he'd brought for her. He was nearly as big as her own horse, and looked trim and fit.

"Will he do?" Wareham asked, a smile on his face.

"I can't be sure until I've put him through his paces," Kat said with a deliberately saucy grin. "Shall we start out?"

Before Wareham could step in and give her a boost, Kat put one booted foot in the stirrup and hoisted herself into the saddle.

"Oh, it has been so long since I rode!" she exclaimed. "I cannot wait until we can gallop."

They guided their horses through the nearly deserted avenues; even the street sellers and merchants were not yet about. Normally bustling Oxford Street was empty of traffic. Up Portland Place they rode until they reached the edge of Regent's Park. An empty expanse of parkland stretched out before them.

"Ready to gallop?" Wareham asked.

Kat nodded. She felt confident she could handle the mount he'd brought; the horse had spirit, yet was well trained and responsive.

With a flick of the reins, she brought the horse to a sprightly trot, then with a tap of her heels urged it into a full gallop. The wind streamed past her face, causing her eyes to tear, but Kat did not mind. *Oh, it was glorious to ride again!*

They flew across the wide field. Kat's mount easily kept pace with Wareham's horse. She glanced over at her escort, who flashed her a mock salute. Kat grinned back at him. Of course Wareham was a good judge of horses and a bruising rider—he'd been a cavalryman.

Like Newkirk. Kat wondered if he was as skilled a rider. She might never know, if her plans went as she hoped. The thought filled her with a surprising pang, which she quickly pushed aside. Newkirk was not going to help her save Eddie, so she did not care if he could do tricks like the riders at Astley's.

All too soon they reached the end of the formal parkland. Reining in their horses, they crossed the road at a gentle trot, then slowed to walk the horses along the lane.

"That's Primrose Hill," Wareham said, pointing to the rise beside them. "One of London's favorite dueling spots."

Kat glanced at him sharply. Did he know about her duel with Newkirk? No, he couldn't; Newkirk would never have told him. His mention of the topic was pure coincidence. Still, she wondered what Wareham would think if he knew. Would he be appalled—or amused? The latter, she thought. She feared she would be the one cringing with embarrassment if he learned the tale. That had been an unfortunate incident.

She glanced sideways at Wareham. He was handsome, in a more rugged and dashing way than Newkirk. Of course, a rake should be handsome; it was part of his appeal.

Kat pondered how to broach the subject that had been on her mind all morning. Was she naive to think that Wareham would even consider marrying her, when he could have his choice of women? Kat told herself that her willingness to not demand husbandly behavior from him was the thing that would win him over.

"I have a proposition for you," she said.

"Oh?"

"I need a husband," she said bluntly, "and I hope that you might be willing to consider the position."

"Me?" Wareham laughed. "There must be scores of young men beating down your doors. Why am I being granted such a singular honor?"

"Because I think you are the one man Newkirk would permit me to marry," she said. "He's already turned down two offers, with the excuse that one gentleman was too young and the other too old. He certainly cannot say either about you."

Wareham laughed. "No, he cannot. I am flattered, Miss Foster, but I do not think that I am ready for such a serious step."

"You must consider the benefits of the situation," Kat continued. "As a single man, you are in the sights of every unmarried woman in the country. Your reputation as a rake only enhances your attraction. A wife—one who would be willing to let you go your own way—would keep you safe from entrapment by an unscrupulous female."

"I think you overestimate my appeal to the fairer sex," Wareham said. "What would you gain from such a marriage?"

"I want to get my brothers away from Newkirk's control," she said flatly. "And I need a husband to do that."

"So you are proposing a marriage in name only," he said.

"Exactly. Once we are wed, and you have custody of my brothers, you are free to do as you please. I'm content to stay in the country and will not bother you."

Wareham regarded her with an expression that made her decidedly uneasy. "And what if I say that I would have no intention of ignoring a wife as delectable as you, Miss Foster?"

She gulped in surprise. *That* was something she had not considered.

He laughed again. "Do not fret. I have no intention of ravishing you here on the grass. I merely wish to point out that there may be more to this 'marriage' than you bargained for."

"I want my brothers back," Kat said. "I will do whatever I must to achieve that."

"That does not say much for your opinion of me," Wareham said with a wry grin. "Any man would suit your need."

Kat flushed. She'd forgotten that men, even hardened rakes like Wareham, needed to hear flattering pleasantries.

"Of course I like you," she said. "You are handsome and charming, dress stylishly, sit a horse well, and—"

Wareham held up a hand. "Enough, enough."

"I feel that honesty is best," Kat said. "I do not think you are the kind of man to dictate my behavior, and I have no desire to restrict yours. You shall be free to do what you wish without any complaint from me."

"An attractive offer." Wareham looked thoughtful. "I shall have the cachet of being a married man, with none of the restrictions. Who could refuse such a convenient arrangement?"

Kat looked at him eagerly. "You will do it?"

"I will consider it," he said. "I do not think you have any idea of what you are getting yourself into, Miss Foster. But if regaining custody of your brothers is so important, I am eager to help you."

"The only way you can help is by marrying me," Kat said. "I promise we shall be no trouble at all."

"If I do decide to go along with your plan, I have to speak to your guardian, and he will not be pleased to see you riding like this. We should get you back to the house before you are missed," he said.

Kat laughed as they turned their horses back toward the city. If Wareham agreed to her plan, it would no longer matter when and where she rode.

She could barely contain her enthusiasm as they returned to town. The ride had been glorious, and she felt certain Wareham was going to help her. Everything looked to be working according to plan.

"I hope you enjoyed yourself," Wareham said as they neared the corner of Newkirk's street.

"Oh, I did! It was so wonderful to have a good gallop. You must promise to take me again, soon."

He executed a mock bow. "It would be my pleasure to take you riding whenever you wish."

"We could do this every day if you married me," Kat said. She gave her horse's neck a pat. "Is he yours?"

Wareham nodded.

"You have the most exquisite horses," she said. "I think I would marry you for that reason alone."

Wareham laughed. "Put in my place again. Miss Foster, you have a great talent for reducing a man's opinion of himself."

Kat smiled at him. "Well, I see no purpose in congratulating you on how handsome you are. *You* had nothing to do with that. But as for being a good judge of horseflesh—now that is a skill I can admire."

Wareham shook his head. "I am beginning to think a future with you would be more amusing than I had first thought."

She smiled back at him, surprised at the sudden look of dismay that crossed his face as he looked past her.

"We are caught out, I am afraid," he said in a low tone. Kat looked and, to her horror, saw Newkirk, standing in front of his house, hands on hips, glaring at them.

"What is he doing here?" she moaned.

"Good morning," Newkirk said icily as they rode toward him.

"Good morning." Kat tried to sound cheerful and unconcerned. "Are you on your way already? It's rather early to be paying calls, isn't it?"

"Get into the house," he ordered.

The tone of his voice was so ominous that Kat did not dare argue. She slid from the saddle, handed the reins to Wareham and dashed past Newkirk, ran up the stairs and into the house.

It was cowardly, she knew, to flee the field of battle. But she preferred that Wareham deflect some of her guardian's wrath before she had to face him.

She told herself it was all Newkirk's fault. If he hadn't refused to let her rescue Eddie, hadn't turned down Morty's proposal, she wouldn't have gone riding with Wareham.

Kat fully intended to tell that to her guardian when he confronted her.

"What in God's name do you think you are doing?" Val gave Wareham a steely look. "Do you have any idea what damage you might have done?"

"Oh, don't get so agitated," Wareham said. "It was an innocent morning ride."

"You know damn well it was anything but," Val said. "How could you let her talk you into this?"

"Do you think she begged me so prettily I gave in and allowed her to have her way?" Wareham laughed. "I've far more experience with women than that, and you know it. No, I suggested this outing myself."

Val shook his head. "I would have at least expected *you* to have more sense."

"Not more than ten or twenty people even saw us at this hour, and certainly no one who knew her—or you. I think you are worried over nothing, Val."

"She is my ward, and it is my job to look after her."

"You are guarding her like a fussy old mother hen," Wareham said. "You can't hold her with such a tight rein for long; she'll bolt. And then where will you be? You should be thanking me. This early morning gallop will soothe her restlessness for a spell."

Val did not need Wareham telling him how to manage his ward. "Oh, now you are the expert on raising daughters?"

"I have as much experience with it as you do," Wareham retorted.

As his friend's voice rose, Val suddenly remembered they were standing in the middle of the street. "Take the horses round to the mews and come inside," he said.

"Can't," Wareham replied cheerfully. "I have to get the horses back, or I'll be late for an appointment. At Whitehall."

"Who in the devil are you seeing at Whitehall?" Val demanded.

Wareham smiled mysteriously. "I shall tell you about it, later. I'll return this afternoon—say about two? We may have something to discuss." He glanced in admiration toward the door through which Kat had disappeared. "She's a marvelous horsewoman."

"And seeking a husband, so she has no use for your attentions," Val said coldly.

Wareham gave him a long look. "Even if my intentions are honorable?"

Val was so stunned by his friend's words that he wasn't able to muster a reply before Wareham mounted up and rode away.

Honorable intentions? Wareham? Val could not believe it. Wareham had never once entertained serious thoughts about a female. And after all the Spanish and French beauties Val had seen him cast aside, it was ludicrous to think that he'd be enamored of Kat Foster. She was not the sort of woman Wareham enjoyed.

No, Wareham was merely having a jest at Val's expense, and he did not appreciate it.

He turned back to the house. He'd talk with Wareham later. Now he must deal with Kat.

Val half expected her to have run out the back while he was talking to Wareham, but to his relief, he peered into his study and watched her nervously pacing back and forth in front of the fireplace. In her preoccupation, she did not notice him standing in the doorway.

It had been a long time since he'd seen her clad in breeches and riding boots, and at that time, he'd merely thought of her as a bothersome brat. But now . . . he realized it was a very good thing that women did not regularly wear trousers, or every man in London would be incapable of coherent thought or speech. Even a pair of rounded breasts peeking out over the top of an indecently low bodice was no match for cloth stretched over a nicely rounded bottom.

Damn. This was not what he'd intended to feel. He planned to berate her for wearing those breeches in town. But at the moment, he was more willing to appreciate the picture she presented, with that shapely rear and long, lithe legs. He felt a shocking stab of desire.

No doubt Wareham had enjoyed the sight as well. Which made Val even angrier. He did not want someone like Wareham ogling Kat. Or anyone else, for that matter. Val vowed to see that those breeches were burned this very day.

He struggled to rein in his emotions. The last thing he needed was to show her his displeasure, and make her even more defiant. Val realized that if he treated this escapade causally, he'd take the wind out of her sails.

He smiled to himself. Perhaps he was finally learning how to deal with her.

Now, if he could only keep his mind on the business at hand instead of those legs . . .

He pushed the door open and strode into the room.

Kat greeted him with a defiant expression.

"I do not care what you say or do, that was the most enjoyable time I've had since I came to London." She gave him a look that dared him to chastise her.

"I do not doubt it." Val gestured to the chairs. "Would you care to sit?"

She eyed him warily.

"I am not going to beat you," he said with a short laugh. "Although you surely deserve it."

"What do you intend to do?" Her gingerly manner of perching on the edge of the chair belied her nonchalant attitude.

He shrugged. "What can I do? The damage is done. If you escaped everyone's notice, you will be safe. If not . . . well, then the tale will be all over London and any punishment I could mete out would be inconsequential compared with that."

Kat stared at him, mouth agape. "You're not going to lock me in my room?"

"And limit you to bread and water?" Val shook his head. "Believe me, the thought crossed my mind, but I realized I would have to explain to all your beaus why you were unavailable. Better that you act normally and wait to see if you got away with this little escapade."

The look of relief on her face was almost comical. Val struggled to keep his own features stern.

"I am honestly more disappointed than angry," he continued. "I had hoped you would think before you acted impulsively."

"Wareham asked me to go with him," she said. "It would have been rude of me to say no."

Val snorted. "I feel certain he would have withstood the disappointment."

"Well, what's done is done." Kat gave him a guileless stare.

Val fumbled for words. How was he going to impress upon this girl that she must never do such a thing again? She might have escaped notice this time, but if she continued to ride in this manner, it was only a matter of time before someone recognized her. And then it would be too late to save her.

"I know what you are going to say," she said. "And it does not matter to me in the slightest if people learn what I've done. I have no intention of marrying a man who will not let me ride as I like, or dress as I please, or curse, or spit, or do any of the other things that young ladies are not supposed to do. How could I marry a man who would not let me be myself?"

"You think you will find such a man?" Val asked.

"I hope so," she replied. "Now, if you are finished, I should like to go upstairs and bathe. I believe we are receiving this morning, and I do not want Sophie to have to entertain alone."

"Go," Val said curtly. There was no point in talking to her now—she had no intention of listening. Perhaps later, he could persuade Sophie to try.

But if that blasted chit was so determined to throw away her chances of making a decent marriage, he was rapidly losing any inclination to stop her. Let her play housekeeper to her brothers until they all grew up and left her. His time would be better spent encouraging Sophie to find a husband. That was starting to look like a much more likely prospect than ever marrying off Kat Foster.

Yet he could not resist watching the enticing sight of her walking out of the room.

At precisely two that afternoon, Val heard Wareham's voice in the hall. Val rose from his chair and walked into the corridor to greet his visitor, striving to appear nonchalant. Yet Val intended to tell him in no uncertain terms that he did not want Wareham to have anything more to do with Kat.

"I believe you wanted to speak to me?" Val asked.

"I thought I should make certain that you had not locked your ward in the dungeon," Wareham said. He set his hat and gloves on the table in the hall and followed Val back into the study.

"You'll be pleased to know that I have not punished her in any manner," Val replied. "Brandy?"

"Of course." Wareham eyed him curiously as he took the glass and his seat. "And allow me to impart a bit of advice, if I may. You need to handle her like a skittish filly; only a light hand on the reins and no whips. Anything more, and you'll break her spirit."

Val gave a derisive snort. "You try to be her guardian and see how far your vaunted advice takes you."

Wareham silently studied the rug beneath his feet for several moments. Finally he raised his head and looked directly at Val. "I am thinking of doing just that."

Val laughed.

"I am serious," Wareham said.

Val stared at him, as if uncertain of what he'd heard. Then he remembered Wareham's words earlier about "honorable intentions." "Marry? You want to marry her?"

Wareham flashed him a rueful smile. "Hard to believe, isn't it? Did I not always swear that I'd never be caught in the parson's mousetrap?"

"Where did you go after you left this morning?" Val demanded. "Straight to the tavern?"

"No, it was to Whitehall, as I said. In fact, it was my business there that put the idea firmly in my mind."

"Have you talked with Kat about this?" Val asked, hoping he had not. He did not want another confrontation with her about unsuitable offers.

"Am I not supposed to petition the guardian before I speak to the lady?"

Val nodded. "And as her guardian, I intend to withhold my permission."

Wareham gave him an incredulous look. "You what?"

"Oh, give on," Val said. "No one in their right mind would approve your suit. Your record with the ladies is dubious, to say the least."

"I am talking about marriage, not a dalliance." Wareham spoke with more vehemence than Val expected.

Was the fellow in love with the girl?

No, he couldn't be. Wareham merely admired her horsemanship and her sense of humor and her jaundiced view of the foibles of society. Which was clearly not enough upon which to build a marriage. Wareham would be too indulgent of Kat's unconventional behavior.

"Don't you think this is rather hasty?" Val asked. "You barely know her."

"We get along," Wareham said. "And I'm a damn sight better candidate than those silly young pups she cavorts with."

Val had to agree with him on that. But, still . . . "Frankly, I was looking for a different sort of fellow for her. A nice settled, country gentleman who—"

"Will seek to dampen her high spirits and turn her into a pale shadow of herself." Wareham rose and strode to the window before turning to face Val. "You want someone who will meet your rigid standards of conduct, but I assure you, Val, there is no such paragon in London. Unless you consider yourself."

Val stared at him, aghast. "Me? Marry her? That is even more laughable than the thought of you doing so."

"Is it?" Wareham raised a brow.

Val felt a sinking feeling at Wareham's accusation. Was his antipathy toward all these marriage proposals motivated by something more personal than a guardian's concern? He struggled to mount an argument, more for himself than anything.

"Marry that hellion? I would rather be back at Waterloo facing the cream of Napoleon's cavalry than take on that task."

"Then let me have her," Wareham said. "I'll keep her spirit intact."

Val shook his head. He didn't like the realization that Wareham knew her as well as he did, knew what she wanted, understood what she needed. The whole idea bothered him. He should be the one to teach her, to guide her into womanhood, not Wareham.

"There is always Gretna . . ." Wareham's voice trailed off.

Val was shocked by the threat. "You would not dare."

"In ordinary circumstances, no. But I suspect that if your ward knew of your refusal, she'd have the horses hitched and kidnap *me* just to spite you."

Wincing, Val acknowledged the truth of his prediction.

Kat was likely to do just that if she learned of this conversation.

"Then you will not speak to her of this."

"I never said I *hadn't* talked with her." Wareham grinned. "She will be awaiting the outcome of this conversation. I wouldn't be surprised if she is at the door now, with her ear pressed against the keyhole."

Val couldn't help glancing at the door before he turned his attention back to Wareham.

Three proposals in two days. He'd despaired of finding her a husband, now suddenly they were banging at his door.

His suspicions deepened. He knew Kat had been behind Mortimer's proposal yesterday. Had she worked her persuasive wiles on Wareham as well?

"What was the offer she made you?" Val demanded.

Wareham looked amused, and Val knew he had been right. *Damn that girl!*

"I suppose she told you that I beat her daily and want to marry her off to some doddering old fool," Val said. "How gallant of you to come to her rescue."

"Actually, it was nothing of the sort," Wareham said. "She offered me the safety of the married state, with the freedom to do as I pleased. A 'marriage of convenience.' "

"Yours or hers?"

"Both, I hope," Wareham said.

"Why would she even suggest such a thing?" Val asked.

"She wants control of her brothers."

"As if I would cede custody to you."

"You need not worry I shall corrupt them. As the lady explains it, I am free to live my own life without interference from her—in return for her ability to do the same."

Val grimaced. Kat was too innocent, too naive to know the dreadful fate that doomed her to. A type of spinsterhood at best; a bitter hatred for the man she'd tied herself to at worst.

Did the girl have no sense at all?

Val realized he was angry—angry at Wareham for putting him in such a position. Angry that he'd been forced into the role of having to find a husband for Kat in the first place. And angry that she was not a more biddable girl who would accept whatever man *he* chose for her, instead of embroiling him in these ridiculous attempts at settling her own future.

Perhaps he should let Wareham have her and be free of the whole sorry mess. But the very thought made him cringe. Val did not want Kat with Wareham. An older, more sophisticated woman would suit Wareham fine, but not an innocent like Kat. She might be a hellion in some ways, but she was not possessed of a great deal of worldly experience when it came to men. Val feared that Wareham would eventually tire of her and, in the process, break her heart.

Wareham was right about one thing, it was going to take a rare man to appreciate her. And to his deepening realization, Val began to realize who he wanted that man to be.

Himself.

He looked back at Wareham.

"Don't say a thing until I've discussed this with Kat. I hope to be able to reason with her."

Wareham nodded. "Fair enough. I think you will find the lady quite determined. I suggest you acquiesce to her wishes. It might save you a great deal of bother in the short run."

"And in the long run?"

"That is not your worry." Wareham smiled. "Then she will be my responsibility." He set down his glass, gave Val a curt bow, and left.

Val paced the room as he fought against the thoughts welling up inside him.

He did not want this. It would be an unmitigated disaster. But the more he argued against it, the stronger became his feelings. It did not matter that Parker was a bore, Mortimer an idiot, and Wareham a rake. Totally unsuitable, all of them.

But Val knew he would have turned all three of them down even if they were paragons of intelligence and behavior.

Because he wanted Kat Foster for himself.

There. He admitted it. Against all wisdom, all sense, he'd fallen in love with the girl.

What in God's name was he going to do now? How could he persuade her that this was right for both of them when she was barely speaking to him?

Val only knew he had to try. Because he honestly believed that the promise of a life with her was too precious a prize to give up without a fight.

Chapter Seventeen

*H*is head was still spinning in confusion when a light tap sounded on the door and Kat Foster marched in.

She presented a picture in complete opposition to the one she had displayed earlier this morning; in place of her grubby breeches and coat, she wore a well-cut gown of pale blue that emphasized her female curves in society's acceptable way. Her hair was neatly arranged, a delicate lace shawl lay across her shoulders, and she appeared the very vision of youthful womanhood.

How very deceiving appearances could be.

She sat down in the chair facing him with a grace he found amusing, knowing she did it on purpose, hoping to fool him into thinking she intended to behave as a female ought.

"I came to apologize for this morning." Kat flashed him a demure smile. "I realize I should not have gone riding in such a manner with Wareham."

Val regarded her with growing suspicion. She was up to her tricks again. What did she have in mind this time?

"I only thought—that since he was the one who suggested it . . ." Her voice trailed off.

"There is no need for this performance, Kat. Wareham has come and gone and been soundly refused."

She blinked at him. "What?"

"Your latest plan is not going to work." Val gave a long, deep sigh. "Although I do have to give you credit for thinking of this one. At first, I almost thought Wareham was serious."

"Whatever do you mean?" she asked.

"You know exactly what I mean." He gave her a shrewd look and was rewarded when her gaze finally faltered and she looked away.

"I would take these offers of marriage more seriously if I could be certain that the gentlemen were speaking on their own behalf, rather than yours," he said.

"You think I can simply persuade any man to ask for my hand?" she asked.

He nodded. "I think you have a genuine talent for it."

"What do you care who I marry?" she asked. "You want me wed. Let me marry whom I will."

Val leaned back in his chair. "I am trying to save you from yourself, Kat."

She stiffened. "I think I am the better judge of what is best for me."

"No, you are not." He glared at her. "If you think Mortimer or Wareham would make good husbands, you are demonstrating an appalling lack of sense."

"What is wrong with either of them?" she demanded. "I could be happy with either one."

Val gave a disparaging snort. "I highly doubt that."

"Since when do you care a whit if I *am* happy?"

"Oh, I care a very great deal," he said. "That is why I seek to protect you from your own folly."

"No one is ever going to meet your exacting standards." Her eyes flashed with anger. "You say you want me to marry, but you turn down all the offers I've received."

"Because the right man has not asked yet."

He was standing on the brink and all he had to do was step back. The girl was a nightmare; she would test the patience of the most sainted man, which he certainly was not.

Yet when he was around her, he felt more alive than he had in years. He'd thought of nothing else but her since she first careened into his life. Thoughts of frustration, exasperation, impatience—but admiration, appreciation, amusement, as well.

And protection. That was what he wanted to do, after all, protect her. Protect her from a poor marriage. Protect her from the worst of her own follies, while guiding her into maturity. Marrying her would cause less wear and tear on his nerves than worrying about what sort of unsuitable candidate or harebrained plan she would come up with next.

"Well?" She still glared at him. "I am right, aren't I? No one is good enough."

Val shut his eyes briefly, steeling himself for the storm to come.

"You are right, as usual, Kat," he said. "Therefore, I think it is time that you accept the inevitable and marry me."

To say she was speechless was an understatement. She stared at him as if he'd suddenly grown three extra heads.

"Cat got your tongue?" he teased her.

She jumped to her feet and stormed toward him. "Are you mad?"

"Oh, most surely," he said. "No sane man would ever willingly agree to such a thing."

Kat glanced at the desk and the decanter of brandy. "Did you drink an entire bottle of brandy this afternoon? Or two?" Her expression turned to one of relief. "That is it; you are drunk. I will send for your valet."

Val took her arm to keep her from leaving.

"I am not drunk, Kat. I almost wish I were. I myself still cannot quite believe what I said."

"Then I shall forget you ever said it."

"The problem is, you are right." He frowned. "Oh, there is a remote chance that somewhere in the city, there is a man who would do well enough for you. But I don't want you to make some horrible mistake before you have a chance to meet him. Marrying you myself is the best for both of us."

Kat gave him a look of utter dismay. "You cannot be serious. I would never marry you."

"Why not?"

"I can think of a hundred reasons," she said.

"Give me a few."

"You won't let me ride as I like."

"In the city, no." Val shrugged. "In the country, I see nothing wrong with it. You are a grown woman, Kat. You can no longer do just as you please. Part of the task of being an adult is behaving in an adult manner."

"You expect me to act like a lady at all times."

"Is that so very difficult? You do an admirable job of it . . ."

She stamped her foot in frustration. "You, you . . ."

"What about me is so terrible?" he asked gently.

She fixed him with a baleful stare. "You took my brothers away."

Val sighed. The boys. "The summer holidays are almost upon us. You'll see them again soon."

"You are no . . . fun. You won't let me do the things I like or act the way I wish. You are always hemming me in with rules and 'shoulds' and 'oughts.' "

"Like the day I took you to Tattersall's," he reminded her.

Kat flushed. "Well, that was all right. But you wouldn't let Wareham take me to a gambling hell."

"*I* wouldn't go to the kind of dens he patronizes," Val replied.

"Cock pits?"

"No respectable woman would be caught near one, I am afraid."

"You won't even let me drive your carriage." She gave him a triumphant look. "I drove Wareham's team in the park yesterday."

"Have you asked me if you could drive them?"

Her smile faded. "Well, no. But you always send the coachman when Sophie and I go out."

"I did not know you wished to drive. Would you like to take the carriage to the park? You can do so this very afternoon if you wish."

He saw the desire raging within her and smothered a smile. Kat would never be one to hold a secret; her feelings were too transparent.

"I should like to drive them to the park," she said at last. "But that does not mean I am going to marry you."

"I promise I shall never write you abominable poetry," he said.

That forced a reluctant smile to her lips.

"As a married lady, you will have a great deal more freedom than you do now as a young unmarried miss," he reminded her. "Give me time. Time to prove to you that I can be the kind of man you would not mind spending your life with."

She regarded him with suspicion. "I do not have to promise anything now?"

He shook his head. "Trust me, Kat. I will show you that there is nothing to fear from me."

She nervously nibbled her lower lip. "This is not a trick? You will not suddenly lay down a new set of rules tomorrow?"

Val slapped a hand over his heart. "On my honor as a soldier of His Majesty's army. If, after a time, you do not find the idea agreeable, I will not pressure you. But in the meantime, you are not to drag every man of your acquaintance before me with new marriage proposals."

She met his gaze with a steady look. "All right. I agree to consider the matter."

"Good. Then get your bonnet and coat, and we will go to the park," he said.

She dropped an elegant curtsy. "As you wish, my lord." Then she dashed out to the hall and tore up the stairs.

Val almost shook with relief. That had not gone too badly. She'd agreed to consider his proposal. Given time, he knew he could win her over.

Because he knew for certain that he wanted Kat Foster as his wife. He'd been fighting the idea from the moment it first crept up on him. But today, with the real threat of losing her to Wareham looming before him, he'd been forced to acknowledge it.

And although she had at first denied him outright, he'd been able to cajole her into agreeing to at least think about the idea. It was a first step, and he felt confident that he'd continue to gain her acceptance at each succeeding step. Until she agreed to become his wife.

Kat could not quite believe what had just transpired in the study.

She had gone downstairs expecting to hear that her plan to marry Wareham had been approved, only to discover, to her total and utter shock, that Newkirk wanted to marry her.

The very idea was ludicrous.

She did not want to marry him. Ever. So why had she agreed to even consider the idea?

Because he'd taken her by such surprise that she'd barely been able to think. If she'd been in her right mind, she would have given him a blistering set-down.

Particularly after such a backhanded proposal. "Accept the inevitable." "No sane man would willingly agree." Certainly not the sort of sentiments one expected in a proposal of marriage.

So why did he even bother? It wasn't as if he had any feelings for her. He was doing what he always did, looking out for his own convenience. And for some strange reason he'd decided it would be easier to marry her himself than find a suitor for her. And, as usual, he expected her to go along with his plans.

Kat shook her head at the man's illogical nature.

Oh, there were women out there who thought Newkirk a great catch, but Kat was not one of them. He might be handsome, a baron, accepted in society and all, but those things meant nothing to her.

She could not really say what she would want in a husband—other than helping with her brothers, but she knew that Newkirk was not the man for her.

He couldn't be.

Because she knew that she would not be able to control him, and the thought scared her. She had never put her life in another's hands, and she had no intention of doing it now. That was why Morty had been such a good prospect, for she knew he would do anything she asked. She'd even have a measure of control over Wareham simply through her indifference.

She could never be indifferent to Newkirk. From the moment they'd met, he'd had the infuriating ability to get under her skin. She'd grown better at controlling her temper in his presence, but it still flared when she thought he was being too heavy-handed, overbearing, or protective.

Like today. He was doing it again. Somehow, she had to show him that he could not order her about.

She had no intention of *ever* marrying him.

Promptly that afternoon, Val began his campaign to convince Kat Foster that he was the kind of man she would like as a husband. One who could be an amiable, cheerful companion. One who allowed her freedom, within reason, and encouraged her curiosity about the world around her. A man she wanted to be with.

Which was why he sat beside her on the carriage seat, mentally clutching the reins with her, while outwardly he strove to appear calm and unruffled as she drove him to the park and around the carriage path. She had a good feel for a team, and while he did not relish the idea of her driving a high-perched phaeton through London's crowded streets during the busiest time of day, he thought she was perfectly capable of taking Sophie to the park.

He merely had to impress upon Kat that she could not engage in reckless behavior while at the reins; no racing through the streets or accepting time challenges to Brighton. He would insist that she at least take a groom with her to forestall any rash actions.

Val nodded at the horses. "What do you think of these fellows?"

"I like them," she said simply. "They're responsive but lively. A pleasure to drive."

"Not quite as showy as those bays of Wareham's," he admitted. "But I think you'll find these will stand you better in the long run."

"Oh, I think they're quite comparable," Kat said.

"You may drive them whenever you wish," Val said. "I only ask that you take a groom with you if I am not along."

"Isn't Sophie a suitable companion?"

"Sophie, I fear, would be of little use if you ran into a problem with the horses," he said.

"I doubt anything could happen that I couldn't handle."

"I agree, but this is London after all, not Gloucester. Abide by my wishes on this, Kat."

She frowned, but nodded in agreement.

"What should you like to do tomorrow?" he asked.

"I want to go to Tatt's again," she declared. "And sit in on the Thistlewood trial. And see the fireworks at Vauxhall."

"Whoa." He held up a hand to stop her. "We can only do so many things in a day. Vauxhall will not be open for a time. I will see if I can learn when the trial is in session. And we could certainly go to Tatt's tomorrow."

"I can think of so many things I'd like to see and do!

I've not been on a picnic, or boated on the Thames, or eaten a bun in Chelsea.''

Val laughed. "We can do all of those things. I see I shall not have a moment's rest with you directing our schedule."

"This was *your* idea," she reminded him. "If you grow too exhausted by such activities, you merely need to let me know."

"You make it sound as if I am in my dotage," he said. "I'm not that old."

She gave him a dampening look. "But you often act like it."

Val clamped his mouth shut. Arguing with her would not further his cause. If she thought him old at his "advanced" age of eight-and-twenty, that had more to do with her perception of him than any reality. It was one more thing she'd misjudged about him; one more thing about which he'd have to convince her she was wrong.

He was not old.

Although Val had no intention of proving it by behaving as foolishly as Mortimer and his young friends, either. After all, his plan was to guide and advise Kat, and he could not do that if she thought of him as her equal in age and wisdom. He wanted her to look to him for guidance, not as a potential co-conspirator in some silly exploit.

Well, persuading Kat to change her mind was the job he'd taken on when he decided to convince her of his suitability as a husband. He couldn't expect that one simple drive in the park was going to affect a drastic change in her attitude. Although her dislike for him had been almost instantaneous at their first meeting, it was going to take far longer to undo her misconceptions.

Val must make certain that he concentrated on changing her mind every single minute that they were together.

It was a task that he would not find unpleasant— merely challenging.

His main strategy would be to keep her off guard as much as possible. As long as he did the unexpected, she would not have time to think or devise excuses to forestall his plans. It was going to take work, but Val was not going to let himself be routed. Napoleon's cavalry had developed a respect for him; he was going to make certain that Kat Foster did, too.

He knew that she had plans already for tonight, one of Sophie's affairs. But starting tomorrow, he intended to take charge of Kat's social schedule. Sophie might have to find another escort for the next few weeks while he danced attendance on Kat.

At least he did not have to worry that his ward would want to attend the sort of affairs he detested, for he knew she disliked most social events as much as he. Something he should pointedly remind her of. Now a card party would do—one that was suitably controlled, of course, so she did not get taken advantage of.

Although that probably was not a serious worry—no doubt Kat Foster was a cardsharp of the first degree and would be fleecing the entire table before he put a stop to it.

Dinner parties would be safe enough—she loved to eat and that would keep her from talking more than she ought. The theater would be equally useful as long as he chose an entertaining play.

That would take care of the evenings. What about the days?

She'd spoken of having a picnic. He could picnic with the best of them—he'd done a great deal of eating alfresco while in Spain. But boating? He did not think he'd ever been rowing in his life. Yet surely, there were boats one could hire. Perhaps one could also hire an oarsman to go with the craft. He would have to ask Sophie.

Since she'd shown herself such a fine hand at the reins, he'd let her drive them down to Chelsea on a nice day. They could stroll along the river and visit the pensioners. And eat buns.

Val realized he'd thought of enough activities already to keep them busy for the greater part of the week. No doubt other ideas would occur to him, or she would mention a new desire he could gratify.

No, there would be no difficulty in devising entertainments for her. The challenge would be to make her view him in a different light. Weaving one within the other was the key to his success.

And Val was not accustomed to failure.

Chapter Eighteen

The morning sun streamed through the drawing room windows as Kat read the racing results in the *Morning Chronicle*. She must ask Newkirk to take her to Newmarket or Epsom to see the races. Now, while he was intent on pleasing her.

Just then he walked into the room, a mischievous smile on his face.

"Kat, get your pelisse—we're going out," he announced.

"Where are we going?" Kat asked.

"As you requested—it's a surprise."

She set the newspaper aside and stood. She rather liked this new Newkirk, the one whose actions grew more and more unpredictable each day.

"Hurry," he said. "Don't keep me waiting."

She looked at him, askance. "I never dally."

Kat hastily grabbed her pelisse and met Newkirk on the front stairs. They climbed into the carriage and drove off.

"Do I get any hints as to our destination?" she asked.

He shook his head. "You will see when we get there."

Kat laughed and sat back against the seat to watch the passing street scene. It was a beautiful May morning, already warm and hinting of the summer to come.

They crossed Oxford Street, heading north. Kat squirmed in her seat, impatient to discover their destination. A simple drive in the country? Was he taking her to some country inn for a special meal?

Open fields appeared before them, and Kat realized they were at Regent's Park, where she'd ridden the other morning with Wareham. Newkirk steered the carriage down a narrow lane and pulled up in front of a small shed, standing beside a strip of water.

"You said you wished to go boating," he said with an eager look. "This isn't the Thames, but it's far cleaner and less crowded."

Kat jumped out of the carriage and walked over to the shed. Behind it was a small dock with several boats tied alongside.

"This will be fun," she said.

The boat keeper came out. Newkirk paid him his fee, and the man led them to one of the boats.

She disdained the hand Newkirk offered and climbed in, sitting in the rear seat. He awkwardly clambered into the center seat, fumbling with the oars and oarlocks while the man untied the small craft. He gave the boat a shove, and they drifted out into the channel.

"Where does this waterway go?" she asked while Newkirk still struggled to get the second oar in the lock.

"It winds its way through the park," he said.

"Have you been rowing here before?" she asked.

He shook his head.

She regarded him suspiciously. "Is it your first time rowing altogether?"

His expression turned sheepish. "I'll manage."

He finally got the oars in place and started pulling them jerkily through the water. Kat rolled her eyes. She could do a much better job of handling the oars.

"Would you rather I rowed?" she asked, trying to hide her amusement.

"No."

The artificial channel cut across the parkland. Kat saw one house some distance from the water, then another, but that was the only sign of habitation in this newly developed section of town.

Ahead of them, the channel split around a large island.

"Shall we go left or right?" Newkirk asked.

"Right," Kat promptly replied.

They crossed under an arched bridge spanning the canal. A Greek-style folly stood on the center of the island, gleaming white in the bright sunlight.

"Such a silly thing," Kat observed. "Who could believe

the ancient Greeks were running around the park building temples?"

As the channel curved around the end of the island, it split again, with another island looming up ahead. A small footbridge passed between the two.

Maneuvering the boat through the narrow channel and under the bridge took all of Newkirk's concentration. Kat fought against the temptation to snatch the oars from him to show him how it was done. The man had to learn to row sometime.

Newkirk awkwardly swung the boat around the narrow end of the first island and headed straight for a small patch of land rising out of the water before them.

"How odd," Kat said. "Why do you suppose they made such a tiny island?"

"Perhaps the ancient Greeks are going to come and build another temple on it," Newkirk suggested dryly.

"Row around it," she commanded.

Newkirk had developed some facility for rowing in a straight line, but rowing in what amounted to a large circle gave him problems.

"Boats were not meant to go in circles," he complained as they headed straight for the bank again.

"Oh, never mind," Kat said. "It looks to be a perfectly empty island. Perhaps they will build something on it later."

With an exasperated sigh, Newkirk bent his back to the oars again, trying to turn the boat in the direction he wished to go. His hand slipped as he swept back for the stroke, and the blade dropped heavily into the water, sending up a large fountain that splashed Kat.

"Newkirk!" she cried. "I'm all wet."

"I beg your pardon," Newkirk said in a tone that told her he was not in the least bit sorry.

She leaned over the side, dipped her hand in the water, and flicked a handful of droplets at him.

"Unfair!" he said. "You did that on purpose."

Kat laughed. "Would I do such a thing?" She dipped her hand again and flung more water at him.

"That's enough!" Newkirk brought one of the oars down onto the water with a loud "thwack." It sent up a huge geyser of spray that splashed over the side and thoroughly drenched Kat's skirt.

"You wretch!" she said between laughs. She began flinging handfuls of water at him as fast as she could, wishing she had a container of some sort so she could get him good and wet.

Her shoe! Kat bent down, quickly untied the laces, dipped it in the water, and flung a satisfying amount at Newkirk. The water hit him square in the chest.

"You brat . . ." He grabbed for the oar again, knocking it loose from the oarlock. It fell into the water and began drifting away from the boat. He lunged toward it, the boat lurched to one side, and before Kat could yell a warning, it tipped both of them into the water.

"Ah!" Kat screeched. "Look what you've done!"

"Are you all right?" Arms and legs flailing, Newkirk swam toward her, concern on his face.

"I'm perfectly fine. Grab the boat before its floats away."

Newkirk reached for the rope. "Follow me over to the island. We can turn the boat over, drain off the water, and things will be right as rain."

He began swimming toward the island, towing the boat behind him. Kat followed, dragging the stray oar with her.

It was a struggle to make progress with yards of heavy, wet fabric pulling her down. Kat was grateful they were in a narrow channel and not the Thames, where she would never be able to reach shore.

She saw that Newkirk had reached the shallows, and she fought onward until her own toes felt solid ground. She swam a few more strokes, then tried to walk, but it was a struggle to put one foot in front of the other.

"This is one more reason why I should be wearing breeches," she called out to him as she fought to move against the leaden weight of her skirts. Val reached out and pulled her onto the shore.

"Look at me!" Kat cried in mock dismay. "You made me lose my shoe!"

"I'll buy you another pair," he said.

She looked at Newkirk, his hair dripping, rivulets of water running off the tails of his jacket. "You look . . ." She burst into laughter at her guardian's bedraggled appearance.

"I look no worse than you," he said with a grin.

Kat glanced down. Her wet clothes were plastered against her body, and her skirts must have absorbed several stones of water. Her dress felt as heavy as one of those suits of armor at the Tower.

"Help me get some of the water out," she said, and started twisting her skirts.

Newkirk made no move to assist, and Kat glared at him with exasperation, intending to chastise him, but he was looking at her with a confused expression on his face. Their eyes met and the look that she saw in his made her quickly glance away and busy herself with wringing water out of her soaked clothing.

She'd never thought to see Newkirk looking at her in such a manner—like a man looks at a woman he admires. And with her wet clothing, he was getting a thorough look.

Kat suddenly wondered if there was more to his offer of marriage than the "mere convenience" he'd admitted.

Was it possible that he actually cared for her? Desired her?

Newkirk? The man who'd insulted her the first day they'd met, ripped her family apart and demanded that she behave like a well-bred young lady? But as Kat tried to heap scorn on him in her mind, she realized that he was not the ogre she kept trying to make him. He'd made a great effort in the last weeks to be amiable, entertaining, and kind. She could almost admit that she considered him a friend.

But a husband?

She felt something brush against her legs. Kat glanced down to see that Newkirk was twining the fabric she'd just wrung, getting even more water out of it.

"I think you are right," he said. "The next time I take you rowing, you can wear your breeches."

The disturbing moment passed, and they quickly squeezed as much water as they could out of her skirts. Then he pulled off his jacket, and she helped him wring it out as well.

"We need to get back," he said. "Before you catch your death of cold."

"Oh, pooh," she said. "A slight drenching isn't going to affect my health."

"Then we should return before *I* get chilled," he said.

Carefully, they tipped the boat onto its side, holding it upright while the water ran out, then flipped it back onto the ground. Only an inch or two of water swirled in the bottom.

Newkirk handed the rope to Kat, then shoved the boat back in the water. She started to wade in after it, but he grabbed her.

"I'm not going to wring those skirts out again." Newkirk picked her up, sloshed through the shallows, and set her down inside the boat. Then he carefully put one leg over the side, pushed off with his other foot, and the boat drifted back into the channel.

If Newkirk really wanted to get back quickly, he should have let her row, Kat thought, but she guessed it was better to salve his wounded pride by not offering. After all, for a first-time boater he had done quite well, except for that minor mishap.

When they at last reached the small dock, the boatman greeted them with a smile.

"Had a bit of an accident, did ye?" he asked.

"The lady grew overexcited," Newkirk said.

"Me!" she protested. "You were the one who tipped us over."

The two men shared a knowing smile.

"Hmmph." Kat flounced toward the carriage.

Val rummaged in the boot and pulled out a carriage rug, which he threw over Kat's lap. He handed her his wrinkled jacket.

"Put this on," he said as he climbed in beside her.

"As if it will disguise the fact that I have been swimming," she said as she shrugged on the damp garment. "My hair is dripping."

"But at least this way no one is going to notice the rest of you," he said. "There have always been tales that some ill-bred ladies dampened their petticoats to appear more alluring, but I think you've gone a bit too far in dampening your whole dress."

"As if anyone finds drowned rats alluring." She swiped a wet lock of hair out of her face.

"Oh, I don't think you look too terrible," he said. "For a drowned rat, that is."

Kat wished she had a fan with her so she could rap him across the knuckles. Smacking him with the wet sleeve of his jacket did not provide the same satisfaction.

Val was glad he had chosen to go boating at the park, so they did not have to drive clear across London to reach home. He did not particularly care if anyone saw them, but despite Kat's protests, he did not want her spending any more time in those damp clothes than she had to. A hot bath was the first thing she needed when they reached the house.

Although he admitted that he hadn't minded in the least being able to admire her drenched form. It was even worse than those breeches. Thanks to them, he had seen the shape of her legs before, but today that wet dress had clung to all her curves like a second skin.

Kat Foster was an enormously attractive young lady. It was all he could do to keep from pulling her into his arms and showering her with kisses. But he did not want to rush her, did not want to frighten her with his desire until she was willing to accept it. And matters had not yet progressed that far.

Why, he'd yet to steal any kiss from her. Probably because he did not know how she would react and dared not risk incurring her displeasure. But eventually—soon, Val hoped—he wanted to show her how he felt.

If anyone had told him a few months ago that he would regard a tipped rowboat as a marvelous piece of luck, he would have thought him mad. But now Val realized that nothing in his life had been the same since the moment she had walked into it. And he would be devastated beyond belief if she walked out of it.

The devil was, he'd fallen in love with her. With a breeches-wearing, hell-bent-on-leather hoyden who wasn't overly fond of art, music, and the strictures of society.

Precisely the same things he disliked.

And she had a sense of humor, a zest for life that he found infectious, and a loyalty to family that he found admirable.

He wanted her more than anything he'd ever wanted in his life. Somehow, he had to persuade *her* that she wanted *him*.

* * *

To Kat's continued amazement and delight, Newkirk proved to be an attentive suitor. No whim of hers was too small for him to gratify, whether it was ices from Gunthers, a trip to the Tower, or a basket of early strawberries sold by a street seller. Newkirk was an enjoyable companion. He'd taken her places she never would have thought to visit on her own—the Iron Works, Massey's steam engine, and the observatory at Greenwich.

Yet she refused to allow herself to be swayed by his concerted efforts to convince her that he would make a suitable husband. Of course he was on his best behavior; he was trying to impress her. He really was not such a bad sort. But definitely not the type of man she wanted for a husband. For that man had to make a place for her brothers in their life. And she could never forget that it was Val's fault that they had all been separated.

So despite bird guns and cream cakes and the promise of a new pair of riding boots, she remained firm against his enticements. There was nothing he could offer her that would take the place of Eddie, Sam, and Thomas. The sooner he realized that, the sooner she could look for a man who would help her get what she wanted.

"I have a special surprise for you," Newkirk announced as he came into the drawing room. Kat was reading the results from the previous day's race meet at Newmarket.

"Oh? I hope it does not involve water again."

Newkirk rolled his eyes. "I promise there are no boats involved. There is a special benefit gala at Vauxhall—they will be open just for tomorrow evening."

She looked at him eagerly. "Will there be fireworks?"

He nodded. "And food and music. Should you care to go?"

"Of course I do!"

Kat could barely contain her anticipation as she dressed the following evening. Vauxhall itself sounded exciting, and the added attraction of seeing the fireworks made her anxious for the night to begin.

She had to admit she was glad she was making her first visit to Vauxhall with Newkirk. He had a way of not making her feel like a gawking girl from the country when she displayed unfashionable enthusiasm over the things she saw. Kat knew she would be amazed by the explosive displays and show delight at all she saw. Newkirk did not mind that. With him, she would feel totally at ease. He'd promised her they would walk all the paths and that she could eat her fill of what he ruefully claimed was the most expensive food in London.

They took the town carriage for the drive south over the river. Kat peered out the window as they drove over the Thames on Regent's Bridge. Lights twinkled from the water below.

"It's a good thing they finally finished building this bridge," Newkirk said. "Else we would have been forced to row across the river."

Kat gave a mock shudder. "That is a frightening prospect. I intend to keep you off the water in the future—unless I am at the oars."

Val gave her a sheepish look.

Carriages were lined up outside the entrance, much like at the theater, and they had to wait until it was their turn to disembark. At last they were able to get out and walk through the entry.

"What do you wish to see first?" Newkirk asked. "I believe there is a nice exhibit of paintings in the Rotunda."

Kat knew that he was teasing her. "Let's explore the grounds," she said. "Give me the full tour."

Newkirk took her arm and led her down the Grand Walk. The pathways were crowded with couples, elderly ladies and gentlemen, parents keeping a close eye on their daughters, and groups of young men eyeing every lady who walked by.

They walked past the colonnades and the supper boxes, down the long, tree-lined path to the far end of the gardens, then back again.

"I don't think Vauxhall looks so dangerous," Kat said. "Why does everyone say so?"

"That is because it is still light out," Val said. "Once it grows dark, it becomes a very different place."

"But you, of course, will keep me safe."

"I will lash you to my side if I have to."

"I promise not to wander off," Kat said. "I should like to sample some of this expensive food you complained of."

"I was afraid of that," Newkirk said with an exaggerated sigh.

Kat laughed.

They returned to the Grove, where Newkirk treated her to biscuits and cheese cakes and bowls of strawberries. Her hunger sated, Kat then dragged him down another of the walks.

"Look, there is Wareham!"

Val stifled a groan and looked where Kat was pointing. Sure enough, it was his friend, sporting a buxom lady on his arm.

Kat tugged at his elbow. "Let's go over and say hello."

"Let us not," Val said.

"Why not?" she asked. "Are you still mad because he was willing to marry me?"

"No." Val turned her about and deftly steered them in the opposite direction. "I do not think that his companion is anyone you should know."

Kat immediately whirled about to stare at the now distant couple.

"Really? Who is she?"

"I have no idea," Val said. "But with Wareham, you can never be too careful."

"I should like to meet a real lady of 'ill repute,' " Kat said. "I think they'd be far more interesting than some of the ladies Sophie knows."

"The key word is 'lady,' " Val said as he led her between two towering hedges. "And while not all of them are fascinating companions, they at least claim that distinction."

She sighed. "When are the fireworks going to start?"

"It is almost dark enough." He patted her hand. "Be patient. Shall I buy you another ice while you wait?"

"Yes," she said, and wrinkled her nose. "I rather thought it would be more interesting. Vauxhall is almost like the park, except no one has any horses. I think the park is even better."

"It is much the same," he admitted. "But once the show starts, you will think otherwise. We can go over to the bandstand and listen to music, if you like."

"Let's get some more strawberries," Kat suggested.

Suddenly, overhead, there was a bright burst of light and

Val fought against the urge to duck. He reminded himself it was fireworks, not incoming artillery fire.

"Oh!" Kat squealed with delight.

Val stepped back against the hedge and pulled her in front of him, laying his hands gently on her shoulders. "Watch carefully," he whispered in her ear. "You don't want to miss a thing."

More rockets exploded in the sky.

Pinwheels of light blazed from tall poles; spinning and hissing, they spewed a halo of sparks. Their fire had barely died when a new series of lights exploded down a length of wire, creating the illusion of a stream of fire racing across the sky.

Kat clapped, shrieked, and jumped up and down at each new display. Val cheered with her, caught up in her infectious enthusiasm.

A final huge burst of flame lit the sky, then suddenly it was dark and quiet.

"Is it over?" Kat asked, her disappointment audible.

"I'm afraid so," he replied.

"Oh, promise me we can come again!"

"Once it opens in June, I shall bring you every night if you wish."

She turned toward him. "Oh, Newkirk, please do."

The pleading tone in her voice tugged at his heart and Val could not help himself. He bent his head and touched his lips to hers. He intended it to be a light, chaste kiss; he did not wish to frighten her. But the moment their lips met, he knew it could never be that for him. He'd warned her of the dangers of the dark walk, not thinking he would be the one she needed protection from. It took every bit of willpower he commanded to rein in his desire for this delightful girl.

He lifted his head and tried to see the expression on her face, but in the dim light, he could not.

"We can sit down for supper," he said awkwardly.

"Yes," she said, in a perfectly calm voice. "I should like that."

Val took her hand and led her back to the bright lights and crowds of the colonnades.

The rest of the evening passed more quickly than he could have believed. Val talked, laughed, and joked with

Kat, but all the time he was acutely conscious of every word she said, every nuance of expression that passed over her face. He saw nothing to alarm him, yet nothing to give him hope, either. It was as if that kiss had never taken place—or that she imparted no special significance to it.

He was shocked when he caught her yawning, and he looked at his watch—half past one! Where had the time gone? He ushered her out the gate to the waiting carriage for the drive back to Bruton Street.

They sat in companionable quiet as the carriage jounced over the cobbles, back across the bridge and then north. Val feared to say anything, not wanting to break the mood. Kat was tired; he could tell by the yawns she tried to stifle. He put his arm around her shoulder and urged her to lean against him. He would not mind in the least if she fell asleep like this.

She managed to stay awake during the drive. He was tempted to carry her into the house, but she took his hand and stepped down from the carriage, then allowed him to lead her into the house.

"I had a wonderful time," she said, standing at the bottom of the stairs.

"So did I." Val bent down and gently kissed her forehead.

She smiled and headed up the stairs.

Val retreated to his lair at the back of the house, deep in thought.

What was he going to do about Kat?

Oh, he had made great progress. She was now as easy and comfortable with him as she was with Sophie, but friendship was not what he wanted from Kat. And while she had not recoiled from his kiss, neither had she responded.

He feared friendship was all he would have from her.

That would not be so bad, would it? Most marriages were built on far less, arranged by parents or relatives among offspring deemed to be compatible—or of like fortunes. At least he and Kat would get along, even if their relationship would be lacking in passion.

But that was not what he wanted—for himself, or for her. For her, most of all. He wanted her to be head over heels in love with the man she married. She deserved that kind of happiness.

And if she could not have it with him, he was going to have to let her find it with another fellow.

But certainly not someone like Mortimer—or Wareham. Val knew she'd only approached those two men because she'd hoped they would aid her to gain her deepest desire—her brothers. Unfortunately, there was only one man who could give her that.

Himself.

Val knew what he had to do, as much for his peace of mind as hers.

He smothered a bitter laugh. He'd sacrificed a great deal in his life for his family, for Sophie, really, sheltering her from the disaster of their parents' marriage. Now he was going to make an even bigger sacrifice for Kat. Where did this streak of martyrdom come from? Surely not from his father, who'd never denied himself anything in his life. Perhaps Val was a throwback to some older, more honorable ancestor.

No matter. Best to get it over with quickly. If they left in the morning, they'd reach St. Giles by midday next. He'd deal with the two boys at Portsmouth later; he knew it was Eddie who most concerned Kat, Eddie whom she wanted back in her arms the most of all.

That was what Kat desired, and that was what he was going to give her. He'd give her the choice to go back to Kingsford with her brothers, give her the choice to never see him again. No matter what it cost him. The chance to be her husband. The chance to show her that she could care for him.

He always thought one was supposed to feel good about doing the proper thing, but it merely left him with a sour feeling in his stomach—and a painful lump in his chest. Giving up Kat was going to be the most painful act of his life.

But he wanted to see her happy.

Kat lay on her bed, staring up at the dark ceiling.

Newkirk had kissed her.

And she had enjoyed it. Had been disappointed when he

released her, placed her hand on his arm and led her back to the bright lights and people, and spent the rest of the evening acting as if nothing had happened.

Hadn't he liked kissing her?

Her growing sense of disappointment was disturbing—disturbing because there was no reason for it. Unless . . .

She could not—would not—dare not—be falling in love with him.

But what else could it be? Over the last week, she'd spent nearly all her waking hours with him while he strove to demonstrate that he could be the kind of man she would marry. And despite all her doubts and reservations, he was succeeding.

She'd started looking at him with new eyes, realizing that what she had first labeled stodginess was really a deep concern for her, and Sophie's, well-being. His emphasis on social propriety was for her sake, not his. He really did not care for society that much, and Kat doubted he would even be in London if he hadn't felt the need to find her a husband.

Deep down, they were very much alike. Oh, the strict military manner was still in him, but what could one expect after all those years of war? In truth, it was a miracle that he was still so genial after such an experience.

Everything he had done, from the day he arrived at Kingsford Manor until now, was done for the sole purpose of helping her and her brothers. She had not recognized it at the time, but it was certainly clear to her now.

And how had she repaid his concern? By shooting him, arguing against his attempts to turn her into a lady, and then trying to get away from him by marrying the first candidate who came along.

What he should have done was toss her over his knee and given her a good spanking.

Instead, he'd put up with her petty rebellions and disastrous schemes until he'd decided, with no lack of exasperation, that the only way he could keep an eye on her was to marry her himself. And she'd had the audacity to laugh at the very idea.

She was not laughing now. If the truth were told, she was rather frightened.

Frightened of the warm feelings she was starting to feel

for him, the understanding, the enjoyment of his company. She had not asked for that—had not wanted it. The very thought left her feeling almost queasy.

Marriage to Newkirk. Spending the rest of her life with him. Being as close as two people could be. Sharing everything—including the marriage bed.

Was that what she wanted?

Kat felt as if she did not know anything right now; all her thoughts were jumbled together like a tangled fishing line, with no hope of being unraveled.

Why did Newkirk have to confuse her so?

Chapter Nineteen

*A*fter tossing and turning all night, Kat awoke to the sound of persistent knocking on her door.

"Yes?" she said groggily.

"Wake up, sleepyhead," Sophie called. "You need to dress and be off."

"Dress and be off where?" Kat stumbled from bed and pulled open the door. Sophie stood in the corridor, still in her dressing gown.

"What time is it?" Kat asked.

"Nine," Sophie replied. "And you can thank me for keeping my brother from pulling you from bed two hours ago. I insisted he permit you to sleep."

"What is going on?" Kat asked.

Sophie held out her hands in a gesture of ignorance. "I do not know. All he said was to dress for travel and prepare to be gone for two nights."

"Go where? And why?"

The maid slipped in behind Sophie and began helping Kat dress while Sophie sat on the edge of the bed.

"Didn't he say anything to you last night?" Sophie asked.

Kat shook her head. "We came home from Vauxhall, he said good night, and that was all."

"A mystery!" Sophie's eyes danced with excitement.

"Are you coming with us?" Kat asked.

"With Lady Ballinger's *soirée* tomorrow night? I should say not."

Kat quickly finished dressing and raced down the stairs. She followed the corridor to Newkirk's office, where she hoped to learn what was going on.

He was sorting some papers on his desk.

"Ah, there you are," he said. "Awake at last. You are becoming as bad as Sophie."

"I am not," Kat said. "We were up quite late last night—this morning."

He arched a brow. "Yes, we were. But I thought you'd prefer to get an early start to St. Giles."

"St. Giles?" Kat gasped. "You are taking me to see Eddie?"

Val nodded.

Kat flung herself at him, mashing his papers as she enveloped him in a hug. "Oh, Newkirk, thank you! Are you ready to depart? When can we leave?"

"As soon as you have eaten some breakfast," he said with a grin.

"Oh, who cares about food? Let's leave now."

"We will not arrive until tomorrow no matter what," he said. "I don't want to have to listen to you complain about being hungry all morning. Go eat your fill of breakfast, and we can leave when you are done."

"I will hurry," she said, and dashed out of the room.

Eddie. He was taking her to Eddie.

Kat skidded to a sudden halt. Why, she wondered? Why now?

While he knew the time dragged for Kat, the hours they spent in the carriage passed far too quickly for Val. He preciously measured each minute spent in her company, fearing they were numbered. After tomorrow, she would have no reason to return to London; once he delivered her and Eddie to Kingsford Manor, she might even order him out of her sight.

And he would obey, without protest, because he desired her happiness above all things.

So he relished every moment they were still together. Val taught her to play piquet, surprised to learn she did not already know how. When that activity paled, he regaled her with severely edited accounts of some of his exploits in Spain.

Not once did either of them broach the subject of Eddie, or the future. Val did not want to ask her plans, for he did not want to hear the answer.

When they finally exhausted all safe topics of conversation, they sat in companionable silence. But Val sensed a new awkwardness between them that had not been there yesterday.

His heart ached with regret for what might have been, but he did not know how he could have acted differently toward her and her family. Unless it was to have ignored his responsibilities as guardian from the start and left the Foster clan to their own devices. And that ran counter to everything he believed.

He could have ignored Kat's outrageous behavior, given in to her pleas to leave her brothers at home. But how could he have known that he'd fall in love with the hoyden to the extent that he'd do anything to please her? Now, while he could undo his actions, he could not undo her memories of them.

Taking her to Eddie was his act of atonement. And if she wanted to take her brother straight home, Val would not object; he'd drive them there himself. And if she asked him to leave the moment they arrived, he would. And if she asked that he fall on his cavalryman's saber, he'd probably do that as well.

He would deal with the pain later.

For Kat, the carriage ride to St. Giles seemed to go on forever. Newkirk made valiant attempts to entertain her, but time still dragged.

At last they stopped for the night at a pleasant country inn. After eating, they strolled through the village, talking of totally inconsequential matters.

Kat was afraid to ask him the most important question— did he intend to take Eddie out of school and bring him home to London? Or would they go back to Kingsford Manor? He'd said prepare for two days of travel; that could cover either option. But in case he merely intended to fulfill his promise to check on Eddie's welfare, she was afraid to ask exactly what he had planned.

Kat spent another restless night, her dreams filled with images of Eddie and Newkirk. In the morning, before they left, she had the innkeeper pack a gigantic hamper with all sorts of sweets and pastries; Eddie would be sick if he ate half of it, but Kat did not care. She was going to see him at last.

At least today they had only an hour in the carriage; Kat did not think she could have stood it much longer.

Newkirk touched her arm when the carriage turned down a gravel drive.

"This is the school," he said.

Kat summoned up her courage to ask Newkirk the question that had been tormenting her all night. "Can he come home?"

Newkirk nodded. "If that is what he wishes."

Kat shut her eyes, tears welling behind her lids. *He was going to let Eddie come home.*

"Thank you," she whispered.

Newkirk had given in at last to her pleas. Then why did she feel this vague sense of dissatisfaction?

The carriage stopped in front of a well-kept building, a Georgian-style structure of brick and stone. Newkirk helped her from the carriage and led her up the broad walk and stairs. Inside, he directed her to wait in the salon while he sought out the headmaster.

Kat paced the room, too anxious to sit still. It had been so long since she'd seen her youngest brother: days, weeks, months filled with apprehension and longing. And in a few short minutes, he was going to be with her again at last.

She heard the door open, and she whirled about. There he stood, his hair askew as always, a patch of dirt on the knees of his pants.

He was the most beautiful thing she'd seen in ages.

"Eddie!" Kat raced toward him, arms held wide.

She grabbed him up and spun him around. "I cannot believe it is you. Look how you've grown!"

"Are you here to take me away?" he asked.

Kat set him down and gave him a close examination. He did not look to be in ill health or starving; his face was almost clean and his clothing, except for that smudge, recently laundered.

Newkirk came up behind him. "That is what we are here to discuss," he said. "Why don't you join your sister and me for a walk, and we can talk about it."

Eddie regarded him with suspicion.

"I've pastries in the carriage," Kat said.

His expression brightened.

They went back outside, and Newkirk retrieved the heavy hamper.

"Eat quickly," he said, handing a fruit pie to Eddie. "This is far too heavy to carry. Your sister must have forgotten there is only one of you."

"What have you learned in class this week?" Kat asked.

"Did you know that Henry VIII chopped off a bunch of his wives' heads?"

"I did," Kat replied.

"Your sister and I saw the very spot where it was done," Newkirk added. "On Tower Green."

"Really?" Eddie regarded both of them with awe. "Did they have the ax and everything?"

"I don't believe it was the same ax," Kat said. "But they had several of them. And suits of armor! You shall have to see them."

"When you come to London," Newkirk added.

"When may I?" Eddie demanded.

Newkirk glanced quickly at her, then turned back to Eddie.

"Did you ever catch any rabbits with the snare I sent you?" Newkirk asked.

Kat stared at him. "You sent him a snare? When?"

He looked embarrassed. "Nick suggested it."

"I caught two, but then Smack took it away," Eddie said.

"Who is Smack?" Kat asked.

"The groundskeeper," Eddie said. "He says he's the only one allowed to catch rabbits."

"Perhaps one day you can come to my house and catch all the rabbits you like," Newkirk said. "We have plenty to go around."

They strolled across the lawn toward the rear terrace,

which looked out over a large expanse of countryside. It was a pretty setting, Kat thought, far more suitable for young boys than the smoke and dirt of the city.

She glanced back. Newkirk and Eddie had stopped and were examining the corner of the terrace wall. Newkirk squatted beside Eddie, who poked at something with a stick.

The scene caused a lump to rise in her throat. It could have been father and son, out for a morning stroll.

Father and son.

Newkirk would be a marvelous father for Eddie—and all the boys. They would get along famously. The boys could show him how to row properly, and the ex-cavalryman would certainly be able to show them a trick or two about riding. They could talk horses, boxing, all manner of manly pursuits. They would soon grow to love him.

She would be the one who did not fit in with their merry group. Because as they had been telling her all along—Newkirk and Nick—Eddie and the twins didn't need a mother any longer. She would always be their sister, but the time for mothering them was over. They were embarking on a new phase of their lives: one that did not require her constant participation.

What then, for her? Not a mother, still a sister . . . perhaps a wife?

She gazed again at Newkirk, who was listening intently to Eddie's involved story. And Kat suddenly knew what she wanted to do for the rest of her life.

"Come on you two," she called. "Stop hoarding the food."

With a look of chagrin, they caught up with her and each helped themselves to another delicacy from the basket.

Eddie perched on the terrace wall.

"Are you going to take me away from school?" Eddie asked.

Kat eyed him cautiously. "You do not look as if you are starving," she said.

"The food is all right, I guess."

"How is the Latin coming?" Newkirk asked.

Eddie made a face. "I don't see the point of knowing Latin."

Newkirk leaned closer. "Neither do I," he whispered.

"Newkirk!" Kat gave him a mock glare. "Knowing Latin is the mark of a gentleman."

Newkirk exchanged a conspiratorial glance with Eddie. "Is your sister saying I am not a gentleman?"

She threw up her hands. "Honestly, you are as bad as he is. You two deserve each other."

"I want to go home," Eddie said.

Kat took a deep breath. "Term ends in a little over a fortnight. I think you should stay here until then."

"What?" Eddie looked stunned.

Newkirk, standing next to him, looked equally surprised.

"Well, it would be rather a waste of time to take you out now with the school year nearly done," Kat said. "If, after the summer, you decide you do not wish to come back, we can find you a different school."

"A different school! I don't want to go to school at all."

"*That* is not your decision," Kat said. "You either go to school or have a tutor, and I would think you'd rather be in the company of a bunch of other boys than home all alone with a prosing old scholar."

"She has a point," Newkirk said. "That's what I did, and I would much rather have been at school."

"I'll come back to fetch you at end of term," Kat said. "Then we shall go to London, and you can see all the marvelous things. Armor at the Tower and the fireworks at Vauxhall."

"Oh, I guess I could wait that long," Eddie said.

"Good. Now, I suspect we are keeping you from your lessons." Kat glanced at the school building. "One more pastry and then you scamper back to class."

Eddie grabbed the biggest frosted cake in the hamper and then gave her a pleading look. "Can I keep them all? I'll share with the others, I promise."

Kat tried to look stern. "You must share."

"I will."

"All right. Give me a kiss and then be off. You've Latin verbs to conjugate."

Eddie planted a swift, sticky kiss on her cheek and tried to run off. But Kat grabbed him and gave him a ferocious hug. "Behave yourself until I come back," she said.

He picked up the hamper and ran back toward the building.

Val reached out and took her hand. "May I escort you back to your carriage, my lady?"

She nodded, and they walked slowly back toward the front drive.

"You know I intended him to leave with us," he said.

She nodded. "I know. But he needs to stay here. *I* need him to stay here."

He stopped next to the carriage and took her other hand. "My brave, honorable Kat. I do think you have finally grown up."

"Finally?" She looked at him askance. "Are you saying I was a mere child before?"

"Not a child," he said with a fond smile. "But not quite yet a woman."

He was right. Somehow, from one moment to the next, she *had* grown up. She had been mother to her brothers long enough. Now it was time to take charge of her own life. To give her heart to the man who had somehow become the centerpiece of her world.

"Take me home, Val."

He looked at her uncertainly. "To Kingsford?"

"No," she said softly, stepping toward him. "To Bruton Street, for now. And then to the Abbey—or wherever else you care to settle. My life is with you."

"Wherever you wish to be," he said, and bent his head for a kiss.

They arrived back in London the following afternoon. Kat had barely stepped into the hall, with Val close behind her, when Sophie came flying down the stairs.

"You are back!" she cried. Then her expression turned puzzled. "But where is Eddie?"

"He's staying at school until the end of term," Kat said.

Sophie glanced quickly at her brother and then back to Kat. "Is that what you want?"

Kat nodded, trying to suppress a smile. "I will be busy enough in the next few weeks without Eddie underfoot."

"What is going on?" Sophie asked.

Val laughed and Kat turned toward him, giving him a warm smile. He took her hand in his.

"You can wish me happy, Sophie," Newkirk said. "I am getting married."

Sophie shrieked with delight and flung herself at Kat.

"It's about time you came to your senses!" Sophie released Kat and gave her brother an equally enthusiastic hug. "I was beginning to think I was going to have to take drastic steps."

"What are you talking about?" Kat asked.

"Don't you see?" Sophie grinned. "I knew the moment I saw you that you were the perfect match for Val."

Kat stared at her. "How could you know such a thing when I just realized it myself?"

Sophie waved her hand. "I know my brother. I've never seen him in such a stir over a female. I knew immediately that he had met his match."

"You might have said something sooner," Val said, with a rueful look. "It might have saved me a great deal of exasperation."

"But it was so fun to watch!" Sophie's eyes twinkled. "Both of you were so determined to ignore what was right in front of you."

"I was reluctant to admit that I was falling in love with him," Kat admitted, giving Val's hand a squeeze. "But now that I know, I shall never forget."

"Oh, I cannot wait!" Sophie clapped her hands. "We shall have to start shopping for your bride clothes at once. I must start making a list of all that you will need." She ran down the hall toward Val's study.

Val pulled Kat into his arms. "Should we get back in the carriage and travel to Gretna?"

Kat shook her head. "Sophie would never forgive either of us. We shall have to endure all her planning."

He planted a soft kiss on her lips. "At least I know that it will be worth all the fuss."

"Most definitely," she replied, and returned his kiss.

A Highly
Respectable Widow

To Ron.
For allowing me to shirk all my
household responsibilities
in the name of "stress reduction."
And I still think you're
cuter than Kevin Costner.

Prologue

For *ennui* is a growth of English roots,
   Though nameless in our language—we retort
The fact for words, and let the French translate
   That awful yawn which sleep cannot abate.
                —Byron, *Don Juan*

*I*t was time to find a new mistress. Edward Warrenton
Beauchamp, the ninth Earl of Knowlton, stared up at the
watered-silk canopy stretched over his head, the delicate floral
pattern dimly visible in the shaded candlelight. The lady sleeping soundly beside him, despite having been under his protection for less than a month, already bored him. Her throaty
lisp, which he had once thought so enticing, now grated on
his ears like the raucous cries of a Billingsgate fishwife. Her
voluptuous curves, which had promised much, now reminded
him of the rotund peasant women he had seen in Belgium.
Even her not-inconsiderable talents in bed inspired no
more than a brief burst of lust. Yes, it was time.

Knowlton rose from the massive bed and quietly dressed.
He pulled the newly fashionable gray trousers over his
tautly muscled legs. The crumpled linen shirt—had he
really been so careless as to drop it in such a heap?—settled
easily upon his shoulders. He did not even bother to button
the front of his richly embroidered white satin waistcoat,
and he stuffed the limp cravat into his pocket. From the
inner pocket of his impeccably tailored coat of black super-
fine he removed a small, flat box and placed it on the dressing table. Picking up his shoes, he left the room without a
backward glance at the sleeping woman.

Easing his weary body against the soft velvet squabs of

his carriage, he found it strange that even such a virtuoso performance as La Belle Marie had given last night should leave him so unmoved. He made a wry grin. Well, perhaps not completely unmoved, he thought as he recalled just how actively he had joined into the exercise. He had the aching muscles to prove it. But the pleasure had fled in an instant, leaving him vaguely dissatisfied, as if there was something more he wanted. Or needed.

He wondered if a long life of excess with women of every shape, size, hue, and class had finally caught up with him. Was this some perverse god's idea of a joke? To turn the once major pleasure of his life into a tedious routine devoid of the element of excitement, imagination, even satisfaction? For there was more to pleasure than that brief physical release, he knew. But now the act of physical union with a woman had become commonplace, almost dreary.

He glanced outside the carriage to the still-deserted streets of London. Knowlton had a fondness for these early-morning hours, having seen enough of them over the years. He liked watching the harsh outlines of the buildings emerge from the concealing shadows of the night. It was unfortunate that people could not be stripped of the shadows they hid behind as well.

A grimace of disgust crossed his face at his maudlin ramblings. He needed something to restore his spirits. Invitations to nearly every estate in the kingdom lay piled on his desk, but somehow he sensed that the discomfort that had so dogged him this spring in London would follow him as long as he remained with the *beau monde*. The thought of a solitary journey across Europe briefly excited him, but then he dismissed that idea as well. Touring alone could be devilish uncomfortable without a companion to take off the rough edges of Continental travel. He absently ran his hand through his light brown hair while he considered. It must be something closer to home.

Of course! He laughed at the sudden realization. Home. The perfect place to restore his restless spirits in comfort and privacy. He had not intended to go to Warrenton until harvest, but what would it matter if he made the journey a few months earlier than planned?

Excitement, which had so long been missing from his life, crept in again. Surely at Warrenton he would find the peace he found so difficult to obtain in London. The placid country-side would be a balm to his soul. Knowlton endured the remainder of the carriage ride to Upper Brook Street with eager anticipation, prepared to issue the order to pack for Warrenton as soon as he crossed the doorstep. He was going home.

Chapter One

. . . the soft breeze can come
To none more grateful than to me; escaped
From the vast city, where I long had pined
A discontended sojourner: now free.
                                        —Wordsworth, *The Prelude*

"*W*hat the blazes?"
    Knowlton ducked instinctively while his temperamental stallion reared in shock and surprise at the sudden attack. As plums flew through the air, Knowlton struggled to keep his seat, grabbing frantically for a handhold as his horse plunged, kicking and stomping at the fruit rolling under his feet.

"Down, you fool," he commanded, swaying in the saddle to the skittered dancing of his horse. Knowlton made a darting grab at the dangling right rein, but at the same moment his mount veered left and he found himself unhorsed. He landed with an ignominious plop in a muddy remnant of yesterday's shower.

"Damn." Knowlton scrambled to his feet, angrily surveying his mudsplattered clothing. Keeping a wary eye on the orchard from whence the attack had come, he sidled toward his mount.

"You are a disgrace to your kind," he said in mock disgust to his horse, who now stood peacefully in the middle of the lane, nuzzling the crushed fruit at his feet.

Knowlton bent down and picked up one of the bruised and battered plums that had so startled his mount, gingerly extricating the pit. He extended the plum cautiously toward the nose of his horse, who sniffed it apprehensively at first, then with relish as he recognized the fragrant smell. Fear forgotten, he grabbed it with his teeth.

"That's better," Knowlton murmured, giving the animal a soothing pat. Carefully tying the reins to a bush, he stood back to survey the trees bordering the lane. Plums did not fly through the air on their own. Someone had tossed them. And he intended to find the culprit.

This section of the estate orchard was little maintained, but the old tree limbs bent groundward with their still-abundant load of fruit. Knowlton quickly scanned the field but noted nothing out of place. The assailant must be hiding, hoping his target would move on. Knowlton advanced with determination. One did not throw ripe plums at the Earl of Knowlton with impunity.

Finding a toehold with his boot, he clambered awkwardly over the low stone fence surrounding the orchard. Once on the other side, he searched the ground and trees, looking for some sign of an intruder. Most suspiciously, he discovered a neat pile of purple fruit under one tree, nestled among the tufts of grass. He knew very well that plums did not fall from trees in clumps.

Those well-timed missiles had put him in perilous danger for a few frightening moments, and Knowlton itched to get his hands on his assailant. There would be no more fruit tossed at unwary passersby from this orchard if he had anything to say about the matter.

Knowlton walked carefully to the base of the tree, circling it cautiously lest any more bombs came his way. Catching a flash of movement in the upper branches, he allowed himself a quick smile of satisfaction. He ducked under the low-hanging limbs and squinted up into the dancing leaves.

"I know you are up there," he said sternly. "It will go easier with you if you come down at once." A deep silence answered his offer.

"I will not ask again," Knowlton said, his irritation mounting. "Climb down and present yourself!"

Some tenant was going to get a tongue-lashing for letting his child run wild, Knowlton mused as he quickly searched for an advantageous foothold. Reaching upward to grab a low branch, he pulled himself up into the tree. Leaves and plums bounced against his head as he scrambled onto the branch. A decidedly loud rustle told him his quarry was above.

Twisting under one branch, Knowlton cautiously sought to rise to his full height. As he did so, a foot came into view and he clamped his hand around the ankle with an iron grip.

"Got you!" he cried. "You come down here now!"

A quick jerk pulled the foot free from Knowlton's grasp, and with a loud crackling of broken twigs, accompanied by the soft thumps of falling plums, a dark shape slipped through the branches with surprising speed.

Knowlton jumped to the ground as the young lad took off running through the overgrown orchard. It took only a few long-legged steps to put the boy within reach and Knowlton grabbed a handful of coat, pulling the lad up short and whirling him about.

An immediate appraisal of the red-haired, freckled-faced youth of perhaps ten told Knowlton he had been wrong about one thing—this was no tenant's son. His shirt, jacket, and breeches, although worn and dirty, were that of a young gentleman.

"You could have caused me serious harm," he thundered at the trembling boy, in mock fury.

"I didn't plan to! I didn't think I could hit you from that distance! I never would have thrown anything if I'd known." The words slid out rapidly.

Something in the boy's glib protestations made Knowlton suspect he was in the presence of a master at apologizing for mischievous behavior. No child with hair that flaming shade of red could be anything else but a rascally scamp.

"Are you familiar with the local magistrate?" Knowlton maintained his stern tone.

The boy shook his head.

"Well, I suspect it is high time you became acquainted. There are the small matters of trespassing, assault, attempted theft . . . If you are lucky, it might only result in transportation."

"Transportation?" the boy's eyes grew wide in alarm.

"You look like an adventurous sort of lad," Knowlton continued, barely able to suppress his grin. "Just the type to enjoy a long sea voyage. Why, I daresay you would find it the adventure of a lifetime."

"I don't want to be transported," the lad protested. "I have to stay here and take care of my mama."

"Oh, I am certain we could arrange for her to travel with you too," Knowlton agreed amiably. "I don't hold with the practice of splitting families up on these occasions."

"I bet if you went to the earl he would not mind too much that I took some of his plums," the boy said. "Everyone says he's a right'un. Maybe if you told him I would never do it again, he would not object."

"I hate to disillusion you, my boy, but I *am* the Earl of Knowlton."

The boy's eyes widened with surprise and he bowed hastily. "It is an honor to meet you, my lord. I could pay you for the plums," he offered eagerly. "Leastwise, not with money, but I could do some work for you. Anything you want. I can pull weeds or scrub pots." He looked at Knowlton with eager apprehension.

Knowlton rubbed his chin as if deep in thought. "I don't know. I have a whole staff of gardeners to pull my weeds. And there is more than one scullery maid to scrub my pots. What else can you do?"

"I could write your letters! Even Mama says I have a neat hand." Then his face fell. " 'Course, you might have to help me with the spelling."

"A secretary who cannot spell. Just what I need."

"I could carve you a whistle."

Knowlton looked skeptical. "A whistle?"

The lad nodded eagerly. "From the willows down by the pond. They make the most marvelous sound when you cut them just right. Mama won't even let me blow them in the house," he announced proudly.

"Well enough, then, you can make me a whistle to pay for the plums. And I will concede you do not know your own strength and did not mean to hit my horse with your missile. But there is still the trespassing . . . although I suspect," said Knowlton, unable to keep a grin from his face, "that someone's mother is going to be extremely perturbed about the state of his clothes."

The lad looked down in chagrin at his dirt-bespattered breeches. "I guess she is going to be angry." He looked up, brightening. "She might not mind as much if I bring her lots of plums."

Knowlton threw back his head and laughed at the logic. He put his arm companionably around the boy's shoulder.

"I remember a few times in my youth when I received a thrashing for ruining my clothes," he confided. "I think plums just might do the trick for you."

"Do you really think so?"

"It is worth a try. Come, I will help you. How many plums does your mother need?"

The lad shrugged. "There are just the two of us. How many can two people eat?"

"Where do you live?" Knowlton asked in curiosity as he reached up to pull a ripe plum from its branch.

"Down across that field there," the boy said, pointing. "In the Rose Cottage."

Knowlton nodded in recognition. He recalled there had been a new renter in the spring.

"If that is the case, you may feel free to help yourself to as many plums as you like, anytime," Knowlton said. "Do you have a name, lad?"

"Robert Mayfield, my lord," he replied. "My mama calls me Robbie. That's 'cause I'm named for my father and it was too confusing to have two Roberts."

"Your father is not living with you?"

"He's dead," Robbie said quietly.

"I am sorry, Robbie," replied Knowlton, berating himself for his curiosity.

"He was killed at Salamanca," Robbie said with a proud air. "He was a captain in the cavalry. I have his sword, except Mama won't let me play with it. And when I am old enough I am going to join a cavalry regiment."

"An admirable goal," said Knowlton. So Mrs. Mayfield was a widow? It might behoove him to look in on his latest tenant. Widows could often be *very* lonely. He stripped off his coat.

"We can use this to carry the plums to your house," he said easily.

Robbie stared at him. "Won't your mama be mad if you ruin your coat?"

Knowlton laughed. "She would if she were still here, Robbie my boy. But I can ruin my coats without fear these days. She died many a year ago."

"I am sorry, sir," said Robbie.

His evident sincerity touched Knowlton. He reached down and picked out a ripe plum from the pile upon the ground. Polishing the fruit on his sleeve, he bit into it and savored the satisfying, juicy tartness. He gestured toward the stack. "Have one."

Robbie eagerly complied. Knowlton eased himself to the ground, stretching out his tall frame on the sweet-smelling grass, leaning back on one elbow while he savored his plum. Lord, it was good to be home.

After the dirt and noise of the city, the country seemed even more peaceful than he remembered. The sound of the breeze rustling the leaves overhead, the nearby trill of a bird, all brought back in a rush memories of his own childhood here at Warrenton. When every new day was an adventure and all was new and exciting. He had never been bored in those days. Maybe he could recapture some of that youthful enthusiasm during his stay this time.

With a disgruntled sigh, Knowlton flung the pit into the far reaches of the orchard, wiping his sticky fingers on his now-filthy buckskins. Between his coat and breeches, his valet would have a fit. That brought a grin to Knowlton's face. The man was far too concerned with his master's consequence.

Knowlton cleared his throat. "Now, Robbie, if you can manage to hold on to the plums, we can probably get that foolish beast of mine to carry us both. I will escort you home and explain matters to your mama." And he could avail himself of the opportunity of meeting the widowed Mrs. Mayfield. Would she have the same flaming red hair as her son? In his experience, the old adage about the passionate nature of redheads held true. With renewed interest, Knowlton started back toward the lane, Robbie half-running to keep up with the lengthy strides.

Knowlton untied his horse and held the reins, then looked expectantly at Robbie.

"Up, boy. We haven't got all afternoon."

"I have never been on a horse, sir."

The revelation astounded Knowlton. "You want to join a cavalry regiment and you do not know how to ride? I think you had better set your sights on a rifle brigade. Of course, you probably have not fired a gun either."

Robbie shook his head. "Mama says both are too dangerous."

Knowlton sighed in exasperation. Hen-witted women could be the death of little boys. He took the parcel of plums and set them on the ground, gave his horse a stern admonition to remain still, and put his hands together. "Step here and I will boost you up."

Robbie did as ordered and managed to creditably scramble into the saddle. Knowlton handed him the coat full of plums, then climbed up behind him.

"This is prodigiously wonderful," Robbie exclaimed with awe, surveying the world from his new vantage point.

"Prodigiously?"

"That is my new word this week," the lad explained proudly. "Mama has me learn a new one every week. The vicar says it is an admirable plan."

"You are friends with the vicar?"

"He is giving me my lessons."

Knowlton's brow furrowed. "You have lessons in the summer?"

"Mama said I missed too much time last spring when we made the move here, so I needed to study all summer if I wasn't to fall too far behind."

"And what is the vicar teaching you?"

"Oh, Latin, Greek, a little history. But I think Mama knows more history than he does."

"And how do you find Latin and Greek?" Knowlton asked impishly.

"Truly?" Robbie asked warily.

"Truly."

"Not very well."

Knowlton laughed. "I shall tell you a secret, Robbie, my boy. I loathed Latin and Greek when I was your age. Hated them. Detested them."

"And did your mama make you study them anyway?"

He nodded. "Not only my mama, but my father and my tutor. And if my lessons were not perfect, I was thrashed. The vicar does not thrash you if you make a mistake, does he?"

"No," said Robbie, with obvious relief. "Do you still hate Latin and Greek?"

"Promise me you will not tell your mother?" Knowlton whispered conspiratorially.

"I promise."

"I still loathe them."

Robbie grinned. "Mama would be very angry if she heard you say that. She says education is very important."

"I did not say education was unimportant," Knowlton said. "I merely meant that cramming Latin and Greek into children's heads is an abominable practice. I much more approve of learning a useful language like French or Italian."

"Or Spanish!" said Robbie excitedly. "I can still remember one time when Papa was home he taught us a few words of Spanish. *Buenas tardes*—that means 'good afternoon.' And *gracias* is 'thank you.'"

"A sight more useful than Latin, I am certain," muttered Knowlton as the Rose Cottage came into view. Stopping his horse at the gate, he dismounted and carefully assisted Robbie down. So Mrs. Mayfield was a mother who did not approve of horses and rifles—yet knew history and insisted her son have a gentleman's education. His interest piqued, Knowlton followed the racing boy down the front path. It was time to make the acquaintance of this intriguing lady.

Chapter Two

She was a Phantom of Delight
When first she gleamed upon my sight.

—Wordsworth

*K*atherine Mayfield rubbed the end of her nose with the back of her hand, leaving a smudge of flour behind. She returned to her rhythmic kneading with renewed determination. Soon she could turn the loaves into the pans, pop them into the oven, and direct her attention to . . .

A frown marred her pale face. There were so many things she needed to accomplish: the washing, the mending, letting out Robbie's clothes for what must be the hundredth time. She shook her head in dismay as she thought how rapidly he was growing. The clothes he had now would last until the weather turned this fall, but then she would be faced with providing him an entire head-to-foot wardrobe. And that meant money. Which meant she must turn from her own chores to her work for Mrs. Gorton, the local seamstress. One more afternoon of stitching delicate lace trim onto some squire's daughter's gown.

Gazing longingly at the bright sunlit yard outside, Katherine wished she could afford to toss her sewing work aside and take the afternoon for herself. It would be heaven to free her mind for a few hours from the never-ceasing struggle to survive. She could pretend she was a grand lady whose servants took care of every minute detail of running the house while she spent her time as she wished.

Katherine shook her head at her futile longings. She could only attach the blame to herself for the state she and Robbie were in. The knowledge that she had done the right thing provided cold comfort when they lived so close to the edge.

With the bread tucked safely into the oven, Katherine turned to wash the flour from her hands. Hearing Robbie's excited chattering through the window, she paused to listen. He had been gone most of the afternoon and she prayed he had not got into any more mischief this week. She froze in mid-step when she heard a strange masculine voice. Robbie had been up to something, the wretch! Hastily rinsing her hands, Katherine dried them on her apron as she hastened through the narrow passageway to the front hall.

Pulling open the door, she saw Robbie dancing down the cobbled pathway, followed by a tall stranger whose demeanor and bearing belied his disheveled appearance.

"Mama, Mama," cried Robbie. " 'Tis the earl; I met him today in the orchard and he says we can have as many plums as we want."

Katherine wanted to sink into the stone steps. How many

times had she warned Robbie against trespassing on the
earl's property? Instead, she gathered her skirts and
bobbed a deferential curtsy to her new landlord, keeping
her eyes carefully averted.

"I am pleased to make your acquaintance, my lord."

The standard greeting he had planned froze on his lips
as Knowlton obtained his first close look at Mrs. Mayfield.
Dear God, an angel had landed on his doorstep! His polite
social smile transformed itself into a wide grin of male appreciation as he perused her from head to toe. He easily
looked past the drab dress, cap-covered head, and flour-
smudged nose to what lay beneath. Mrs. Mayfield was quite
one of the most stunning women he had ever seen. The
straggling red curls peeking out from under her cap set off
a flawless complexion unmarked by the trace of a freckle.
And her form . . . It looked to be ample in all the right
places, soft, and curving where it should.

Returning his gaze to her face, he found himself staring
into the loveliest pair of blue eyes he had ever seen. The
mingled expression of anger and wariness he saw there bemused him.

Katherine lifted her gaze and caught her breath at the
appreciative look in the earl's eyes. Was it going to start
all over again here? She struggled against her anger. "Have
you seen quite enough, my lord?"

Her tone was icy, but as Knowlton expected, the accent
was cultivated.

"You don't have to call him 'my lord,'" Robbie piped
up. "He's not toplofty at all. See all the plums we gathered?
And I got to ride on his horse! It was ever so high in
the air. And I did not fall off. Can I get a horse of my
own now?"

"Do not bombard your mother with so much information
at once, you scamp," Knowlton said, ruffling the boy's hair.
"If you know what is good for you, you will run off and
make yourself more presentable before your mother has a
chance to take a good look at your appearance."

Katherine caught only a brief flash of Robbie's stained
clothing as he raced by, and she grimaced in dismay. Turning back to the earl, she smiled coolly.

"I can only surmise you found him stealing plums in your
orchard," she said. "I am very sorry, my lord. He has been

told time and time again not to wander onto the estate grounds, but he—"

Knowlton raised a forestalling hand. "I do not mind in the least. He was in the oldest portion of the orchard. I always allow my tenants free access to the fruit there. He did nothing he should not have." Knowlton had already determined not to alarm her with the plum-throwing incident. He thought Robbie had already been properly chastened for that indiscretion.

"Thank you, my lord," Katherine replied. She noted the expectant gleam in his cool gray eyes. "Was there another matter?"

"It is a hot afternoon," he said. He wanted to linger in her presence, to determine if his first reaction had been overhasty. He could simply not believe his good fortune. "Perhaps a glass of something cool . . . ?"

He watched carefully as dismay momentarily flitted over her face; then her previous closed expression returned.

"I beg your pardon, my lord. Please come inside. I can bring you a glass of water, or there is some May wine, if you prefer."

"Water would be most welcome," he said, following her over the threshold and into the parlor.

Katherine hastily retreated to the kitchen, searching to find a glass that was not cracked or chipped. So here was the great Earl of Knowlton. He did not look at all like she had imagined. In his shirtsleeves, with the casually open collar, stained buckskins, and windblown hair, he looked more like a country squire than one of the richest men in the kingdom. And one of the most notorious womanizers. A frisson of apprehension gripped her. Katherine prayed there would be no trouble here, as there had been in the last two places she had lived. She had been all too aware of his appreciative appraisal on the front steps. Those scrutinizing gray eyes made her uncomfortable.

She hoped the intentional drabness of her costume had given him pause. It was only a pity she could not do something to her hair. One sight of that color and all men thought one thing. She did want to stay in this neighborhood for a while, at least; another move would be ruinously expensive.

During her absence, Knowlton's sharp eyes appraised the

shabby parlor, noting the worn upholstery on the two chairs and the tallow candles on the highly polished but conspicuously bare table. It was very clear that Mrs. Mayfield was not a widow of means. She might have an interest, then, in improving her financial station. This promised to be a most propitious situation.

When Mrs. Mayfield reappeared with his water, Knowlton gestured for her to sit, sensing her wariness. He did his best to put her at ease.

"Is the cottage to your liking?" He noted approvingly that a few recalcitrant locks of hair crept from beneath her kitchen cap, giving her a less-than-matronly appearance. Particularly since her hair was the same flaming shade as Robbie's. There was something elementally exciting about red hair on a woman.

Katherine nodded politely, uncomfortably aware of his close examination.

"No leaking roof? Sticking windows?" He arched a quizzing brow.

"Everything is satisfactory, my lord."

"You have only to speak to Mr. Taggert if you encounter any difficulties." Knowlton smiled easily. "I want my tenants to be happy. Any justified repairs will be performed."

"Thank you, my lord." Katherine relaxed her guard slightly. If he remained true to his word, Lord Knowlton would be a vast improvement over her last landlord. She suppressed a shiver at the memory of the old, drafty, and damp cottage in which she and Robbie had spent the previous winter.

"You have a lively son," Knowlton commented. "He must lead you on a merry dance."

She smiled and he observed how that action brought a glow to her pale face. He longed to reach over and pull off that ridiculous mobcap so he could see her hair in all its glory.

Robbie bounded into the room at that moment, his face and hands showing signs of a less-than-thorough wash.

"Robbie!" Katherine exclaimed in dismay, forgetting the earl for a moment. "Look at your clothes!"

He looked down sheepishly at his filthy breeches, with a tear across one knee. "I am sorry, Mama." He set down

Matt

1-510-789

1199

the bundle of the earl's coat on the table. "Here are the plums we picked. Will you make a pie for us, Mama?"

She looked in horror at the misshapen garment. "What did you wrap these in?"

"My coat," said Knowlton with a grin.

"You will have ruined it," she scolded.

He shrugged. "It was not my favorite coat."

She stood up, reaching for the bundle. "I will do what I can to clean it for you," she said, and whisked her armload out into the hall before he could protest. She was grateful for another excuse to leave the earl's presence.

Katherine dumped the plums into a bowl and surveyed the ruin of the earl's coat. Brushing off a stray leaf, she grimaced in discouragement. It was not terribly dirty; a good brushing would remove most of it. But the weighty plums had done things to the coat that its tailor had never intended. The earl would never wish to be seen wearing it in polite company again. With a shake of her head at the folly of the nobility, she took her clothes brush to the inside. The price of this coat would have kept her and Robbie in clothes for years.

"I fear your coat is ruined," she said woefully when she returned to the parlor. "I did what I could."

"And much more than you needed to, Mrs. Mayfield. I thank you." His gray eyes twinkled with suppressed amusement.

Robbie was bouncing on the edge of his seat. "The earl says I can visit him at his house anytime I want."

"That is very kind of you." Katherine eyed the earl with a wary glance, her suspicions reawakened.

"Truly, I mean it," Knowlton interjected, hearing the doubt in her voice. "I do not stand on ceremony with my tenants. There are a good many things at Warrenton to interest a sharp lad like Robbie. He is welcome at any time." As are you yourself, he thought silently. Most welcome.

He saw a fleeting spasm of alarm cross her face and feared he had acted too precipitately by inviting Robbie. True, it was not the thing one would expect an earl to do, but Knowlton thought he had explained himself well enough. Robbie did amuse him, and he was sorely in need of amusement. But Mrs. Mayfield sat there glaring at him as if he had asked her to dance naked on the table. His reputation, no doubt. The country gossips would surely have apprised her of that. It might take some time to repair the damage, but he already suspected it would be a worthwhile campaign.

"Thank you for the water, Mrs. Mayfield." His mouth curved into a sensual smile. "And for the chance to meet your son."

"Thank you again for the plums," Katherine replied, quickly rising to her feet to hasten his departure. His smile disconcerted her. With relief, she escorted the earl to the door. "We will very much enjoy the preserves they will make."

"Ah, yes, I surmised you were an accomplished cook," he said with an air of mystery.

Katherine's expression became puzzled.

"I might have said it was the delicious aroma of baking bread with which you tortured me throughout this visit," he said with a roguish twinkle in his eyes. "But actually, it was the dab of flour on your nose that gave it away." He reached out and brushed the offending spot with his finger, gratified to see the blush that rose to her cheeks. She looked even lovelier with color in her face.

Katherine willed her voice to remain calm, the skin on her nose still tingling from that gentle touch. "Thank you for pointing out that flaw in my appearance, my lord. I would hate to think that an important person might happen by and find me in such disarray."

He admired her aplomb and his grin widened. "It was no less a social crime than having your landlord drop in uninvited and in his shirtsleeves. Shall we call it even, Mrs. Mayfield?"

She nodded, amused in spite of her wariness. He sketched her a low bow and exited the cottage. Katherine returned to the kitchen, sinking weakly into the corner chair.

This was far, far worse than she could ever have imagined. In the other places where there had been difficulties, at least she had been personally repelled by the men. But the earl . . . It was not difficult to see why he was such a success with women. That devastating smile had sent even her pulse racing. He was handsome, witty, and knew exactly how to set off his not-inconsiderable charms to best advantage. In short, he was every inch the rake his reputation labeled him. She had the sinking feeling that remaining impervious to his charm would be one of the most difficult tasks of her life. But ignore him she must. Men of his station had only one use for poor widows.

Robbie followed the earl into the yard, watching with worshipful eyes as he mounted his horse and rode away with a farewell wave. He slowly sauntered back into the house, heading straight for the stairs.

Katherine waited at the bottom. "There is a *small* matter we need to discuss," she said sternly. "Were you not told to stay off the estate grounds?"

Robbie nodded glumly.

"And haven't I asked you countless times to take better care of your clothes?"

He nodded again.

"Robbie, those clothes have to last you until I make your winter ones." Katherine shook her head in dismay. "You are already starting to look like a ragamuffin. You will be reduced to wearing your Sunday best soon, and that will mean you shall be confined to the house. I will not allow you to ruin those."

"Yes, Mama." He turned to make his escape.

"Robbie?"

"Yes?"

"Three pages in your Latin grammar. For disobeying me."

"The earl didn't mind," he protested. "He said it was all right."

"But I did not, and it is my word that counts in this house. Now, you march into the study this minute and finish that work, or there will be no supper for you."

"Yes, ma'am."

Knowlton nearly laughed aloud as his horse trotted toward home. He had not been so highly diverted in an age. Robbie was a scamp. In fact, he reminded Knowlton all too clearly of himself at that age, when his mother had sworn he would be the death of her and his father had birched him regularly for some transgression or other. He was willing to bet Mrs. Mayfield did not birch Robbie. She had probably devised some equally devilish punishment for the lad—like incarceration in his room on a bright, sunny summer's day. Knowlton had much preferred a birching to that.

He was captivated by his short acquaintance with Mrs. Mayfield. She had done nothing to dash the hopes that had blossomed when he had first heard that a widow lived on his property. He could not wait to see her with her hair down. The color reminded him of firelight and sunlight mixed and would look most enticing spread out upon a white pillow.

Her demeanor, however, gave him pause. He suspected she was exactly what she appeared—a very respectable widow, struggling to raise her son alone on too little money. He would have a quick word with Taggert and see what assistance they could offer her.

Yet there had been a brief glimpse of something else— her flash of wit at his departure showed there was more to Mrs. Mayfield than first appeared. There had been a hint of mocking amusement in her voice when she gently chastised him for arriving uninvited on her doorstep. She was not afraid to trade barbs with an earl. He liked that.

The more he thought on it, the deeper his interest grew in Robbie's mother. Knowlton had little experience with ladies of her ilk—he preferred experienced women of the *ton* to impecunious widows, for the former knew the rules of the game. He had heard too many tales of the danger of going outside that tight circle, of raising expectations that would never be met.

But Mrs. Mayfield posed a challenge. He had ample proof of the stories of redheaded women, that they had a nature more fiery and passionate than even his own. Why else did so many ladies of less-than-virtuous honor dye their hair that color? He rather thought he liked the idea of testing Mrs. Mayfield to see if that adage always held true.

In fact, it would be a welcome challenge. Could he overcome her widow's reticence to expose the sensual woman that lay beneath? A lazy smile crept over his features. It was exactly the scheme he needed to bring himself out of his boredom. A true test of his seductive skills. He had no doubt of his success—the only question would be the length of time it would take to bring Mrs. Mayfield to his bed. Cheered as he had not been in weeks, Knowlton whistled a lively tune as he guided his horse toward home.

Chapter Three

And, after all, what is a lie? 'Tis but
The Truth in masquerade. . . .
—Byron, *Don Juan*

"*M*y lord?" Knowlton's imperious butler stood immobile inside the study door.

"What is it, Hutchins?" the earl drawled in a bored voice.

"There is a young person here, my lord." The butler's tone clearly indicated his disapproval. "He insists he is here at your invitation and wishes to see you."

Knowlton looked up with interest. "And what does this importuning guest call himself?"

"He says he is Robbie Mayfield, my lord."

"As I thought," said Knowlton, lowering his booted feet from his desk. "Send him in, Hutchins. And, Hutchins . . . unless I give instructions otherwise, Mr. Mayfield is to be admitted whenever he calls."

"As you wish, my lord."

Knowlton grinned as Hutchins departed. So, the rascal was here already. He pushed away the London papers he had been reading.

Robbie walked into the study, his head swiveling this way and that as he examined every corner of the room.

"Good morning, Robbie." Knowlton's smile widened at the boy's avid perusal.

"This whole house is yours?"

"Every inch of it," replied Knowlton.

"How many people live here?" Robbie breathed.

"Only myself," said Knowlton.

Robbie's eyes widened. "You live here all by yourself?"

"Only if you discount an army of servants."

"Don't you ever get lonely?"

Knowlton laughed. "Rarely. I usually am not here long enough to grow lonely. If I am, I invite a houseful of guests to stay with me."

"How do you keep them from getting lost inside the house?"

"I have to be very careful of that," the earl admitted. "I always count heads at the dinner table. I would hate for someone to starve to death and die in some lonely corner." He casually walked to the far wall and opened a cupboard door, peering cautiously inside. "I always like to double-check," he told Robbie in a confidential tone. "Just in case there is the skeleton of some former guest that I missed."

Robbie shuddered at the thought.

"I am roasting you." Knowlton clapped the lad on the back. "Come, I am certain you did not wish to spend the morning in the house. I will show you the stables."

Robbie ran to keep up with the earl's long strides as they crossed the rear lawn. The boy stared in wide-eyed wonder at the paddock, where several horses frolicked and gamboled in the morning sunlight.

"How many horses do you have?" he asked with awe as they stepped into the seemingly endless stable block.

"Several," replied the earl blandly. He was growing uncomfortable with Robbie's awestruck wonder at every sight. Knowlton had always taken Warrenton's magnificence and the excellence of its stables for granted.

"What do you do with them all?" Robbie inquired as they walked past grays, bays, blacks, and chestnuts.

"They all have their special purposes," the earl explained patiently. "There are riding horses, horses for hunting, horses for the light carriages, horses for the heavy carriages, and horses for whatever other special need may arise."

"I would like to learn how to drive a carriage someday," Robbie said.

"You had better learn how to ride first," Knowlton reminded him. "You are getting a late start as it is, for a cavalry officer."

Robbie scuffed his boot against the packed dirt floor. "Mama says we cannot afford a horse," he said glumly.

"You do not need your own horse to learn on," the earl

said, making an instant decision. What better way to gain the boy's confidence? "There must be some beast in this stable that would be quite suitable for you."

"You mean you would allow me to ride one of your horses?" Robbie's eyes grew big.

"I think I can arrange it," the earl said, smiling at the boy's unfeigned eagerness.

"And you will teach me how to ride?"

Knowlton hesitated for a moment, then nodded, offering up a silent self-congratulation at this unexpected opportunity. What better way to get on Mrs. Mayfield's good side than to take an interest in her beloved son?

"Frank, have Alecto saddled," Knowlton ordered.

"Alecto?" Robbie asked. "Wasn't she one of the Furies?"

Knowlton smiled. "Far enough in your Greek studies for that, eh? An apt name for a mare, don't you think?"

The groom soon led out the medium-size bay, saddled and bridled.

Seeing the eager expression on the lad's face, Knowlton remembered how he had been set on his first horse before the age of three, and felt a brush of compassion for Robbie. How long had Mrs. Mayfield lived on the edge of poverty? Long enough that her son had never learned the basic points of horsemanship. He gave Robbie an encouraging smile. "Ready for your first lesson?"

Robbie nodded.

"The first thing to remember is: never jerk on the reins," Knowlton explained to his avid listener. "It hurts the horse's mouth. Use gentle pulling. And always be firm in your intentions. A horse will sense your hesitation and will use it to take advantage."

"Firm but gentle," Robbie repeated as the groom led the horse over to the mounting block. Now that he stood next to the horse, her back looked a long way up. There would be no Knowlton in the saddle to hold him on this time. Swallowing hard, he stepped onto the block and grabbed the reins. Knowlton helped him slip his foot into the stirrup, then Robbie swung his right leg up and over.

Knowlton waited patiently while the groom adjusted the stirrups to accommodate Robbie's short legs. Then he nodded to have the mare led about the yard. He watched Robbie with a critical eye, seeking to take his measure as a potential horseman. He was pleased with what he saw. Despite the lad's understandable nervousness, his seat was natural and unforced.

"Take up more slack in the reins," he commanded. "Hold your hands low, in a relaxed position."

Robbie complied readily, looking eagerly at Knowlton for approval.

The earl nodded his satisfaction. The lad would learn fast, Knowlton thought. He just might make the cavalry after all, despite the fact he was a good seven to eight years late sitting on his first horse. With careful instruction . . .

"Try a trot, Frank," Knowlton instructed the groom. "Hang on tight, Robbie."

Knowlton grinned as Robbie bounced along at the quickened pace. He saw the gleam of excitement in the boy's eyes and felt an unfamiliar sense of satisfaction at Robbie's pleasure. Remembering his own early riding lessons, and the grateful fondness he retained for the old groom who had taught him, Knowlton experienced an odd wish that perhaps someday this boy would look back with the same emotion on the man who had first set him on a horse.

"You are looking good, lad," he called in encouragement, rewarded by Robbie's wide grin of pleasure at the commendation.

Katherine was pleased that Robbie applied himself so diligently to his studies these days—and if he worked hard only to make certain he would have more time to get into mischief, at least his work was not suffering. She could not ask more of him; she knew how much she already asked by insisting on schoolwork in the summer.

She knew he spent most of his time with Sam Trent, one of the farmers' sons. Katherine did not mind the difference in social station; Robbie needed to be with boys of his own age, and if only farmers' sons were available, well, they would do.

Sighing, she picked up her basket, preparing to walk to the village. It was probably debatable exactly which class she and Robbie belonged to anymore. The requirements of survival were more important than paying homage to the beliefs of one's class. Food was more important than status. She had learned that lesson well.

Katherine accomplished her errands at a leisurely pace, knowing there was no need for haste this day. It was warm and sunny and the sky the brilliant blue of high midsummer. She could not blame Robbie a bit for wanting to be out on such a glorious day. Even she was tempted to follow some childish pursuit—like wading barefoot in the stream or climbing a tree to reach the topmost fruit.

Unfortunately, neither pursuit was suited to the image of responsibility she assiduously tried to cultivate. With a regretful toss of her head, she ambled down the lane toward home. Mothers were not allowed to behave like children, no matter how much they might wish to.

Katherine heard the sound of an approaching carriage, and she stepped automatically to the side of the road to let it pass, hoping it would not leave her covered in dust. She relaxed when she heard the vehicle slow.

"Good day to you, Mrs. Mayfield."

Katherine turned in surprise at the sound of the earl's voice. "Good day, my lord."

"Fine weather, is it not?" He doffed his hat.

"Very fine," Katherine assented, willing him to drive on.

"Almost too fine a day for driving," the earl continued, holding his horses at a standstill. "But alas, without my groom I am doomed to be a-wheel. Should you care to join me?"

"Thank you, but I will walk."

Her reluctance spurred his determination. This was a perfect opportunity to allay her apprehensions. "Oh, come now, Mrs. Mayfield. You have been to the village, I see, and I suspect your basket is growing heavier by the moment."

"I am quite capable of carrying my basket," she protested, firmly intending to resist his cajolery. Lord Knowlton only boded danger for her.

"Now, do not be churlish, Mrs. Mayfield. I am only trying to be a good neighbor." Knowlton gave her his most innocent smile. "Contemplate how much more pleasant your afternoon will be if you arrive at your home rested and refreshed, instead of worn and tired from a hot, dusty walk."

His persistence irritated Katherine.

"Surely you are not nervous about driving with me?" Knowlton flashed her an injured look. "I would understand your hesitation if I was inviting you into a closed carriage, but I hardly think you are in much danger from me in the curricle."

As her reluctance stemmed precisely from her apprehensions about the earl, Katherine was at a loss for a civil reply. Why would he not leave her alone?

Knowlton shook his head sadly. "I see that I have misjudged you, Mrs. Mayfield. I thought you were the type of lady who would not judge another merely on the basis of hearsay. How can you be so certain that I am not a suitable companion?"

"You mean to suggest otherwise?" she asked dryly. She could not resist the temptation to bandy words with him. Words, after all, were perfectly safe.

He flung a hand to his breast. "You wound me, my lady. You impugn my honor."

The rakehell *had* no honor, she thought, amused nonetheless by his protestations of injured innocence.

"You can rely on my complete trustworthiness," he promised, pleading for her capitulation.

"I thank you for your concern, Lord Knowlton," she said coolly. "But I much prefer to walk. Good day, my lord." After bobbing a slight curtsy, Katherine turned and resumed her steps down the lane.

Despite his disappointment, Knowlton's admiration rose a notch. This was to be no easy conquest. He picked up the reins and urged his horses into a slow walk. Mrs. Mayfield would find that he was not readily discouraged.

"You have not yet asked me what drew me into town this afternoon." His voice held a slightly mocking tone.

Katherine kept her eyes facing forward, grateful that her bonnet hid most of her face. She would not give him the satisfaction of seeing her reluctant curiosity. "Do tell."

"I was visiting with the vicar."

She resisted the urge to laugh. Did he really think to impress her with such a ridiculous tale? "I see."

"You sound rather doubtful."

Katherine glanced with undisguised skepticism at the earl. "Pardon me for seeming so, but in all the tales I have heard of you, my lord, not one has mentioned your propensity for the religious."

"Did I not tell you it is unwise to listen to idle gossip?" Knowlton looked at her, his face full of wounded vanity. "I always make it a point to attend services when I am in residence at Warrenton. I feel it is my obligation to set an example for the lower orders."

Katherine's eyes held a challenge. "Then I shall look forward to seeing you this Sunday," she replied, thinking to trap him with his outlandish boasts.

"I certainly hope so!" Knowlton smiled at his success in finally gaining a reaction from her. "I was speaking with the vicar about that very matter. I feel it incumbent upon me to visit him whenever I return, to remind him that I am now here and he can no longer get away with the boring drivel he spews from the pulpit during my absences."

Katherine's lips twitched in suppressed amusement. "How do you know it is so dreadful if you are not here?"

"I have my sources," he said with a mysterious air. "The vicar knows that he dare not bore me, for whatever good example my attendance sets would be dashed to pieces if I fell asleep in the process."

"I am certain the vicar appreciates the challenge."

"I daresay he does."

All too soon, to Knowlton's mind, they reached the gate of the Rose Cottage. How he would have liked to continue this conversation for another hour—preferably with Mrs. Mayfield in his carriage, not walking alongside it. But he congratulated himself on the progress he had made this day, and determined not to be too greedy for success. He must allay her apprehensions first.

"Perhaps next time you will not be so reluctant to accept my offer of transportation," he said, watching her face carefully to see how she reacted to his suggestion. "Now that I have demonstrated my respectability to you."

It would take more than a few boastful remarks about a visit to the vicar to overcome *his* reputation, Katherine thought. "We shall see," she said noncommittally. "Once again, I bid you good day."

Knowlton watched as she walked down the flagstone path to the cottage door. He resisted the impulse to laugh aloud. She was such a skittish thing, terrified of his reputation as

a man no lady could feel safe with. Which was highly un-
true. He knew any number of women who had never been
forced to fend off an unwelcome advance from him.

Of course, they were outnumbered entirely by those who
had accepted the advance, or even begged for it, but that
was not the point. He needed to convince Mrs. Mayfield
she was perfectly safe with him. The fact that this was a
total untruth did not bother him one whit. With a wide grin
he urged the horses homeward. The pursuit of Mrs. Mayfield was already proving to be a delicious antidote to
boredom.

Katherine set her basket down with a thunk on the
kitchen table and struggled to untie the ribbons of her bonnet, which had become hopelessly tangled.

Drat that man. She had sensed the danger from him at
their first meeting, and he had done nothing to dispel that
image today. Oh, he had been as polite as could be, but
she knew that behind that facade lurked a man who only
ached to get his hands on her. He was just like all the
others. She should have ignored him completely, instead of
trading sallies. Why had she been so foolish?

Because you wanted to be, a small voice said. *Because
despite the danger, you are intrigued by the man. And secretly flattered that he finds you attractive.*

Katherine shut her eyes. It did not help in the least that
Knowlton was a devastatingly handsome man. He had
looked every inch the lord today in his polished Hessians,
form-hugging pantaloons, and expertly tailored coat; quite
a contrast to the muddy and disheveled man who had
graced her parlor only a few days ago. But the look in
those expressive gray eyes had not changed. The admiring
gleam she saw there did nothing to dispel her
apprehension.

The years since Robert's death had taught her to be increasingly wary of men. She had grown adept at politely
fending off their advances. If a situation grew too intolerable, she moved. Now, she feared she was in the midst of
her worst situation yet. It had been easy to turn up her
nose at bumbling squires and lewd old lords. Now, for the
first time, she found her pursuer dangerously attractive.
And that would never do. She reminded herself she had a

son to raise now, and there was no time for dreams. She must make it quite clear to Lord Knowlton that she held him in disinterest.

She only hoped he would not see that for the lie it was.

Chapter Four

O, what a tangled web we weave,
When first we practice, to deceive.
                                        —Scott, *Marmion*

*I*f Katherine found herself looking forward to the Sunday service with more than an ordinary interest, she assured herself it was mere curiosity over how the vicar would respond to Knowlton's charge to improve his sermons. She told herself she was quite content not to see the earl again.

After leading Robbie to an empty pew, Katherine noticed with a mixed twinge of disappointment and satisfaction that the earl was not in his box. All his talk of a public display of piety had been just that—talk. As she had suspected. Then she grew aware of the sudden hushed silence of the congregation. Trying to dismiss the small thrill that raced through her, she slowly returned her gaze to the earl's box. There he stood, surveying the assembly with an amused smile at the stir his presence created. He caught Katherine's eye and gave her an ostentatious wink. She abruptly dropped her gaze to the hymnal in her hands, wishing she could hide her flaming cheeks. Drat that man!

The service seemed to last for an interminable time. Katherine was unable to appreciate whether Knowlton's talk had had any effect on the vicar, for her attention and her eyes kept straying to the lone man in the Beauchamp family box. She knew she could not allow the earl to dis-

concert her so, yet she felt powerless to control her
thoughts. Even here in church, when her mind should be
on holy matters, she was more aware of his clean, pure
baritone singing "A Mighty Fortress Is Our God" than she
was of the words of praise.

When at last the congregation was dismissed, Katherine
grabbed Robbie and nearly raced out of the church. She
did not want to risk another encounter with the earl while
her thoughts were so disordered. But Robbie darted from
her side the moment they reached the steps, and she was
forced to wait.

"A most edifying sermon, I do declare." Knowlton
stepped up behind her, pitching his voice low so only she
could hear. "Did you not find it so, Mrs. Mayfield?"

Whirling to face him, Katherine did not miss the wicked
twinkle in the earl's eye.

"Most edifying, my lord," she replied, primly lowering
her gaze.

"I must say, I thought the vicar's sermon incorporated
a highly instructive lesson." Knowlton smiled at her discomfort. She was not half so reluctant to be in his presence as she pretended, he knew. It provoked a desire to
see how far he could push her. "It shall be a rare pleasure
to listen to the next sermon if he continues in this
manner."

"Perhaps the repeated exposure to such edifying
thoughts will do you good," she retorted, turning away
abruptly. How dare he express his interest in her by blatantly striking up a conversation in full view of everyone
in the parish? If her name ever became linked with Knowlton's, her reputation would be in tatters. No single woman
was deemed safe with him. Spotting the vicar and his wife
at the church steps, Katherine hastened to join them.

Knowlton determined not to allow Mrs. Mayfield to get
the better of him this time. With quick steps he once again
stood at her side.

"Robbie has made a decided improvement in his Latin,
Mrs. Mayfield," the vicar said to Katherine. "I may make
a scholar of him yet."

"He has been working very hard," Katherine acknowledged, uncomfortably aware of Knowlton's presence again.

"Excellent sermon, vicar," Knowlton interjected with an approving nod.

The vicar beamed at the compliment. "Thank you, my lord. It is a pleasure to have you with us again."

"I think you will have that pleasure often," Knowlton said, with a pointed glance at Katherine. "I have a mind to remain at Warrenton for some time. I find I am learning to enjoy the simpler pleasures of country life."

Katherine frantically glanced about, looking for her son. She could not leave without him, yet every moment she spent in the earl's presence was torture. She nearly collapsed with relief when she heard Robbie's voice. "I will tell him you are pleased at his progress, vicar. If you will excuse me . . ." She executed a brief curtsy and hurried toward her son.

"I want to play with Sam," Robbie announced.

"You can see Sam another day," Katherine said, hastening him toward the lane. "There are chores to be done at home. And I want you to gather blackberries for me today."

"But I wanted to—"

"You will do as I say," she snapped, and then instantly regretted her harsh words. It was not Robbie's fault that the earl disconcerted her so. She would have to take greater care to avoid him next time. In a conciliatory tone she added, "If you pick berries for me as soon as we arrive home, you may have the rest of the afternoon free."

"All right," he said grudgingly. He had secretly nourished hopes of being able to catch a ride in the earl's curricle today. At least there would be time to walk over to Warrenton and maybe talk Knowlton or his groom into another ride in the paddock.

The following morning, Knowlton stretched lazily in his bed, leaning back against the soft pillows. Country living was having a decidedly harmful influence on him—he felt downright slothful having slept so late. If he was not careful, he would soon be rising at farmer's hours. And that would never do.

With a resigned sigh he tossed back the covers and swung his legs over the edge of the bed. As if on cue, Rigsby, his valet, entered. Without a word he picked up Knowlton's blue brocade robe and helped his master into it, then stood aside as Knowlton padded across the thickly carpeted floor into the bath chamber.

It was the only improvement he had installed here at Warrenton, and was worth every penny, the earl thought. The bathing tub itself, fashioned from Italian marble, was large enough for two, as he had proved to his satisfaction more than once. However, it was not the tub itself but the newly installed shower bath of which Knowlton was most fond. The craftily arranged cistern in the attic, combined with the warming stove, provided ample hot water at his command. And there was something very refreshing about drenching oneself in water rather than soaking in it like a stewed chicken.

A discreet knock came at the door while Knowlton toweled himself dry.

"Young Robert is here, my lord," Rigsby announced.

"Has he been to the stables yet?"

"I think not, my lord."

"Have him wait in the morning room, then," said Knowlton, reaching for the clothing Rigsby had laid out on the bed. Smiling to himself as he dressed, Knowlton anticipated Robbie's reaction to the new pony in the stable. He only hoped that Mrs. Mayfield would not cut up too strongly when she discovered the gift. He suspected she was not comfortable with her impecunious status, and would resent anything that she would consider charity. He would have to tread carefully to avoid alienating her.

Knowlton dressed quickly in buckskin breeches and Hessians. Disdaining the formality of a cravat, he tied a simple Belcher scarf around his neck and shrugged himself into his chocolate-colored riding coat.

He exited his room and hastened down the stairs, eager to see the young lad's response to the surprise that awaited him. It would make up for the abominably boring afternoon Knowlton had spent yesterday at Squire Moreton's acquiring the animal.

"Good morning, Robbie," Knowlton greeted, with a laughing glance at the plate of crumbs on the boy's lap. "Breakfast?"

Robbie rose to his feet, his face flushing. He gestured at the tea tray. "They brought this in . . ."

"Excellent idea," Knowlton agreed, taking a large bite of one of the spiced buns. He poured himself a cup of tea and took a seat facing Robbie. "I surmise you are here to continue your riding lessons."

Robbie vigorously nodded his head.

"Did you finish your Latin this morning?"

"Yes, sir. I did five whole pages."

"Admirable, admirable." Knowlton nodded, privately thinking it a miserable task to set before an adventurous boy. It was a measure of Robbie's respect for his mother that he had complied. Knowlton never would have.

The earl quickly drained his cup, snatched another bun from the tray, and rose from his chair.

"I had a slightly different plan today," he explained to Robbie as they walked across the yard to the stables. "Alecto is not the perfect horse for one just learning to ride, so I thought—"

"I know I will do better today," Robbie interjected. "It is only . . . well, it was so high up and she'd never moved so fast before."

"And you performed with creditable skill. I am not taking you off her as punishment, Robbie." Knowlton smiled gently. "I only thought a more suitable mount would speed your progress. Do not fear, I have no more a liking for slugs than you."

He paused before the stable entrance, peering into the darkened corridor.

"Shall I bring the new 'un out?" Frank asked.

Knowlton nodded. "But not saddled or bridled. The lad needs to learn that task as well."

Robbie's eyes grew wide as Frank reappeared with a horse that looked every bit as lively as Alecto but a great deal smaller.

"Does he have a name?"

"He has none," Knowlton replied. "I thought you would perhaps wish to name him."

"Should it be Greek or Latin?" Robbie asked, tentatively reaching out to stroke the chestnut pony's nose.

Knowlton shrugged. "I always believe the master should name his own horse."

"He is mine?" Robbie's eyes widened in wonderment.

The earl grinned. "Now, what use would I have for a

horse this size? Granted, he has a good deal of spirit and
I daresay he could hold his own with nearly any mount in
the stable. But I fear it would be a comical sight with my
legs dangling near the ground."

"Really mine?"

"Really."

The sunny look that had brightened Robbie's face suddenly faded. "But . . . but Mama will not approve, my lord.
I know we cannot afford to keep a horse. Thank you very
much, anyway."

"Now, would I make a gift of something and expect you
to pay for it?" Knowlton chided his young guest. "As long
as he resides in my stable, he is entitled to my hospitality."

"Mama will still say no," Robbie reiterated. "She does
not wish me to join the cavalry."

"Not every lad who rides joins the cavalry," Knowlton
explained. He hesitated over his next words. "I think, Robbie, there is no need for your mother to know about this
present. She really would not understand, would she?"

Robbie grinned at the earl's conspiratorial tone. He understood what a deuced bother mamas could be at times.
"I think that is a capital idea."

"I will expect you to take charge of the creature,"
Knowlton explained. "Frank here will tend to his feed and
watering, but it shall be your job to saddle and bridle him
for riding, and to cool him down and groom him after
every ride."

"I will be glad to do that," Robbie said. "Can I start
now?"

At Knowlton's nod, Frank took the bridle and gave Robbie a quick demonstration on how to put it on the horse.
Even if the animal was a pony, he was still tall enough that
Robbie needed the mounting block to fasten the strap behind the ears. The same procedure was followed with the
saddling, as Knowlton himself checked the tightness of the
girth. Robbie beamed with pride when the earl congratulated him for a job well done.

Knowlton remained in the paddock for an hour, gently
instructing Robbie in the finer points of horsemanship.
With his natural seat, combined with the fearlessness of
youth, the lad would soon make up for his lack of earlier
training, and be a bruising rider within a year's time.

As he watched Robbie's wide grins of delight, Knowlton realized he took genuine pleasure in pleasing the lad. He felt a twinge of guilt, knowing he had first sponsored the connection as a method of ingratiating himself with Mrs. Mayfield, but he found he quite liked Robbie for his own sake. Robbie still carried the wide-eyed wonder of childhood, the fascination with the world that Knowlton had lost so long ago. Maybe Robbie could show him how to see the world through those eyes again, if only briefly.

At last relinquishing Robbie's tutelage to Frank, Knowlton saddled his own mount and headed out across the estate for his own belated morning ride. The ripe heads of grain were close to bursting with their seeds. Harvest would start in a few short weeks. It was a project involving skilled teamwork, a joy to watch as well as participate in.

And once the last shock was tied, the last load hauled to the granary for threshing, there was the celebration. Knowlton looked forward to it with eager anticipation. It was one of the few times of the year that the aristocrats and gentry rubbed elbows with the laborers, as class barriers tumbled down with foaming mugs of ale and the riotous contests of strength, skill, and speed that made up the annual Warrenton Harvest Home. And perhaps during the evening there would be the opportunity for a dance with the lovely Mrs. Mayfield. He really needed to accelerate his attempts to undermine her resistance. The harvest festival was the perfect setting. He made a mental note to remind the musicians to play lots of waltzes. He intended to dance them all with her.

Katherine fought against her concern at Robbie's lengthy absences from home. She suspected he and his crony Sam were up to the usual boyish pursuits—fishing or some such activity—and she did not want to smother Robbie with too much mothering. It was a constant effort to fight against her need to keep him close. Robbie had bloomed over the summer, rapidly losing some of the boyishness within him. It momentarily saddened her to see her baby beginning to show signs of the man he would grow into. But it was the lot of every mother to experience that bittersweet sense of pride and loss.

She reached again for her sewing. There had been time,

at least, for her to start making Robbie some new shirts for the winter. With any luck she would have his wardrobe in good order before the rush of sewing for the fall and winter assemblies began. It was peaceful to sit in the sunlit yard in back of the cottage and do her own work, for a change.

Katherine looked up in pleased surprise when she heard the rear gate thud shut. "Hello, Robbie."

He started guiltily.

"Did you have an entertaining afternoon?" Katherine asked.

"Yes," was his faint reply.

Katherine patted the bench next to her. "Tell me about your fun," she said invitingly.

Robbie's face took on a reluctant expression. "Let me wash up first," he said.

His response aroused her suspicions. Robbie never liked to wash unless he was reminded.

"Oh, no, come talk now," she said pleasantly.

Warily he took his place at her side.

Once in the closer confines of the garden bench, it was obvious to both her eyes and nose that Robbie had been up to some amazing mischief.

"You smell decidedly of horse," she observed.

"Oh, well, we were walking and . . . um . . . we stopped and petted this horse that was in the field."

She frowned. "Do you wish to try again?"

He looked at his toes. "No, ma'am."

"Robert Mayfield, I want to know where you went and whom you were with."

Still staring at his feet, he mumbled, "At Warrenton."

"You were at Warrenton?"

"The earl said I could visit there anytime I wanted," he said defensively. "Remember?"

"I am certain the earl was only being polite when he issued that invitation," she said. "He has more important concerns than to be pestered by ten-year-old boys."

"But he does not mind," Robbie protested. "He says he likes my visits. And when he is busy, Frank is there to help me with my po . . ."

"Your what?"

Robbie clamped his mouth shut.

Katherine closed her eyes, willing herself to retain her temper.

"Robbie, what exactly goes on when you visit Warrenton?"

He stood silent, his eyes wary and defiant.

"Robbie, if you do not tell me this instant what is going on, I will forbid you to leave this house again."

"Lord Knowlton is teaching me to ride," he admitted.

Katherine bit down on her lip to restrain her anger. "You did not think to ask my permission for embarking on this project?"

"I thought you would say no."

Katherine sighed. Robbie was right, she probably would have. That was no longer the point. Robbie had been lying to her about his whereabouts for several weeks now.

"I am disappointed that you could not see your way clear to telling me what you have been doing—and that you have lied to me."

Robbie frowned. "I did not want to lie, Mama. But it is so wonderful to ride! Knowlton says I have a natural seat and it will not be long before anyone is unable to tell I have not been riding since I was little."

As the enthusiastic words tumbled out and his eyes lit with excitement, he reminded Katherine of his father. Robert had always responded with the same animation when he was excited. She knew what he would say if he was standing here beside her now. That she was coddling the boy. That Robbie was ten and needed to spend less time with his mother and more time with boys his own age—and other grown-ups as well. And that he should learn how to ride.

Katherine sighed, knowing that to say no now would cause more harm than good. "You should have spoken to me about this earlier," she said, attempting to look stern.

"Yes, ma'am." Robbie looked at her with apprehension. "Will I . . . will you still let me learn?"

Katherine nodded, then found herself nearly knocked off the bench as Robbie flew at her, grabbing her in a grateful hug.

"Oh, thank you," he gasped. "I promise I will be very, very

careful. That is why Knowlton bought the pony—because the other horses were all so big, he said even if I did fall off it would not be such a long way to the ground, and—"

His words finally registered. "Lord Knowlton bought you a pony?"

Robbie reddened at his untimely revelation.

"Robbie?"

"Just a small one," he whispered.

Katherine's control snapped. This was outside of enough. Knowlton must have known that she would not be pleased with Robbie's riding lessons. But to actually buy him his own horse to ride . . . Tears of anger and humiliation stung at her eyes. She took a deep breath.

"Robbie, I should like you to go and wash up now. Dinner will be ready soon."

As soon as Robbie entered the house, she gave vent to her anger with an elaborate oath. Damn Knowlton and his charity. She was well aware she could not afford to provide Robbie with the usual possessions of a young boy of his class. But that did not give the earl the right to do it for her. Her cheeks burned with humiliation. Why was it that every time she thought she had reached an accommodation with her current status, something like this came along to remind her of all the things that were no longer possible?

She clenched her hands in an attempt to still her rage. This life had been her choice, she reminded herself. She had known at the outset that there would be times like these, when the poverty she had sentenced them to would grate on her soul. But there were worse things in this life than poverty. She and Robbie were still together, and that was more important than all the ponies in the world.

Robbie would be unhappy with her, she knew, when she informed Lord Knowlton that her son could not accept such a present from him. But she could not allow her love for Robbie to overcome her scruples. Tomorrow she would tell Lord Knowlton exactly what she thought of his gift.

Chapter Five

Virtue, how frail it is!
  Friendship how rare!

—Shelley, *Mutability*

*K*atherine's fingers trembled slightly as she struggled to fasten the tiny buttons on the back of her gown. A night's sleep had not lessened her anger with the earl. He had no right to involve himself so deeply in Robbie's life, teaching her son how to ride and presenting him with a pony. Such arrogance! She would put an end to it once and for all. Robbie would be disappointed, but this was something she simply could not tolerate.

She was almost grateful to the earl, in a way, for precipitating this crisis. For now she truly had a reason to be angry with him. At every encounter, Katherine had found it more and more difficult to retain her firm barrier against his immeasurable charm, despite the danger he represented. Today, after such a provocation, it would be easier to keep him at arm's length.

Anxiously, she surveyed her appearance in the cracked glass above her dressing table. In her Sunday best gown of dove-gray silk, a survivor from her days of mourning for Robert, she made a respectable sight. There would be no flour smudges to amuse the earl today. And with her outrageous hair tucked under her bonnet, she would present the very image of a responsible, concerned, and efficient lady. A lady whose words would be heard and heeded.

Hastening down the stairs, she gathered her cloak and bonnet and moved into the dining parlor to use the sideboard mirror to ensure she had tied her ribbons just so.

Satisfied at last with her presentation, she grabbed up her reticule and stepped outside.

Despite the bright sky, there was a fall chill in the air and she was glad to have her cloak about her shoulders. With businesslike strides she set out for Warrenton. The lion would be bearded in his den.

"Excuse me, my lord, but there is a Mrs. Mayfield here to see you."

Knowlton started with surprise at the butler's announcement, and he stepped from behind his desk. He could barely believe his good fortune. He had been trying to think of a reasonable excuse to invite her to Warrenton, and now she appeared as if in answer to his wish.

"Please escort the lady in, Hutchins. And have a tea tray sent up."

From the moment she had stepped over the threshold of Warrenton, Katherine's courage had begun to desert her. As she followed the butler up the stairs, she suspected there were few country homes that matched the splendor and opulence of this house. Katherine found it odd to have a rakish bachelor in possession of such worldly magnificence. She fleetingly longed to turn tail and run; then she mentally shook herself. It was she who had a grievance, not the earl. It was she who dealt from a position of strength. He was the one who had acted in error.

Knowlton's lips curved into a welcoming smile as she entered his study.

"Good day, Mrs. Mayfield. How delightful to have you visit me at last." He nodded to Hutchins to withdraw and bring the tray. "Allow me to take your bonnet and cloak."

"That will not be necessary—"

He cut her off with a peremptory wave of his hand. "No, I insist. You must stay for tea and whatever else Hutchins brings from the kitchen." He reached out an imperious hand for her outer clothing.

Katherine ignored his outstretched hand, clutching her reticule tightly in her nervousness. She felt all her confidence draining and she strove to regain control of the situation. She was here with a complaint, and she would not let his honeyed words soothe her into forgetting her purpose.

"I am not here for a social call, Lord Knowlton," she

began, fixing him with a stern look. "I have come because I was very upset to discover that not only have you been teaching my son to ride but also you have purchased a mount for him with all the attendant accoutrements. I simply cannot allow such a thing."

"And pray tell why not?" Knowlton kept his expression blank.

"You have no right to present my son with expensive gifts."

Knowlton suppressed the urge to grin at the indignant look on her face. He did not think she would appreciate humor at the moment. "You find it improper? I would agree with you—had I given *you* a gift. But I hardly think it wrong for me to present Robbie with a token of my friendship."

"A horse is hardly a 'token of friendship,' " she retorted angrily.

"It is also a gift not worthy of such anger." He knew his deliberate calmness would ruffle her further.

"Certainly, you are aware that I have no means to maintain a horse for Robbie. Why else do you think a ten-year-old boy raised in the country does not ride?"

"Robbie's horse may reside in my stable. That was my intention when I purchased it for him."

"And for how long?" Katherine lifted her chin indignantly. "At some point in time, responsibility for its care will devolve upon me." Her expression turned bitter as she acknowledged the truth of her situation. "I cannot afford it. It is better that he should never have access to an animal, for he then will not know what he is lacking."

"He will be a poor cavalry officer if he cannot ride." Knowlton could not hide his mocking smile.

"I have no intention of allowing Robbie to join the military."

He watched her stiffen into a prim position, so in contrast to that distracting hair that peeked teasingly from under her outmoded bonnet. His hands itched to free it.

"Oh, come now, Mrs. Mayfield. Your own husband was an officer in the cavalry." He smiled more benignly now, his head tilted to one side. "It is an honorable career."

"It is a highly unsuitable one for a young man of little means," she retorted. "It is an air-castle dream without any foundation in reality. If there is no money to maintain a horse, there is even less to purchase a commission."

Knowlton hesitated, wishing to choose his words carefully. He could easily lose whatever advantage he had gained if he misspoke. "I realize, Mrs. Mayfield, that your financial situation is precarious and I respect the economies it forces you to follow. I fail to see where the gift to your son of something you are not capable of purchasing yourself can be such a problem."

"Perhaps because you have always been able to buy everything you want," she said heatedly. "When have you ever had to measure out your pennies and make the choice between a serviceable pair of shoes or a sack of flour?"

"I am aware that I live a fortunate life." He flashed her a self-deprecating smile. "But if I can afford to give a horse to your son, what is your objection?"

"It is far too expensive a gift for him to accept. Had I known of it from the beginning, I would have instructed him to refuse it."

"To what purpose? Should Robbie suffer because your pride is wounded?" He gestured to his booted foot. "Do you have any idea what one of these boots cost, Mrs. Mayfield? More than I paid for the horse, saddle, bridle, and a year's worth of feed. And I have a closet full of boots like these."

He continued speaking in a softer tone. "I know it is galling to want to provide the best for one you love, and not be able to. If a friend is willing to present a gift, it is only churlish to refuse. It gave me great pleasure to present the pony to Robbie. Do not sacrifice Robbie's happiness on the altar of your pride, Mrs. Mayfield. Do you honestly think you will achieve anything noble with your stubbornness?"

Katherine considered the wisdom of his words. He was right in saying Robbie would suffer because of her inability to accept what was in effect charity. Tears stinging her eyes, she shook her head.

"Then we will consider the matter settled. Robbie may keep his pony. And I promise I will consult you before I make any more purchases on his behalf. Agreed?"

Katherine nodded slowly. "Agreed, my lord."

Knowlton flashed her a warm smile. "That was not so

difficult, was it? Now, please, Mrs. Mayfield, take off your bonnet and cloak and we can sit and enjoy the refreshments that should be arriving momentarily. I do not want your enmity. Can we not be friends?"

She stood silently, wavering in her resolve. Despite his air of wounded innocence, she still sensed that danger lurked in a "friendship" with Lord Knowlton. His reputation precluded the idea of an innocuous friendship with a woman.

"Come now, Mrs. Mayfield, I will not bite. Despite the lurid stories I am certain you have heard, I am not in the habit of seducing ladies in my study. At least, not unless they are willing. Stay and have some tea." He again extended his hand for her bonnet and cloak.

Surprised at how little shocked she was by his bold manner, Katherine had a sinking feeling that she had somehow lost the fight as she untied her bonnet ribbons. She did not want to be at her ease with this man. She was angry—nay, furious—with him. Yet his friendly smile was most disarming.

"I had hoped you would grace Warrenton with a visit one day." The earl smiled as he guided her to a chair. "We are beginning to think of Robbie as another member of the household. It is only fitting that his mother should be a familiar face as well."

Katherine opened her mouth to speak but closed it again as Hutchins came in with the tea tray. For the next few minutes she busied herself with the tea and filling her plate with the dainty cakes Knowlton insisted on pressing upon her.

"My weakness," he confessed as he popped one of the richly buttered delicacies into his mouth. "It is fortunate I allow my cook to prepare them only once a week or I would be as fat as a prince in no time."

She raised an eyebrow at his sly dig at the Regent.

"So tell me, Mrs. Mayfield, why did you and Robbie decide to settle in Lincolnshire? Do you not have family elsewhere?"

Katherine stiffened slightly at the polite interrogative. "The lease terms on the cottage are very generous," she replied evasively.

He sighed imperceptibly, knowing he would get no more

information out of her. There was a slight air of mystery
about Robbie's mother that intrigued him. For a brief moment he wondered if she really was a widow—perhaps she
had merely been the mistress of that dashing cavalry officer.
It would explain her straitened financial circumstances. Yet
would a cavalry officer have left his sword to his mistress?
It was a puzzle.

"I understand Robbie is taking lessons with the vicar,"
he said, trying to hit on a conversational topic that would
elicit a positive response from her.

"He is. I fear Robbie fell behind in his studies this last
year when we were in the process of moving. I tried to keep
him caught up, but he is well beyond my limited abilities in
Greek and Latin."

"He will be ready for school one of these days, then."

She flushed. "Perhaps."

Knowlton berated himself for such a stupid remark.
School was very likely just the type of luxury that Mrs.
Mayfield could not afford. He felt a fleeting twinge of anger
at that unknown cavalry officer for leaving his widow in
such precarious financial circumstances.

Katherine busied herself with refilling her cup. She hated
Knowlton's solicitous concern. She had deliberately chosen
her path; if she was beginning to have doubts that she had
made the right decision, she was still unconvinced that it
was a disaster either. It was much easier to forget her situation without his subtle references to her poverty.

"Harvest will start next week," Knowlton said, attempting to ease the awkwardness in the air. "It is tradi-
tional that the lord of Warrenton throw a party for his
tenants and laborers at its completion. It has developed
into a rather ostentatious affair, I am afraid," he said with
a self-deprecating grin. "Footraces and pie-eating contests
for the lads, more brawny competitions for the men, while
the ladies display their talents in the culinary and domestic
arts. I fully expect you and young Robbie to attend."

"I do not think—"

"Consider it an order," he said sternly. "From your
landlord."

"Put that way, how can I refuse?" She flashed him a
withering glance.

Ignoring her irritation, Knowlton allowed a slow, sensual

smile to light his face. "Your presence will make it a memorable event."

Katherine concentrated on sipping her tea. What a provoking man! He expended considerable effort to disarm her concerns about Robbie and the horse, then reawakened all her fears with his broad hints of interest and that wicked smile. What kind of a devilish game was he playing?

After Mrs. Mayfield's departure, Knowlton sat back in his worn leather chair with a self-satisfied smirk. The victory over Robbie's pony pleased him. Whatever else came between him and Mrs. Mayfield, he did not want to see Robbie hurt. He must keep his relationships with the lovely widow and her son separate. He knew that now, and felt a twinge of guilt for ever thinking he could use Robbie to ingratiate himself with his mother. It simply would not do.

There were other methods of conquering Mrs. Mayfield's fortress. His face broke into a broad grin as he remembered how her emotions had swung from one end of the pendulum to the other and back during their conversation. He meant to keep her off balance, so she would not be able to readily marshal her defenses. Let her wonder just what his game was. As long as he did not rush his fences, it might be just the proper strategy to take.

He did not know when the pursuit of a woman had so entertained him. Perhaps that had been the source of so much of his boredom in London—there had been no need of pursuit. From the diamonds of the demimonde to the leaders of the *ton,* they had pursued *him.* His only problem had been in deciding where to bestow his favors among the many offers. No wonder he had grown jaded. The pursuit of Mrs. Mayfield was just the thing he needed to restore his enthusiasm.

Despite her present poverty, he suspected she had known much better times. It would certainly account for her stubborn refusal to accept assistance. Her adamant attitude only showed how much she resented her current situation. That was something he could easily rectify.

She would not be as skilled a lover as he was accustomed to, but that was no matter. Technique could easily be taught, if the pupil was willing. And with that flaming hair, he had no doubt of her suitability. It would be only one more delightful advantage to the situation—the opportunity to awaken a less-experienced woman to her sensual nature. Although he had been often pleased, satisfied, and sometimes even a little amazed at the skills of his many bed partners, there was something to be said for molding a partner to suit his own particular preferences. It would be a most pleasurable task.

The anticipation of the prize—for he held no doubts of his ultimate success with Mrs. Mayfield—began to have a decided effect. Briefly, he contemplated a minor dalliance to take the edge off his growing hunger. There were several delectable prospects within easy riding distance of Warrenton. But no, he decided. It was all part of the game. His enforced celibacy would only heighten his pleasure at the pent-up release. He would await Mrs. Mayfield's capitulation with growing eagerness.

It was time, however, that he did take steps to further his aims. He must move quickly to solidify the gains made today. With the Harvest Home less than two weeks away, if the weather held and the crops were brought in on time, he had a perfect goal to aim for. He would slowly reel Mrs. Mayfield into his net, then pounce when he judged her sufficiently entangled.

Knowlton shifted in his chair, his mind caught in a reverie that involved removing every last hairpin from Mrs. Mayfield's upswept tresses, allowing that flaming mass to swirl about her shoulders. Then, with a shrug at such precipitate thinking, he cleared his mind of her. He would never admit to being *bored* at Warrenton, but he did concede he would not mind some company. That matter could easily be remedied; the shooting would be excellent in a few weeks and he knew there would be no lack of takers for any invitations he tendered.

Seb Cole would come—if he was not already committed to a rendezvous at some other house with whatever new flirt he had acquired. And he really should ask Hartford, and Drummond—and Pelham was never averse to a convivial gathering. And of course, Wentworth.

At that name, he paused. He thought Somers would come, but now that he was married, with a fat, drooling little daughter ensconced in his nursery, he might not wish to. Marriage had a way of changing a man. Knowlton would never criticize his closest friend for marrying, although that event had shocked Knowlton to the core. It was too close for comfort.

Knowlton had nothing against marriage, actually. It was a useful institution—for some. He had a deep certainty, though, that it was not for him. Constancy was not a part of his nature, and no woman had ever captured his interest long enough for him to doubt that supposition. He preferred matters as they were—even if his last mistress had driven him to boredom in less than a month. Knowlton shrugged. He would take care to choose more carefully in the future. He suspected Mrs. Mayfield would not begin to bore him for a long, long time. That thought set off another reverie, this one involving the creamy white shoulders that he knew must lie beneath Mrs. Mayfield's high-necked gowns.

Katherine was not surprised to find Robbie waiting in the parlor when she returned to the cottage. She saw how he struggled with his desire to know what had transpired at Warrenton, and his very real fear that she had put an end to his riding.

"I talked with Lord Knowlton," she said, knowing she must put his fears to rest at once. "And we both decided that for now, you may keep the pony and continue your riding lessons."

"I can?"

"You may."

Robbie hurtled across the room and embraced her in a breathless hug. "Thank you, Mama."

"I want you to continue to be very polite to the earl," she continued. "He is very generous, and I want to make certain that he knows how well you appreciate his efforts."

"Oh, I will," Robbie said. "Can I go up to Warrenton now? Atlas will need his exercise."

She smiled lovingly at his eagerness. "Yes, you may go. Be careful, now."

"I will," Robbie called back over his shoulder as he raced out the door.

Katherine sat down with a sigh. He was growing and changing so before her eyes. It would not be so long before he was a young man, and what then? She was going to have to do some very serious thinking about Robbie's future. Knowlton's innocent remark had only reminded her of the difficulties ahead.

Her mind drifted back to her talk with the earl. The man was most exasperating, and she suspected he acted so deliberately to goad her into some unladylike reaction. Yet his interest in Robbie seemed sincere and she could not honestly say that she minded. Robbie had so little contact with adult men; the vicar was the only other alternative. And although she was quite aware that Knowlton was not a stand-in for a father, she did appreciate the time and trouble he took with Robbie. It was difficult for a lad to be without a father, particularly one as enthusiastic and adventurous as Robbie. Knowlton did not seem to be dismayed by the boyish high spirits that often threatened to overwhelm her. It was only one more example of how much Robert's death, and her own actions afterward, had affected them.

For Robbie's sake, at least, she would try to maintain an amiable relationship with the earl. She did not need to have much contact with him, which she thought was all to the good. His presence made her uneasy, as if he could see through all her carefully built defenses to the woman inside. The very part of her that she did not want him, of all people, to see. It would only encourage him.

She half-believed, after his protestations of friendship today, that they could meet in amiability, without her having to fear any untoward behavior on his part. And she was forced to acknowledge that he had not overtly done anything to cause her alarm. He had jokingly talked of his reputation as a rake, implying that the rumors were overblown, and always assuring her that he would never act against her will. But it was the unuttered aspects of his communication that most disturbed her, the knowing grins, coolly appreciative glances, and appraising looks that caused her the most distress. That man could say more with a glance than with all the words in Christendom. And none of it proper.

Chapter Six

When we arise all in the morn,
For to sound our harvest horn.
We will sing to the full jubilee, jubilee;
We will sing to the full jubilee.
                    —Nineteenth-century harvest song

*K*nowlton's valet awakened him in the cool hours before dawn on the first morning of harvest. Shivering at the chill in the room, Knowlton quickly donned his well-worn breeches and gratefully pulled a warm woolen coat over his shirt. Once the sun rose, the coat would be quickly discarded, but at this moment it was a welcome bar against the predawn air.

The rest of the house was beginning to stir as Knowlton made his way to the kitchen for a hasty breakfast of bread and cheese. He simply could not stomach the massive harvest breakfast that was presented to the laborers at the granary. He would take a more substantial repast at the noontime dinner. Knowlton was filled with an eagerness to be off to the fields.

Ever since he could remember, he had loved the harvesttime. Beginning in June with the first hay cut, harvest continued in one way or another until October, when the last of the fruits had been pulled from the trees. But it was the corn harvests of late August that really defined harvest for him. The glorious golden fields were at their peak, the stalks of grain drooping under the weight of their ripe heads. Even the smallest breeze sent rippling waves across the land, like the waves radiating from a stone tossed in a pond. In less than a week it would be gone, the fields re-

duced to bare stalks of stubble. It was a massive undertaking, a true test of teamwork and organization, a symbol
of man's mastery over nature.

He had watched the workers in his youth, sneaking out
of the house before dawn and not returning until the men
had stopped for the night. His father could not understand
his fascination with the harvest. Corn was money, and the
previous Earl of Knowlton had had no opposition to that.
However, he cared little for the process by which it was
earned, as long as everything went well and his coffers were
filled. But to his son, there was something elemental in
watching the men with their razor-sharp sickles moving
down the rows like a giant tide, felling everything that
stood in their path. As he grew older, he became more and
more involved in the process, bringing beer and ale to the
workers in the fields, taking the sickles to the smith for
sharpening in the evening. Then, in that glorious summer
when he was sixteen, he had been given his own sickle by
the indulgent bailiff and let loose on the fields.

The men had not laughed at him, though he could not
cut at nearly the same rate as the more experienced laborers. His hands had been bleeding and blistered by the end
of the day, and he could barely straighten his back, but he
doggedly, if foolishly, kept coming every day until the last
stalk had been cut. And in the process, he had earned the
grudging respect of the workers, who looked upon the
young lord in a new light. Many of those same men, or their
sons, still worked for him, and the bonds forged during the
yearly weeks in the fields had lasted through the years.
Knowlton treated his tenants well, and they knew it was
due to personal interest, not self-serving obligation.

Most of the workers had finished their breakfast and already gathered at the foot of the first field when Knowlton
arrived. He greeted the men with a wave or nod or a
friendly call of a name. He saw Robbie Mayfield standing
beside the fence, looking a bit awed and forlorn. Knowlton
guided his horse to him and dismounted. It would increase
Robbie's status to be seen with him.

"Excited?" Knowlton asked.

Robbie nodded. "I hardly slept a wink last night," he
confided.

"That will not be the case tonight, I'd wager," said

Knowlton, suspecting the boy would be ready to drop with exhaustion by midafternoon. He would learn. "Is your mama to be here today?"

"She will be here to help the parish ladies serve dinner," Robbie said.

"The men are ready, my lord," Taggert, the bailiff, called to Knowlton.

The earl clapped Robbie on the shoulder. "Do not try to do everything today," he cautioned. "Harvest lasts many days and we do not want to lose you too soon."

Knowlton stripped off his coat and poured himself a foaming tankard of ale from the barrel at the edge of the field. Raising it in salute to the workers, he took a large swallow of the strong brew, then gestured for the work crew to take their own sample. It was customary, this first tasting of the harvest beer. As the day wore on and their throats choked with dust and chaff, they would not appreciate the taste, but only the moisture. When all had sampled the brew, Knowlton took the sickle handed him by Taggert and raised it above his head as a signal to the workers to form their staggered line. Behind the men stood the women and children, who would bundle the cut stalks into sheaves. Stepping to the edge of the field, Knowlton bent to cut the first swath. Harvest had begun.

At the sound of the dinner horn, Knowlton straightened cautiously. After stooping for hours, his back ached horribly, if the truth were told, but he would never complain aloud. He no longer worked the entire harvest; it was an indulgence that he could not justify when he knew there were men more skilled than he who could accomplish the task with greater ease. But Knowlton persisted in cutting on the first day, and the last, to remind his workers that their lord was not too proud to toil alongside them, and to remind himself of the value of the land that was the source of his family's wealth.

He pulled off his sweat-soaked shirt and wiped his face. God, it was hot today. The thought of cool water, wet beer, and the noonday meal quickened his steps across the stubbled ruin that marked the workers' path.

Katherine had arrived at the field an hour ago, curious to see this ritual labor and willing to lend her hand in the feeding of the workers. She hoped Robbie had fared well. It had been thoughtful of Lord Knowlton to invite him to participate.

"Mama, Mama." Robbie raced up to her, his face flushed with excitement. "Is it not wonderful?"

She smiled at his enthusiasm. In truth, there had been little for her to see, for the workers had moved an impressive distance down the field. After the meal, perhaps she would stay and watch for a while.

Robbie danced at her side as they followed the wagon hauling the food and drink to the workers. The sheer quantity of food provided by the earl impressed her. Knowlton did not stint his workers. There were cold meat and pies, bread, cheese, puddings and, of course, the ubiquitous beer and ale. She wondered dryly how the workers could even stand at the end of a harvest day with the quantity of beer that they drank. Eight quarts was a prodigious amount for anyone to consume.

She could see the workers now as the laden food wagon rolled to a stop. They stood in small groups, laughing and joking while they traded gibes about each other's prowess with the sickle. A few men stood about the water barrels on the wagon, eager to wash the grit and dust of the field from their bodies before the noonday meal. Katherine turned to speak to Robbie, when she caught sight of the earl.

He was standing beside the wagon, his hand curled about the ladle he dipped into the barrel of fresh, cool water. Katherine could not tear her eyes away from him. The form-fitting breeches, riding low over his narrow hips, only emphasized the hard, muscled plane of his abdomen. As he turned, she nearly gasped at the sight of the dark, curling hairs that trailed down his belly, disappearing into the waistband of his breeches. It was an all-too-clear reminder of what lay lower, and Katherine was stunned to have such thoughts enter her mind. She quickly raised her eyes, but the sight of his upper torso did little to settle her equilibrium. She watched in fascination as he poured water over his upper body and arms, her eyes following each rivulet as it traced its path down his bronzed skin.

As if sensing her gaze, Knowlton turned slowly. His gray eyes met hers and a lazy smile creased his face. Katherine's cheeks flamed, but she did not turn away quickly enough to miss the ostentatious wink he directed at her. She wanted to take to her heels and not stop until she was safely back at the cottage, with every door and window bolted against him. But she knew that would be no protection against the traitorous thoughts that danced through her mind.

"How nice of you to offer your help with the harvest, Mrs. Mayfield."

Knowlton's words caused Katherine to freeze, afraid of what her eyes would reveal if she faced him. Yet she would look foolish beyond belief if she tried to converse with him with her back turned.

Turning toward him, she took care to keep her eyes averted. "I think I will find it an interesting experience."

Katherine realized her mistake instantly. There was no relief in keeping her gaze lowered, for it directed her glance to that thatch of dark, curling hair that swept up across his abdomen from the edge of his breeches. Katherine hastily raised her eyes to meet Knowlton's knowing gaze.

"Poor Mrs. Mayfield," he teased. "She cannot decide what is worse—a half-naked man's chest or his face." Deliberately he began to towel the droplets of water off his chest with his crumpled shirt.

Katherine's cheeks flamed. "If you had any decency, you would not be parading around in such a state of undress," she said through clenched teeth.

"If I had any decency, Mrs. Mayfield, you would not even think twice about the situation." He grinned wickedly. "Why, if Mr. Ashe removed his shirt, I doubt you would have any reaction at all."

She had a strong urge to slap that silly smirk off his face. He did this on purpose, she knew, but his aim puzzled her. If anything was guaranteed to cause her to draw away in alarm, it was his outrageous behavior. He took such pains to deny his rakish reputation, yet now he rashly dispelled his protestations with his actions. What was he trying to accomplish—beyond leaving her inarticulate with irritation?

He pulled his damp shirt over his head, covering himself, but for Katherine the damage had been done. The image of that muscled chest, the dark hairs swirling into patterned whorls, was emblazoned on her mind.

Knowlton casually took her elbow and led her to the other side of the cart.

"I am hungry," he said. "And it is your job to feed me." He thrust a plate into her hands.

Katherine fumed silently, filling the plate to overflowing with every bit of food she could. Watching him from the corner of her eye as he leaned casually against the wagon side, his arms folded over that now-hidden chest, she again rued the day she had decided not to quit the neighborhood. She busied herself with the food, studiously avoiding the earl until she shoved the heaping plate into his grasp.

"Oh, good," he said, eyeing the pile of food with feigned enthusiasm. "I am starved. And thirsty. Some ale, if you please, Mrs. Mayfield?"

Her hands itched to dump the foaming mug over the top of his aristocratic head. But she somehow knew that if she did, it would be his victory and not hers. She contented herself with ignoring him for the remainder of the work break.

Knowlton grinned inwardly every time he caught a glimpse of her bustling about the food wagon. He knew she avoided him intentionally, and reckoned that a triumph. Mrs. Mayfield must be closer to surrender than he had thought, if the sight of his half-naked body could inflame her so. There had been time to catch a glimpse of the look in her eyes before she turned from him. He recognized admiration—and desire—when he saw it. He could not have planned things better if he tried. He was almost tempted to remain with the harvesters for the duration, if it would quicken the outcome of the campaign.

But fruits too often displayed might pale with familiarity. Far better that she have time to think on and remember what she had seen today during the next week. It would make the last day of the harvest all the sweeter. He was becoming a master at controlling his anticipation, and if it had half the effect on Mrs. Mayfield that it had on him, she would be a quivering blob of jelly by next week. The thought cheered him as he picked up the sickle. His muscles were already beginning to stiffen, and if he did not get back to the field, he doubted he would be able to continue for much longer.

    *   *   *

Robbie could barely keep his eyes open when Katherine finally dragged him home. The men were still cutting when she left the field, but there was no point in Robbie exhausting himself the first day. Katherine stood over him while he scrubbed his arms and face, then tucked him into bed. She was certain he was asleep before she reached his door.

She smiled at his enjoyment of the day. He had been so eager to help. Harvest was a fascinating process; she had been glad to participate herself. If working at the harvest meant she and Robbie could eat with the workers and avoid the expense of a week's meals, all the better.

Today, trading gossip with the other women, Katherine for the first time felt a part of the community. At first she had been surprised to learn the vicar's wife and daughters always attended harvest, but they explained it had long been a tradition in the parish. The earl's household prepared the food, and the parish ladies served. It made harvest go faster, and by freeing up the laborer's wives to help in the field, it put a few extra pennies in the farmers' coffers. And since the earl held the living, it was only thoughtful on their part to help him with the harvest.

They had also told her more about the Harvest Home, the premier celebration in the neighborhood each year. Knowlton intended it for the tenantry and villagers, but Mrs. Ashe said the gentry came from miles around as well. It was the only festivity at Warrenton that the mothers felt comfortable sending their daughters to, she confided. Not that she wished to speak ill of the earl, for he was a good man. But there had been more than one party at the house with women that no God-fearing member of the parish would wish to associate with. Mrs. Ashe did give the earl credit for keeping his hands off the local lasses. He had done nothing to earn the enmity of the neighborhood.

Unbidden, the image of Knowlton, with rivulets of water rolling down his torso, rose again in Katherine's mind. She shook her head as if to rid her brain of the mental picture. He was even more audaciously attractive than Robert, she realized with a start, shocked that such a comparison came to her. Knowlton knew the power of his attraction, and used it with a skill she was forced to admire. Those expressive gray eyes, which could change in an instant from cool cynicism to smoky warmth, haunted her thoughts.

Her pure, physical reaction to Knowlton shook her more than she cared to admit. It stirred up emotions and passions that she had struggled to subdue during the six long years of her widowhood, for passion was a luxury she could not afford. At best, it was a transient emotion, and at worst, it could bring disaster. But today the earl had shown her just how close to the surface those feelings lay, and how easily they could spring back to life.

It was foolish in the extreme, for there was no respectable outcome to any passing fancy he might entertain of her. She had no illusions whatsoever about her status in his eyes—dalliance perhaps, but nothing more. She knew his reputation as a womanizer, and he had done nothing to dispel that notion from the day they met. On the contrary, he had done everything to confirm it. If she had not been a fool, she would have packed up their belongings and hustled herself and Robbie into the next county within hours of that first meeting.

Yet she had not, and it became apparent to her that she was being drawn deeper and deeper into his web, losing her will to resist his blatant charm. She was lonely; she did want for companionship, and the earl would only be too eager to provide it. She simply could not let him disturb her so. She would have to keep her own emotions firmly in check during her dealings with him. From now on, she would be immune to his wiles and tricks. Buoyed by her new confidence, she picked up the lamp and made her way up the stairs to bed. As long as she remained steadfast in her resistance, she was safe.

So why did that thought depress her?

Chapter Seven

The Mellow Autumn came, and with it came
The promised party, to enjoy its sweets.
—Byron, Don Juan

*T*he day of Warrenton's Harvest Home dawned clear and sunny. Knowlton hummed a bawdy ditty as he wrapped the intricate starched length of cravat around his neck, weaving it into an impeccable knot *à la Warrenton*. It was deucedly foolish to dress so formally for an outdoor party, but the tenantry expected their lord to look like, well, a lord. He could only be grateful they did not expect him to appear in white satin knee breeches with a *chapeau bras* under his arm. Ah, well, by the early evening he would have discarded most of this tomfoolery. He stuck a fine ruby stickpin in his neckcloth, fastened two fobs to his chain, and looked to Rigsby for assistance in donning his skin-hugging coat.

Taking the back stairs, Knowlton quickly made his way to the kitchen. That room was full of bustling servants, with Cook up to her elbows in flour as she prepared the last-minute dainties for the feast. Knowlton grabbed a piece of sugared apple out from under her nose, earning himself a scowl, which he returned with a laugh. He exited the house and circled around to the front, noting with approval that the long tables were already set out on the south lawn. His staff bustled about, laying out the tablecloths and setting up the serving dishes. Across the drive, the livestock pens awaited their customers. Satisfied that all was going according to custom, Knowlton strolled back into the house through the terrace doors.

The large drawing-room table was piled high with wrapped packages, cups of silver, and beribboned medallions. He smiled. It gave him great pleasure to hand out the various prizes and awards. The trinkets were not much, but they were treasured and valued by their winners. He knew many a farmhouse that still displayed prizes won during his grandfather's day. It cost him little, yet cemented his tenants' loyalty.

He circled the room, glancing in dismay at the mantel clock. The guests would not be arriving for at least an hour, and there was no way of knowing when *she* would arrive. He had no particular plans for dealing with Mrs. Mayfield today, preferring to wait and see what opportunities developed. But he was quite certain that he would have made significant progress in his pursuit by the end of the evening. He had let the anticipation build for long enough. It was time to reap the fruits of his sacrifice.

"Now, Robbie, promise you will not eat too many sweets." Katherine could see the tables groaning under the weight of the food upon them. The earl's party promised to be as lavish a display as rumor held. "And be careful of your clothes. I do not think those breeches will stand for another patching."

"Yes, Mama," Robbie replied absently, his mind on the delights ahead. Sam had said there would be more food than he could imagine, and games and races. He wished there had been some pony races, for then he could ride Atlas. But Knowlton said there were too few lads in the district with ponies and they would have to race on foot instead.

Edging away from his mama's watchful eye, Robbie desperately hoped he would win some contest, for then he could receive his prize from Lord Knowlton. Sam had said the earl always gave out the prizes. And after the prizes they could eat their fill and watch the grown-ups as they danced and sang. Sam said it could get pretty entertaining later in the evening, when most of the men were in their cups. The party would grow loud and boisterous and no one would care what the younger boys did. Robbie did not think his mama would allow him to stay that long, but he hoped he could stay out of her way long enough to have fun.

Katherine looked about her with growing interest. Across the drive, makeshift pens filled with farm animals covered one section of the lawn. She saw Robbie and Sam reaching over one barrier to pet the enclosed sheep.

She deliberately tried to avoid spotting the earl, averting her gaze whenever she saw a man who looked to be dressed remotely as she thought Knowlton might be. Yet when she had not seen him after a half-hour, she grew anxious. He was here today, was he not? Perhaps he only made his appearance in the evening, after the dining. In which case all her silly posturing to avoid him had been most foolish and—

"Good day, Mrs. Mayfield." Knowlton was suddenly in front of her, sweeping an elegant bow.

Katherine started. Had she conjured up the man out of thin air?

He gently clasped her elbow. "Shall we stroll about the grounds? I believe you have not seen the gardens yet?"

"I do not think—"

" 'Tis a pity. I appreciate a beautiful woman who can think."

"I see it is to be a day of flummery from you, sir," she said, but made no move to free herself. She could firmly control the situation. "Can you afford to ignore the rest of your guests in such a cavalier manner?"

"They have already seen the gardens," he said with a wicked grin. " 'Twould be only a dull procession for them."

"While I shall be filled with transports of delight?"

"Undoubtedly," he replied. "My gardeners do their work well."

They crossed the gravel drive, following the flagged path that led around the house to the rear terrace and the gardens spread below.

"I have yet to thank you for allowing Robbie to help with the harvest. He enjoyed himself immensely." She offered him a grateful smile.

It was such a rare reward that he nearly caught his breath. How he would like to have that dazzling smile bestowed upon himself more often. In reward for other achievements. He patted her hand. "Harvest was my favorite time of year when I was his age," he said.

"And now?"

He looked at her quizzingly.

"Do you still enjoy harvest above all?"

A flicker of amusement danced in his eyes, "No," he said slowly, his voice low and seductive. "There are other pursuits I find more enjoyable now."

Katherine quickly averted her gaze. Fool, she chided herself. She had walked straight into that one.

Knowlton smiled and took her hand in his, leading her down the terrace steps as if nothing had been said. Knowing he needed to quickly redeem himself ere she fled, he calmly pointed out the organization of the garden as if he were unaware of the attractiveness of the woman at his side.

"I should like you to see it in high summer, when the blooms are at their fullest," he said as they strolled back toward the house. "Or in spring, when the first color appears. I shall have the gardeners send you some bulbs for the cottage."

"That is kind of you, my lord," Katherine replied with a wary look.

He laughed aloud. "Kindness is rarely the virtue ascribed to me. There are those who would say that even the simple gift of some flowers to a delectable widow is only a sign of my baser intentions."

"Is it?" Katherine stopped and calmly surveyed him. It was what she herself believed. Would he have the honesty to admit it?

"You wound me with your suspicions." Knowlton placed a hand over his heart. "Here I have behaved with the utmost circumspection for at least ten minutes, yet you still doubt my intentions? Have I given you any cause to question my actions?"

Katherine had to admit he had not. Overtly. But she knew he was watching her, wanting her, seducing her with his eyes and his wickedly innocent—and not-so-innocent— words. Yet to accuse him on such grounds would make her look a fool.

"I thought not." He tucked her hand in the crook of his arm again and led her back toward the front lawns. "I think, for that slur, Mrs. Mayfield, that you owe me a boon."

"What did you have in mind, my lord?"

He eyed her with amusement. She knew perfectly well what he had in mind, the saucy witch. It was all part of this game that they played, the verbal sparring, the penetrating glances, the averted gaze when he had crossed the line. He thrust, she parried in as excellent a display of swordsmanship as he had seen in a long time. But he would slip past her guard eventually and his lance would hit home.

"A simple dance, my lady. An unexceptionable request."

Nothing he did was unexceptionable, thought Katherine suspiciously. Still, it was only a dance. There could be little danger in that.

"I will grant you a dance, my lord. But nothing more."

"Knowlton," he responded. "Certainly, Mrs. Mayfield, after an acquaintance of our duration, you can find it within yourself to call me by my name, at least. No one would find it the least bit forward."

She frowned. He was doing it again, teasing her and skirting around the edge of a blatant flirtation.

"Very well, *Knowlton.*"

He flashed her a grin of triumph before they were once again enveloped by the gathering on the front lawn. He deftly instigated a polite conversation with the vicar, drew Katherine into it, then drifted off as if that brief interlude in the garden had never happened.

Katherine wished it had not. Every moment spent in his company was a moment closer to disaster. He could disarm her with a word, and despite the fact she knew exactly what game he played, she was powerless to withdraw from it. Had it not been the nineteenth century, she would have accused him of witchcraft.

She drew herself up with a start. This was ridiculous. She was perfectly able to deal with Knowlton. Her reluctance stemmed only from her foolish desire to fill the void left in her life after the death of Robert. Six years was a long time to be alone, with only her son for company. But Knowlton was no answer to that problem. His presence in her life would be only temporary, and she had no wish for that.

"I believe this is my dance?"

Knowlton stood before her, his face as eager as any little boy's. He had doffed his jacket at some point during the evening, his cravat had vanished from his neck, and only his elegantly embroidered waistcoat hinted at his aristocratic veneer. In the wavering lantern lights, he had a slightly raffish air.

"I am not certain . . ." Katherine began.

"You promised." Even in the dim light she could see the challenge in his eyes.

That put too fine a point on a simple agreement, but Katherine nodded her acquiescence. She had seen him earlier, joking with the squires and farmers as they hoisted mugs of foaming ale, and she suspected Knowlton had drunk his share. Pray he was not foxed enough to make a spectacle. Guests parted to allow him to lead her out into the middle of the dancing platform, and the musicians struck up another tune.

"A waltz," she said as he pulled her into his arms. "I should have guessed."

Knowlton grinned. "I like to waltz, Mrs. Mayfield. And it is very obvious that you are at least acquainted with the dance."

She nodded, allowing the magic of the music to take hold as she twirled in his arms. There was something dreadfully disconcerting about waltzing with a man in shirtsleeves. Her fingers sought only the lightest contact with the soft linen of his shirt, but it was all too easy to feel the heat from the skin below. She wished she had worn her gloves—but Mrs. Ashe had said few ladies bothered for this party. With Knowlton half-undressed, they were rapidly becoming a necessity.

"Has it been an enjoyable day for you?" Knowlton asked as the pattern of the dance brought them together again.

"Yes," she said. "I have never been to such an event and it is . . ."

"Marvelous?" He eagerly fished for the compliment.

"Fascinating," she continued, smiling softly. "The entire neighborhood is here, and all the barriers are down for a day."

"Are your barriers down, Mrs. Mayfield?"

She looked guiltily into those deceptively calm gray eyes. Sometimes it was as if he could read her mind. "I believe I have not forgotten that I am a lady."

"Neither have I," he replied, and subtly tightened his hold on her waist.

"I believe you are holding me too close, my lord," she said in protest.

"I do not think such a thing is possible," he replied, his eyes twinkling. "After all, this is a waltz, the most scandalous of dances, precisely because it allows one to hold one's partner close."

His slow, seductive smile mesmerized her. He was not completely sober, yet he was as lithe and agile on his feet as if he had abstained the entire evening. But there was a new gleam of appreciation in his eyes when he looked at her that made her uneasy. Before, he had teased her with words, which could easily be deflected. Now those eyes . . . Without leaving her face, she knew his gaze was raking her frame, mentally stripping her. She *felt* naked as he circled her around in the motions of the dance, the warmth from their bodies radiating whenever they drew together in the intimate movements. She was almost tempted to pull free and flee, before it was too late.

Katherine uttered up a grateful prayer when the music ended at last. Knowlton lightly held her arm and led her to the side of the platform. He stopped and said a word to a man here, teased a lady there, and before Katherine quite knew what had happened, they were very alone in the empty garden he had shown her earlier in the day. Discreetly placed lanterns lent just enough light to the scene.

"My lord," she began in protest.

"Knowlton," he corrected softly. "Or even Edward. I answer to both."

"It is highly improper—"

"Not unless you wish it to be so," he replied with a husky rasp to his voice.

Katherine moved to walk away, but he grabbed her wrist and drew her to him.

"Stay for a few moments," he pleaded. "I would like to hear my name just once from those rosy lips."

"You are being ridiculous," she snapped, but he drew her even closer until it was all she could do to keep their bodies from touching.

"It is not such a bad name," he whispered. "It has been borne by kings and dukes."

"And rakes who tempt women in the dark."

"Tempt?" he laughed. "Do not say you can be tempted, Mrs. Mayfield? Or may I have leave to call you Katherine?"

"No."

He nodded agreement. "You are right. Katherine does not quite suit. Kate is better. Although you are not the least bit shrewish."

"My lord, you are foxed," she said, her alarm growing. How could she have been so incautious as to have allowed herself to be alone with him?

"Edward."

"*Edward,* you are foxed." She tried to pull away from his grasp, but the hand on her wrist tightened.

"No, just a trifle elevated," he insisted. "It is the nearness of you, not the ale, that flummoxes my senses and leaves my brain in such a state of disarray." He lifted her imprisoned hand to his mouth, pressing a gentle kiss on the palm before folding her fingers over it. He planted another kiss upon the bent digits before his lips traced a searing path down her thumb to her wrist.

"Enough!" she cried when the pleasure-pain became more than she could bear. "You know that I am not inclined toward a dalliance with you."

He eyed her with amusement. "Why, my dear Kate, how interesting that you should hint of such a thing. The thought had not crossed my mind."

"And pigs have wings," she muttered.

"One kiss. 'Tis all I ask. Surely not an overly demanding request?"

She opened her mouth to protest, knowing already that he had won. Because she did not want to say no. She wanted to kiss him, to feel the lips that had traced such fire across her hand. Would their touch be so potent when pressed against her own?

"One," she said shakily. "And then you will escort me back to the front lawn."

"Assuredly," he agreed.

He made no move to take his boon, but merely looked into her face with his now-familiar amused grin. Then he pulled her close, crushing her against his body as his strong arms wrapped around her. His mouth lowered to hers, softly touching, caressing, brushing her lips with the faintest of pressure until her reluctance faded. His tongue teased against her mouth, begging, pleading for entry until she granted him that favor too.

Katherine nearly jumped from the shock of the gentle invasion, relishing the sensation, yet afraid of the intimacy she had allowed him. She felt herself relaxing in his embrace, her arms creeping up to wrap themselves around his neck, pulling his head farther down as she responded to his demanding mouth. She refused to listen to her doubts, her fears, instead giving herself up to the sheer exquisite pleasure of his nearness. Katherine nearly cried aloud when he finally tore his mouth away.

He held her clasped against him; she felt his thudding heart beneath her ear and heard his labored breathing mingled with her own.

"We should go back," she whispered when she could take air to speak again,

"I fear it will be a short while before I can escort you back into polite company," he said slowly. "Perhaps we can take another turn around the garden?"

Katherine's gaze flew to his face and she saw the smoldering desire that lurked within his eyes, frightening in its intensity. It was that which returned her to her senses at last. She stepped away from his embrace.

"I shall see myself back," she said hastily, turning toward the house.

Knowlton watched her go with a mixture of regret and hope. He had cast down the gauntlet this evening; the next days would tell whether she would pick it up or not. Drawing in a deep breath of cool night air, he smiled at the darkened garden. He would take it as an encouraging sign if she did not commence packing on the morrow.

On one matter he had been right: Katherine Mayfield was as passionate as her red hair indicated. It was going to be a delightful experience to unleash the full force of her desire.

Chapter Eight

Folly is an endless maze,
Tangled roots perplex her ways.
How many have fallen there!
—Blake, *The Voice of the Ancient Bard*

Sleep did not come easily to Katherine that night. After the kiss in the garden, she had wished to flee immediately from the party, only to recollect that she needed to wait for a ride home with the vicar and his wife. So she stayed close to Mrs. Ashe until it was time to depart. Katherine caught no further sight of Knowlton, for which she was grateful.

What must he think of her after her wanton response to his kiss? She should never have allowed him to kiss her so, should have drawn back at the first sign that it was to be more than an innocent brush of his lips. Instead, she had allowed him an intimacy that frightened her.

She dreaded their next encounter, fearing that the naked desire she had seen in his eyes that evening would be there always now, when he looked at her. She must make it very clear to him that her behavior had been an aberration, a foolishness born of the hour and the circumstances. He must not think he could ever dare such a thing again.

Her first impression of him had been correct: he was dangerous. He had pierced her armor as easily as if she were an innocent child, rather than an experienced widow who had grown adept at fending off improper advances from all manner of men. Yet Knowlton had the power to disarm her at a glance. No, Katherine could never allow him to get so close to her in the future.

If she had an ounce of sense, she would pack up her own

and Robbie's meager belongings and find another cottage, in another county, where she would never have to worry about seeing the earl. Yet she was reluctant to do so. She liked it here in Lincolnshire; she had made friendships in the short time she had lived here. And she hated the thought of wrenching Robbie away from another home.

Ironically, it was Robbie who made their departure difficult, precisely because of his fondness for the earl. Robbie idolized the man. Katherine should have anticipated that sooner and cut the connection earlier, when she had the chance. Now it was too late; Robbie would be hurt and resentful if she refused any further contact.

Still, it would not be a bad thing to try to ease Robbie away from the man. She suspected Knowlton's interest in her son was more of a whim of the moment, one that would fade over time. They could not expect the earl to remain indefinitely in the neighborhood; he would be returning to the excitement of London ere long, and Robbie would be bereft. It would be best to prepare him now for the eventual disappointment.

As for the earl and herself . . . She would inform him quite succinctly that she was determined to keep him at arm's length in the future. His attentions might be good for Robbie, but they were nothing but troublesome for her.

By Sunday, Katherine seethed with frustration. She had agonized over what she would say, how she would react when she saw the earl next. Yet there had been no opportunity for an encounter over the last four days. She had not been able to greet him in the coolly correct manner she planned, to indicate to him that whatever madness had seized her in the garden had faded upon reflection. Robbie finally divulged the news that the earl had left Warrenton for a brief trip to Nottingham. The truth left her strangely deflated.

So now she would be forced to confront him at church, with all the neighborhood in attendance. She would not put it past him to make some sort of embarrassing scene, just to cause her discomfort. She simply did not trust him to behave anymore, whether in public or in private. Her stomach churned with apprehension as she and Robbie traced the lane toward the village.

Katherine spotted Knowlton the moment she entered the church, lounging in solitary splendor in the family box. His face bore a trace of resigned boredom, which changed when his eyes lit upon her. He smiled, inclining his head a fraction in greeting. Katherine nodded politely in turn and turned her attention to Robbie.

The service lasted for an excruciating passage of time, the vicar's words no more than an endless drone in Katherine's ears. Every time she tried to concentrate on the service, Knowlton's presence distracted her. One could not look toward the vicar without seeing the earl. In desperation, she cast her gaze onto her hymnal, but before long her eyes were drawn toward the front once again.

She wanted to escape to the safety of the cottage the moment the service ended, her resolve draining away with each passing moment. But she had to talk with him, in order to put an end to this foolishness once and for all. Katherine forced her steps to slow as she took Robbie's hand and led him down the aisle. The earl was behind her, she knew, taking his time as he stopped and greeted nearly every member of the congregation, as if he knew how it would only increase her agitation. Stepping into the warm sunshine, she had half a mind to dish out the same treatment, and strike out for home without confronting him, but Robbie had already vanished somewhere with Sam, and she needed to wait for his return.

She watched with growing apprehension as Knowlton finally appeared in the church door, deep in conversation with Mr. Ashe. If he put on this facade of piousness to impress her, he was failing miserably. Knowlton looked up for a moment and caught her gaze. A slow smile lit his face. He mumbled something to the vicar and slowly ambled toward her.

"Good morning, Mrs. Mayfield." He doffed his hat.

"Good morning, my lord," she replied coolly.

"Young Robbie has abandoned you already?" He lifted one mocking brow.

She nodded. "He and Samuel Trent are up to some mischief, I am certain."

"It is fortunate, for there is a matter I wished to speak with you, without Robbie present."

"Yes?" she strove to remain cool. What would he dare now?

He smiled in his most disarming manner. "I have invited some friends for a small shooting party next week. I wished to ask you—beforehand this time—if you will permit Robbie to accompany us."

She stared at him as if she had not heard. He wanted to speak about Robbie joining a shooting party? He was going to stand here and pretend that nothing had happened that night in his darkened garden?

"I thought he could help with the game bags or carry the shot," Knowlton continued, a smile teasing at the corner of his lips. "I assure you, he will not be allowed near any of the guns."

Katherine quickly gathered her wits. It was a heaven-sent opportunity to put one part of her plan into effect.

"It is kind of you to ask," she said slowly, "but I think it would be best if Robbie did not participate. He is about to resume his studies with the vicar, and a little extra preparation would not be amiss."

"I see," Knowlton said.

Katherine was certain she was mistaken. That could not be disappointment she saw in his eyes.

"Robbie has had a most enjoyable summer," she rattled on, "but it is high time he settled down again. And truly, my lord, I do not think your guests will wish to be bothered with a ten-year-old pest."

"Perhaps you are right, ma'am. I trust the lad will still be coming to Warrenton to ride?"

She hesitated. "Perhaps for the duration of your party, it would be best if he stayed away."

He frowned. "Are you taking out your anger with me on your son? If so, it will not do."

"Anger?" she asked in some surprise.

"I believe I behaved with less than circumspection the last time we spoke."

His eyes lit with a teasing laughter that belied his apologetic words. Katherine's irritation rose.

"The only anger I felt over that incident was with myself, my lord, for allowing such an untoward situation to occur. Who could blame you for taking advantage of such a foolish soul?"

"Who, indeed?" he asked, and there was a hint of that wicked gleam in his eyes.

Katherine did not avert her gaze. "I am concerned more about Robbie," she explained. "He adores your company, and I am most grateful for the attention you have lavished upon him. But I know that the situation cannot continue. You have your own interests, and we can hardly expect you to remain here in the country forever. This will allow Robbie to see that matters will change as the year wears on."

"A good point," he said, although he had yet thought little of leaving Warrenton. "But I hate to deprive the lad of his horse while the lesson is learned. I meant it sincerely when I said the animal was a gift to your son. If you do not wish Robbie at Warrenton, perhaps I can make some other arrangements for the stabling of the beast."

"There is the small shed at the rear of the cottage garden . . ."

"Of course. 'Twill be just the thing. Robbie is adept at caring for him now, and I can have Frank amble over from time to time to make certain he is carrying out his duties properly."

"Then it is arranged."

"I will take care of matters this week, then." Knowlton took her gloved hand and bowed over it in departure. "Oh, there is one more thing, Mrs. Mayfield."

"Yes?"

A roguish twinkle lit his eyes. "It was a very lovely kiss."

Katherine's cheeks flamed as he took his leave, a broad grin upon his face. He had done it again—disarmed her completely, then struck with lightning speed. Drat the man!

Knowlton's grin lingered for most of the ride home. How he loved to bring the color to her cheeks. She blushed more prettily than any woman he knew. He had noticed her studied casualness in her treatment of him, knew she was remembering their last encounter the entire time he nattered on about Robbie and the pony. He had not been able to resist that little reminder, just to make certain she knew he had not forgotten it either.

Lord, he was glad he had availed himself of that bouncy barmaid in Nottingham. There were limits to what one man could endure, and he had reached it long ago. That simple kiss in the garden had shaken him more than he could ever have imagined. He was quite certain he had the delectable

Kate Mayfield wavering, but a precipitate move on his part could still scare her into flight. With his hunger assuaged, he could now behave with a modicum of restraint until he had her willing acquiescence.

He honestly did regret her refusal to allow Robbie to participate in the shooting party. He genuinely liked the lad. Yet he agreed with Mrs. Mayfield's concerns: he had no intention of staying forever at Warrenton, and Robbie would have to realize that eventually. Knowlton had noticed with growing dismay the worshipful way Robbie regarded him. It was flattering and frightening at the same time. His gradual withdrawal from the boy's life would be the best thing. But how was he to reconcile that with his pursuit of the mother?

Quite simply, Robbie needed to be out of the way. He was old enough for school, and it would do him good to be with more lads of his own age and class. Samuel Trent was a spirited lad, but a farmer's son was not the best companion for Robbie. He came from gentry stock at the least, and in spite of their poverty, he should be consorting with those of his own kind.

Knowlton was certain, however, that Mrs. Mayfield did not have the funds to send Robbie away to school. That would be the problem he must tackle. He knew her pride would not allow him to finance such an endeavor—even if it was not uncommon for a noble to finance several charity students at the premier schools. Somehow, he would have to find a way to provide her with the means to purchase the lad's education without letting her know it came from him.

Then, with Robbie away, he could avail himself of the widow's charms without restraint. The Rose Cottage would make an admirable love nest. Cheered by the thought that his designs might yet succeed, he broke into most ignoble whistling.

Katherine watched Robbie with sympathy as he moped about the house. He had deeply resented her order that he stay away from Warrenton while Knowlton entertained his shooting party. Even moving his pony to the makeshift stall in the shed had not improved his disposition. It worried her, for it showed that he had grown as attached to the earl as she had feared. And that would never do.

"Why don't you see if there are any late apples left on the trees?" she suggested helpfully. "I could bake a pie for dinner."

"They are probably all gone," he grumbled.

"We will not know for certain until you look," she reminded him. "Put on your coat and take the basket. And do not get yourself dirty!"

She watched his reluctant form as he ambled down the walk. Once again, she was filled with regret—and doubt. Had she chosen the life that was best for him? As he grew older, she grew less certain. Their lack of funds grew more critical the older he became. Lessons with the vicar would suffice for only so long. How much easier it would be for the both of them if she had the money to pay for Robbie's schooling. She had heard the tales of the horror of scholarship life, the boys no better than unpaid slaves to the other students. Katherine did not want a life like that for Robbie. She determined that there would be no Eton or Harrow for him under those circumstances.

But the price that would be exacted for the money to send him off properly had been too much for her to pay six years ago, and she still thought it was too heavy a burden now. She could delay a final decision for a few more years. Perhaps there would be some miracle in the intervening time . . .

She shook her head wistfully. Her father would have reprimanded her for thinking of so worldly a miracle as money to send a boy to school. But she did not think the miracles of holy angels would be of much use to her. There were other schools, with endowed openings, that would put Robbie on the same standing as the paying students. It was time she began to investigate these matters.

At least with Robbie out of the house today, she could finish with her fall cleaning. There were only the upstairs bedrooms to finish, and the cottage would be gleaming from top to bottom. Then she would have to devise some other project to occupy her time. There was little extra sewing at this time of the year, and matters would not improve for another month. Yet it was a glorious relief not to have to sew more lace and trimmings on the elegant gowns that she could never afford for herself.

She had just succeeded in turning the mattress in Robbie's room, noticing the increasing lumps in the matting feathers and knowing she did not have the funds to purchase a new one, when a strange male voice hailed her from below.

"Mrs. Mayfield?"

She came down the stairs warily. A disheveled but expensively clad man stood in the front hall.

"Mrs. Mayfield?"

She nodded.

"Lord Knowlton sent me, from Warrenton. We were out shooting and there has been an accident. Your son—"

"Robbie?" she gasped, a wave of dizziness sweeping over her. "Shot?"

"Oh, good God." The man scowled. "I am making a mull of this. Your son has a broken leg, ma'am, from falling off his horse. Knowlton took him up to the house, sent for the doctor, and dispatched me to bring you to Warrenton."

"I will come at once," she said rapidly, tearing off her mobcap and darting into the kitchen to grab her cloak.

By sheer force of will, Katherine forced down her panic. Robbie would be all right, she told herself as she followed Knowlton's guest to the waiting curricle. It was only a broken leg. Boys broke their legs all the time and suffered no lasting harm. But the calming words had minimal impact.

She sat quietly on the rapid carriage ride to Warrenton, only her firmly clenched hands betraying her anxiety. She was grateful the man beside her was disinclined to speak. Katherine did not think she could have carried on a conversation if her life had depended upon it.

She was poised to leap from the carriage before it came to a clattering halt at the bottom of Warrenton's steps. Throwing a grateful thank-you over her shoulder, she jumped from the coach and raced up the stone steps. Knowlton's imperious butler awaited her at the front door and ushered her quickly up the stairs.

Robbie looked so small in the massive canopied bed, eyes closed, long streaks marking the path of his tears across his dirty face. Knowlton sat beside him, Robbie's small hand clutched protectively in his.

"Robbie." Her voice came out as a choked whisper.

"Mama?"

Knowlton stood up, motioning her to take his place and

placing Robbie's hand in hers. "The doctor should be here at any moment," he said quietly, then retreated to the far side of the room.

Katherine reached out and brushed back the hair from Robbie's forehead. "You are being a very brave boy," she said. "I know it must hurt dreadfully."

He nodded. "I cried, a little," he confessed, and those very words brought the tears back to his eyes. "I'm sorry, Mama."

"Hush," she said. "Do not worry about anything now. Is it only your leg that hurts?"

"My head hurts a bit too," he said. "And my side."

She felt under his hair, flinching when he winced at her touch. There was a nasty bump.

"What happened?"

"Atlas heard the shooting and he got scared and started to run and I . . . I fell off."

"And were you not told to stay away from Warrenton while there was shooting?" the earl asked sternly.

Robbie nodded.

"We will talk about that later," Katherine said, surprised that the earl chastised Robbie. Did he fear she would hold him at fault?

"The doctor is here," Knowlton announced after looking out the window. "I will bring him up."

An hour later, Katherine again sat next to Robbie, his small hand curled securely in hers, while she watched him sleep. As soon as the preliminary examination was finished, the doctor had given him laudanum to deaden the pain of splinting his leg. Now Robbie lay with his leg straight and bandaged. The bump on his head was little more than that, and his ribs were only bruised. He had been very fortunate, if "fortunate" could describe the plight of an active ten-year-old who was to be confined to his bed for several weeks. It would not be difficult at first, but as he convalesced and the pain eased, Katherine knew it would be a taxing experience, for both her and Robbie. He would grow to loathe his small room at the cottage, and she knew her days would be an endless succession of trips up and down the stairs as she sought to do her own work while she kept Robbie entertained.

"Is he asleep?" Knowlton's voice was soft as he slipped quietly into the room.

She nodded. "The doctor said he will probably not awaken until tonight. He wishes to keep him dosed with laudanum for a day or two until the pain subsides."

"He was a brave little boy," Knowlton said.

"How did you find him?"

"Purely by chance. We had achieved little success in the upper field and were heading toward the corner when Somers—Lord Wentworth, the man who brought you here—noticed Atlas wandering about."

"I feared something like this would happen if he began riding."

"You cannot protect him from everything, Katherine. I do feel at fault, for I had not thought that blasted pony would be so skittish. I never would have wished Robbie harm."

"I know," she replied, and gave him a comforting smile.

"Are you comfortable? I can have a tea tray sent up."

"Thank you, that would be nice. Would it be a dreadful imposition for me to beg the use of your carriage to take Robbie home? I thought he would be easier moved after his next dose—"

"Absolutely not," he said sternly. "I talked with the doctor and he made it very clear that Robbie was not to be moved about."

"But I must take him home," she said. "We cannot stay here. You have done enough, for which I am grateful."

Their eyes met and he saw the apprehension in hers. Damn! Did she think he would dare to take advantage of the situation?

"I will take care of matters," he said noncommittally, then rose from his chair. "The tray will be sent up."

Katherine nodded and looked back to the pain-etched face of her sleeping son. How lucky they had been. She brushed his tousled hair back from his forehead.

Knowlton's sincere concern for Robbie's welfare touched her. She remembered all his past kindnesses to her son, and her often ungrateful responses. She might justifiably question Knowlton's interest in her, but they both seemed to be of the same mind regarding Robbie. And as her knowledge of Knowlton increased, her power to resist him weakened. Katherine rightly feared the close proximity remaining in his house would entail. It was well, then, that she would be taking her son home tonight.

Chapter Nine

What is virtue but a calculation of the
consequences of our actions?
            —Mary Hays, *Memoirs of Emma Courtney*

After arranging for tea and some food to be sent up to Mrs. Mayfield, Knowlton went in search of Lord Wentworth, finding him alone in the study. The other guests were still tramping through the fields.

"Is there any chance your lovely lady would be willing to join you here, Somers?" Knowlton asked, his voice light. "The doctor has recommended that the lad not be moved until the leg heals, yet it is a highly improper situation for his mother to remain in a bachelor household. She is determined they leave, and I cannot help but feel it would not be good for the lad."

"Elizabeth would come in a moment—if she can bring Caro."

Knowlton winced. "I suppose it is too much to hope that your lovely daughter is one of those quiet children who never exercise their lungs?"

Somers laughed. "The vain hopes of a confirmed bachelor. I shall let you in on a secret, my friend. The main reason to have one of these monstrously large houses is that you can tuck the infants into a far corner. Out of sight, out of hearing. Distance works wonders."

Knowlton sighed. "I will allow the chit, only on the condition that word of her presence does not leak out. Too many ladies would see it as a sign of hope."

"Little do they know that there is nothing better to encourage a man in his bachelorhood than exposure to a small child."

"That bad?" Knowlton lifted a sympathetic brow.

Somers shook his head. "I am afraid to say I was captivated from the first moment I saw her. You cannot know the feeling, to hold your own child in your arms, to know that you had a hand in her creation. It is an awe-inspiring experience." He clapped Knowlton lightly on the shoulder. "We shall have to get you married off one of these days, so you can discover it firsthand."

"Spare me that joy." Knowlton gave a mock shudder.

Somers laughed. "I will write to Elizabeth."

"I shall dispatch a groom today." He eyed his friend hopefully. "Do you think she can be here within a week?"

"Of a certainty. She was rather put out at my leaving in the first place, so I am assured she will be willing of an early reconciliation."

"Under the cat's paw already?"

Somers raised a knowing brow. "Someday, my friend, I hope you will understand," he said enigmatically, and seated himself at the desk to pen his letter.

Knowlton stared out the window while Somers prepared his missive. Marriage had wrought a change in his friend, and he could not say whether it was for good or ill. Still, Somers was barely two years into his marriage, and the thrill of new fatherhood had yet to wear off. What tune would Somers sing five years hence?

As soon as the letter was finished, Knowlton rang for a footman and ordered its delivery. Now, if Lady Wentworth cooperated, he only had to protect Kate's reputation for a week. Knowlton realized he should ride to the vicar's and see if Mrs. Ashe would be willing to play duenna.

What a laughable situation. He had been scheming for weeks to get Kate into his arms, and his bed. And now here he was, presented with a perfect opportunity, with her son's sickroom a hairbreadth away from his, and he felt obligated to treat her with all the honor and respect he would pay any noble guest. It would be intolerably funny if it was not going to be so damn difficult.

Mrs. Ashe was perfectly willing to settle for a time at Warrenton, agreeing with Knowlton that the boy should remain where he was. Knowlton returned home with a lighter heart, knowing he could forestall Kate's every argument. Robbie's recovery was of the utmost importance. He was certain he and Kate could adjust to the awkward situation. Besides, she would be preoccupied with her son and he had his own guests to entertain. They would see little of each other.

"Everything is arranged," he announced as he slipped into the room. Robbie still slept his drugged sleep.

"Thank you, my lord." Katherine smiled gratefully. "I appreciate your efforts. I shall let you know when I give Robbie his next dose. He should be ready to travel within half an hour of that."

"Mrs. Ashe will be arriving within the hour to play propriety for you, Mrs. Mayfield. There is no need for you to disturb your son. You may stay as long as the doctor thinks is necessary for Robbie's leg to heal properly."

Katherine surveyed him with dismay. "Is it not rather presumptuous of you to have arranged such a thing?"

"I am doing what is best for Robbie, which is what we both desire. If you take him home, apart from the danger of the journey and the struggle to get him into his room, have you thought about the effect it will have on you? To play nursemaid for him as well as perform all your other duties at home?" Knowlton struggled to rein in his real anger. "Here you need to do nothing beyond sit with him for as long as you like. Your meals will be prepared for you, your laundry will be washed, your every whim accommodated. I think you would be a fool to leave."

"You would." Her blue eyes filled with anger.

Knowlton walked over to the window, his arms folded across his chest. He looked out over the lawn for some time in silence, then turned and leaned against the sill. He had created this awkward situation between them, and however much he regretted the need, he knew he must reassure her.

"I wish you to know that I will remain out of your way," he stated. The promise pained him, but he knew it was the only way he could convince her to stay. "You need not fear that I will be anything but a gracious host."

She studied him for a moment. Could she trust him?

Better yet, could she trust herself to remain under the same roof and not fall further under his spell? It was a risky proposition. But with Robbie's health uppermost in her mind, it was a chance she would have to take. "Thank you," she said at last.

"Then it is agreed? You and Robbie will stay?" He cringed at the eagerness in his voice.

"We will stay," she agreed. "But I shall need to return home, to pack some things."

"I will take you now. My housekeeper can sit with Robbie until you return."

Katherine was grateful that Knowlton remained in the curricle while she raced about the cottage, gathering up the clothing and items she and Robbie would need for an extended stay at Warrenton. She was still apprehensive about the matter, not completely trusting Knowlton to behave himself, nor completely trusting herself to be in such close proximity to him for any length of time. She had already learned how easily he could overcome her defenses, and she would have to take great care to stay as far from him as possible. Fortunately, since she would be busy with Robbie, that would not prove too difficult. She hoped.

"Lord Wentworth has written to his lady, to ask her to come and stay," Knowlton told her on the drive back to Warrenton. "I think you will enjoy her company. She will be busy with her young daughter, but I imagine you will have some time to talk together. You are very close in age, I believe."

"We are ruining your shooting party," she said with dismay.

He shrugged. " 'Twill not be much disruption. I fully intend to ignore the presence of you ladies until the evening meal. Does that set your mind at rest?"

She smiled. "It does, my lord. Although I hope Lady Wentworth does not mind having to come."

"Somers assures me she will not. He claims that as long as she can dote on her daughter without interference, she will be content in any location."

She could not stifle her laugh.

"Yes?" he arched a brow.

"It will undoubtedly be an interesting experience for you, I am certain, to have your house overrun with children."

"I hardly think one lad in a splint and a toddling child will have much power to disrupt my household," he said.

"We shall see."

The first week at Warrenton sped by with rapidity. Katherine and Mrs. Ashe sat together in Robbie's room, sewing and talking quietly while he lay abed. Knowlton, despite his plan to ignore both Robbie and his mother, dropped by several times each day to ascertain that they were managing well. Both Katherine and Mrs. Ashe preferred to eat with Robbie, and they saw little of Knowlton's guests.

By the end of the week, after several days of unwanted rain put a damper on the hunting, matters changed. Lord Wentworth was the first to pop his head into the room.

"Thought I would see how the lad is getting along," he said. "Bored to flinders yet, Robbie?"

Robbie glanced at his mother, as if wondering what she wished him to say. She nodded in encouragement.

"Only a bit, sir. Mama and Mrs. Ashe are doing all they can to engage my interest."

"But it is not enough for a lively lad stuck in bed, is it? Do you play chess?"

Robbie shook his head.

"Then I shall teach you," Lord Wentworth assured him. "Knowlton must have a set around here somewhere. If you do not mind, Mrs. Mayfield?"

"Goodness, no," Katherine replied, pleased that Robbie would have the opportunity.

Yet it was Knowlton who appeared half an hour later, carrying not a chess set, but a backgammon game.

"I know there is a chess set somewhere in the house," he said by way of apology, "but it will take a bit longer to locate it. We will start with backgammon."

Katherine smiled uneasily. This was precisely the situation she had wished to avoid during their enforced stay at Warrenton. But her dismay was replaced by gratitude as Knowlton studiously ignored her. He patiently taught Robbie the rules of the game, and played with him for over an hour, until it became obvious Robbie was tiring.

Katherine walked Knowlton to the corridor. "Thank you so much for entertaining Robbie."

"He is a bright lad," he said. "When I find that blasted chess set, I am certain he will learn as quickly."

"And what will come next?" she asked in a teasing voice. "Whist?"

"A capital idea!" Knowlton returned her teasing. "Drummond lived for a time on his skill with the cards. He will prove a most instructive teacher."

Katherine shuddered in mock horror. "I hate to think what other skills your guests are qualified to teach."

"Only those suitable to a ten-year-old," Knowlton promised.

"He will enjoy the company," Katherine admitted. "He has already grown bored with my efforts, I fear."

"We will soon chase away his boredom," Knowlton promised. He caught her gaze, his eyes twinkling. "But whatever shall we do to relieve your boredom, Mrs. Mayfield? A stroll in the garden, perhaps?"

Katherine paused. She had hoped that this sojourn at Warrenton would pass in an unexceptional manner. Knowlton would keep to his friends; she would tend to Robbie in the isolation of his room. As long as they were not forced into close contact, she could deal with Knowlton. But his words, his nearness, brought back in a rush all the memories of the feel of his body pressed close to hers as they exchanged kisses in the garden. She saw his gray eyes coolly watching her, as if he could discern her thoughts, and her cheeks grew redder. Knowlton was becoming far, far too dangerous for her to deal with. Precisely because she was losing her will to fight against him. Avoidance was her only defense.

"I shall suggest that to Mrs. Ashe," she said, consciously stiffening. "Perhaps this afternoon we shall act upon your suggestion."

Knowlton bowed graciously, but Katherine saw the flicker of disappointment that crossed his eyes. She must keep firm in her resolve.

The elusive chess set was finally unearthed and the following day Lord Wentworth began teaching the game to Robbie. His visit was soon followed by appearances by the other men of the party: the flirtatious Seb Cole, who struck Katherine as a rogue of Knowlton's ilk, the rakish, wid-

owed Duke of Hartford, who talked proudly of his own
son away at school, and the rather aloof Viscount Drummond, who managed to look cynical and sad at the same
time. Katherine marveled at their patience as they taught
Robbie chess and whist, regaled him with stories of valor
and glory at Waterloo, and generally inspired hero worship
to rival Robbie's feelings for Knowlton. And they never
once made her uncomfortable with unwanted attentions.

Lady Wentworth arrived in due time, in a carriage
Knowlton laughingly insisted was crammed to the roof with
baby paraphernalia. He did not miss the eagerness with
which Somers leapt to his feet at the announcement of her
arrival. Knowlton·shook his head in dismay. Somers was
well ånd truly caught.

Despite all Knowlton's intentions, the presence of Lady
Wentworth altered the nature of the previously idyllic bachelor retreat. Whereas Kate and the vicar's wife had remained
upstairs, Lady Wentworth joined the men for dinner most
nights. That forced the gentlemen to be on their better behavior, and the easygoing bachelor life of their first week in residence reformed itself into a more restrained atmosphere.
Lady Wentworth graciously stayed out of the way as much
as possible, but the mere fact of her existence disrupted the
household. Knowlton was not surprised when the duke cor-
nered him in the library one morning.

"I cannot say that it was not entertaining, Knowlton, but
it is time to be gone." Hartford extended his hand.

"Ladies driving you away, eh?"

"More a reminder of what is waiting back in London,"
the duke replied. "One of the most delectable morsels I
have had in years. Good thing you were here in the country
when she made her debut, else you would have tried to
snap her up."

"You can only be glad I was here," Knowlton replied.
"Else she would not have taken a second glance at you."

"But I am a duke," Hartford protested loftily.

"But I am Knowlton."

They both burst into laughter.

"Take care, Hart, on the journey home. And I promise
that the spring shoot will be more convivial."

Knowlton sighed as his friend left the room. Hart gone

today; Cole and Drummond would not be far behind. He was now struck with entertaining the Wentworths, whose cozy domesticity was rapidly growing tiresome. Knowlton had been more than startled by Somers' defection from the bachelor ranks, but this new role of blissfully besotted husband shook Knowlton to the core. Somers, with whom he had drunk, gamed, and wenched for years, was becoming an unknown quantity. Knowlton could not help but harbor a bit of resentment against Lady Wentworth. She was an admirable lady, strikingly lovely, intelligent, and witty, yet she had brought his closest friend to such a pass.

One thing for certain, he was going to have to drag Kate out of her seclusion and into the drawing room. The thought of spending the evening in the sole company of the Wentworths while they made calf's eyes at each other, was more than he could stomach. If Kate joined them, they could at least play cards or drum up some other diversionary program.

Besides, he looked forward to spending more time in her company. He had remained studiously circumspect these last two weeks, playing the correct host and never overstepping the bounds of propriety. With three other bachelors in the house, he dared not do else. Now that only Somers and his lady were left, he could lower his guard a bit. There would be no word of gossip from the Wentworths. While he would not take full advantage of Kate's presence in his home, it would take more of a saint than he to continue to ignore her. He had come too far not to press for her final capitulation. Despite that trip to Nottingham, he found his body ached for her as much as ever.

Knowlton set about advancing his scheme on the very morning his other guests departed, bounding up the stairs to the invalid's room as soon as the last carriage cleared the drive. Robbie, his recuperation far enough along that he was back working on the dreaded Latin, was frowning over his books while his mother sat near the window, reading.

"If you will excuse your mother, Robbie, I have a matter I should like to discuss with her."

Robbie nodded glumly. It made no difference whether his mother was in the room or not; he would have to finish his Latin.

"I hope you do not want to ring a peal over me for driving all your guests away," Katherine said when she joined him in the hall. "I am truly sorry."

He waved a dismissive hand. "They rarely stay longer than this. Too many other amusements to draw their attention."

"Are we keeping you from your diversions as well?"

Not for long, he hoped. "I fear there has been a sad want of requests for my presence this fall," he said with a rueful expression. "I had planned to stay here at least until the start of the new year, so you have not overset my plans."

"I am glad."

"I am certain you have grown tired of your confinement in that room," he continued. "Now that there are no debauched males lurking in the hallways, I wish you would make yourself at home in the house."

"I fear your guests were so gracious at entertaining Robbie that he will be suffering from increased fits of boredom if I do not keep him close company."

"Nonsense. He is a sensible lad and knows he cannot rely on you for constant amusement. I think it is high time that you began to act as a proper guest."

She eyed him cautiously. "And how does a proper guest act?"

"She joins her host in the drawing room in the evening, for conversation and companionship," he said. "And allows herself to be taken for a tour of the house. You have been here for over a fortnight and have yet to see more than a fraction of Warrenton. It is enough to make a more sensitive man take offense."

Katherine could not resist him when he was determined to be charming. She told herself she would be safe with him; she had his promise that he would not misbehave while she was under his roof. He had behaved admirably up until now; there was no reason to think he would alter his behavior.

"I would very much like to see your home," she said.

He took her hand in his and led her along the corridor to the wide, curving staircase that rose from the ground floor. "From the cellars to the attic, or from highest to lowest?"

"I hardly think I need to peruse the attics *or* the cellars," Katherine replied.

He shrugged. "Do not complain, then, that I gave you less than a thorough inspection."

Knowlton rushed Katherine through most rooms, giving her an almost self-deprecating tour, as if he felt embarrassed at being the owner of such a magnificent estate. She stopped him occasionally to linger over a fine piece of furniture or a collection of curios, but she mostly let him have his way until they reached the portrait gallery. There she forced him to slow and explain each and every painting.

"I do not know who half these people are," he protested.

"Then you should," she retorted. "Show me the family, at least."

He led her past an endless array of portraits, starting, inexplicably, with his grandfather, the seventh earl.

"Gambler," Knowlton explained. "Lost and won the family fortune several times over."

"I trust he was on the winning side when he passed on."

"Most assuredly. He'd just won ten thousand pounds at a game, stood up from the table, and dropped dead. My grandmother always claimed it was by the grace of God or he would have lost it all the next night."

Katherine gave him a sidelong look.

"Now, this rogue," he continued, pointing to a man with the long curls of Charles II's age, "was a crony of Lord Rochester's."

"Who was he?"

Knowlton stifled a smile. "One of the minor poets."

"He must be *very* minor; I have heard naught of him."

"He was not prolific," Knowlton admitted. "And his poems were mostly circulated privately."

Katherine could only guess at what scurrilous scribbling his ancestor's friend had prepared. "Were any of your ancestors respectable?"

Knowlton laughed. "I doubt it. There seems to be a streak of misbehavior that runs from father to son."

"Where is the portrait of your father?"

"I had it removed."

Katherine busied herself with studying the next portrait. Another clue to the mystery that made up Knowlton. For despite his reputation, Katherine was beginning to understand that there was a far more complex man lurking behind the rakish facade than he let on. That was the man she wanted to know.

"What of the women in your family?" she asked loftily. "Whatever possessed them to align their lives with such a packet of rapscallions?"

"Need you ask?" His gray eyes twinkled mischievously. Knowlton took her hand in his, rubbing his thumb across her upstretched fingers. "We Beauchamps are decidedly impossible to resist."

"Are you so certain of that, my lord?"

An amused smile flitted across his lips. "Would you care to put the matter to a test?" His fingers tightened on hers.

Katherine looked into his eyes, trying to capture a glimpse of what he really thought. Did he truly believe he was irresistible to any woman? Or did he only think she was less than firm in her resistance? Had he sensed the doubts and longings that plagued her?

They stood for long minutes, their gazes locked together, without moving and barely breathing. Katherine knew that one step forward would take her into his arms, and her will wavered. But still she stood her ground.

Knowlton brought her hand to his lips, brushing them softly against her fingers, while his eyes never left hers. His expression was enigmatic; Katherine saw neither desire nor pleading there. Only curiosity.

A voice echoed down the long, paneled corridor and broke their concentration.

"Shall we call it a draw—for now?" Knowlton asked, a knowing smile spreading across his face.

Katherine nodded silently. He placed her hand on his arm and led her from the room.

Chapter Ten

And for marriage I have neither the talent
   nor the inclination.

                           —Byron

*I*f Katherine had been honest with herself, she would
have taken Robbie that very day and fled not from the
mansion, but from the entire neighborhood, without a backward glance. She knew she was playing with fire, but like
the moth drawn to the flame, she could not tear herself
away.

So instead of quietly remaining in Robbie's room in the
evening, she allowed herself to be drawn into the convivial
atmosphere of the drawing room, playing whist or other
card games with Knowlton and the Wentworths. Often
Katherine remained with Knowlton after the others retired
for the night. He made no overt physical approach toward
her, but his mere presence in the room was enough; she
was acutely aware of his every move and look. She often
caught him watching her with a knowing smile on his lips,
which brought a flush to her cheeks.

And if his presence discomfited her, it also lured her into
more and more intimate discussions. More than once they
talked long into the night, Knowlton almost eagerly revealing more and more of himself to her.

"I am no saint," he said to her one evening.

"I would not have thought to label you such," she replied
dryly. "But why veer so far in the opposite direction? You
are not an evil person."

"Why?" He shrugged. "I think it is much easier to lead

a life of debauchery than to walk the straight and narrow. And it is infinitely more entertaining."

"Does it not bother you to have such a dreadful reputation?"

"I have found that there is nothing more alluring to the ladies than a dreadful reputation." Knowlton's face creased in a self-satisfied smile.

"I do not understand the reasoning behind that. Why would any woman be interested in a man who she knows will treat her only as a casual interest?"

"Perhaps because that is all they wish from him."

She sighed. She had hoped to gain some insight into her own attraction to the earl, but his explanations did not enlighten her. Casual dalliance was not a thing she favored. "I am afraid that I simply do not understand the *ton*."

"You are operating under a severe handicap," he explained with an amused smirk. "You were one of those rare creatures who actually had a marriage based on love. Many couples do not, and therefore think little of casting their vows aside for a bit of fun."

She knew he taunted her with his flippant remarks, knew also that he was hiding behind them as well. Could she goad him into an unexpected revelation? "I refuse to believe that the entire world is like that. Look at Somers and Elizabeth."

"A very rare exception," he murmured, shifting in his chair. "Look at Hartford, a doting father, but he rivals me for the numbers of mistresses he has kept."

"But he was once married, so he must have formed some regard for a woman."

"To his great regret."

"Truly?" Katherine's eyes grew wide.

"He discovered quite shortly after the wedding how eminently unsuitable they were. When it was far too late."

"And you, of course, will never allow such a thing to happen." The bitterness in her voice surprised Katherine. Why should she expect Knowlton to behave any differently than his rakish reputation allowed?

"Precisely. What need have I of a wife when I can have nearly every woman I wish in my bed?"

Katherine was long past having the shocking nature of Knowlton's conversation disturb her. What did bother her was Knowlton's callous dismissal of the possibility of love and happiness with another. She pitied him more than anything. It strengthened her to know that she had more experience and wisdom in one area, at least.

"I have shocked you," he said. "I am sorry."

"No, it is not that." Katherine self-consciously twisted her fingers. "I find that it is I who am sorry for you. You cut yourself off from the possibility of ever finding lasting happiness."

" 'Tis an impossible dream," he replied, the sarcasm heavy in his voice. "I will wager in five years' time Somers and Elizabeth will appear as any other bored couple."

"I do not believe so."

"You sound as if you desire a wager."

"Do not be foolish," Katherine snapped. "How cruel to actually wish unhappiness on someone, if only to be proved right in a silly wager."

"I am not wishing unhappiness upon them," Knowlton protested. "I am merely stating the unlikelihood of their besotted state continuing much longer." He leaned forward, the intensity of his look startling Katherine. "Good Lord, they have been wedded for nearly two years now. I have seen newly married couples less in each other's pockets."

"I think it speaks well of Lord Wentworth that he holds his wife in such esteem," Katherine said archly.

"And did Captain Mayfield live in your pocket in such a way?"

Katherine paled, averting her eyes. "He was not at home long enough."

Knowlton set down his glass and took her hands in his. "I am sorry, Katherine. My damnable tongue. I am certain the captain was an admirable husband; you are too fond of the married state for it to have been otherwise."

She offered him a wan smile, captivated by the warmth in his voice. If only he knew just how much he tempted her to cast caution to the winds, to once again act on her impulses and not her wisdom. Particularly when he looked at her in the way he did now, his eyes pleading for forgiveness. She glanced down at their joined hands, then raised her eyes to meet his gaze, nearly recoiling at the new expression she saw there.

His expression of pleading had changed to one far more

deadly. There was pure, naked desire in the look he gave her now. He was doing nothing to hide it, showing her blatantly how much he wanted her. She felt a long-remembered thrill race through her and she could not tear her eyes away from his penetrating gaze. Those cynical gray eyes made silent love to her, causing the heat to rise within her at the very thought. The power in his look was almost hypnotic, and Katherine did not think she could glance away even if she wished. His thumb rubbed a sensuous pattern along her palm, and every nerve in her body tingled with growing anticipation and apprehension. She swayed slightly as the struggle raged within her.

"Katherine," he whispered hoarsely.

The sound of his voice jolted her back to her senses and she wrenched her gaze away. Her breathing was fast, her pulse racing. He had totally, utterly seduced her with only a look.

"I think it is time I said good night," she said a trifle breathlessly.

"Must you?" His thumb kept stroking suggestively along her palm. "There is so much more we could discuss."

Katherine snatched her hand away and jumped to her feet. She had to get away. Now. "Good night, my lord."

"Edward," he corrected as he politely rose.

"Edward," she whispered as she fled through the doorway.

Knowlton sank back into his chair, his mind and body disordered. Yes, she had fled from him, but not before he had clearly seen how she reacted to his advance. He had watched her breathing quicken, watched the soft rise and fall of her breasts increase as her awareness grew. She had responded to him physically, and he knew he had made progress. After all her talk of love and marriage, she had not been averse to his invitation.

She had declined it, to be sure, but not with any note of ringing finality. She had been interested, of that he was certain. The passionate nature she had shown him during that long-ago kiss in the garden still lurked within her, barely hidden under the surface. It would not be a torturous struggle to bring it to the forefront again. A few more *tête-à-tête* evenings like this, a glass or two of warmed brandy, and she would be falling into his arms and bed like a ripe plum from a tree. And once he had fully awakened her to the pleasures to be found there, he could look forward to a very satisfying relationship. Very satisfying. He had great hopes for Kate. She would not be a boring companion.

Katherine avoided Knowlton the next day, her thoughts still too jumbled from what had transpired the previous evening. She knew that a firmly worded set-down would cool Knowlton's ardor; he was too much a gentleman to press forward where he was not wanted. But she could not bring herself to say the words that would free her from his attentions.

Knowlton was an enigmatic man. He was, without a doubt, one of the most blatant rakes she had ever met; at the same time, he was a responsible landlord and a thoughtful and caring gentleman. She was beginning to learn about the man under the flippant facade, the Knowlton that few people ever saw. The Knowlton who could buy a little boy a pony and spend endless hours teaching him the finer points of horsemanship. The Knowlton who would cut hay alongside his workers, then entertain them with all the pomp and hospitality a royal guest would receive. The man who would allow his hunting party to be broken up and his home invaded by women and children, just to ensure that a young boy's broken leg healed properly. There was more depth to him than most people imagined.

She wanted to probe those depths, to bring out the hidden Knowlton who possessed tenderness and consideration. She wanted him to openly acknowledge that side of himself; the side he was afraid to face. He disclaimed interest in marriage, yet he had the patience of a doting parent when he dealt with Robbie. He would make a marvelous father, Katherine decided, and it was sad to think that he would not allow himself the joy of that relationship. Why was he so dreadfully opposed to admitting to his feelings?

She refused to accept that he was as satisfied with his libertine existence as he claimed. Surely there were times when he must wish for something as simple as companionship, a woman who was there for more than just the pleasure of her body. Abruptly, Katherine recalled the sensual gaze that had held her transfixed last evening, rekindling

the very real attraction she felt for him. He almost could
make her believe that a physical relationship would be
enough, almost convince her that the pleasure would be
worth whatever it cost.

Almost. But she had paid dearly for her hard-won widow's respectability. Knowlton would take all that from her,
leaving nothing in return. If only she could reach his
heart . . .

"I find the idea of a dinner party wholly ridiculous,"
Katherine complained to Lady Wentworth as they sat in
the drawing room the next evening after dinner.

"Humor the man. He is dying here in the country without the social diversions of the city."

"Then why does he not go back to London?" Katherine
restlessly prowled the room. "He insists he is perfectly
happy rusticating away here."

Elizabeth shrugged, calmly setting another stitch in her
embroidery. "Sometimes I think Knowlton does not know
his own mind. But if he wishes to have a neighborhood
dinner party, who are we, as his guests, to gainsay him?"

"I never said he could not have a dinner. I merely said
I think it is foolish to expect me to attend."

"Nonsense." Elizabeth smiled. "It would be good for
you. We are all getting a little too familiar with our enforced company. It will be a welcome respite to swap gossip
with some new faces."

"Think how it will appear if I am at dinner!" Katherine
whirled to face her new friend. It was one thing for her to
remain at Warrenton as nurse for her son. To be a guest
at a formal dinner would put her on a much different footing. It was a sharp reminder of how she could move in
Knowlton's world—if she chose.

"Katherine, the entire neighborhood knows you are staying here. And they know that I am here as well and that
the situation is entirely proper."

"But to appear at the dinner table like I am an honored
guest? It will engender untold gossip."

"It would inspire worse gossip if you did *not* appear at
the table."

Katherine sighed at the thought. She had not realized it
before, but what Elizabeth said was true. "You are right, I

believe that would look worse." She thought for a moment. "But whatever shall I wear?"

Elizabeth laughed, recognizing the battle had been won. "Show me your wardrobe. I imagine we can contrive something."

There was no question it would have to be Katherine's gray silk, years out of date and much the worse for wear. With new trimming it would be passably acceptable, she thought, though nothing could transform it into the quality suitable for a formal dinner at an earl's table. Yet she had little choice. A new gown for such a singular occurrence was out of the question. A trip to the village with Elizabeth produced some new lace, which Katherine quickly stitched to the drab dress. It would have to do.

By the time she had finished the alteration, Katherine actually looked forward to Knowlton's party, after a fashion. The doctor had decreed that Robbie would probably be released from his enforced leisure by then and could return home. Katherine decided they would depart the day following the dinner. So the party would be a farewell of sorts—to Warrenton, Knowlton, and the leisurely life she had led here. It had been lovely to be so free of duties and responsibility, spending a few weeks living the life she had turned her back on before even knowing its delights. If she felt the tiniest regret for that decision, she pushed her qualms to the back of her mind. She dared not look back.

Katherine stretched carelessly and shifted in her chair. She had deliberately remained with Robbie this morning. It would not be long until they returned to the cottage, and she must begin to accustom herself to not being in the earl's presence each day.

"Katherine, darling, would you be a dear and rescue Knowlton?" Elizabeth stood in the doorway to Robbie's room. "I left Caro with him in the drawing room and I am afraid he will take fright and run at the least provocation."

"Certainly," said Katherine, smiling in anticipation of the earl's discomfort.

"I will not be above ten minutes," Elizabeth replied. "Caro tore my lace and she is sure to destroy the rest of the gown if I do not get it out of her reach."

Katherine set down her book, glancing over to Robbie. He

was absorbed in his own reading. "I will be back when Elizabeth has repaired her dress," she said to him. "Unless you would like me to bring Caro up here to keep you company."

Robbie wrinkled his nose. "I do not want any babies in my room."

The drawing-room door stood ajar and Katherine was able to look into the room without attracting Knowlton's attention. She brought her hand to her lips to smother a laugh. There he sat, Caro perched gingerly on his lap while he tried to keep her active hands off his neatly tied cravat.

"Here, now," he said in dismay as she managed to grab one of the ends. He disentangled her pudgy fingers, but the moment he released her hand, she grabbed again.

Katherine could hear Caro's gurgle of delight. The look of panicked frustration on Knowlton's face was priceless.

"Stop that, Lady Caroline," Knowlton said, his face mirroring his helplessness. "Men do not like ladies who destroy their cravats for no good reason." He fumbled at his waistcoat and pulled out a gold pocket watch. He dangled it in front of the quickly enraptured girl, who followed every motion with her bright eyes.

"That is a watch, my lady. Can you say 'watch'?" Knowlton half-laughed. "Of course you cannot. You can barely lisp 'mama.'"

"Mama?"

"Oh, the devil take it," Knowlton mumbled. "Try to say 'Knowlton.' 'Knowl-ton.'"

"No-ton," Caro parroted.

"Very good. You are a smart girl." He allowed her to grab hold of the watch. "A watch is for telling time. A very important thing you will learn when you get older. If you do not know what time it is, how can you ever contrive to arrive fashionably late at a ball?" He leaned closer and whispered in a conspiratorial tone, "That is as important as learning how to pick out the most expensive item in a shop. Your papa will be paying for your things for a very long time, so you must learn at an early age to ask for the best. Papa would never say no to his girl." Knowlton's face broke into a wicked smile. "You must insist on having the nicest bonnet and the fanciest lace for your dresses. How else is your papa to show you he loves you?"

Katherine was almost tempted to interrupt his outrageous advice, but she knew Caro did not understand a word of it. Yet his words gave her pause. Did he think all women were like that?

"Oh, Elizabeth, where are you?" he sang in mild despair as Caro fixed her attention and her hands on his cravat again. "This female seems to be impervious to my charms. How can you insult me so, dear lady?"

Caro answered with a chortling laugh.

"Now you try to flirt with me, you saucy baggage." He grinned and tapped her cheek with his finger. "You are going to lead your papa on a merry dance when you get older, I will wager. He will find his hall littered with your admirers. But none of them will be good enough for his precious baby, will they?" He wrinkled his nose at her and she did the same in return.

A new sensation, not laughter, but something more like astonishment, swept over Katherine. She had seen how patient Knowlton was with Robbie, but had taken that for granted. Most men did well with boys his age. But watching him now with Caro, she saw that it was not just older boys, but also baby girls who brought out the hidden side of him. He had been ill-at-ease initially, but the longer she watched, the more relaxed he became.

He would be a marvelous father, she realized. Patient and understanding with his sons, teasing and loving with his daughters. A mixture of sadness and longing swept over her. He protested so vehemently against marriage, yet by turning his back on it, he was rejecting this experience as well. Would he ever admit, deep down inside, that he might like to bounce his own daughter upon his knee? Want to be cajoled by sweet smiles and demanding pouts into buying her the most expensive bonnet in the shop? Katherine knew if she asked him, he would deny such thoughts. But she would call him a liar.

Caro rapidly lost interest in the ruined folds of Knowlton's cravat and slid off his lap, landing with a plop on her well-padded bottom. She grinned up at him.

"What, leaving so soon?" He peered down at her clear blue eyes. "I cannot believe I am such a failure with a lady. Perhaps you would rather take a stroll, Lady Caroline? Shall we take a walk through our domain?" He stood up, reaching down to pull her to her still-unsteady feet.

"Now, if what your doting papa says is true, you can march like a trooper." Knowlton stood behind her, holding her tiny hands in his fingers. "Shall we make a circuit of the ballroom, my lady?" He shuffled behind her awkward, high-stepping gait. "Look, there is Lady Barnham. Isn't she wearing the most dreadful head ornament? And look at Lady Welmore! Such a shocking display. You will have to remember to tell your papa you wish to patronize the same modiste. That will keep the lads interested. Oh ho," he said, reaching down to catch her as she stumbled. He swept her up into the air. "Shall we waltz instead, my lady? I know we have not been properly introduced, but I assure you that I am the very model of good manners and restraint. Just ask your papa."

Holding Caro in his arms, Knowlton whirled her about the room at a dizzying pace, the girl's delighted laughter goading him to ever greater speed.

Katherine stepped back in alarm when they came in her direction, but she was too slow.

Knowlton spotted her as he twirled past the door, and was flooded with chagrin to have such a witness to his foolishness. He stopped and looked at her quizzically for a moment; then he turned his head to Caro. "Uh-oh. It is that mean dragon of a chaperon, come to take you away from me."

Katherine stepped into the room. "Why, I would not dream of such a thing. You two make such an adorable couple." She was delighted to see the faint traces of color cross Knowlton's cheeks.

"It is true," he said, setting Caro down carefully. "I seem to be notoriously irresistible to the ladies." He flashed her a wry grin. "Except for one."

"Ah, we are a fickle lot," Katherine said airily, kneeling down to give Caro a hug. "Why, I daresay if her papa came into the room, she would bolt from you like a shot."

"No," he said in mock disbelief. "Lady Caroline would do no such thing. Would you, my dear?"

"Bapa?"

"Bapa is off somewhere, Caro. But I can take you to your mother now." Katherine grinned in delight at Knowlton's bedraggled cravat. "You seem to have decidedly adverse effects on people's clothing," she scolded the girl. "Look what you have done to Lord Knowlton's cravat."

"Oh, do not scold her for that," said Knowlton, a wicked gleam lighting his eyes. "I have never yet objected to a lady removing my cravat. Or any other article of clothing, for that matter."

Katherine planted a noisy kiss on Caro's cheek to avoid a reply. "Shall we find Mama?"

"Outright rejection from two ladies." Knowlton placed his hand over his heart. "Ladies can be so cruel, but do not despair. I know one day I will recover from the wound to my vanity."

"Do not listen to your Uncle Knowlton when he is being so silly," Katherine warned Caro.

"Uncle Knowlton?" his eyes mirrored his disgust.

Katherine flashed him an impish smile. "But assuredly. You performed an excellent rendition of the doting uncle. I cannot wait to tell Elizabeth and Somers of your achievement."

"Kate . . ." he said warningly.

She quickly sidestepped him and headed for the stairs.

Chapter Eleven

Take heed of loving me,
At least remember, I forbade it thee.
— John Donne, *The Prohibition*

Katherine was eager to talk with Knowlton about what she had seen and heard while he entertained Caro. Surely, confronted with such irrefutable evidence, he would acknowledge that he was not completely averse to family life. As if coming to her aid, Somers and Elizabeth had retired early again—ostensibly because Elizabeth was fatigued. The knowing glance the two exchanged before leaving made it clear to Katherine the real purpose of their departure. She gave a longing sigh at the marked sign of their affection and, picking up her sewing again, edged her chair infinitely closer to the candles.

"I begin to wonder if I have unknowingly committed some grievous offense," Knowlton said while he refilled his brandy glass from the decanter on the table. "They flee from me with such ease."

"I rather think they prefer to be alone with each other," Katherine said.

Knowlton frowned and leaned negligently against the mantel. "They remind me of someone newly converted to Methodism, with their superior attitude and smug smiles." He tossed back his head for a long swallow of brandy.

Katherine stuck her needle into the cloth and looked at him with a quizzical expression. "Why do you make mock of their happiness?"

"Because I know it will not last," he said curtly.

Katherine picked up her needle again, forcing herself to concentrate on taking neat, even stitches. Knowlton hated the evidence that Somers had a heart. Was it because he feared to discover that he had one of his own? Or was he envious because he had none?

"My father once said that one should never question the strength of another's love," she said quietly. "For the answer was more often a reflection of the questioner's own desires, rather than a true measure of the other's."

"But there is nothing at stake for me in this matter," Knowlton said, his gray eyes darkening.

"Are you so certain?" she asked quietly. "Perhaps it is envy that causes your irritation. You covet what Somers has."

Knowlton glared at her oddly. "Are you implying that I desire Elizabeth?"

Katherine shook her head. "Of course not. I meant what they have together, a settled marriage, with a family."

"What would I do with a collection of brats?" He grimaced. "Noisy, loathsome creatures that only cut up your peace, spend enormous sums of money, and then run off with unsuitable partners."

"Your protestations are weak, Edward." Katherine was determined to draw him out, to force him into an explanation or at least an admission of his antipathies. "I have seen how you deal so patiently with Robbie. And after this morning, Caro worships you. All she could say after I restored her to Elizabeth was 'No-ton, No-ton.' "

"I do have a way with the ladies," he replied with a smug smile.

"Why are there so many?" she persisted. "Is not the admiration of one woman enough for you?"

"But how could I be so cruel as to confine my attentions to only one?" he said in feigned indignation. "When there are so many others who would welcome it as well? It would hardly be the gentlemanly thing to do."

Katherine sighed in exasperation. "There has not yet been one lady who captured your heart?"

"You are looking at an anatomical miracle—I have no such organ. Or so it has been claimed." Knowlton presented a front of calm indifference as he strolled to the table and refilled his glass. Kate's piercing questions made him edgy. He had not wanted an inquisition this evening, he only wished to pass the time amiably with a woman whose company he enjoyed. Kate seemed determined to spoil all that.

"Besides, by bestowing my interests in several directions, I perform a valuable service," he said, turning back toward Kate. "For who else would listen as disappointed wives tell their troubles? And only think of all the young ladies who would be forced into the streets if deprived of my generous subscriptions. I could not be so unfeeling."

"You are quite the philanthropist," she said dryly.

"Let us talk of you for a change," said Knowlton, eager to deflect her attention. "For someone who is so eager to trumpet the joys of the married state, you set a poor example. Alone for six long years . . ."

"There are not many who would offer for an impoverished widow with a son," she said.

"Have there been any?"

"No offers I would deign to accept," she said quickly,

focusing her gaze on her sewing so he would not see her heightened color. Oh, she had received offers aplenty. But none of them respectable.

"Of course, the prim-and-proper Kate Mayfield would not listen to an improper offer." Knowlton stepped closer, reaching out his hand to stroke his fingers lightly across her cheek. He had caught a glimpse of the passion that lay beneath her surface calm. Could she really be content to remain alone forever? "Sometimes I wonder about the woman who hides behind that facade. She must long to come out at times. I wager she would enjoy herself very much if she did."

Katherine's skin burned under his touch, his nearness making it difficult to collect her thoughts. He came so close to the truth. And each moment she spent with him made it harder to hide her yearnings. But as he remained closed to her, she must remain the same to him.

"Perhaps not every woman is susceptible to your entreaties," she said quickly, fighting against the distracting feel of his fingers as they caressed her neck.

"I have never yet met a woman who was indifferent to me," he said in a seductive whisper. "Are you so certain you can be?"

No, she thought. She was no more impervious than any other of his conquests. But she still had the strength to resist him. Barely. "Yes."

"I think otherwise," he said, withdrawing his hand from where it rested on her neck.

"Only a fool would express interest in a man with a self-proclaimed lack of heart."

"Perhaps no one has ever wished me to possess one," he said lightly, taking a step away from her chair.

His comment jolted Katherine. Could it be that no other woman had desired or demanded his love? A wave of sympathy rushed over her. No wonder he protested so vehemently against that which he had never known. Yet it also stirred hope within her—for it was possible that he would one day acknowledge that he could care.

Knowlton gazed at Katherine, wanting to reach out and touch her fiery curls, the reflected firelight streaking them with gold. The brandy, the warm room, and Kate's nearness wreaked havoc with his senses. It had been so very long since that kiss in the garden. His self-imposed restraint grew more difficult with each passing moment in her presence.

Looking at him, Katherine saw the desire in his eyes and she was afraid. Not of him, but of herself. She grew less certain of her willingness to tell him no.

"I fear the hour grows late," she said, folding up her sewing and gathering her threads.

"Tarry awhile longer," he urged. "If our discussion bores you, we could play cards."

"Thank you, but I should be to bed. Robbie will waken early."

He nodded, accepting her departure with regret. He saw her to the door, pressed a swift kiss on her hand, and watched her walk up the stairs. Returning to the room, he sank down into the chair she had only recently moved from.

Was it possible that Somers and Elizabeth would continue to live for years in their besotted state, as Kate seemed to think? The possibility sent a cold chill through his heart. For if Somers, the laughing, teasing, amatory expert he had known so long, was snared by love, it meant that at last there was a barrier between them that could never be breached.

For Knowlton held no illusions about his ability to love. He could no more confine himself to one woman for any length of time than he could avoid eating, or breathing. It was variety that had always been the siren call in his life. Endless variety, sampled with an appetite bordering on voracious. He had been fonder of some than others, he was willing to grant, but no more than that.

And, admittedly, he was fond of Kate. She had intrigued him from the first, generating a mixture of lust and need that surprised him with its intensity. After his disturbing *ennui* in London, it was comforting to know he could still desire a woman as deeply as he desired Kate.

Yet there was more than sheer lust guiding his dealings with her. He had never danced attendance on a woman for such a length of time without slaking his physical need. But it was possible, in the middle of a drawing room conversation, or a walk through the garden, to forget for a moment how much he wanted her and to simply enjoy her company.

It was the novelty of the situation, surely, that made it

so enjoyable. He had never lived in such a domestic situation with another woman. It was, he thought wryly, something like having a wife. They took breakfast together at times, shared a luncheon now and again, and were always together for dinner. After he and Somers enjoyed a companionable glass, they then joined the ladies for a quiet evening. And Knowlton found it all eminently enjoyable. Particularly when the Wentworths departed and he had Kate to himself.

He grinned in rueful amusement. If he was not careful, Kate would have him half-believing that it was possible to be content with only one partner. *Perhaps* it was possible for Somers. But not for him. Kate might hold him for longer than any other woman had. But "forever" was a word used only by poets and dreamers. It had no basis in reality—for him.

The next afternoon, Katherine noted with surprise the large box resting on her bed. It had not been there when she went down to lunch. Puzzled, she lifted the cover, unwrapped the paper, then drew back her hand in stunned surprise. It was a dress, of a deep, rich plum hue. The bodice and sleeves were ornamented with ribbons and lace of a shimmering silver. Her hand trembling, Katherine drew the gown from its wrappings. With its high waist and deeply flounced hem, it was of the first stare of fashion and the most exquisitely beautiful dress she had ever seen. She had looked at enough of Elizabeth's fashion books over the last weeks to recognize that.

Tears of humiliation stung her eyes. Elizabeth knew she did not have a proper dinner dress and had purchased this for her. It was a generous gesture, but hateful just the same. Katherine knew she should be filled with gratitude, but her pride would not allow her. How hateful it was to be poor.

"Katherine, have you seen . . . ? Oh, what a beautiful creation!" Elizabeth stepped through the door. "You decided on a new dress after all! I like it so much better than the gray silk."

Katherine turned toward her, a bemused expression on her face. "It is not from you?" she asked in confusion. "It was here on my bed."

"Had it been mine, I never would have given it away,"

sighed Elizabeth, running her hand over the silky fabric. "Did you think that I . . . ?"

Katherine nodded.

Elizabeth smiled. "I had thought to do such a thing, but I feared you would say no if I asked. Obviously the giver did not bother to ascertain your desires."

Katherine instantly knew from whom the dress had come. "I will be back," she said, dashing from the room.

Knowlton was in the library, his head bent over a pile of papers. His face lit with a warm smile as Katherine entered.

"Did you order that dress?" she demanded angrily.

Knowlton leaned back in his chair, his arms crossed over his chest. "We are direct and to the point, are we not? No time spent in idle chitchat or greetings for Kate Mayfield. We must immediately reach the heart of the matter." The smile never left his face as he capped the inkwell and folded his hands upon the desk. "Now, my dear, what dress is it that you refer to?"

For a minute Kate's assurance faltered. Yet if not he, then who? "There was a dress upstairs, on my bed. A very elegant, fashionable, and expensive dress."

"Oh, that one. You came in here with such a flurry, I was afraid I might have switched it with the one that arrived for the housekeeper. That certainly would have been an error."

Katherine trembled with her anger. "How can you possibly think I could accept such a gift from you?"

"Now, Katherine, you are not going to get on your high ropes and throw out all those loathsome remarks filled with pride and injured vanity and such things?" Knowlton's smile took on a mocking cast. "I am having a dinner party. You are an invited guest without a suitable garment to wear. Therefore, I have provided you with one. I found it to be a rather simple solution."

"It is highly improper." Katherine glared at Knowlton. "You cannot buy clothing for me as if I were your . . . your . . ."

"Mistress? *Chère amie?*" His smile widened. "I assure you, I am quite aware that you hold no such position in my life." He uttered a long, regretful sigh. "Since you do not, what does it matter?"

"What will the other guests think?"

"I highly doubt, unless you wear a neatly lettered placard

stating, 'This dress purchased by Lord Knowlton,' that anyone will have the foggiest notion that the dress did not
come from your own closet."

"Everyone knows I could not afford such an elegant
gown." Humiliation began to war with her anger.

"Then let on that you borrowed it from Lady Wentworth. I understand it is not unheard-of for ladies to share
their clothes."

"But I will know!"

"And it bothers you greatly, doesn't it?" Knowlton tilted
his head to one side and examined her closely. "Kate, Kate,
Kate. When are you going to learn how to be a gracious
recipient? Were you never taught that it is always polite to
say thank you for a gift, even if the present you receive is
not one that you particularly want? Lord knows, I have
been accused of all manner of rudeness, but I am still able
to remember that particular rule."

She wrung her hands in frustration. "It is not that I object to the gift, Edward, but what it represents."

"And what does it represent?" he asked, his voice light
and teasing.

"That . . . that there is more than friendship between us."

"Is there?" he arched a querying brow.

"We are merely *friends*," she insisted hastily. "Friends
do not exchange such intimate gifts."

Knowlton laughed. "I would hardly call a dress 'intimate.' Now, had I given you a chemise, or stockings, or
garters, you might have cause for complaint."

He sat silently for a moment, as if appraising her
thoughts. "I know! It is the color to which you are averse.
I had thought to consult with you on the subject, but I
knew we would have a tiresome argument along these lines,
so I thought to trust my own judgment. I *knew* I should
have ordered the green."

"You simply do not care a whit about my feelings on
this matter, do you?" She made no attempt to hide the
anger in her voice.

"No, I do not." Knowlton grew exasperated with her
obstinate refusal to accept his gift. "You are being stubborn
to the point of stupidity. You were given a gift—take it
graciously and leave off with this argument." He stood and

took a menacing step forward. "I assure you, Kate Mayfield, that if you do not wear that dress to dinner tomorrow,
I will announce that fact in front of the entire company
and bring down worse embarrassment than you could ever
imagine upon your head. You can toss the thing in the rag
bag the next day, for all I care, but you will wear that
damned dress to dinner!"

Katherine scowled angrily. Could he not see that his persistence only caused her further humiliation? "How can you
continue to offer help to me when you know I do not wish
it? First Robbie's pony, then your invitation to remain here,
and now this."

"I interfere because I want to," he said, his gray eyes
softening. "I know this will be difficult to believe, but I
have a great weakness for ladies in distress. They bring out
whatever vestiges of respectability are still left within me.
It would be immodest of me to recount some of the good
works I have performed, but I assure you, there are several
ladies in the kingdom who have me to thank for rescued
lovers, restored incomes, and salvaged brothers."

"So now I am your current charity project? That is almost a worse insult."

"I assure you, Kate, I am not acting out of charity." His
eyes darkened to a smoky gray. "If I told you that I desire
you more than I have ever desired any other woman, and
long to see that rich fabric draped over your soft curves so
that I may further admire them, would you then consent
to wear it?"

Katherine clenched her fists. "You are impossible!"

"I agree," he said, his eyes twinkling at her discomfort.
"But since you are so opposed to 'charity,' I thought lust
might make a more appealing motive."

The ridiculousness of the whole situation suddenly struck
her. He was impossible. Impossible and irresistible. She
laughed. "You could talk an angel into marrying the devil
if you set your mind to it."

"What a mocking thought! I would never do such a
thing." Knowlton's eyes danced with merriment. "Now, I
might talk her into becoming his mistress . . ."

Katherine shook her head and turned toward the door.

"I will think on it," she said, and hastily quit the room.

Not ready for the confining walls of the house, she sought out her cloak, and then stepped out into the gardens again. Here she would be free to think.

Knowlton's candid acknowledgment of his desire for her grew more and more disturbing. And she had only herself to blame. Their talks had outstepped the bounds of propriety long ago, yet she had never stopped him. Each time they talked, he grew more and more bold, as if trying to see just how far he could take matters before she objected. And she truly could not imagine what he could say that would accomplish that. It was flattering to know that he wanted her. If only she did not want him equally as much. She could deal with his desire. Her own wants were the problem.

It was foolish beyond extremes. She would never be more than a casual dalliance to him, she knew that. It was not what she wanted from life. However rash the manner of her marriage to Robert had been, she did not regret it, or the closeness that came to a couple only through the bond of matrimony. She would never know that with Knowlton.

But she had no doubts that he would be a skillful and exciting lover. Once her maidenly hesitation and ignorance had been overcome, she had quite enjoyed that aspect of married life. Those feelings had lain dormant since Robert's death, but Knowlton had awakened them until they burned hotter than ever. Katherine reddened to find her thoughts straying in such a wanton direction, but she could not help herself. After all, it was what Knowlton wanted of her. He knew the allure of the prize he offered.

It was frighteningly tempting. All she had to give up was her conscience. And her dream of finding love again. But it was not the initial step that threw fear into her heart, it was the eventual parting that chilled her. For she knew that if she allowed herself to succumb to Knowlton, she was lost. Now, knowing only part of the man, she could almost convince herself that her feelings for him were formed from gratitude and friendship and nothing more. It was merely his bold, suggestive remarks that made her skin grow warm and her face grow heated whenever they were together. It was only her physical desire, not anything more lasting. She had to fight it. She could not love a man who offered her so little.

Love? The idea was patently absurd. She was certainly not hen-witted enough to fall in love with a man who neither wanted nor would return such affection. Yet she had. How could she feel so strongly about the worst possible sort of man? She knew full well what he was: a womanizer, a connoisseur of the fair sex, who looked at women as bedmates. One who offered her a temporary future at best, to be followed by a lifetime of longing and regret. It was madness.

As Katherine walked past the fading roses, she could almost laugh at her folly. Here she was, at eight-and-twenty, behaving as rashly as she had at seventeen, when she had fallen top-over-tails for the dashing Robert Mayfield, ignoring the disapproval of his family and hers. At least then she had the excuse of youth to explain her actions. She had no such convenient explanation for her present predicament. It was as if her very determination to resist Knowlton had led her in the opposite direction. And now she was foolishly, futilely in love with a man who would not be flattered by that declaration.

How she wished she could reach his heart. For despite his protestations, she knew he had one. She saw it in his patience with Robbie and in that teasing time he had spent with little Caro. And she thought, too, that he must feel some affection for her. Despite her earlier anger, the gift of the dress had been a generous gesture. It would make her feel more at ease in the glittering company, would make her look as if she belonged to their society. And why would he do such a thing if he did not have a care for her?

As she thought further, her smile deepened. He wanted to see her dressed in finery, looking like a lady of the *ton*. It was churlish of her to refuse to wear such an honorably intentioned gift. It would please him to see her in the dress, and she was suddenly deeply eager to please him.

Katherine briefly closed her eyes, dizzy with excitement and anticipation. If only she could get him to admit he cared. Once past that monumental wall, anything was possible. Even capturing the heart of a self-proclaimed heartless man.

Chapter Twelve

One Kiss, dear Maid! I said and sigh'd—
Your scorn the little boon denied.
Ah why refuse the blameless bliss?
Can Danger lurk within a kiss?

—Coleridge, *The Kiss*

*K*atherine's stomach churned with nervous anticipation as she put the finishing touches on her toilette. She could scarce believe the elegant lady reflected in the pier glass was herself. It was not merely the fashionable dress; everything about the woman in the mirror looked unfamiliar: the hair that Elizabeth's maid had coaxed into an elegant concoction of braids, curls, and ringlets, the cheeks, with their faint application of color, or the eyelashes she had allowed Elizabeth to darken. Even the simple jewelry—a filigree silver necklace and ear bobs, brought from Spain by Robert—looked dazzling on this stranger.

Katherine deliberated about waiting for Elizabeth and her husband before she went downstairs, but then shrugged off her cowardice. It was best to get the matter over with quickly. She resolved to enjoy this last night at Warrenton and not allow nervousness to rule her actions. After six weeks in Knowlton's company, it would be foolish to develop apprehensions at this late date. She had elected to wear his dress, and therefore he was entitled to see it. Gathering up her gloves and the shawl lent to her by Lady Wentworth, Katherine proceeded down the stairs to the drawing room.

Knowlton was already there, waiting. He stood with his back to the door, staring into the flickering flames of the fire. Katherine could not help but admire the picture he presented: his pantaloons set off his nicely formed legs; the tight-fitting coat revealed his narrow waist and muscled shoulders. Unbidden, in her mind rose the image of Knowlton at harvest, naked to the waist, with the mingled droplets of water and sweat sparkling on his chest. She took a deep breath to still her pounding heart.

Sensing her presence, Knowlton turned, but the greeting he had been prepared to utter stuck in his throat.

She was, by far, one of the most beautiful women he had known. He had recognized that at their first meeting, despite her severe coiffure, cap, and dowdy gown. Dressed now as a lady of the *ton,* she truly took his breath away.

It was not entirely the dress—although that daring neckline, skimming low over the swell of her creamy breasts, was enough to set his blood pumping. Her decision to wear it pleased him. He was not even certain he liked her hair fashioned in such an upswept style. It was something more indefinable that made her look different. It came out in her carriage, her bearing. Katherine walked and stood as if she had finally realized just how alluring she was, and found security instead of fear in that knowledge.

He hastened to her side.

"You look exquisitely lovely tonight, Mrs. Mayfield." His gray eyes raked her with frank admiration.

"Thank you, my lord," she replied with a faint smile. "You look quite handsome yourself."

"All for you," he whispered, raising her gloved hand to his lips.

God, how he wanted her. She was quickly driving him mad with need and desire. Not for the first time he damned his noble promise not to take full advantage of her presence under his roof. He had not known then what a sweet temptress she would be. Her skittishness, her modest blushes, only served to inflame his desire. The dress he had forced upon her had been pure folly, for it set off her curves in maddening detail. His hands and lips ached to cover those breasts . . .

He felt the slight tremor in her hand and realized just how intently he stared at her. Lifting his eyes to her face, he felt a thrill of satisfaction as she met his gaze without flinching. His mouth widened into a broad, sensual smile.

"Your gown fits . . . nicely." His smile grew broader as she modestly looked away. "One would think—"

"Thank goodness, we are not late." Somers' voice caused Knowlton and Katherine to step back from one another with a start. "Elizabeth insisted on tying my cravat, and I fear she is sadly out of practice."

His wife shot him a knowing smile.

"The other guests should be arriving momentarily," Knowlton said, half-relieved that the Wentworths had arrived when they had. He was afraid he might have sadly crumpled Katherine's gown if they had been left alone much longer. "A glass of wine?"

Elizabeth drew Katherine aside while the men sauntered to the side table. "You look marvelous."

"Thank you," Katherine replied.

"Nervous?"

Katherine nodded. "A little. I feel as if I am in the middle of a masquerade; I barely recognized the woman in the mirror. I am grateful it is only the neighbors here tonight. I do not think I could face strangers in this new guise."

Elizabeth gave her a reassuring squeeze of the hand as they turned to greet the newly announced visitors.

Knowlton had kept the party small—the vicar and his wife, Squire Moreton, his wife and two daughters, and Sir Richard and Lady Court. It was a "duty" dinner, designed to maintain amiable relationships in the neighborhood. Not that Knowlton ever looked down upon or disdained the other residents of the county. If they were not frequent guests at Warrenton, it was more because the usual entertainments there were unsuitable for family attendance. Tonight he made every effort to demonstrate just how respectable the present situation was.

The vicar and his wife were the first to arrive, and immediately greeted Katherine.

"And how is young Robbie doing?" the vicar asked.

"Quite well," replied Katherine. "Bored beyond belief. But the doctor says the splints may come off tomorrow and we shall be able to return home." She directed a smile at Knowlton. "It has been most gracious of Lord Knowlton to extend his hospitality to us for so long."

Katherine turned back to the vicar. "Robbie has done

an admirable job of keeping up on his studies. I shall have to wait for the doctor's advice, of course, but I think he will be able to resume his work with you soon."

"It will be good to see the lad again," Mr. Ashe replied. "Although I expect he may prove more rambunctious than usual this fall after such a long period of forced inactivity." They all laughed.

The other guests soon arrived in a flurry of greetings.

"It is a surprise to see you here, Mrs. Mayfield." The voice of the squire's wife held a slightly condemning tone. "I would have thought your son's leg healed by now."

"I anticipate the doctor will say we can return home when he visits tomorrow," Katherine said politely, choking back her irritaiton.

"There is nothing quite like being in your own home," Mrs. Ashe sympathized. "And you must call on me, my dear, if you need any assistance. I know how exhausting Robbie can be."

"That is such a lovely dress," the squire's wife commented, drawing attention back to Katherine. "Surely it is not sewn by Mrs. Gorton's hands Did you make it yourself? I hear you do such exquisite work."

Katherine stiffened, knowing that she had stitched the lace on the very gown Mrs. Moreton wore, and that lady was probably aware of it as well. "Lady Wentworth was gracious enough to share her wardrobe," she lied smoothly.

"Interesting," murmured the lady, casting a sly glance at Elizabeth.

Katherine was relieved when Hutchins entered and announced dinner.

Knowlton chose to seat Katherine partway down the table rather than next to him. To have seated her in the place of honor would only have raised troublesome questions about her status in the house. He knew how grindingly respectable the situation was, but the Wentworths were an unknown entity in this part of the county. Unfortunately, his neighbors were all too familiar with the typical cut of guests he entertained. He must do all in his power to ensure no harm would come to Katherine's name.

The slight distance had the added advantage of making it easier to watch Katherine unobserved. He looked with interest while she chatted amiably with the vicar while waiting to be served, then alternated her attention between him and the squire's younger daughter during the soup course.

"Mrs. Mayfield," the squire's wife began as the soup was removed, "I understand your late husband served during the Peninsular campaign?"

"That is correct," Katherine replied with a trace of wariness.

"My own eldest was there also, as you know, although fortunately he returned to us. What regiment did your husband serve in?"

The next course, of stuffed pheasant, was set before her and Katherine took advantage of the slight pause to calm her thoughts. "He was in the Eighteenth Hussars."

"The Hussars, you say?" Squire Moreton looked at her curiously. "That's a mighty difficult regiment to join."

Katherine did not miss the implication. The Hussars were notoriously selective. Why had she not claimed a less-exalted regiment?

"Regimental commissions are such a strange thing," Knowlton interjected, noting Katherine's discomfort. "One tries for ages to buy one without success, then one day there is suddenly an opening and at a bargain besides." He smiled warmly at her. "I am certain Captain Mayfield was pleased with his luck."

"Yes, he was," Katherine said, grateful for Knowlton's rescue. It had been purely family influence that eased Robert into the Hussars, but she did not want to admit that. It would lead to too many other questions.

"I understand your son has received a new posting?" Knowlton turned the conversation and the attention back to Mrs. Moreton, who he knew could rattle on for hours about her son. But his mind pondered Katherine's surprising revelation. The mysterious Captain Mayfield had purchased a commission in the Eighteenth Hussars. A rather intriguing story, one that implied a certain family background. Someday he must question her more thoroughly about it.

Katherine still appeared at ease, Knowlton noted with relief when he dare to glance in her direction again. He had not wished this party to make her uncomfortable, and for a moment he feared it would have that result. The squire's wife was a gossipy worm.

But as he watched, he observed Katherine talk and smile and look as unconcerned as if this type of entertainment were a daily occurrence in her life. She looked very much as if she belonged at the table. With the possible exception of Elizabeth, Katherine outshone every lady there in grace and manners, let alone beauty. In that, she was unparalleled. The golden glow from the candles gave her hair a fiery luminescence that constantly drew his eye. How he wished she had worn her hair down so that it floated in soft waves about her shoulders. He ached to bury his hands in its silky softness.

Knowlton clenched his fingers to control his burning desire. How was he going to allow her to leave tomorrow? He had grown accustomed to her presence, the knowledge that he could seek out her company at any time during the day, that they would dine together in the evening, and talk long into the night. And despite the torture it inflicted on his body, he loved to sit and savor the sight of her.

"May we count on your support, my lord?"

The vicar's voice broke into Knowlton's distracted thoughts. "Certainly," he mumbled. Seeing Katherine's amused smile, he wondered what he had committed himself to. Repairing the church organ? The Christmas Fund? He dared not ask.

"Perhaps Mrs. Mayfield would be willing to assist with the new altar cloths," Mrs. Moreton suggested.

"I am not certain I shall have the time," Katherine protested.

"Oh, but you do such beautiful work," the squire's wife said with a sly smile.

Katherine fought down her anger at Mrs. Moreton's deliberate taunting. Remembering the long hours spent in her mother's parlor, sewing every manner of altar cloth imaginable, Katherine never wished to see one again. She no longer had the luxury of sewing for free. The squire's wife knew perfectly well that she needed to devote her time to the paid sewing given her by the seamstress.

"Perhaps your lovely daughter would be willing to lend her talent," Knowlton said, smiling in an avuncular manner

at the young lady seated at his right. He did not know if
the chit could even thread a needle, but it grew apparent
that Mrs. Moreton was determined to discomfort Katherine
this evening. He offered up a prayer of relief when the next
course arrived.

"We sponsor a school in our district for the local girls,"
Elizabeth offered. "Sewing is one of the skills they are
taught. Perhaps you could establish a similar program here,
and thus have many willing hands for your cloths."

"Capital idea," said Knowlton, looking pointedly at the
vicar. "Perhaps we could discuss such a thing next week?"

"Will your son be going to school soon, now that his leg
is better?" Mrs. Moreton pressed on with her inquisition,
disregarding the efforts of the others to turn the conversation. "Our youngest is presently at Eton."

"Robbie is doing quite well with Mr. Ashe, at present,"
Katherine replied.

"It is never too early to plan ahead for these things,"
Mrs. Moreton continued. "Particularly if Robbie is to attend on a scholarship."

Knowlton winced at the tactless reference to Katherine's
lack of funds.

"Not all schools are as expensive as Eton," Katherine
replied coolly. "And based on my husband's experiences,
Eton is the last place I would choose to send Robbie."

"Quite right," Knowlton interrupted, cutting off Mrs.
Moreton before she could open her mouth. "I detested
Eton myself."

"Hartford sent his son to an interesting school," Elizabeth interjected, and launched into a lengthy description of
that place.

Knowlton inclined his head to listen absentmindedly to
Elizabeth and the squire's wife, but his attention remained
on Kate. She had revealed another clue about her late husband—he had attended Eton. That knowledge only added
to the mystery surrounding her current circumstances. Circumstances he hoped to change soon.

Once or twice her eyes strayed to his, and he reveled in
the intimacy of their shared look. He watched the gentle rise
and fall of her chest, noticing her quickened breathing when
she became aware of his gaze. Her cheeks colored with that
maddeningly enticing rosy glow when their eyes met again.

Damn propriety. He was going to have to find a way of furthering their relationship in such a way that no attention was drawn to them. But he was damned if he was going to let much more time pass before he pursued her in earnest. He had promised to remain a gentleman while she was under his roof, but tomorrow she repaired to her own house. The constraints on his behavior would be gone and he intended to make every use of the opportunity. He would waste no more time before he learned if she was as passionate in bed as her hair would indicate. Modest blushes or no, he had no doubts that she would be.

Knowlton was relieved that he had included a chilled dessert on the menu. He needed the cool ice to dampen the fire in his body. That brief interlude in Nottingham seemed centuries ago. He belatedly jumped to his feet when he realized the ladies were taking their leave.

He endured the remainder of the evening with growing impatience. Knowlton called the private gathering of the men to a close in an indecently short interval, and did nothing to promote a lengthy evening entertainment. Lady Wentworth was prevailed upon to play the pianoforte, which she did with consummate skill, but Knowlton only wished that everyone would go home so he could have Kate to himself for a time.

She thwarted him in that endeavor, for when the vicar and his wife took their leave, she pleaded the need to check on her son and fled the drawing room before Knowlton could protest. The other guests rapidly departed as well, Somers and Elizabeth retreated to their rooms, and he was left quite alone in front of the dying fire with an unwanted glass of brandy in his hands. Whatever hopes he had held for the evening, he had not envisioned a scenario like this. He might as well seek his bed; perhaps he could find a moment alone with Kate on the morrow.

As he reluctantly passed down the corridor, he noticed that the door to Robbie's room was slightly ajar, and Knowlton could not resist the temptation to peek inside. Kate was probably safely in her own bed by now. But as he quietly pushed open the door, he saw she had not yet retired. He stood silently in the shadows, watching her as she stood in front of the window. With the curtains thrown open, the blue-white light of the moon cast her corner of the room into almost daylike brightness. She was looking out onto the moon-drenched grounds of the estate, her arms loosely clasped about her. She still wore her dinner gown, although she had taken down her hair and its soft curls fell in flaming clouds about her shoulders. She looked so fragile and delicate. He clenched his fingers. If he retreated quietly, she would never know he had come . . .

He silently crossed the carpeted room.

"Robbie has dropped off at last, I see," he whispered softly as he came up behind her.

Startled by his presence, Katherine turned to face him.

"It was a long battle," she confessed, then returned her gaze to the moonlit scene outside. Her skin prickled in the knowledge of his nearness.

He rested his hands lightly on her shoulders. "I hope you enjoyed tonight."

She smiled warmly at the night. "I am glad you persuaded me to attend. I did enjoy myself."

"Your presence certainly made the evening more enjoyable for me," he whispered softly, brushing back her hair to expose one creamy white shoulder. "I scarcely noted what I ate. It was too difficult to tear my eyes away from your beauty."

She laughed nervously. "Of a certainty, my lord."

"Set off to great advantage by the lovely dress you are wearing," he said, stroking his fingers across the bare skin of her shoulder, then tangling them in her fiery curls. "I have been longing to bury my hands in your flames all evening."

"Edward, I—"

"Shh," he said quickly, turning her so she faced him. They stared at one another for an eternity of silence; then with a slow, seductive smile he cupped her chin in his hand and covered her lips with his before she could protest further. Feeling her initial hesitation, he kept his kisses light, feathering them across her lips until he felt her relax. He drew away, looking into her face for her acquiescence before he went further. Her blue eyes were wide with surprise, yet he saw a flicker of desire there that encouraged him.

Dropping his hands to her waist, he gently pulled her against him, bringing their mouths together once more.

This time, she responded, and his kisses grew more demanding, more possessive. His senses reeled in a way he had not thought possible from a few mere kisses. He softly flicked his tongue over her lips, teasing, pleading until they parted beneath his and he could probe the warm moistness of her mouth.

Katherine almost jumped at that all-too-obvious invasion of her body, yet she did not resist Knowlton's bold advances. She would regret her weakness later, but for now she did not want to think coherently, only wanted to give herself up to the sensations coursing through her veins. Deliberately ignoring all the warning voices in her head, she raised her arms and curled her fingers in the hair at his nape.

Cold shivers ran up Knowlton's spine at her touch. She was a redheaded witch, casting a spell of sensual pleasure over him that he was powerless to resist. He buried his fingers in her hair, drawing her even closer. His other hand, pressed in the small of her back, held her pinioned in an embrace that scorched along the length of their touching bodies.

Katherine trembled as she willingly pressed her body against his. She leaned her head back, closing her eyes against the warm sensations of his lips, her breath catching as he trailed kisses down her neck, pausing to nibble her ear before he once again claimed her mouth. She burned with fire; she was filled with an all-consuming need and want that overcame all rational consciousness.

Knowlton grew bolder, kissing her with growing urgency, his tongue twining with hers as his hands roamed over her body.

"Kate, Kate," he whispered as his hand sought the softness of her breast. Through the thin silk of her gown he felt the nipple go taut beneath his seeking fingers, matching the growing tightness in his groin. Dear God, it had been so long . . . She was like a drug, sapping his mind, his thoughts. He was burning with a fire that only she could quench.

A low moan issued from the shadowed corner of the room. Instantly, Katherine wrenched herself from Knowlton's arms and quickly crossed to her son's bed.

Knowlton berated his stupidity for choosing such a poor location for his lovemaking. But he had not intended such a thing when he had paused at the slightly open door—or had he?

"He is asleep." Her whisper broke into his thoughts.

Knowlton hesitated. The spell had been weakened, but not broken. Then slowly he brought her hand to his lips, kissing first her curled fingers, then pressing his mouth to her palm.

"I apologize for my inopportune choice of place," he said quickly, willing his rapid breathing to slow. Kate stood there silently; in the shadowy light it was difficult to read the expression on her face. He exhaled slowly. "These rooms connect with mine, you will recall. We could be more private there."

She knew what he asked, what he wanted. And knew that she half-wanted it as well. But she still held on to the last vestiges of her resolve. If only she could hear the words she wanted from his lips. "It is late," she demurred.

He accepted his dismissal with grace. "Then I shall bid you good night, my fair Kate." Knowlton pressed another kiss on her fingers, exiting silently into the corridor.

Katherine stood in the middle of the room, unmoving, staring at the door. She had nearly lost all her control this time. If Robbie had not stirred . . . She had no doubt that she would have found herself in the earl's bed. And she truly was not certain which outcome to the evening disturbed her more.

With only the shadowy moonlight lighting his bedchamber, Knowlton stripped off his neckcloth and tossed it onto the dresser. Every nerve in his body still flamed with the memory of Kate's shape pressed close to his. She had been so close to capitulation. Only his incredibly stupid move of attempting a seduction within feet of Robbie's bed had cost him his prize. And tomorrow Kate would be gone from his roof.

Unbuttoning his shirt, Knowlton considered. He grew tired of this clever game they played; he advanced, she parried, but they progressed toward the goal nevertheless. After tonight, there was no point in disguising his aim. She knew exactly what he wanted of her. And, he felt confident, she wanted the same of him. Kate had been just as passionate as her red hair indicated. He smiled quickly. Once again, his judgment had not failed him. Kate Mayfield was as delectable a morsel as he had desired in an age, and would be every bit as delicious as he hoped. His anticipation grew as he divested himself of the rest of his clothing and crawled beneath the covers of his solitary bed. Tomorrow he would finalize matters.

Chapter Thirteen

Come live with me and be my love,
And we will some new pleasures prove.
                    —John Donne, *The Bait*

*K*nowlton awoke the next morning and stretched lazily beneath the covers, a smug smile of satisfaction crossing his face at the memory of Kate's heated embrace. He had to have her, had to possess her.

He had never before taken a mistress without first sampling her talents, but he held no fears that Kate would be a disappointment. He had seen and heard and felt enough last night to have no worries in that area. Whatever skills she lacked could be easily taught, and the pleasure would be in the teaching. His imagination stirred at the thought.

He experienced a momentary doubt over Kate's willingness to become his mistress, but quickly set it aside. With her straitened circumstances, it should be easy to work out a satisfactory arrangement. He knew how her poverty grated upon her. His offer would put an end to all that. And if gowns and jewels and money were not enough, there was always Robbie's future to consider. Knowlton felt a twinge of apprehension at using the boy again to further his own interests, but quickly ignored it. It would benefit everyone if he paid for Robbie's schooling. And if it meant that the lad would be away for a good part of the year, giving Knowlton uninterrupted access to Kate, all the better.

With a low chuckle, Knowlton threw back the covers and padded across the room to the bell rope. He must plan his strategy carefully. He was determined to win the prize at last.

Katherine looked up in trepidation when Knowlton entered the room. She was afraid to face him this morning, uncertain how she should react after her wanton behavior the night before. He would never believe her protestations now.

She owned she had been more than a trifle surprised at her reactions to his lovemaking. Granted, Knowlton was a skilled practioner of the art, and it was to be expected that he would know all manner of tricks to get a lady to respond. But she had responded with all the pent-up yearnings of the last six years. And now she must face the ramifications of her recklessness.

Knowlton was pleased to find Katherine at Robbie's bedside when he entered the room. "Good morning, Mrs. Mayfield. Robbie."

Katherine did not turn her head. "Good morning, my lord."

Knowlton sat down next to Robbie on the bed. "Ready to do battle with grammar again this morning?"

Robbie made a disgusted face.

Knowlton laughed. "Cheer up. I promise I will come up to play you a game of chess later, before the doctor comes."

Robbie turned an apprehensive gaze toward Knowlton. "Will we . . . will we be able to play chess again after I go home?"

"Certainly," Knowlton reassured him. "That is, if your mama does not object."

Katherine shook her head, knowing future contact with the earl would only further her folly. "You have done more than enough for us, Lord Knowlton," she protested weakly.

"But not nearly as much as I wish," he said in a low voice.

Katherine turned away. It took only a look from

him to set her pulses racing. Last night had been madness. How could she have allowed herself to do such a thing?

Knowlton rose, pleased at her discomfort. It meant she was as affected by his presence as he was by hers. For a brief moment, seeing her averted gaze, he feared the morning would be full of recriminations. But Katherine Mayfield did not look like a woman filled with anger. On the contrary, she looked like a woman who very much needed to be kissed, again and again. He could not wait for the next opportunity.

However, it was as if events conspired against him. Whenever he thought to draw Kate away and discuss his plans for her, some other matter always intervened. He seethed with frustration. Once the doctor gave permission for Robbie to go home, Kate would be gone before Knowlton had the opportunity to talk with her.

When he finally freed himself from the latest minor crisis, he raced to Robbie's room, only to discover Kate was elsewhere. He searched the drawing room and library before realizing she was probably in her favorite haunt—the garden. He quickly slipped outdoors. Relief flooded his face when he spotted her, and he hastened to her side.

"I had hoped to find you here."

Katherine turned away slowly from her contemplation of the last brave roses scattering their color across the landscape. She could not keep the soft smile from her lips. "And why is that, my lord?"

Taking her hand and placing it upon his arm, Knowlton led her along the graveled path. He prayed she would accept his offer. She would be a fool not to. Even he acknowledged that the terms he proposed were more than generous. He doubted there was another lady in the kingdom who had been offered as much. Yet he knew that the idea of becoming his mistress might be difficult for her to accept. She had been a properly married lady once, and throwing off the mantle of respectability, no matter how carefully he disguised their relationship to others, would give her some pause. He wished there had been more time to entice her with the pleasures of the flesh. Had they not been interrupted in such an untimely manner last night, he was certain the evening would have ended in his bed.

But it had not, and now it was up to him to convince her that was where she belonged.

Katherine walked nervously by his side, but did not draw away from him. They had but a few short hours more together. She wanted only to revel in his presence this one last time. She wanted to store away all the memories of him that she could, to warm herself with on those long, lonely winter nights.

"My bed was such a cold and solitary place last night," Knowlton said at last, a wistful smile creasing his face. "I kept thinking how much more pleasurable it would be with a lovely lady to keep me warm."

Kate closed her eyes for a brief moment. He was not going to let her forget last night, after all.

Knowlton stopped abruptly and turned toward her. Cupping her face in his hands, he brushed her lips briefly with his, then kissed her with a searing intensity that brought back all the passion of the previous night. Katherine swayed against him, helpless to stem the sensations rising within her. To deny him now would take more strength than she would ever have.

"I know what I want, Kate," he said when he released her, his breathing erratic. "And last night proved beyond a doubt that I want you very badly."

He flashed her that wickedly seductive smile that sent a tingle of anticipation through her body. Her heart leapt at his words. He wanted her. He *cared* for her.

Knowlton took her hands in his, his gaze caressing her face. "I should like to take you under my protection. Know that I do not make the offer with any intention of causing you insult, Katherine, for I mean it as the highest compliment. I realize there are some . . . uh . . . different circumstances here than I usually deal with. I am quite willing to make arrangements for Robbie as well. For you, there will be a house in town, or a country cottage, if that is what you prefer. And I shall pay for Robbie's schooling."

Kate heard the words, but they registered only feebly on her brain once she caught his meaning. Something inside her crumbled like a discarded piece of paper. He wanted her for his mistress. He was willing to pay her to come to his bed.

Of course it had been foolish of her to ever think she

could have more from him. She had manufactured that expectation out of her own longings. But like the reckless girl who had once raced off to Gretna Green, she had clung to her hopes that somehow she could reach into his inner self and touch him as no woman ever had before. Had she not been so close to tears, she would have laughed at her folly.

"The idea does not offend you?" Knowlton asked with a tinge of apprehension.

"Offend me?" she asked, her voice sounding as numb to her ears as she felt inside. "How could I possibly take offense? You have offered to feed me, clothe me, house me, and send my son to school. And you ask so *very little* in return."

"True," he cheerfully admitted, oblivious of the sarcasm in her voice. "But I learned long ago that when one wishes the finest quality, one must be willing to pay for it."

"Like fine horseflesh or impeccably tailored clothes?" Katherine struggled to keep herself from trembling, the anger in her voice rising with every breath. "How does it make you feel, my Lord Knowlton, to know that you cannot have a woman without paying for her first? Do you ever calculate the cost of each touch? How much do you spend for a kiss?"

She reached out and grabbed his hand, drawing it to her breast. "Is that worth a shilling? Or a new pair of stockings?"

Knowlton jerked his hand back and stared at her in surprise, his gray eyes widening in bemusement at her vehement reaction. "Stop it, Kate."

"I would be very wary of anyone I had bought," she continued in the same biting tone. "Does the price include my emotions, my lord? Or my loyalty? You would never know when a more lucrative offer might tempt me away. Or whether my pleasure was real or feigned—or do you not care about that?"

"I had only thought to ease your circumstances, not insult you," he said with a touch of irritation. "You are quite free to refuse."

"And refuse you I shall," she cried, feeling the tears beginning to well in her eyes. She struggled against them. "I would rather starve and send Robbie to school as a scholar than whore myself to you. At least I would have my pride intact." She took a few steps toward the house, then turned to him again.

"I pity you more than anything," she said, her voice cloaked in sadness. "For you are never going to know anything beyond the mere exchange of money for sex. There is so much more to life." She turned again and sped toward the house before her tears fell.

Knowlton stared after her, anger and confusion dancing through his brain. He had sadly misjudged her after all. Kate was as hopelessly respectable as he had first thought her. Foolish woman. She would rue her refusal one day, when the shadows of the poor house loomed darkly over her. Pride was a poor substitute for food and shelter. With a disgusted scowl, he kicked up a spray of gravel, listening to the clattering stones crack against the others on the ground. There was an abundance of other women who would jump at the chance for such an opportunity.

Katherine fled to the sanctuary of the library, knowing she could be alone there. Sinking down into one of the comfortable leather chairs, she gave full vent to her tears of anger and sadness.

Mistress. An elevated title for a woman who sold her favors as easily as a common street whore. Fine clothes, fancy houses, and flashy jewels could not hide the basic transaction. Money for sex. A simple trade. But one she could not accept.

Had she cared for him less, his offer would have provided less insult. She still would have been shocked and angry, to think that he thought he could buy her in such a way. And to dangle the dream of school for Robbie had been cruelly taunting. Yet it was the simple fact that he wanted their relationship to be on the level of a tradesman's exchange that caused the deep hurt inside her. She was, after all was said and done, nothing more than a temporary plaything for him.

It had been pure folly to delude herself with the hope that he would come to care for her. She had allowed her love to blind her to his true nature. How arrogant an assumption on her part, that *she* would be the one woman to engender tender feelings in him. He had always claimed he had no heart, and for once, she saw it was true. At this moment, she wished she did not either. For then it would not hurt so very badly.

A noise in the hall alerted her to the doctor's arrival. Katherine glanced quickly into the mirror to make certain her face no longer showed the ravages of her earlier tears. Satisfied that no one could see how deeply she bled inside, she exited the library and hastened to her son's room.

Katherine watched eagerly while the doctor removed Robbie's splint, examined the leg, and pronounced himself satisfied with its healing. He cautioned against overactivity, warned the lad to make use of a crutch or cane while he strengthened the weak muscles, and said Robbie would be fit as ever within a month.

Even though she had expected the news, Katherine uttered a deep sigh of relief when the doctor said Robbie could go home. She knew she could not have remained for another night under Knowlton's roof. She only wanted to get as far away from him as possible.

Katherine was also grateful that the Wentworths would be departing for their home today as well. She knew she would not be able to hide her damaged heart from Elizabeth, who was uncannily perceptive about such matters. Making her good-byes to the Wentworths, Katherine promised to consider accepting Elizabeth's invitation to their home for Christmas. She knew she would miss the countess; in their short acquaintance Katherine had found the closest thing she had ever known to a friend her own age.

Knowlton did not make an appearance as the preparations for Katherine and Robbie's return to the cottage were put into motion. There was little enough to do, she thought, but acquiesced for the last time to the assistance of the Warrenton servants. There would be plenty of time for her to take care of herself in the future.

It was only when they gathered in the entry hall, waiting for the coach to be brought round, that Knowlton made his appearance.

He tousled Robbie's red mop. "Eager to be off, eh?"

Robbie nodded.

"Now, you promise to take good care of your mama." Knowlton shot a quick glance at Kate, standing tight-lipped against the wall. "Do not make too much extra work for her, do you hear me?"

"Yes sir," Robbie replied.

"I will keep a good eye on Atlas for you," Knowlton said, wondering if Robbie would ever be allowed to set foot at Warrenton again. "When the doctor says you are ready, we will go riding."

"You will come and play chess at the cottage?"

Robbie's plaintive query seared Knowlton. How much had changed since the lad had first asked the question this morning.

"I will be gone for a space. There are some business matters I need to take care of in London." He patted Robbie companionably on the back. "But as soon as I return, we will meet again across the board."

A footman carried Robbie to the now-waiting carriage. Knowlton turned to Kate. Her closed expression gave no indication of her feelings. Was she still angry?

"I am sorry to see both of you go, Mrs. Mayfield."

Katherine met his gaze without flinching, even though it took every ounce of strength she had not to let him see how disturbed she was. "It was most generous of you to extend your hospitality for so long, my lord."

"It was no imposition," he said. "I enjoyed it very much."

Keeping her expression calm, Katherine pasted a polite smile upon her face. "I am certain you are a gracious host to all your guests." She turned and took her bonnet from the hovering footman. "I bid you a safe journey to London, my lord." Tying the ribbons firmly under her chin, she walked down the steps, her back rigid.

With long strides, Knowlton caught up to her just as she approached the coach. Smiling blandly, he took her hand to help her into the vehicle.

"If I can offer you or your son any assistance in the future, do not hesitate to let me know," he said. Lowering his voice, he added, "I still have a care for your welfare. And I ask nothing in return."

Katherine bit her lip to keep it from trembling. Nodding briefly, she took her seat, refusing to look out the window after the door closed. She needed no last look to imprint Knowlton's features on her mind. They were etched in her heart forever.

Knowlton stood on the steps watching the carriage until

it vanished from sight. There was nothing he could say or do to put matters right again, he knew. He let out a long, resigned sigh. He had held such high hopes for Kate; it was unfortunate she had turned out to be such a disappointment. It had all been an interesting diversion, but nothing more.

He rued the day he had laid eyes on that redheaded witch. His initial reservations about dallying after a lady of her ilk rushed back over him like a reproach. That was what came of dealing outside the circle of experienced ladies. He would have to remember that lesson for the future. With a careless shrug, he turned and mounted the stairs.

Robbie showed more enthusiasm at returning to the cottage than Katherine had thought he would. Even a ten-year-old appreciated the familiarity of home. The Warrenton cook sent along a cold collation so Katherine would not be faced with too many tasks on her first day home. Katherine noted in shocked puzzlement that the cottage gleamed. There was even, she noted with surprise, a new mattress on Robbie's bed. Knowlton had taken care of matters, of course. She was forced to admit a grudging gratitude for his thoughtfulness.

Robbie, worn out from excitement and the work of exercising his newly healed leg, fell asleep early. Katherine sat alongside his bed until he drifted into slumber, then made her way to the parlor.

She looked around her, really opening her eyes to what she saw. A tiny room, filled with cast-off furniture. It was the typical residence of a lady who had not the means to support a proper establishment. "Genteel poverty"—was that not the expression? Now it seemed more intolerable than ever.

Katherine had tried to count herself lucky to have a roof over her head, thinking that as long as she had Robbie with her, it was all that mattered. Material things were not important. Love and family were.

Yet she barely had either. Only Robbie. And as much as she loved her son, he would one day leave her side to make his own way in the world. And she would be so dreadfully alone.

Would it hurt so badly then, after all the years had

passed? Would she look back upon this as just a foolish interlude in her life, the last gasp of her impulsive girlhood? She sincerely prayed it would be so.

But whatever the future held in store, she knew it did not include the Rose Cottage. She could tarry no longer in this neighborhood. Where, then, to go? To another cottage, in another county? To another life on the edge of poverty, scrimping and saving every penny in order to clothe Robbie? Begging and pleading to find a school somewhere that would take him without fees? Discouragement bowed her shoulders.

Katherine had caught a glimpse of what another life could be like during her stay at Warrenton. It was not the opulence of the furnishings or the expensive clothes that meant so much to her. It was the element of comfort, the security of knowing that there would be a roof over her head in the morning, that there would be ample food on the table at night, and that one could easily replace a pair of worn shoes or a torn coat without throwing the household budget into havoc. It was knowing that there was a point and purpose to the long hours Robbie spent struggling with his Latin and Greek, for there would be school and university in his future. Knowlton had offered all that, but she could not accept his terms.

The events of six years ago washed back over her. The angry words, the veiled threats, the fear and the distrust. Could she take the chance now? For there was one other place where she could find security. One other person she could turn to in order to ensure that at least Robbie had a future in which he could seek his own happiness. She had enjoyed four blissful years married to Robert. Perhaps that was all the happiness she was destined to achieve in this life. But Robbie was still young, with his whole life before him. She could still hope for more for him.

Six years ago, she had scornfully turned her back on her only other source of assistance. Now she would have to go hat in hand, pleading her case. But if Robbie benefited, it would be worth the damage to her pride.

Her pride. Katherine smiled ruefully. She had made so many decisions based on pride, and what had it earned her? A life where she and her son lived on the precarious edge of survival. A life where she was subjected to offers of the type Knowlton had made. Pride was an expensive commodity in her situation. Too expensive.

With a sigh, Katherine rose and picked up the candle. She followed the eerie shadows it threw on the wall as she mounted the stairs to her room. It was time to confront the past. She and Robbie would leave for London tomorrow.

Chapter Fourteen

'Tis time, I feel, to leave thee now,
   While yet my soul is something free. . . .
                    —Thomas Moore, To— — — — —

*K*atherine nervously clenched her hands together, staring blindly out the window as the hackney wound its way toward St. James Square. For the thousandth time, she prayed she was making the right decision. For both Robbie and herself.

As the coach pulled up in front of the modest building, a liveried footman opened the door and assisted Katherine from the carriage. He followed her up the few stone steps, where another footman held open the front door.

Adjusting her eyes to the dim light in the entry hall, Katherine looked about for her first view of the town house of the Marquess of Winslow. A silent, stern-faced butler motioned for her to follow him up the stairs. With tight self-control, she refrained from gawking at the ancient paintings and ornamental vases lining the staircase walls, but she was helpless not to come to a dead stop when she saw the painting at the head of the stairs. There was no question it was Robert—at ten or eleven, perhaps, posing with his older brother, Frederick. The painter had captured his boyish enthusiasm, the *élan* that had so swept her off her feet when she was seventeen. How she hoped Robbie could see this portrait. Despite the differing hair color, they looked so much alike.

"My lady?" The butler was correctly proper.

She started self-consciously, embarrassed at having been caught gawking like a visitor on open day. "Proceed," she directed.

While the butler held open the door to the marquess's study, Katherine halted momentarily outside the room. What fate awaited her inside? Would she be welcomed home as the prodigal daughter, or tossed out on her ear as an unwanted relative? Whatever the outcome, there was no changing her mind now. Her last hope rested inside the room. Squaring her shoulders, she stepped through the doorway.

The man behind the desk rose as she entered. Katherine struggled to suppress a small cry of shock at his appearance. In the six years since she had seen him last, he looked to have aged twenty. His hair was completely white now, and his shoulders were stooped with age. Still, he projected the aura of command that she remembered so well.

"So, my dear, you have decided to come out of hiding at last." He did not conceal the derision in his voice.

"Yes, my lord."

"Your letter mentioned that you are interested in discussing the future of my grandson. He is well, I trust."

She nodded, fighting down her nervousness. "He is still recovering from a broken leg earned in a riding accident, but otherwise enjoys excellent health."

"Trying to crowd his fences, eh?"

"Not anything so dramatic." Katherine forced a tentative smile. "He only learned to ride this past summer, and a shooting party startled his mount."

The Marquess of Winslow shook his head in a display of sympathy, and motioned for her to sit. He took his own chair and surveyed her with an assessing gaze. "Well, madam, what exactly is it that you wish to discuss?"

Katherine took a deep breath and met his piercing stare without flinching. So much depended on the outcome of this interview; if she made a mistake, antagonizing him further . . .

"Robbie needs an education, my lord. And I simply do

not have the funds to send him to a school commensurate with his station—or his abilities." She unconsciously played with the folds of her skirt. "He is doing quite well at the present, taking lessons with the vicar, who has no doubt that Robbie will be able to take his place at school with no shame to his studies."

Katherine looked down briefly, steeling herself to say the words. Raising her gaze, she again met the marquess's imperious gaze. "I am asking you to pay his tuition, and perhaps use your power to find him an adequate position when he finishes his schooling."

"Hmm." The marquess sat silently for a moment.

Relief flooded Katherine at having at last made her request. It was all in his hands now; she had done what she could. She searched his lined face for a clue to the fate of her mission, but he gave no hint of his feelings.

"What career does the lad envision?" he asked at length.

"He wishes to be a cavalry officer." She gave him a small, apologetic smile. "I think he would do well at law, my lord."

The marquess toyed with his penknife, which only served to increase Katherine's agitation. Her fingers continued their nervous fumbling.

"Why now, after all these years?" His deep blue eyes stared at her coldly.

"It is school," she said simply, having practiced this answer numerous times. "Robbie deserves to have a proper education. I do not care if it is Eton or Harrow—there are other schools just as fine. Since there are so few scholarship opportunities . . . I thought I would appeal to you first."

"Have you forgotten your last words to me?" The marquess's face grew harsh.

"No, my lord, I have not." Katherine lifted her chin defiantly. "And I still believe them to be true. You had no right to accuse me of being an unfit guardian for my son, or to attempt to take him from me. If you still feel that way, I shall take my leave." She rose to her feet.

"Sit down, Katherine. You have not completely outgrown your impetuous nature, I see." The marquess leaned back in the chair, forming his fingers into a steeple. "I believe I shall make you a bargain, madam. Let me make young Robert's acquaintance. If I think that you have done an acceptable job of raising him to this point, I will do as you ask."

"And if not?"

"I will wash my hands of the both of you." His tone was abrupt.

"I think this is a bargain I shall easily win," she replied with the hint of a smile. Hope leapt within her. "He is bright, inquisitive, and eager for new experiences. Very much like his father."

"Who was also a hotheaded young fool without an ounce of common sense when he got the bit between his teeth," the marquess countered.

"I am beginning to learn, with Robbie, that opposition only makes children more determined." Katherine spoke carefully, afraid of alienating the marquess now that she had gained a tentative victory. "As a parent, you have to learn when to let them find their own path."

The marquess fingered his penknife, then sighed. "There is no question I dealt poorly with Robert on the matter of your marriage," he admitted. "Perhaps it is time I make amends to you—and his son."

"I think Robert would have been pleased to hear you say that," Katherine said, her voice catching.

The marquess stood up quickly.

"Where is the lad? Did you bring him with you to London, or do you still have him secreted somewhere in the countryside?"

"He is here," Katherine replied, allowing the first tremors of encouragement to surge through her body.

The marquess pulled out his watch and consulted it. "Bring him around today at five," he ordered. "The two of you may stay to dinner. Leave your address with Harlow and I will have the carriage sent round."

"Thank you, my lord," Katherine said.

The marquess waved her out of the room, immediately turning his attention to the piles of papers on his desk as if she were no longer there.

Katherine's knees felt weak and wobbly and she was astounded they were able to carry her out into the corridor and down those intimidating stairs. She could hardly believe that the interview had gone so well. For six years she had hidden herself and her son from this man, and in the

matter of a few minutes all that had been passed over as
if it never happened. Has she been a prideful fool? Had
those last six years of struggle and sacrifice been totally
unnecessary?

Yet she still retained some nagging doubts about the
marquess. He had tried to take Robbie from her once;
would he do so again? She could be playing right into his
hands. He could send Robbie off to school, hire the most
expensive legal help in the country, and wrest him away
from her—forever. The thought chilled her.

But the elderly man she had encountered today was not
the same man who had threatened her after Robert's death.
She was willing to concede that grief and anger had held
him in their sway at that time; the years would have soft-
ened that blow. And of course, there were other grandsons
now, to carry on the name. Robbie was no longer so close
to the title. Perhaps the marquess spoke now in complete
sincerity.

She would have to hope so. For by returning tonight, she
was casting Robbie's fate, and hers, into the marquess's
hands. She prayed she was not making a dreadful mistake.

"Where have you been?" Robbie's voice demanded
querulously as she reentered their sleeping chamber at the
posting inn.

"Visiting," Katherine replied briefly, laying her warm
winter cloak carefully over the back of the chair. "Did you
finish with your Latin?"

He scowled. "Almost."

She shook her head, but she was not angry. What boy
of his age would be interested in Latin grammar when there
was all of London to explore? Yet his leg was still weak,
and not up to a rigorous traverse of the city's streets. The
Latin would occupy his mind while he recovered his
strength.

"We will be going out tonight," she said casually, groping
for the best way to explain things to Robbie. How best to
tell him all that had transpired between her and the Mayfield family? Would he understand the reasons for her actions six years ago? Or would it all be too confusing?

"Will I have to wear my new clothes?" He grimaced.

She nodded, and sat down facing him. "Robbie, there is

something important I need to discuss with you. You are ten now, and very nearly a young man, and therefore old enough to know most of the story." She took a deep breath as she regarded her son's quizzical eyes.

"Your father was more than a captain in the cavalry," she began. "He was also the son of a marquess."

"A marquess? Papa?"

"The *son* of a marquess," she reiterated. "And only a younger one, which is why he was in the cavalry, for the titles and estates will go to his elder brother. When your father and I married . . ." She paused for a moment, watching his face carefully, fearing his reaction to these revelations. "Neither his family nor mine was very happy about it. The marquess, in particular, was very angry."

She halted in her narrative. It would be pointless to tell Robbie just how angry the marquess had been, and the words that had been exchanged between father and son when Robert had brought home his Gretna bride to the family estate. It would be best if Robbie never heard that story—or what had transpired between herself and the marquess after Robert's death.

"That is why I have not spoken of him before. But he is your grandfather, Robbie, and you have aunts and uncles and cousins here in London and in the country. I spoke with your grandfather this morning, and he is very eager to meet you."

She would not tell him what the outcome of the meeting could mean for the both of them. School was not a primary concern of Robbie's; he was too young to know the advantages that would accrue from consorting with his peers. Or the doors that could be opened to him at the word of a marquess. Better that he looked forward only to having a family around him at last.

"Is my grandfather still angry?"

Katherine shook her head and smiled encouragingly. "He is not. That was long in the past. He has invited us to dine with him tonight, which is a great honor, for not everyone has the opportunity to dine with a marquess. That is why I wish you to wear your new clothes and demonstrate your best manners, so I can be proud of you."

"Tell me about my cousins."

"I know very little about them, I am afraid. Your papa had

several sisters, and they all have children even older than you. I know there are two young boys—the sons of your uncle. You can ask your grandfather about them tonight."

She studied him closely, trying to gauge his reaction to the news. But Robbie's face only reflected his boyish curiosity.

"Does this mean," he asked at last, "that we are not going to go back to Rose Cottage?"

"Yes, Robbie. The marquess will probably find us another place to live, closer to his house." And far away from the Earl of Knowlton.

"What will happen to my pony?"

"When we are settled, you can write to the earl and ask him for your pony. You will not be able to ride until your leg is stronger anyway. And I would not be surprised if the marquess has some ponies of his own that he might let you ride."

To her relief, that answer appeared to mollify his concern. She had felt a twinge of guilt at leaving Robbie's pony behind, knowing that he might never see the animal again. If the marquess did take them in, the pony could be retrieved. She knew it would reveal her location to Knowlton, but by then it would not matter. She was certain he would have little to say to her in their changed circumstances. And there was little she wished to say to him. She wished to avoid any future contact with the earl for as long as possible. Until all the dreams he had so thoroughly dashed faded from her memory.

Katherine noted with a self-conscious start that Robbie was watching her closely. This was no time for what-might-have-been, she chided herself.

"I promised I would show you some of the sights of town today," she said, brightening. "Shall we see what we can see from the windows of a hackney?"

Robbie scowled. "My leg is fine, Mama."

"And I intend for it to stay that way. We shall save it for more important endeavors like the Tower and the waxworks. It would be a pity to tire it out now and have to miss those sights."

"All right," he grumbled.

Katherine sympathized. He had been inactive far too long. But he still favored the healing limb, and walked with a slight limp, particularly when he was tired. Until he was perfectly well, she did not want to take any risks.

She managed to find a hack that was not too worn or filthy inside, and once the driver got over his surprise at being ordered to drive about the streets so they could gawk like tourists, it was a pleasant journey. It was a wanton extravagance as well, Katherine noted ruefully, but if all proceeded as planned, money would no longer be of such pressing concern. With Robbie's schooling paid for, she could exist quite easily on the small competence she had, so she even had the man stop at Gunther's, where she treated Robbie to his first ice.

They dallied so long that it was a mad scramble to get themselves ready for their visit to the marquess. Katherine slicked Robbie's wayward hair to his head in hopes of his making a more presentable appearance and of disguising its brilliant red shade. She dressed herself in her serviceable gray silk, twisting her hair into a demure chignon. For once, she wished she had a decent cap she could wear. It would make her look older and more responsible. And hide that devilish red hair.

As if that would impress the marquess. Despite the favorable outcome of the morning's visit, she was still more nervous than she wished to be. As she herded Robbie into the waiting carriage, his eyes had widened at the sight of the grand town coach with its coat of arms upon the door and the liveried grooms.

"Is the marquess rich?" Robbie whispered when they were settled inside on the padded velvet seats.

She nodded. "He is."

"Will he give us money, then, so we do not have to be so poor?"

"In the first place, Robbie, we are not poor." Katherine could not keep the defensive tone from her voice. "We just do not have enough money for frivolous whims. And the marquess will do whatever he pleases with his money. It is not our concern."

What a dreadful lie, she scolded herself. Money was precisely what she was asking the marquess for. But somehow the thought of asking for tuition money did not sound so crass.

"Damn that witch!"

Knowlton stormed out the door of the Rose Cottage, his

face contorted in anger. What kind of a monster did she think he was? He had accepted her refusal, had acknowledged that she considered it no compliment. There was no need for her to pack their belongings and flee from him as if he posed a danger.

Why? Why had she left, without a word to anyone, or a message to him? He knew now he had sadly misjudged her. His offer of protection had been received as a mortal insult. Knowlton felt a spasm of regret for that. But certainly she would realize her angry rejection had effectively stilled his intentions regarding her?

Had something else gone wrong while he was gone? Knowlton felt a stab of concern. He knew Kate had little money. Her furniture was gone; that would have entailed the expense of a cart for the journey to wherever she had fled. Rents could be low at this time of year, but food would grow dearer as winter neared. He knew she had supplemented what income she had with sewing, but would she have that opportunity in the new place she settled? He cringed at the thought of her and Robbie in need, hungry and cold throughout the harsh months to come.

And what was worse, he would probably never know her fate. Pain shot through him at the dismal thought. If she and Robbie arrived at some pitiful state, he would never know. It would not take many reversals to reduce them to paupers; they could find themselves on the parish rolls in short time. Why was she being such a fool? He would never have forced his intentions upon her. She was safe after she made it clear she did not want him.

But she *had* wanted him. That had been no feigned passion that night in Robbie's room. She had been as bold and wanton as any lover he had bedded, wildly exciting, achingly tender, and firing such a yearning in him as he had never known before. Even now, in the cold October wind, his body raged with desire at the remembered feel of her. He had struggled against the burning heat of his memories during his absence from Warrenton, consoling himself with knowledge that he could douse the flames in the softness of a more willing female body if he so desired. That he had not done so was his own folly.

Knowlton mounted his horse and took a long, last scowling look at the Rose Cottage. He had been driven with such plans, such ideas. Once Robbie was settled in school, he had thought to travel. Kate would have enjoyed that, he was certain. Paris, Switzerland, Italy. He wanted to share with her all the delights he had discovered there, and search for new ones they could both share. And now . . . now . . .

With a vicious tug at the reins he set his heels to his horse. He had better things to do than worry about the fate of such an ungrateful woman and her son. He had offered to help, and his offer had been refused. Very well, he would spend no more time with them. Let them seek their own fate.

Chapter Fifteen

Wherefore hast thou left me now
    Many a day and night?
Many a weary night and day
'Tis since thou art fled away.

—Shelley, *Song*

*K*atherine could not shake her last-minute jitters as she and Robbie entered the marquess's town house. She was not worried about her son's impression upon the marquess—she knew that Robbie's deportment and manners were all she could wish, and he would not shame her. It was her own behavior she concerned herself with. If things began to go wrong, she did not know if she could rely on her good sense to still her tongue. The marquess still had far to go in earning her trust.

"This is even fancier than Knowlton's house," Robbie whispered to his mother as they followed the butler up the stairs. "Did my papa really live here?"

She nodded. "Not often, though. He grew up at the country estate."

"Will we got here sometime too?"

"Perhaps," she said, her lips compressing in a thin line. Her memories of her one visit to that house were bitter.

At the top of the stairs she motioned for the butler to halt, and she turned Robbie toward the picture that had so captured her imagination that morning.

"That young boy is your papa, Robbie."

"Really?" He stopped and stared. "He looks different from the miniature."

"The miniature was painted much later," Katherine explained. "Why, he must have been near your age when this painting was done. The older boy is Frederick, your uncle."

"I don't look much like him, do I?" Robbie asked with a note of regret.

"Of course you do," Katherine hastened to reassure him. "You have my hair, but otherwise you look very much like him. See how full of mischief he looks? I wager he was nearly as big a scamp as you."

The butler coughed and Katherine shot him a sharp look.

"Lord Robert could be quite a handful," he said.

"Did you know my papa?" Robbie asked eagerly. "What do you remember about him?"

"That he was always a very inquisitive lad," the butler said, and a ghost of a smile crossed his face. "Stubborn as could be when he was thwarted, and always in and out of trouble."

Katherine smiled fondly. Robbie and his father were very like—and both took after the old marquess. Her amusement faded as she remembered the confrontational scenes between Robert and his father. Would Robbie carry on the strife into the next generation? She prayed she had successfully leavened some of his willfulness. She gently nudged him forward.

"Your grandfather is waiting," she reminded him.

Robbie took one last look at the portrait and followed her down the long corridor to the drawing room. Katherine stood aside nervously to allow Robbie to enter. She had said her piece in the morning. The outcome of this evening depended upon Robbie and his grandfather.

The marquess rose from his chair as they entered, surveying his grandson with a skeptical look.

"So," he said at last. "I suppose it was too much to hope that you would have inherited your father's coloring."

"I have my mama's hair," Robbie said proudly.

Katherine knew that no matter the outcome of this interview, she would forever be proud of her son for that defiant remark.

"So you do," said the marquess, nodding his head.

"Mama says I look a lot like Papa. We saw the portrait at the top of the stairs. Was he really my age then?"

The marquess looked startled. "You may have the right of it, my boy. He could not have been more than ten or eleven when it was painted. And you are ten now?"

"Almost eleven," said Robbie. "In January."

Katherine could almost hear the marquess mentally ticking off the months. "A full ten months after the marriage," she remarked with a tinge of sarcasm.

He had the grace to look embarrassed, then turned back to Robbie. "Is this your first trip to London?"

Robbie nodded.

"And how do you find the city?"

"I have not seen that much," Robbie confessed. "Mama and I took a hackney and drove through the city this afternoon. She does not want me walking much because of my leg."

"Ah, yes, your leg. Came a cropper, did you?"

"It was my fault," Robbie said. "Mama told me not to ride near to where they were shooting, but I forgot."

"Sounds like your mama gave you some sensible advice," the marquess said. "Do you always forget what she tells you?"

"No, sir. Only once in a while."

Katherine stifled a smile.

The marquess motioned for them to sit. Katherine settled upon the low sofa, but Robbie took a chair next to the marquess.

"Mama said I was to ask you about my cousins," Robbie said. "Are there any my age?"

Katherine realized with a pang how few opportunities there had been for Robbie to develop friendships among youths his own age. It was one more thing her stubborn pride had cost him.

"Georgie's eldest is nearing eighteen," the marquess mused. "There are a gaggle of females ranging from five to fifteen, but no lads your age, I am afraid. Frederick's two boys are still in short coats; too young to be of much interest to you."

"Oh," Robbie said with a crestfallen expression.

"Wanted a playfellow, eh?"

Robbie nodded. "I miss my friend Sam."

The marquess shot Katherine a questioning look.

"One of the neighbors' boys," she explained hastily. She could only imagine what the marquess would say if he knew Robbie's playmate was a rough farmer's son.

The marquess appeared satisfied. "Your mama says you are doing well in your studies. How is your Latin?"

Robbie glanced at his mother. "Adequate," he said.

"Greek?"

"Tolerable."

"Mathematics?"

"He has outpaced his tutor in that field," Katherine said proudly, not adding that she had been that person. But she had no qualms about Robbie's ability in that area.

The marquess nodded in satisfaction. "Your mama thinks you ought to be going to school soon. We sent your papa off at eleven. What do you think of that idea?"

Robbie looked at his mother in surprise, and Katherine groaned inwardly. She had known there would be a stumbling block somewhere this evening, and they had just run straight into it. She returned Robbie a rueful smile, refusing to indicate what response she desired. Thank goodness she had never repeated Robert's stories of how he had hated life at Eton. Robbie was on his own.

"Well, I . . . I think that might be all right," he said doubtfully. "What kind of school? Would I have to leave Mama?"

"It would depend on which school you were suited for," the marquess responded. "Perhaps the best thing to do is have you examined by a qualified tutor to see how far you have progressed in your studies. If there are any deficiencies, you will need to make them up first."

"Do you really want me to go away to school?" Robbie asked his mother.

"It would give you the opportunity to be with boys your own age," she said cautiously. "You would have the chance to make many friends."

Robbie sat quietly, considering. "I will think about it,"

he said finally. He turned back to the marquess. "Are Mama and I going to come and live with you now?"

Katherine suppressed a grin. She was pleased to see the marquess put on the spot for once.

"It may be," he said. "Do you want to live in the city?"

"Can I have a pony in the city?"

"Still eager to ride after your accident?"

Robbie nodded. "I had to leave my pony when we came here, but Mama said you might let me bring him here. May I?"

The marquess nodded silently, and Katherine saw the ghost of a smile flit across his lips.

The butler appeared at the door. "Dinner is served, my lord."

"About time," grumbled the marquess. "You would think they wanted a body to starve around here." He eyed Robbie skeptically. "Have you creditable manners at he table, boy?"

Robbie nodded.

The marquess held out his arm to Katherine and she took it shyly.

"He'll do," the marquess whispered to her in a low undertone as they stepped into the corridor.

Katherine and Robbie moved to the town house the following day, to Robbie's great delight. He insisted on exploring every nook and cranny of the four-story building. Katherine admonished him against pestering the servants, for his first question to all of them was whether they had known his father. Surprisingly, a large number of the house workers remembered Robert and filled the eager boy with tales of his father. It did much to ease Katherine's worries about how Robbie would adjust to the change in their situation.

She had barely had the opportunity to adjust herself to their changed surroundings when Lady Durham descended upon her. Katherine had never met the wife of Robert's older brother—they had married after Robert's death—and she was curious to meet her sister-in-law for the first time. Smoothing down the skirts of her unfashionable day gown, Katherine repaired to the upper saloon to meet the woman whose children had supplanted Robbie in the inheritance.

What could she expect from the countess? Acceptance, dismay, or outright resentment?

An elegantly garbed and coiffed woman, short and slender, with dark hair, was gazing with rapt attention out the window to the activity in the square below.

"Lady Durham?" Katherine questioned.

The lady turned and surveyed Katherine with an inquisitive and appraising stare. At the moment when Katherine felt her anger rising at this rude perusal, Lady Durham broke into a musical laugh.

"I can certainly see why Robert chose you over his family!"

"Can you?" Katherine's voice was icy.

"Oh, dear, I have bungled matters already, haven't I?" Lady Durham tossed her head gaily. "I always make such a mull of things. What I meant to say was that you are far more lovely than I could have imagined. It will be a delight to take you in hand."

"Take me in hand?" Katherine felt her anger rising again.

"I did not phrase that well either, did I? The marquess wishes me to advise you on the matter of your new wardrobe."

"Since he obviously does not trust me to competently choose my own. He need not fear, I will not disgrace him."

"And there is no reason to think you should," Lady Durham murmured soothingly. "I really am making a botch of this. I am certain you have excellent taste. But I do so love to shop, and Frederick is being positively *gothic* about my overrunning my allowance again this quarter and has forbidden me to make any more purchases. Helping you choose your new wardrobe will be almost as much fun. Please say you will let me accompany you."

Katherine smiled in spite of herself. She began to suspect her younger sister-in-law was a bit of a scatter-wit. "I would enjoy it if you came along, Lady Durham."

"Oh, please, call me Castalia. After all, we are sisters of a sort. Your name is Katherine, is it not? May I call you that?"

Katherine nodded, growing more and more amused by this chattering young woman.

"Do you wish to begin this morning? I know they have

received some new silks at the warehouse, and I saw the most exquisite lace shawls at Plummer's last week, and—"

"I need only a few things."

Castalia paused. "The marquess said he had given you *carte blanche* for everything, top to toe. My goodness, you do not intend to turn down such a generous offer?"

"It is a munificient gesture, but I hardly see the need." Katherine shook her head doubtfully. "I own I would like to purchase a few dresses. However, my remaining needs are small."

Lady Durham laughed. "I can see why the marquess wished me to accompany you. You cannot possibly do without at least a dozen outfits." She ticked off the list on her fingers. "Two walking gowns, at least, and a carriage dress. Dinner gowns . . . three, I think, and three evening dresses as well. Do you ride?"

Katherine shook her head, too astounded by the woman's grandiose plans to say anything.

"Well, perhaps another carriage dress, then. And some morning gowns. With all the matching gloves, bonnets, shawls, and shoes, it will make a prodigious collection." Her eyes glowed with excitement. "It should entail a full week of shopping, at least."

"But I have no need—"

"Of course you do. You do not want to disgrace the Marquess or the memory of your husband when you are presented into society?"

"I hardly think I shall be much in society," Katherine protested. "Once the matter of Robbie's schooling is settled, I will be returning to the country."

"You do not wish to remain in London?" Incredulity lit Lady Durham's face. "Why ever not?"

"I have no reason to be in the city. I have no connections with whom to renew acquaintances."

"Then you will have ample opportunity to make new ones," Lady Durham declared emphatically. "Goodness, Katherine, the Little Season is in full swing already. If we do not get you about soon, everyone will have deserted the city for country estates and you will have to wait until spring."

Katherine suspected that she was going to be swept along into whatever plans the marquess and Castalia had for her, whether she wished to be or not. This woman might be frivolous, but Katherine suspected she had a will of steel beneath her flighty exterior.

"I will acquiesce to perhaps half that number of outfits," she said firmly. She did not wish to be more indebted to the marquess than she had to.

Castalia airily waved a hand. "Six, eight, twelve. It is much the same. Shall we leave now?"

Katherine suppressed the urge to laugh at her sister-in-law's determination. "I will get my cloak."

Katherine was much less in favor of Castalia's enthusiasm when they finally returned to St. James Square. It was not the countess who had been required to stand stiff as a statue while she was being measured, poked, prodded, and pinned for what seemed an eternity. Despite Katherine's protests, Castalia proceeded to order all the gowns on her required list, plus a few extra. When measurements had been taken, the fabrics chosen, and delivery dates promised, Castalia then dragged her to the vast warehouses where she forced stockings, handkerchiefs, chemises, gloves, and every manner of item on the protesting Katherine. She had wondered at the two footmen who had accompanied the carriage, but saw the wisdom in their presence when they followed the two ladies from the shop with an enormous burden of packages in their arms.

Katherine sank back against the carriage cushions in exhaustion.

"Now, of course, we will have to plan your entrance into society." Castalia bubbled with enthusiasm. "I know Lady Trumball is having a rout next week; that might make a nice beginning. We can have our own ball the following week, and—"

"Castalia, it really is not necessary to go to such trouble. I assure you, I have no desire to cut a dash in society. I am merely a simple country widow."

"But Frederick has been so reluctant to give his permission for a ball. If it was in your honor, he could hardly refuse, could he?"

The pleading look Castalia directed at her did little to alleviate Katherine's misgivings. Her only desire had been for Robbie's future when she repaired the breach with his grandfather. She had never intended for the marquess to provide for her; now she had acquired this overwhelming wardrobe and her in-laws were determined to introduce her to society. Katherine feared she would be woefully out of place among the elevated reaches of the *ton*.

Katherine's protestations were ignored and Castalia merrily planned a ball more suitable to the debut of an Incomparable than the mere introduction of the inconsequential widow of a long-dead younger son. And Katherine began to have grave suspicions as to the reasoning behind this. No one had actually said anything outright to her, but it did not take long for Katherine to notice that Castalia, and the marquess himself, took great pains to introduce her to every bachelor they met.

Katherine shook her head at their faulty reasoning. She had given them no indication that she wished to remarry. And she grew suspicious of their motives. Marriage would cut her legal ties to the Mayfields—would they use that as an excuse to attempt to take Robbie from her again?

And even if she did not have that worry, she saw no reason to take another man to husband. Short as it had been, her marriage to Robert had been all that she could have wanted. It would be an impossible task to attempt to recreate that magic with another man. And if the image of a pair of cynical gray eyes belied her protestations, she had the cold comfort of knowing that he held out no offer of marriage.

She felt as if she were being swept along by a swift river current. With no hope of struggling against it, she was forced to acquiesce and follow where it led her. And if it involved routs and balls and theater parties, well, there was a growing part of her that admitted that the enjoyments of even the Little Season were more than she had ever hoped to experience. As long as she accepted that they were to be a temporary happenstance, she could relax her qualms and attempt to enjoy herself. It might be her only opportunity.

Despite his growing dissatisfaction, Knowlton felt himself strangely reluctant to leave Warrenton, even though he felt restless and bored within its walls. In the past few weeks the servants had learned to tread lightly when in the presence of the earl. The merest slip, an awkward appearance, or a perfectly respectable performance of their duties was likely to earn them a blistering tirade from Knowlton.

He sought comfort in exhaustion. From morning to afternoon he was in the saddle, riding about the county in a reckless manner that left him physically tired but mentally alert. When not ahorse, he stalked the estate with his shotgun, bagging enough birds to feed the entire county. By dinnertime he could barely keep his eyes open, and it took only small quantities of brandy or port to tumble him into sleep, usually in his chair in the study.

He studiously avoided Katherine's old cottage on his wild rambles, riding miles in the other direction to avoid any place associated with her. Yet every sight of his own stable brought Robbie's abandoned pony to mind. How could she have been so cruel as to leave the poor beast behind? Robbie would be grieved at the loss. She was intolerably selfish, thinking only of herself. If he ever got his hands on her again, he would be sorely tempted to throttle her.

Knowlton grew more discontented with every passing day. Warrenton held too many reminders of the pleasant hours he had spent in Kate's company. Every night, as he took to his bed, he was assailed with vivid reminders of that impassioned kiss in Robbie's room. Knowlton's body ached for her. He struggled against his desire, willed his body to obey his mind, but more often than not his efforts resulted in dismal failure.

The peace of mind he had thought to find at Warrenton when he arrived from London all those months ago completely eluded him with Kate's abrupt departure. And short of filling his house with an assortment of unwanted guests, there was little he could do to restore his sympathy with life here. Perhaps it was time to return to London. There would still be a flurry of activity before the *ton* left town for the winter holiday. Time enough to sample the pleasures of the city. After a four-month absence, they might not look so discouraging.

Yes, he decided, he would go to town. It was only the solitude of Warrenton that made the memories of Kate Mayfield so difficult to abandon. He would wager that within a week of his arrival in the city, her memory would cease to taunt him. In London, there was no shortage of ladies who would be quite willing to accept his patronage. With a sudden spurt of enthusiasm, he rang for Rigsby and ordered him to prepare to depart the following day.

Chapter Sixteen

Woman, that fair and fond deceiver
How fond are striplings to believe her!
— Byron, *To Woman*

*K*atherine's arrival on the scene was greeted by the *ton* with curiosity and questions, which the family explained away as a lengthy period of mourning for the long-dead Robert. This explanation was met with complete acceptance. Katherine continued to make mild protests against the family's attempts to turn her into a social matron, which Castalia dismissed as the typical nervousness due any young lady making her bow in London. Katherine *was* nervous about it. Raised in a simple home, the grandest entertainments she had ever attended were the local assemblies, where she had met Robert. Her subsequent life as an underfunded officer's wife had not been overly exciting. And certainly since his death she had lived as retired a life as one could imagine. Those weeks at Warrenton had been her only contact with members of the *ton*. Now her in-laws expected her to take that association as a matter of course.

It was not that Katherine did not wish to enter society. She confessed she enjoyed the small dinners and musical entertainments she attended, and the theater was as entrancing as she remembered from her lone visit with Robert. It was only the lack of purpose for her participation that caused her to pause. All she wanted from Robert's family was a gentleman's education for her son; she never planned to ask for anything for herself. But they acted as if it were all a matter of course, and Katherine suspected that only downright defiance would cause them to lay down their plans. And there was just enough of a luxury-loving woman in her not to go that far. She would never take her new position for granted, but while it was offered, she would be foolish to refuse. When Robbie went off to school next year, she could take up the threads of her own life again.

Katherine felt the tiniest twinges of doubt about the ball that Castalia organized in her honor. It seemed to be far too grand an affair for introducing a widowed sister-in-law. Indeed, it looked more appropriate for the come-out of the daughter of an exalted family. But Castalia just laughed off her protests and blithely went her own way. Katherine submerged her doubts and followed along. And she had to admit that the gorgeous green silk Castalia forced upon her was made up into an admirable dress.

Katherine fought against her nerves as she followed Castalia into the main drawing room. No other young lady making her first bow into society could feel more apprehensive. The falseness of her position plagued her. She was *not* an innocent miss in search of a husband. Why, then, had she allowed them to subject her to this public perusal?

Because it pleased them, and that pleasure reflected on what the marquess was willing to do for Robbie. And that was why she found herself at the Earl of Durham's house, dressed in all her new finery, waiting for the ball in her honor to begin. At least this sacrifice was more pleasant than the one she had made six years ago. The results of her current capitulation were worth it, of course, for the marquess was completely reconciled to her guardianship of Robbie. She had achieved all she could have asked for.

Still, she felt the stirrings of regret for Knowlton and what might have been. If only she had been able to reach his heart . . . even a few months in his arms would have been worth the lifetime of loneliness that followed. But he had made it abundantly clear that he felt no emotion for her beyond lust. Once again she wished she had listened to her head instead of her heart in her dealings with him.

Castalia's voice intruded into her thoughts.

"Now, Katherine, I will take it upon myself to introduce you to a number of suitable dancing partners. Rumors of your presence have already been circulating among the *ton,* so you can be assured of a great deal of interest."

"How wonderful," Katherine responded dryly. Just the thing to set her at ease.

Castalia laughed. "I assure you, it is much more pleasant to be making your debut at twenty-eight than at seventeen."

"I still find the whole idea foolish," Katherine said. "I would much rather cultivate the role of secluded widow."

"Nonsense," Castalia replied, tapping her lightly on the arm with her fan. "You deserve to have what Winslow's stubbornness and Robert's untimely death deprived you of. You are the daughter-in-law of a marquess, remember, and that gives you enormous social consequence. And with my backing, you will go far."

"You will be a wicked marchioness," Katherine said, a smile lighting her face.

"I know," Castalia responded with a self-satisfied smile.

By midnight Katherine was laughing at all her earlier nervousness, swept up by the excitement of the evening, the attentions of her numerous partners, and the glittering company she found herself in. She had often wondered what her life would have been like if not for the estrangement between Robert and his father, if they had taken their rightful place in society. She was rapidly discovering that it might not be such a bad life after all.

Fanning herself against the heat generated by too many people crowded into too small a space, Katherine scanned the crowd for a familiar face. She would be forced to navigate the crush herself to find the punch if she could not find a willing assistant. Resigned to the trek, she turned toward the door, then stopped, frozen in place.

He was the last person she had ever dreamed of seeing this evening, and she instantly acknowledged her foolishness. She had assumed they would meet again, someday, but not so soon. He'd said he planned to winter peacefully on his estate—so why was he here now in London, in November? And why, oh why, was he at this house?

Katherine edged her way back into the center of the room, her gaze darting about in frantic search of Castalia.

But fatally, she looked in his direction one more time, and their gazes locked.

She did not mistake the brief shock that registered in his eyes before his usual cool, mocking expression returned. Ignoring the image she presented, she turned and pushed her way through the crowd. Flight was the foremost thing on her mind.

She found Castalia in the next room and grasped her arm in relief.

"I am feeling unwell," she gulped.

"It is this heat," the countess murmured sympathetically. "Let me find someone to get you a glass of punch."

"No, really, I think I would feel better if I—"

"Ah, Lady Durham." Knowlton crossed the room with impatient strides and took Castalia's hand and raised it to his lips. "A dreadful crush, as usual. Your reputation as London's premier hostess is in no danger tonight."

"Nor is yours as a flirt," she responded, rapping his knuckles with her fan until he released her hand.

He turned expectantly toward Katherine.

"I do not think I have had the pleasure of meeting your exquisite companion," Knowlton said with a mocking smile. "Please, do the honors."

"Certainly. But I warn you, Knowlton, do not try to set up one of your flirtations with her. She is a highly respectable lady, not your type at all. Do you remember Frederick's younger brother, Robert? This is his widow. Lord Knowlton, may I present Lady Robert Mayfield."

"Enchanting," he said, drawing her hand to his lips. "How could such a fair light have denied us her presence for so long?"

"Now, Katherine," Castalia warned, "do not take a word he says seriously. Knowlton is an incorrigible flirt, and terribly spoiled by the adulation of countless women who are less than ladies. In short, he is a rogue."

He brought his hand to his chest as if reeling from a blow. "You wound me, Lady Durham."

Katherine felt like a tongue-tied idiot, but she could not have uttered a word if her life depended on it. She prayed he would go away.

"It is quite warm in here," he said, taking in her pale

face. "Let me escort you to the refreshments, Lady Robert."

"Thank you, but I shall be fine," she whispered, preparing to flee.

"No, I insist," he said, grabbing her elbow in a firm grip and leading her none too gently across the room.

In the relative emptiness of the corridor, Katherine tried to shrug his hand loose, but he only clasped her arm tighter.

"Unless you want an embarrassing scene, you shall come with me," he said between gritted teeth, dragging her down the hall. Pushing open the first door he came to, he gave a satisfied sigh as he shoved her inside the room and firmly shut the door.

Katherine rubbed her arm. She would have bruises tomorrow.

Knowlton turned his steady gaze upon her. God, she looked beautiful. That flowing emerald gown accentuated every luscious curve; the fashionably low décolletage did more than hint of the full breasts that lay below. It took no imagination at all to envision her naked form. Anger, hurt, longing, and lust warred within him as he confronted the woman who had so disturbed his life these last weeks.

"I suppose you want an explanation," she said lamely.

"I? What right do I have to demand anything from you?" He glared at her fiercely. "I have no claim on you, *Lady* Robert."

She fumbled with the clasp of her fan. This was going to be as dreadfully awkward as she had feared.

"I assume you really *are* Lady Robert? Or is it only another of your false identities?"

"I never lied about who I was," she retorted. "I am Robert's widow."

"Of course, *Mrs.* Mayfield," he said sarcastically. "The fact you are the daughter-in-law of a marquess is irrelevant."

"It was and is," she said angrily, trying to brush past him.

"You fool." He grabbed her arm roughly. "What game were you playing, masquerading as an impoverished widow?"

"It was no game," she said. "The marquess did not approve of my marriage to Robert, and dealt with me accordingly."

"And left you totally without funds at your husband's demise? Difficult to believe."

"It is true!" Damn his arrogant assumptions. "When

Robert died, the marquess tried to take Robbie from me. I had to live in hiding, else he would have found me."

"Now suddenly you are cozy as an inkle-weaver with the whole family? It does not wash, Kate."

Her name on his lips sliced through her like a knife.

"I did it for Robbie," she said quietly, turning away to get hold of her emotions. "He has a right to know his family and his heritage."

"Of course, there is the added advantage to you of the sponsorship of the marquess's family." He coolly appraised her elegantly clad form. "I must say, Katherine, you have done well for yourself."

Anger boiled up inside her. "I did not do this for myself," she said icily.

He stepped back a pace and subjected her to a long, lingering perusal. "I suppose they forced that gown upon you."

Katherine's cheeks flamed. How dare he accuse her of mercenary motives! "Had I wanted only elegant gowns, I recall you were only too eager to provide them."

She turned away again, running her fingertips along the edge of the rosewood table. Katherine did not want him to see how, even now, his presence disturbed her composure.

Knowlton realized with a sudden stab of pain that his improper proposal had driven her back into the family circle. His offer to pay for Robbie's schooling no doubt reminded her of the advantages that would accrue to him as the grandson of a marquess. What had he forced her to do?

"Kate," he said with a new degree of warmth in his voice, "are they treating you well?"

A twinge of irony touched her laugh. "In point of fact, they are. The marquess has virtually apologized for his actions six years ago and made me feel like the veriest fool for not getting in touch with him sooner."

Relief crossed his face. This forced reunion with her husband's family was not hateful to her. She would be well-taken-care-of, and protected. Yet he felt a trace of sadness, knowing she had no need of his help now. The one thing he could offer her—an easy life—had been taken care of.

"So now you can return to the life you left," he said lightly. "There will be more fine dresses of silk and lace, parties and—"

"I had never set foot in this house before last month," she said, sighing with remembrance and regret. "Neither the marquess nor my own parents countenanced my marriage to Robert. We eloped, a true Gretna Green marriage. The scandal alone would have put us beyond the pale, but the marquess exacerbated the situation by publicly disowning Robert for 'lowering' the family's standards by marrying a mere country vicar's daughter."

"You are a vicar's daughter?" Disbelief washed over his face.

"A rather rebellious and willful one, I fear," she acknowledged with a sad smile.

Knowlton's guilt over what he had proposed to her deepened. How could he have asked the daughter of a *vicar* to become his mistress? "What did your parents do? Certainly they must have been pleased to see you married so well."

"They sided with the marquess, about both the marriage and Robbie. They thought it a folly for me to try to raise him alone on the mere pittance Robert left me." She shrugged. "I managed to reach a tolerable accommodation with my father before he died."

Pity and guilt washed over Knowlton. He had not known how deep an insult his offer had been. It had endangered not only her own respectability but also her son's entire future. No wonder she had rejected him so vehemently.

"Under the circumstances," he began, "I find that my previous offer to you was highly inappropriate. I apologize if I offended you, Lady Robert. I had meant it as a compliment."

"I hardly took it as such." Her gaze met his without flinching. Only she knew how much her studied dispassion caused her. He looked as calm and unperturbed as always. Her defection had not troubled his dreams, she was certain. She was the only one filled with regret and longing.

"I regret we parted on such violent terms. You never did allow me to say good-bye properly, you know," he chided in a voice suddenly grown husky. He had been living on dreams of her for weeks now; certainly, once he experienced the reality again, it would banish those foolish flights of fancy. The real Kate Mayfield could not come near to his maudlin imaginings. He could free himself from her spell once and for all.

Katherine was unable to turn her gaze away from the grip of those piercing gray eyes, and when he took a step toward her, she did not fall back. He would never know of the storm that raged within her as she fought against her longing.

"It is not necessary," she said hastily. His nearness wreaked havoc with her senses. She must get away from him. But her feet would not move; she watched him, entranced, as he took another step toward her.

"Oh, but I insist." He laid his hands lightly on her shoulders, drawing her toward him while he lowered his head to kiss her.

He nearly groaned at the moment of contact, knowing instantly that this had been an act of pure folly. He was still ensorcelled by this redheaded witch. Just the touch of those soft lips to his brought back a flood of memories of her passion. Heat diffused through his body; his hold on her shoulders tightened as he pressed her against him. Kate, Kate . . .

He released her so suddenly she nearly lost her balance.

"Our paths will undoubtedly cross here in town," he said, covering his unsteady voice with a mocking smile. "But you need not fear I will touch you again. This is good-bye, Kate." He turned on his heel and left the room.

Katherine stood for she did not know how long, staring at the closed door through the mist of tears in her eyes. She had been fooling herself in thinking she could maintain her composure when she saw Knowlton again. No amount of time would ever make it easy. It had been pure, hellish agony. Every portion of her body screamed for his touch, his caress. She touched her shoulder, where the mark of his fingers still remained. She longed to be in his arms again.

It had been sheer madness for her to think she could enter the elevated reaches of the *ton*. She did not belong here, for she did not have the skill to play the game. Like a foolish young chit, she had lost her heart to Knowlton, and neither shimmering dresses nor glittering jewels could ease the aching pain of knowing he would never be hers. A wiser woman would have been able to match Knowlton's indifference with her own, conducted a discreet affair, and not have lost a night's sleep when it was over. But she could not overcome the rigid upbringing of her childhood that easily. She had veered so very close, but she had wavered out of love—an emotion most of the *ton* held in disdain. No, she was not meant to live in this world. And knowing she would eventually encounter Knowlton again in town, she only wanted to flee to the farthest reaches of the island.

Knowlton went directly from his talk with Kate to the door, ordering his carriage brought round immediately. He stood on the steps, the cool night air working like a bucket of cold water on his overheated soul.

How could one simple kiss disconcert him so? He half-believed she was a witch. He had kissed her not above a dozen times, and the memories of those encounters were burned into his brain as if they had been lovers for years. What strange hold did Kate Mayfield have over him that no other woman had ever had?

Scowling, he stepped into his carriage. He needed a woman. Badly. It was the only cure to this madness that held him in its grip. One night in the arms of a skilled practitioner of the art of love would wipe out all memories of his modest little widow. He leaned out and gave his coachman the address of a house in the north end of Mayfair. He would find what he needed there. By morning his desire for Kate Mayfield would be only a dim memory.

Chapter Seventeen

One struggle more, and I am free
　From pangs that rend my heart in twain;
One last long sigh to love and thee,
Then back to busy life again.
　　　　　　—Byron, *One Struggle More, and I Am Free*

"Mama, Mama!" Robbie bounced exuberantly into the front drawing room. "Atlas is here. In the mews."

A sharp shaft of pain shot through Katherine and she

closed the book in her lap. One more reminder of Knowlton to add to her torment. And a reprimand to her as well. She should have sent for Atlas as soon as she and Robbie were ensconced at the Winslow house. But she had hesitated to make Knowlton aware of her present location. He must have sent word to Warrenton the morning after the ball. "How nice of Lord Knowlton to have arranged such a thing."

"May I ride in the park today?"

"I do not think you are quite ready for riding yet, Robbie." She ignored the pleading look in his face. There would be time and enough for riding after his leg had healed further.

"Of course he is," the marquess said, peering over the top of his newspaper. "You are coddling the lad."

Katherine's lips compressed into a thin line. "Perhaps you are right."

"Of course I am right," the marquess chortled. "Get Hodges to saddle up your pony and take you to the park, lad."

Robbie glanced nervously at his mother. "May I?"

She nodded reluctantly. Robbie gave her a swift hug and raced out of the room as quickly as he had arrived.

"Must you contradict me at every turn?" she demanded icily of the marquess when Robbie was gone.

"Only when I think you are doing the lad no favors," the marquess retorted. "He's been clinging behind your skirts long enough. If he's to be off to school next year, he will need some toughening up."

"And you think that teaching him disrespect for his mother is going to help?" Katherine cringed at the shrill tone of her voice.

"You saw how he looked to you for the final word," the marquess said. "He still knows who is in command."

Katherine sighed. It did seem petty, arguing over these minor points. But every day they remained in this house, she felt her control over Robbie undermined at every turn. The longer they remained, the more she would be pushed into the background. She yearned for the freedom of her own establishment. Tomorrow, maybe, she would broach the subject with the marquess. They had availed themselves of his hospitality for far too long. She was eager to be out of the city—particularly now that she knew Knowlton was here.

"You are sorely blue-deviled of late," the marquess said, scowling. "Order the carriage and go shopping. Always used to put the marchioness in a better frame of mind."

"There is nothing I have a need for. You have provided me with so much already." There was a hint of reproach in her voice. She could not help but feel she was living on the marquess's charity.

"Go visiting, then. Castalia will welcome you. You are giving me the fidgets."

Katherine considered the idea. "Perhaps I will," she said slowly, setting her book on the table. There was little else to occupy her time. She was rapidly discovering just how dull life as a "lady of leisure" could be. It was difficult to remain glum in the young countess's presence. Castalia could charm anyone out of the crotchets.

Katherine was forced to admit she did feel better after talking with Castalia. Infectious gaiety and amusing gossip were exactly what Katherine's bruised spirits needed. And despite her earlier protestations, she was quite willing to join her sister-in-law for a morning of shopping. Anything to keep her mind off that disastrous meeting with Knowlton. She began to understand why so many matrons overspent their allowances. A new parasol overcame a multitude of hurts.

Upon exiting the shop where Castalia had ordered another two winter bonnets, Katherine recognized Lady Wentworth alighting from a carriage.

"Elizabeth!" she cried joyfully.

Lady Wentworth looked bemused for a moment and then recognition creased her face. "Katherine! Whatever are you doing in London?"

"It is a complicated tale," Katherine replied, turning to Castalia. "Are you acquainted with my sister-in-law, Lady Durham? This is the Countess Wentworth."

"It is a pleasure to meet you," replied Elizabeth. "But how is she your sister-in-law?"

"My deceased husband was a son of the marquess of Winslow," Katherine confessed.

"Oh," said Elizabeth, her eyes widening. "And you never told me. Shame on you, Katherine."

"The marquess and I had not been on friendly terms for years," Katherine explained defensively. She did not miss the slight hurt in Elizabeth's eyes, and felt a pang of regret for having deceived her friend.

"And now you are?"

Katherine nodded.

Elizabeth raised a questioning brow. "Does Knowlton know?"

Katherine did not miss Castalia's unveiled look of interest at the mention of the earl's name. "He does," she replied softly, hoping Elizabeth would say no more.

"What a delightful surprise this all is," Elizabeth said. "I insist you visit tomorrow and tell me the whole story."

"Are you to be in town long?"

"Somers insisted that we come up, since I have been too wrapped up with Caro to even care much for society this last year." Elizabeth laughed. "Spending the Little Season in town is my penance."

"Did you bring Caro with you?" Katherine had grown fond of the little girl during her stay at Warrenton.

"Of course. And you will have to visit her as well tomorrow. The town nursery is a great big barn of a room, but she has settled in rather well. I shall see you then, Lady Durham." Elizabeth nodded her farewell and continued on her way.

Castalia said nothing until she and Katherine were seated in the carriage.

"You did not tell me you were acquainted with Lord Knowlton." The reproof in her voice was strong.

Katherine ducked her head deferentially. "We were merely neighbors."

"Katherine!"

"Robbie and I rented a cottage on his estate," Katherine said quickly. Elizabeth would keep her counsel. Castalia would not. She had no need to know about what was now firmly in the past. "He was very kind to Robbie."

"Knowlton never struck me as the type who would put himself out for a small boy." Castalia surveyed Katherine with open suspicion.

"I own his reputation with women is dreadful, but he is well-thought-of at his home." Katherine felt odd defending the man who once wished to make her his mistress. But it was the truth. Just as she had come to know the Knowlton who lay beneath the cynical exterior, she wanted Castalia to know that there was more to him than his reputation allowed. "He is a conscientious landlord, liked by both tenants and neighbors."

"What stories I will have to tell the *ton*." Castalia's eyes twinkled. "The dreadful Lord Knowlton befriends young boys, widows in distress, and farmers."

"Do not say anything," Katherine pleaded quickly. She did not want her name linked to Knowlton's in any manner. He would detest such gossip as much as she.

Castalia eyed her curiously but said no more.

Katherine was pleased to find Caro with Elizabeth when she arrived at their elegant Grosvenor Square house the following morning. She played games with the girl for half an hour before Caro was returned to the nursery.

"Now, tell me about your estrangement from the marquess," Elizabeth eagerly leaned forward in her chair. "It all sounds so deliciously mysterious!"

"It is all rather silly, in retrospect," Katherine said, shaking her head in self-deprecation. "Winslow was less than delighted when Robert and I eloped, and when Robert was killed, the marquess tried to take Robbie from my care."

"How dreadful!"

"Frederick had not married then, and Robbie was next in line to the title," Katherine explained, although even after six years she still did not completely absolve the marquess for his actions. "Now that Castalia has the boys, Robbie is not so important."

"So the old marquess accepts you now?"

"More for Robbie's sake than mine, I fear." Katherine smiled wryly. "But we are able to tolerate each other. And I cannot complain about his generosity. He is allowing us to make our home with him until Robbie goes to school next year."

"How interesting, to discover such a similarity in our lives. For I was estranged from my family for the longest time, until Somers drew us back together." Elizabeth smiled fondly. "Perhaps that is why we developed such a quick friendship."

Katherine nodded. She had felt it also, that sense of having found a kindred spirit in Elizabeth.

"What are your plans after Robbie goes away to school?"

Katherine contemplated her fingers. "I am not certain. There is a dower house on Winslow's country estate—"

"Do not say you intend to lose yourself in the country again?" Elizabeth's eyes flashed in protest. "You are much too young and pretty to settle for such a thing. You should be on the lookout for another husband."

"The idea does not appeal to me," Katherine replied stiffly. Was she to be badgered on this topic by Elizabeth as well?

"Nonsense. Surely Winslow would set you up with a reasonable dowry. I know any number of men who would be interested, no matter what size settlement you brought." She gave Katherine a sidelong glance. "Although I rather thought that you and Knowlton—"

"There was never anything between the earl and me," Katherine interjected hastily.

"And pigs fly," Elizabeth retorted. "I am not blind, Katherine. I noticed the way he looked at you. And the way you viewed him in return."

"Knowlton has no inclination to marry," Katherine said, more vehemently than she intended.

"And you wish it otherwise, don't you?" Elizabeth squeezed Katherine's hand in sympathy. "Are you dreadfully fond of him?"

Katherine nodded, swallowing against the lump in her throat. "I know it is pure folly, but I could not help myself. He has such a dreadful reputation, but he is one of the warmest, most caring men I have ever known."

"I shall have to speak to him and knock some sense into that brain of his."

Katherine grabbed Elizabeth's hand. "Do not! He never misrepresented his intentions. I have only myself to blame for my foolishness."

"Do not worry, Katherine. I will say nothing to Knowlton if you do not wish it. But I still insist the man is a fool to allow you to slip from his fingers."

"He is doing it of his own volition."

"Have you seen him in town? Does he know of your connection with Winslow?"

Katherine nodded. "Knowlton is determined to remain free from the chains of wedlock," she said, a thread of sadness in her voice. "There is nothing I can do to change the situation. So I have resolved to think of him no more."

"Then we shall have to find you a husband elsewhere," Elizabeth announced emphatically. "I am certain there will be several suitable candidates in town this fall. This makes me look forward to the Season even more."

"I do not wish to marry again," Katherine protested, knowing that it would be as futile to argue with Elizabeth as it had been with Castalia. Trust her luck to have fallen in with such confirmed matchmakers.

"We shall see," Elizabeth said dryly. "Now that you have family around you, I assume it is too much to expect that you will visit with us over Christmas."

"I own I had not thought that far ahead," Katherine said. "I do not know what sort of celebration the family plans. I would like to visit you."

"It will be quite sedate, I fear." Elizabeth leaned closer and patted her abdomen. "It seems we are to be blessed with a permanent reminder of our stay at Warrenton."

Katherine winced inwardly at Elizabeth's happy news. Another joy she would never experience again. "How wonderful," she said with unfeigned enthusiasm to Elizabeth, and the conversation turned toward domestic matters.

Knowlton expertly guided his prancing stallion through the empty park lanes. The early-morning gallop went far to restore his equanimity and clear his head, as did the cool morning air. His thinking had been woefully fuzzy these last few days, since seeing Katherine again.

It had been more than a shock to discover that his prim little widow was connected with one of the premier families in the realm. He felt a measure of satisfaction in knowing that his dishonorable pursuit had driven her back into the secure hold of her husband's relatives. They would take good care of her. It was the one thing he had worried about when he discovered Kate's precipitate flight—that she would be in want. Knowing now that she was well-taken-care-of, he could rid his mind of her once and for all.

He chose to ignore the fact that he had thought the same thing at Lady Durham's, when he had hastened from the ball into the arms of one of London's leading Cyprians. If that liaison had proved less than satisfactory, it could only be because of his disordered mood. The lovely lady had performed with admirable skill and talent, and he had merely not been in the proper frame of mind to appreciate it. He suspected he would be more entranced with the lovely opera dancer he planned to see tonight. He had deliberately waited a few days to make his conquest of her, knowing how well anticipation whetted his appetite. He had no doubts that tonight's adventure would be very pleasurable.

"Knowlton! Knowlton!"

The earl's head twisted around to identify his importuning caller.

"Robbie!" A genuine smile crossed Knowlton's face at the sight of the tousled redhead. Knowlton reined in his mount and watched with amusement as Robbie bounced along on his pony, a groom dutifully trailing behind him.

"Thank you for sending Atlas! It is ever so wonderful to be back on him again."

"He was eating me out of hay and oats." Knowlton laughed. "How is your leg? Healing properly?"

Robbie nodded. "Mama did not want me to start riding so soon, but my grandfather said I could. Do you know I have a grandfather who is a marquess?"

"Yes, I do," Knowlton said. "It must be pleasant to discover you have a family."

Robbie considered. "Well, Grandpapa is nice, and I like Aunt Castalia and Uncle Frederick. But most of the cousins, well, they are either girls or babies."

Knowlton laughed inwardly at the note of disgust in Robbie's voice. It would not be many years before he changed his view.

"I did not know you were in London," Robbie said with a faint hint of accusation in his voice.

"It was an unexpected trip," Knowlton lied. He keenly felt the boy's disappointment. He had not stopped to consider how the break with Katherine also affected his relationship with Robbie. "Are you practicing your chess and whist?"

Robbie scowled. "Grandpapa will not play with me. Uncle Frederick played a game of chess with me last week, but he is not at our house very often." His face brightened hopefully. "Could you come to the house and play with me?"

Knowlton winced at that plea. "I am afraid not, Robbie." The lad's crestfallen face smote him. He must do something for the boy. "Perhaps there is something else you and I could do together. Have you been to Astley's yet?"

Robbie shook his head, his eyes widening with hope. "Will you take me?"

"You shall have to ask your mother," Knowlton said. "If she approves, we shall go. Ask her if Tuesday will be acceptable."

"Oh, I am certain it will be." Robbie's face beamed with pleasure at the anticipated treat.

Knowlton felt a twinge of regret for the relationship that must, by necessity, die away. Robbie was a good lad. In other circumstances, Knowlton would not mind keeping up the friendship. But it took only one glimpse of Robbie's unruly red hair to bring the image of his mother to mind. He would take him to Astley's to soothe his conscience. Robbie would gradually acquire his own circle of friends and not need him anymore.

"Send a note round to Upper Brook Street when you find out," Knowlton said. "And you be careful with that leg. We don't want you laid up again."

"Yes, sir," said Robbie. "Thank you again for sending Atlas."

"My pleasure." Knowlton touched his hat and urged his horse forward. He could feel Robbie's hero-worshipping gaze boring into his back as he trotted down the path. Damn!

It had not seemed to be such a bad idea back at Warrenton, befriending the boy as he had. Even if he and Katherine had not made an arrangement, Robbie could have come and gone as he pleased at the house. But here in London, with eyes and ears everywhere . . . Any attention he directed at Robbie would be instantly scrutinized and analyzed with an eye to his mother. From Lady Durham's introductions at that disastrous ball, it was quite apparent that Kate had said nothing of him to her new family. He hoped that the revelation of this chance meeting with Robbie would not cause her distress.

He knew that Kate would not like the proposed trip to Astley's, but hoped that she, like him, would see the necessity of a gradual sundering of his ties with Robbie. As he and his mother were drawn deeper into the Winslow circle, there would be little need for Knowlton to entertain the boy. And Knowlton was certain that Robbie would be headed off to school soon, which would effectively solve the whole problem. There was no deep cause for concern.

Then why was he filled with such regret?

Chapter Eighteen

Is it thy will thy image should keep open
My heavy eyelids to the weary night?
—Shakespeare, *Sonnet 61*

*T*he death of the old queen brought an abrupt halt to Katherine's debut into society. Not that the *ton* called a complete stop to their entertainments. The theaters closed for a respectable length of time, and dancing parties were curtailed, but little else changed—except the necessity of acquiring an entire new mourning wardrobe.

However, the Winslow circle considered the event a chance to retreat to the country earlier than planned, so before December arrived, Katherine found herself back where she had longed to be—in the English countryside. To her dismay, the removal from London did not bring her the peace of mind she desired. She had thought that in the country, with no chance of another awkward encounter with Knowlton, she would be free from her memories. But it proved otherwise. Perhaps it was because her only other visit to the country home of the Winslows had been in Robert's company, and had ended with the permanent breach between father and son. There were no fond remembrances here to lull her into serenity.

And the country brought with it too many memories of the summer and fall in Lincolnshire. London was not fraught with experiences shared with Knowlton. But the country abounded with reminders. Neatly tilled fields evoked the heated days of harvest. The well-tended flowerbeds suggested the garden at Warrenton, where she and Knowlton had walked and talked, and where he had kissed her for the first time. And every sight of Robbie and his precious pony brought Knowlton's face to mind.

Even the gaiety of the Christmas and Twelfth Night celebrations did not soothe her spirits. Katherine treasured no fond memories of such opulent markers of the season; Christmas in the rectory had been a time for quiet reflection, and there had been only one Christmas with Robert. Like everything else, the Winslows celebrated the season with uncommon enthusiasm. Katherine allowed herself to be drawn into the merriment, accepting chaste kisses from her relatives under the kissing ball, playing charades long into the night. But her enthusiasm was forced. The country did not bring the enjoyment she had hoped for.

Yet she loathed the idea of returning to the city even more. Indeed, she managed to find any number of excuses to remain in the country while the rest of the family drifted back to the city. Castalia's younger son developed the sniffles and Katherine volunteered to stay with him when the marquess returned to town for the opening of Parliament. Unfortunately, Castalia decided to remain as well, so Katherine was not freed from her sister-in-law's determined plans for her future. At least there was little opportunity for them to be put into action while Katherine remained out of town.

The long months of separation did little to dim her memories of Knowlton. Katherine did not think there were enough years left in her life for that to occur. But she reached an accommodation of sorts with her wayward heart. The sharp pain of the early parting receded into a dull ache, and she realized one day that she no longer thought of him every hour. Yet memories flooded back over her at the oddest times. The first spring flowers peeking their heads aboveground reminded her of the Harvest Home, when they had walked in his garden and he had promised to send her bulbs. The aroma of brandy brought back their lengthy cozy chats in the library at Warrenton. And every fond glance exchanged between Castalia and Frederick reminded Katherine with a pang that she was quite alone.

When at last the countess announced that Katherine simply must accompany her to London, she could not bring herself to refuse. Particularly since Robbie had been begging her with every breath to return to the fascination of the city. With children and tutor in tow, they made the journey.

Knowlton grimaced with relief as his carriage clattered down the driveway. He had endured enough country parties to last him for the remainder of his life. The forced conviviality of the drawing room before dinner drove him mad, the mad scramble for partners in the long hours between dinner and bed grew tedious. Even cold, dirty, midwinter London held a greater appeal. In the house at Upper Brook Street, he could lock himself away for days at a time without fear of interruption. If he went a week without seeing another face, he would not complain.

His face twisted into a grimace. Holidays were an intolerable invention. The insistence on trying to outdo all others in Christmas cheerfulness escaped his understanding. There was not much to be gay about during this dark time of the year, when one was tucked away in some damp, cold house in some wretched corner of the country, where the chimneys smoked, the ladies giggled inanely, and the food was bland. He should have stayed at Warrenton.

But it was precisely Warrenton he wanted to avoid when he had ill-advisedly accepted all those invitations in December. He did not want to spend any more time in the empty corridors, with the ghost of Kate still haunting them the way she haunted his mind. In the company of other revelers, surely he would easily forget her.

Yet even in the midst of the largest groups, his thoughts often strayed to her, quite against his will. At the oddest moments something would trigger his memory, and images of Kate would torture his mind. Her embarrassment when he had bared his chest in front of her at harvest. Her gentle chiding over his past excesses when they talked long into the night at Warrenton. That first, lingering kiss in the garden.

Never had a woman so filled his mind for such a length of time. Usually women were nothing more than amusing creatures who provided entertainment and pleasure and then were forgotten as quickly as they had come. But Kate . . .

It was her abrupt departure from Warrenton, the long weeks of worry and anger, and the final discovery of her subterfuge that so embellished her memory. She was the first woman in years to have refused him, and he theorized it was that which made her so unforgettable. Had matters run their normal course, he would have grown tired of her and brought their liaison to an end. The fact that *she* had ended it, before it had barely begun, rankled.

He shrugged. Ah, well. London lay at the end of the road, a city full of the most beautiful and willing women in the world. He was bound to find another to capture his fancy before more than a few days passed. His attempts last year had been too halfhearted. This time he would find a lady who could drive even the memory of his own name from his brain.

The difference between the Little Season last fall and the full Season of the spring quickly became evident to Katherine. Invitations arrived at St. James Square in a never-ending stream. She thought that by staying with the marquess she would draw little attention, but those she had met in the fall were eager to see her again and those who had not were curious about the widow. Katherine limited her attendance to those events that either the marquess or the Durhams graced with their presence. She was determined to preserve the mantle of respectability she had paid for so dearly.

Katherine inwardly groaned when she saw Castalia bearing down on her at Lady Winthrop's musicale. She had hoped to spend at least one night free from her sister-in-law's matchmaking. Be it musicale or rout, Castalia never abandoned any opportunity to present Katherine with promising suitors.

"Katherine, dear, I would like you to meet Lord Belton."

Castalia grabbed Katherine's hand and virtually dragged her across the carpeted music room. "He is a viscount, dreadfully plump in the pockets, and most polite."

"He sounds irresistible," Katherine said through gritted teeth.

"Belton! How nice to see you this evening. A sad crush, is it not?" Castalia beamed in anticipation. "I must make you known to my sister-in-law, Lady Robert Mayfield. Poor Robert was killed in the Peninsula, you know, leaving Katherine alone with a small child." Castalia attempted to stiffle a sigh. "Katherine has done such a marvelous job raising the lad on her own, but we are well pleased she has joined us in London at last."

Katherine turned three shades of red at Castalia's ridiculous babbling. It made her sound like some bedraggled heroine in a poorly written tragedy. She simply must have a long talk with her sister-in-law.

"Lady Robert." Belton bowed low in greeting.

"My lord." Katherine fitted a polite social smile on her face. He looked exactly as one of Castalia's candidates would—conservative dress, a pleasing but not overly handsome countenance, and an aura of placid respectability.

"Oh, there is Lady Wallace. I must speak with her." With a wave of her fan, Castalia flitted across the room.

Katherine dared to raise her eyes to Lord Belton's and was struck by the look of amusement in the blue depths.

"I am afraid Lady Durham is—"

"As transparent as a sheet of glass?" Lord Belton offered.

They broke into shared laughter.

"She almost had me wishing to make a donation to the poor widows' fund," Katherine confessed, taking a closer look at the viscount. His light-brown hair was nearly the shade Robert's had been. "I pray that you will not hold her dramatics against me, my lord."

"Not at all. I have known Lady Durham long enough to know to discount three-quarters of what she says. However, one must pay attention to the other quarter. You have a son, then? How old is he?"

"Eleven," Katherine replied.

"And probably a bundle of mischief, if I remember life at that age," Lord Belton said kindly.

Katherine smiled. "That he is. But I am certain you do not wish to hear of my son, my lord. Are you in town for business or pleasure?"

"I am not certain," he said. "I came up last week for an auction, intending to stay for only a short while, but I might have reason to reconsider that plan."

Katherine vainly fought against her blush at the appreciative look she saw in his eyes. "What type of auction did you attend?"

"A book sale. An unfortunate gentleman outspent his income and was selling off his library."

"You must be a collector of books, then." Katherine relaxed slightly. There was something comforting in such an innocuous endeavor.

He smiled. " 'Collector' may be too formal a term. 'Accumulator' is more apt. I do not have many rare or fine works, but I like them all the same."

"Do you collect books on special topics?"

Belton shook his head. "Whatever strikes my fancy, I am afraid. Or whatever is offered for sale. But certainly, Lady Robert, you did not plan to discuss books when you attended a musicale. Did you enjoy the soloist?"

"I own I am rather indifferent to operatic airs," she admitted with a rueful smile.

"I also!" Belton looked around in mock dismay. "But it would not do either of our reputations good to have that overheard."

Katherine laughed again.

"Did you plan to eat with the Durhams, or may I take you in to supper?"

His suggestion delighted Katherine. It was wonderful to find someone she enjoyed conversing with. "I should like that very much," she said, extending him her hand.

As they entered the supper room, Katherine felt a moment's hesitation, remembering Castalia's deliberate maneuvering to bring her together with Lord Belton. Then she willed herself to relax. Lord Belton *was* nice and it was foolish for her to deny herself pleasant company out of some vague apprehension. He was certainly the least intimidating man Castalia had introduced to her.

*   *   *

Katherine was not certain how it happened, but over the next few weeks it seemed she saw more and more of Lord Belton. It was rarely by prearrangement. Oh, he took her for an occasional drive in the park and even consented to accompany her and Robbie on a visit to the British Museum. Katherine still retained the Durhams' escort to the parties she attended, and they always saw her home, but she found she spent more and more time in Lord Belton's company during the intervening hours. If she entertained suspicions about Castalia's connivance in alerting Belton to their plans, she did not complain.

She did enjoy his company. He was amusing, modest, and eminently likeable. What was more, Katherine felt totally safe in his company. He treated her with polite circumspection, and any fears she may have entertained about his interest in her soon faded after hours of his unexceptionable company. He made no untoward moves, treating her in the same refined manner he did Castalia. Katherine even dared to look forward to seeing him whenever she went out.

Katherine genuinely began to enjoy herself in the hectic social world of London. She dampened the pretensions of any importuning men she met, and could always rely on Castalia, Lord Durham, or the marquess to provide her with protection if she needed it.

Tonight's fete was a severe crush, which of course made it a great success. Katherine fanned herself unsuccessfully, too hot and uncomfortable to concentrate on Castalia's bright chatter. It had been a long week and she looked forward to spending tomorrow night at home. Robbie had complained more than once that he saw little of his mother. She felt a nagging guilt at her unintended neglect and resolved to spend more time with him. In the fall he would be away at school and she would seldom see him.

Katherine's languidly waving fan hesitated fractionally as she caught a glimpse of Knowlton across the room. The mere sight of him caused a tingling awareness to sweep over her body. Forcefully, she willed herself to calm. It was inevitable that they would encounter each other in society; they could certainly behave in an amiable manner when it happened. That thought did little to still the pounding of her heart. Dismayed at her reaction, she turned and addressed an innocuous remark to Castalia.

Normally Katherine enjoyed listening to Castalia's artful prattle, but she was no longer in the mood for any polite chatter. Her glimpse of Knowlton had ruined the evening for her. She was torn between expectation and dread that she would suddenly find him at her shoulder. How could she decently extricate herself and return home?

She almost collapsed in relief when she saw Lord Belton standing at the door, looking about with an air of expectant anticipation. But when she saw the smile of recognition that lit his face when he spotted her, she felt the tiniest qualm in her stomach. It seemed . . . No, she was reading too much into an innocent smile. She would have greeted him in the same way if she had picked him out in a crowded room. She valued his friendship, as he did hers. There was nothing more to their relationship than that.

"Lady Durham, Lady Robert." Belton greeted them with an affable smile. "A sad crush, is it not?"

Castalia nodded. "I am certain Lady Steventon had no intention of hosting half of London here tonight."

"If I may offer my assistance in trying to clear a path to the refreshments . . . ?"

Castalia shot a knowing glance at Katherine. "We would be most delighted, my lord."

Katherine dutifully followed them into the crowded supper room, where Belton appropriated three chairs. She fidgeted with her gloves while she waited for his return. Why, of all nights, had Knowlton chosen this one to appear? Her initial relief at seeing Belton soon changed to dismay. She felt uncomfortable at the idea of Knowlton seeing them together, which was in itself ridiculous. One could not read into the situation that which was not there.

Katherine stifled the thought with a surge of anger. It did not matter *what* Knowlton thought. If he even thought of her at all. A man who only wanted her for his mistress would have little reaction if he saw her receiving the attention of another. Katherine smiled weakly. It might even please him to discover he need not fear any chastisement for his dishonorable proposal. She knew that fear had been uppermost in his mind when he first discovered her identity. Let him see he no longer concerned her either.

Katherine talked herself into a state of composure until she saw Knowlton enter the supper room—this time in the company of an exquisitely beautiful lady. She nudged Castalia.

"Who is that with Knowlton?"

Castalia turned and stared boldly, to Katherine's chagrin. "Do not be so obvious," she commanded.

A mischievous smile flitted across Castalia's face. "That is Lady Taunton. A lovely lady, married at a young age to an aging lord who then conveniently died, leaving her a *very* rich widow."

"Do you know her well?"

Castalia wrinkled her nose. "She is not, shall we say, of the highest *ton*. She is much more popular among the gentlemen than their ladies."

"Is she Knowlton's mistress?" Katherine asked bluntly, inwardly berating herself for wanting to know.

Castalia shrugged. "Who knows? It is said Lady Taunton prefers to have several men at her beck and call at any one time. Goodness, you know Knowlton better than I. Why do you not ask him?"

Belton's arrival with their food saved Katherine the necessity of a reply. She looked up and thanked him with a radiant smile.

Knowlton sensed Katherine's presence in the crowded saloon even before he saw her in the far corner of the room. God, she looked beautiful tonight. Every time he saw her she looked even more ravishing, her creamy white skin begging to be touched, her golden-red hair a living, glowing flame. Involuntarily, his body responded.

He struggled against his impulse to glower across the room at Belton, who bent over Katherine in a very proprietary way. Damn, he had no right to feel this way. He knew perfectly well why she had rejected him. No respectable lady would entertain an offer such as he had made. It had been a grievous insult.

And if respectability was what Kate truly wanted, she could not do better than Belton. Knowlton doubted the viscount would even dare to kiss a woman without having first offered a declaration of marriage. And marriage, the one thing he himself was unprepared to give her, was what Katherine wanted most of all. So let her look for it elsewhere—in Belton she had a likely candidate.

"I am feeling sadly neglected, Knowlton." Lady Taunton's voice was soft in his ear.

"You were the one who insisted on coming here tonight," he growled. "I told you I would be a poor substitute for Seb."

"You also promised Seb to keep me entertained while he was gone," she warned. "He will not be pleased if I expire from boredom before he returns."

"I am sure Seb will be reasonable about the matter," Knowlton drawled in bored tones.

She rapped him on the arm with her fan. "You are incorrigible." Lady Taunton glanced quickly across the room. "Who is the fair lady who inspires such a look of gloom upon your face? Surely not Lady Durham—apart from being a widgeon, she is boringly happy in her marriage. Perhaps the lovely redhead at her side?" She smiled as Knowlton's scowl deepened.

"And Belton is so attentive. Do not tell me you two are engaged in a rivalry for the favors of such a striking lady?"

"Not at all," Knowlton said smoothly, taking her arm and steering her out of the room. "No lady who could be content with Belton's placid nature would ever interest me."

Chapter Nineteen

Fill for me a brimming bowl
And let me in it drown my soul:
But put therein some drug, designed
To banish woman from my mind.
　　　　　　　—Keats, *Fill for Me a Brimming Bowl*

"*L*ook, Mama, there is Knowlton!"
　　　Katherine looked across the park to where Robbie pointed, then quickly averted her eyes from the two mounted riders.

Damn him. Why today, of all days, did she have to encounter him in the park, when she was in the presence of both Robbie and Lord Belton? Robbie would demand to stop, Belton would notice her discomfort. He would be too polite to ask why, but he would wonder just the same. She looked up, startled, when she felt the carriage speed up.

"Why did we not stop?" Robbie asked plaintively.

Belton exchanged a quick embarrassed look with Katherine. "I do not think your mama wished to," he said quietly.

Katherine clenched her fists to resist the urge to swivel her head around and catch a better glimpse of the woman who rode at Knowlton's side. She wished she had taken a longer look when she had the opportunity. Belton's reaction left her with no doubt of the woman's status.

So. Knowlton was openly displaying this latest mistress in the park. At least Katherine now knew he entertained no regrets for her refusal. He had obviously found a suitable replacement.

Katherine remained quiet as they returned to the house

in St. James. Robbie bounded from the carriage while Katherine waited for Belton to assist her.

"Thank you," she said, giving him a grateful smile.

"I did not want to place you in an awkward situation," he said. "I did not know how best to explain things to your son."

She sighed. "I imagine that it is time he learned of such matters."

Belton cleared his throat. "If you like, I could . . . I could explain the situation to him."

Katherine was touched by his offer, yet felt a twinge of apprehension at the same time. It was not the action of a casual friend—and she hesitated to think of him as more than that. "Thank you, my lord, but I believe that is something I will have to undertake on my own—unless Robbie grows uncomfortable. I will certainly not hesitate to send him to you with questions in that event, if you do not object."

"I would be most willing to assist you," Belton said, pressing her fingers slightly.

Katherine gathered her wits and edged away toward the house. "Thank you for the drive. I look forward to the theater tonight."

"So do I," said Belton as he climbed back into the carriage and drove away.

Why had she felt the need to feign enthusiasm for their outing tonight? At times, she found Belton's solicitous kindness overwhelming. She was grateful and appreciative, but also felt guilty that those were her only reactions to his attentions. His tentative squeeze of her fingers had not sent a thrill of delight up her spine. His offer to explain the role of impure ladies to Robbie had been generous, but bordered on an intimacy with her family that she was not certain she wished to acknowledge.

Why was it that whenever she began to imagine she could find some form of happiness with Belton, or someone like him, Knowlton always appeared on the scene and exposed her wishes for the lies they were? He loomed as a nemesis in her life, unwilling to free her from his unnatural hold. She had never been one to pursue lost causes, but for some reason her heart had been frozen forever with the image of Knowlton engraved upon it. She fought, railed, and kicked against his hold, but she could not free herself from his grasp.

And now he flaunted his present mistress in front of all the town, a constant reminder to Katherine that he had once intended her for that role. It only marked her failure as complete. She had been nothing more than a passing fancy to him. How she wished she could say the same of Knowlton. Memories of that torrid embrace at Warrenton were ground into every fiber of her body. She could no more cut them away than she could cut off a finger or toe. Would she have to live with them for the remainder of her life?

By the time she had reached her room, Katherine felt the beginning of an enormous headache. Her temples throbbed and it was all she could do to grit her teeth and endure while the maid helped her from her dress. Katherine gratefully curled up in a ball and pulled the covers over her head to shut out the world.

The last person Knowlton had expected to encounter in the park that morning was Katherine—and Robbie. What fool impulse had guided him into taking that Cyprian riding? He had been less than enchanted at their first dealings, but since that seemed to be his reaction to every woman he took to bed these days, he had decided to give her another chance. By the time they returned to her set of rooms, any flickerings of desire had fled. He gave her a vague promise of a future engagement, and returned the horses to the mews.

What was wrong with him? This was a thousand times worse than his *ennui* of the previous spring. Then, it had been a general but vague dissatisfaction. Now it was a yawning chasm of disinterest. He had spent the better part of a month working his way through the muslin company, and not one single woman had inspired him to a repeat visit. In fact, he had more than once been inclined to depart before the activities commenced. But he soldiered on, needing to prove to himself that this was only a temporary aberration.

And what was worse, these numerous liaisons did little to slake his burning need. His expression darkened. Even at the moment of release, he felt the dissatisfaction welling up within him again, his desires unsatisfied. Not since Kate . . .

As he entered his bedchamber he rippled off his cravat and flung it across the dressing table in a fit of anger. There was nothing special about her. It had only been that long, seductive courtship that had heightened his interest so. He laughed derisively. How could he possibly compare a few fumbling kisses with a prim-and-proper widow to the pleasures of the most skilled courtesans of the city? It was obvious that his mind merely exaggerated the effect of Kate's kisses.

He only needed to look to her escort to convince himself of that. Belton was as dull a fellow as he could imagine—and it seemed every time he saw Kate she was in the prosy bore's company. He laughed harshly. They suited each other. She might be breathtakingly beautiful, but her manner was quite ordinary. She only wanted a respectable husband, a house full of screaming brats, and the usual round of ladies' teas and gossip. He was lucky she had refused him—else he would have been forced to cast her off quite soon, he was certain.

No, he had made a great error in judgment regarding Kate Mayfield. He had allowed lust to blind him to her true nature. It angered him that he had wasted so much time and thought on her.

To her regret, Katherine's headache departed during the long afternoon, and she could devise no valid reason to excuse herself from the theater that evening. A night of Castalia's lighthearted prattle and Belton's increasingly overwhelming attentions would do little to improve her spirits. Despite her misgivings, she found herself that evening seated next to Belton in the marquess's box at Drury Lane.

Katherine sat deep in her own musings throughout the production, oblivious of the words spoken onstage. It was a surprise when the final lights rose and the theatergoers began to stream from their seats.

"You were very quiet tonight," Belton remarked as he escorted her through the corridor.

"I found the play very diverting," she lied smoothly. "Did you not find it so?"

She turned to look at Belton, and was startled to see the man who stood by his side. Katherine's step faltered at the sight of Knowlton and the overdressed woman with him, and she gripped Belton's arm tightly to keep from stumbling.

"Belton, Lady Robert." Knowlton inclined his head in greeting.

In the crowded corridor she was trapped, and short of ignoring him completely, there was little Katherine could do to make her dismay known. Giving Knowlton the cut direct would cause worse gossip than to be spotted here chatting with him as if . . . as if he did not have *that* kind of woman on his arm. She nodded in a fractional acknowledgment.

Appraising the woman at his side, Katherine realized with a shock that it was not the same one he had been with that morning. The brunette was brazenly beautiful, expensively dressed, and clinging to Knowlton's arm as if her life depended upon it. Which it might, Katherine thought wryly, remembering how generous his offer to her had been.

She was grateful for Belton's gentle tug on her arm. Katherine could not have consciously moved.

Knowlton smiled his mocking grin. "So nice to see you again, Lady Robert." He stepped aside to let them pass.

"The nerve of that man." Belton was furious. "The insult to you . . ."

"I did not perceive it as such," Katherine replied, trying to compose her own shattered nerves. Had Knowlton sought her out deliberately to flaunt his lightskirt before her? Did he taunt her on purpose, showing her that he had no problem finding other women to fill his bed?

"It was not at all the thing."

"The less said, the better," Katherine replied curtly, which only had the effect of eliciting an odd glance from Belton. She firmly directed her gaze straight ahead. This day had been an unmitigated disaster and she only wished to go home.

But the mansion in St. James Square provided no refuge, and Katherine lay awake long into the night. Today had been full of revelations. Knowlton was certainly doing nothing to demonstrate the qualities that had so endeared him to her. In fact, it looked as if he was embarking on a course of dissipation that surpassed even his own reputation—two ladies in one day! It was outside of enough to have been in Belton's presence at both encounters.

Belton's reaction to each situation gave her pause. He cared for her, she knew. There was every likelihood he would make her an offer. Katherine only wished to stay his hand for a while longer, until she could bring some semblance of order to her confused mind. She was in no position to make any critical decisions right now.

Especially since she had discovered just how strong her feelings for Knowlton still were. It would take only the slightest encouragement from him to bring them to the fore again. She had thought she had resigned herself to the situation. After all, he had brutally dashed all her hopes with his cold-blooded offer of protection. She wondered if there was any way to accomplish that task. She would pay gladly for the solution.

Over the next weeks it seemed she encountered Knowlton everywhere. He was often in the park, driving a carriage or riding alongside a changing panoply of women, each lovelier than the last. At the parties where their kind would not be welcome, he was seen at the side of various ladies about whom rumors circulated, but who still were held to be of the highest *ton*. The only mote of comfort Katherine could derive from all this was that she rarely saw him with the same woman twice. Was that significant? Or was he just embarking on a new streak of licentiousness that would put his old reputation to shame?

The unexpected arrival in town of Elizabeth and her husband was one of the few bright spots in Katherine's existence. She eagerly accepted their invitation to dine, hoping there would be time for a long chat with Elizabeth.

"I am so pleased you could come on such short notice," Elizabeth greeted Katherine warmly. "I had no intention of being in London this spring, but when Somers needed to come to town, I decided to accompany him. It may be my last chance to get out in a while!"

Katherine smiled warmly as Elizabeth patted the notable bulge in her abdomen. She had missed Elizabeth's company, particularly over the last month, as her misery over Knowlton grew.

"I understand you have acquired a very attentive suitor." Elizabeth's voice was teasing.

Katherine ducked her head modestly. "It is an unexceptionable relationship."

"Unexceptionable?" Elizabeth laughed heartily. "Katherine, the entire town is talking about you and Belton. I would not be surprised to find it in the betting book at White's."

Anger crossed Katherine's face. "Do not those silly men have better things to do with their time?"

Elizabeth patted her hand. "Now, now. You must admit that your mysterious appearance last fall had all the tongues wagging. People were bound to notice, whatever you did."

"How many are coming for dinner tonight?" Katherine firmly changed the subject.

"Oh, a few close friends." Elizabeth airily waved her hand.

Elizabeth's idea of a "few" was slightly different from her own, Katherine shortly discovered, for it numbered closer to twenty. Most were familiar faces, and Katherine soon found herself drawn into conversation.

She had just accepted a glass of wine from her host when a familiar voice caused her to freeze. Knowlton! She was instantly filled with anger. Elizabeth had deliberately not told her he would be here. She scanned the crowded drawing room, trying to catch her friend's eye. Their gazes met momentarily, then Elizabeth looked away in embarrassment. Katherine vowed to give Elizabeth a piece of her mind when they were next alone.

Katherine's discomfort reached new heights when she saw the seating arrangements had placed her on Knowlton's left! She halted beside the table, looking for any other place to sit, but it would have caused a dramatic commotion to displace another. Biting back her anger, she allowed the footman to seat her.

"I believe Elizabeth is playing games this evening." Knowlton leaned imperceptibly toward Katherine, speaking in a low undertone.

"Quite," she replied stiffly.

"I do not find it a totally intolerable situation. Do you not concur, *Lady* Robert?"

Katherine winced at his inflection. "You know perfectly well how awkward this is—for both of us."

"How so?" His eyes lit mischievously. "I am never averse to sitting beside a beautiful lady." His voice dropped lower. "And you are exceptionally lovely tonight, Kate."

"Do not call me that," she hissed, keeping her gaze firmly on her plate.

"My apologies, Lady Robert. I forget you hold a more exalted position these days."

Katherine fought down the overwhelming urge to empty her wineglass over his head. He knew exactly how uncomfortable she was, and he was doing everything he could to make her discomfort worse. She would throttle Elizabeth when this was over.

As if to confound her, Knowlton conversed with her no more for the remainder of the meal. But he made his presence constantly known. With only a hairbreadth of distance between their chairs, it was no challenge for his muscular thigh to press against hers. The first time he made contact, Katherine nearly jumped at the shock to her senses. He turned slightly, surveying her with a mocking grin before returning his attention to the lady on his right. Then all too soon she felt his foot rubbing against her ankle.

"Stop that!" she whispered. He did not indicate he heard, but she no longer felt his touch.

Whatever appetite she had once possessed vanished completely. Katherine toyed with the idea of feigning illness, but such an announcement would only draw unwanted attention. Perhaps if she ignored him . . .

She nearly jumped up from her chair when she felt his fingers stroke sensuously along her leg while he pretended to fumble for his napkin. She quickly slipped her own hand down to her lap, but he caught her fingers in his, squeezing them so tightly she nearly winced.

As the dinner dragged on for an interminable time, Katherine grew close to tears. Why did he seek to humiliate her so? He knew she had put their relationship behind her; knew that when she had refused his offer she had determined on a life that did not include him. She had made her choice; why would he not accept it?

Knowlton kept Katherine under close study. She was thoroughly uncomfortable, he noted with malicious pleasure. He had felt her startled movement when he furtively rubbed her thigh. His touch still had the power to thrill her. Despite the modest front she maintained before the *ton,* it was obvious that there was still a trace of passion left within his wanton little widow. He fought down the heat rising in his own body. He was *firmly* in control of this situation. He only wanted to see how far he could push her. Knowlton blessed Elizabeth's seating arrangement. This was the most entertaining evening he had enjoyed in weeks.

"Pardon me," he said, reaching past Kate for the salt cellar. He made certain his arm brushed against hers. He smiled at the faint flush that rose in her cheeks, and pressed his thigh against her again, watching her heightened color. Lord, she blushed like an angel.

Pretending to pay attention to his food, he surreptitiously watched the gentle rise and fall of her chest. Whoever was making her dresses certainly knew how to set off those snowy breasts to perfection, he thought. Kate was obviously not covering her assets with a demure neckline. Of course, he thought scornfully, she was more likely to snare a husband with such a prominent display of her charms. He rubbed his leg against hers and saw how quickly her breathing increased.

He knew he could get her alone if he wished. Her reaction to him tonight told him she was less indifferent to his presence than she pretended. It might be just the thing to stifle this maddening obsession he had for her. He had the opportunity now to make a very deliberate comparison of her talents. He felt certain she would not live up to his inflated memory.

The more he thought on it, the more he embraced the idea. He could contrive some excuse for drawing her away from the other guests. It would take only a few moments to whisk her away to some unoccupied room, where he could avail himself of another sample. He needed to set his mind at rest about her once and for all. Knowlton grinned in anticipation.

When the ladies at last rose to retire to the drawing room, Katherine immediately sought out Elizabeth.

"What could you have been thinking of to seat me next to Knowlton?" she demanded.

"Oh, dear. Did I create a problem?" Elizabeth was all wide-eyed innocence."

"The man is a total boor," Katherine said bitterly.

"How dreadful." Elizabeth sounded truly sympathetic. "I had thought you were friends, at least."

"We are not," Katherine said stonily. "I feel perfectly dreadful, I have a throbbing headache, and I only wish to go home. Can you order the carriage round?"

Elizabeth nodded. "Wait in the library. I will explain to the other guests that you are unwell." She pressed Katherine's hand. "I am truly sorry. I had no idea I would create such a disaster."

Katherine offered her a woebegone smile. "I know you meant no harm. But he has changed, somehow, from the man I knew last fall, and I do not like the new Knowlton."

After making her way to the library, Katherine gratefully sank into one of the deep upholstered chairs. It would be some minutes before the Wentworths' carriage would be ready to take her home. At least here, in the darkened shadows, she could relax and try to will her headache away.

In the cozy heat of the room, the tension drained from her body and the pounding in her head was reduced to a mild tapping. Katherine lay back in the chair, eyes closed. Shortly she would be home in her own bed; by tomorrow she would feel quite the thing again.

Knowlton slipped silently into the room, grinning at his discovery of Katherine's hiding place. "So this is where you have hidden yourself." He stood before her, hands on hips. "You need not have gone to such great lengths, Kate. You could hardly expect me to ravish you in full view of all the company."

Her eyes snapped open at his mocking tones. "With your behavior at dinner as an example, I would not put such a thing past you," she said, her voice filled with scorn.

"My, we are upset. What you need is a good glass of brandy to relax you." Knowlton turned to the side table and filled two glasses.

Katherine looked down as he forced a tumbler into her

hand, and she did not see him circle behind her. She jumped when she felt the touch of his hands on her shoulders.

"Do not touch me." She shrugged out of his grasp.

"Oh, but, Kate, you are so tense. Let me ease the knots from those muscles." He began kneading the base of her neck.

Even with his gloves on, the touch of his fingers sent a delicious thrill dancing through her body. Perhaps if she ignored him he would tire of this new game and go away.

"Drink," he commanded, and she obediently took a swallow from the glass in her hand.

Despite her intentions, Katherine found herself relaxing beneath the ministrations of his hands. A slow languor crept over her as he stroked away the stiffness in her neck. Her eyes drifted shut and her shoulders drooped in a relaxed attitude. She did not move when he removed his hands, feeling almost as if she were floating along on an airy cloud. Then she jumped in surprise and pleasure as his warm fingers stroked along her neck.

"Much nicer," he murmured into her ear. "Gloves are *such* a nuisance."

His heated breath against her neck left gooseflesh in its wake. "My lord . . ." she began in protest. She simply must send him away.

"Hush," he commanded. "Relax."

She complied, her body drained of will. His stoking fingers had a hypnotic effect. It did feel so wonderful . . .

Katherine sat bolt upright when Knowlton's lips brushed her neck. Swiveling around, she glared at him in anger. "I did not give you leave to do that."

His lips formed an apologetic, almost boyish smile. "My pardon, Lady Robert. I sometimes forget myself when I am so close to such loveliness."

Katherine stood up, setting her half-finished brandy on the table. She let out a deep sigh. "I suppose it was too much to expect that you would behave yourself." She leaned over to pick up her shawl, but Knowlton laid a staying hand on her arm.

"Are you so certain my behavior offends you?" he asked, his gray eyes dark in the shadowed room. "Methinks the lady doth protest too much."

She reached again for her shawl, but he quickly drew it out of reach.

"You should have watched yourself more closely in the mirror at dinner," he said, his voice low and seductive. "You would have seen how that lovely flush crept over your cheeks every time our bodies touched. Or how your breathing quickened when I ran my hand down your thigh."

"The only feeling I entertained was disgust at your boorish behavior," she retorted.

"I think not, Kate." He stepped out from behind the chair and lifted her chin with his finger. "I think you were recalling how very pleasurable the touch of my hands could be on your creamy skin." His voice dropped lower. "I think you remember exactly how much you enjoyed our little interlude at Warrenton."

"Never."

"Prove it." He pinned her with a challenging stare.

"You are being foolish," she said with a nervous laugh.

"I think not. I think behind the elegant and reserved Lady Robert is the redheaded Kate who came so eagerly into my arms. Do not pretend you would not like my lips and hands caressing you again."

She struck him a ringing blow across the cheek.

"Damn you," he cried, grabbing her arms and jerking her against his body. He forced his lips on hers, brutally grinding them against her tightly closed mouth. As his grip on her arms tightened, she moaned in pain and he forced his tongue between her lips. Burning lust quickly replaced his anger as he held the woman who had driven him to near-madness. He pressed his body against her, letting her feel the hardness in his groin. His tongue thrust rhythmically; the taste and smell of her built the heat inside him to the boiling point. He felt her resistance crumbling against his physical onslaught and felt a thrill of triumph.

He would succeed now. He berated himself for not having locked the door behind him when he entered. She would be close to capitulation in no time, yet they risked discovery in this room. With a muffled groan he tore his mouth away and planted hot, wet kisses across her neck and face. He enfolded her in his arms.

"Come away with me tonight," he whispered, nipping at her ear. Without waiting for her reply, he again sought her mouth, seeking, teasing her own tongue into a flurried response.

"Katherine, the carriage is . . ."

Knowlton looked up in surprise at Somers, standing in the doorway with a look of mingled shock and amusement on his face. Katherine immediately pulled free from Knowlton's arms and fled past Somers into the corridor.

"Not quite the thing to be seducing the guests." Somers grinned.

Knowlton turned away, struggling to control his impassioned breathing. "Take a damper, Somers. It is none of your concern."

Damn. Knowlton expelled his breath in a loud whoosh. He had been within minutes of having Kate fall into his hands like a ripe plum. He could have spent an enjoyable evening sampling the delights of his redheaded witch before he sent her on her way like all the other women whose charms faded in the cool light of morning. Now he would be forced to the trouble of seeking out another female to sate his lust this night. Such a bother.

As he turned to exit the room, he spied Kate's shawl, crumpled in a heap on the floor. Bending down, he picked it up and held it to his nose, reveling in the faint scent. Lavender. Kate.

Chapter Twenty

O, Beware, my lord, of jealousy!
It is the green-ey'd monster which doth mock
The meat it feeds on.
                                        —Shakespeare, *Othello*

*T*he spring sky was lightening in the east when Knowlton dragged his body from the carriage. He staggered slightly as he climbed the stairs, fumbling in his inner pocket for his key, which seemed to have vanished. With

an angry snarl he jerked the bell rope and in moments a
sleepy-eyed footman opened the door. Knowlton quelled
him with a fierce look and stumbled up the next set of
stairs to his room. He flung himself backward onto the bed,
his legs dangling down over the sides.

He was doomed. There was no other word for it. He was
totally, utterly, miserably doomed. For the rest of his life.
Because only death could release him from Kate Mayfield's hold.

He had been a fool to think that a successful seduction
last night would drive her from his thoughts. My God, it
would only have wrapped the chains tighter. Although he
wondered if that was possible.

He had tried, oh, how he had tried to free himself of her
memory. He had picked the loveliest lady from the milling
crowd in the Green Room, one who was new and fresh
and eager to please a noble client. But when the moment
came, he had only wanted to bolt from her room in dismay.
Only by imagining that it was Kate's lips he kissed, Kate's
breast he suckled, Kate's body he sheathed himself in,
could he find a trace of pleasure in the transaction. And
even then the pleasure was so transitory as to be almost
nonexistent. One chaste kiss from Kate was more enjoyable
than three bouts of sexual gymnastics with any dancer.

He laughed harshly. After his cruel treatment of Kate,
there was little chance she would ever look upon him with
favor again. He had tormented her at dinner, then rudely
insulted her with his forced attentions in the library. He
could still feel the stinging slap of her palm against his
cheek. He had deserved far more than that. It would take
a man of more diplomacy and tact than he to erase the
humiliations of that evening from her mind. He might
spend a lifetime at it and never succeed in regaining her
respect. What had he done?

Katherine awoke with a deep, unnamed yearning in her
breast that was painful in its intensity. Memory of Knowlton's erratic behavior washed over her. He had been cruel
in his taunting, brutal in his attentions. And she had still
responded, still clung to him as if her life depended upon
it. Had Somers not intruded when he did . . . There was

no doubt she would have done whatever Knowlton had asked of her.

Her cheeks flushed with shame. How could her body behave so traitorously, rebelling against all her sense? No matter how much temporary happiness she would find with him, Knowlton would eventually cause her deep, searing pain. He would never give her the only thing she wanted—his heart. If he had ever possessed such an organ, it was buried so deep within him that she doubted it could ever be found again.

She turned her face into her pillow, tears stinging at her eyes. How could she continue to be so foolishly in love with him? It was maddeningly pointless, yet no matter how hard she fought against it, it was impossible to free herself.

Katherine resolved, when going down to breakfast, that she would be most careful with her social calendar in the future. She would avoid any entertainment that might draw Knowlton's presence. That this would bar her from most events did not cause her dismay. In truth, the excitement of life in the fashionable world had paled. It was frivolous and fun, but now that she was in the middle of it, she realized that it was no more satisfying than her old life had been. It would be all too easy to let herself drift along, following in Castalia's pattern. But she did not want that for herself. A nice quiet cottage in the country sounded like heaven.

The sight of the enormous container of creamy white hothouse roses caused Katherine to pause upon entry into the breakfast parlor. The marquess eyed her with an eager expression.

"You have made an impression on someone, my girl."

"For me?" she asked with a sinking feeling. Her trembling hand reached for the card.

> *Words cannot express my regret over my insufferable behavior last evening. Know that I never wished to hurt you, Kate. My only excuse is that your bewitching presence does strange things to my judgment. You have my promise that there will never be a repetition.*
>
> *Knowlton*

Clutching the note to her bosom, Kate fled from the room, tears streaming from her eyes. Her initial relief at Knowlton's promise was overlaid with sorrow that she would never again be encircled by his arms. Yet that was what she wanted—was it not?

Katherine kept to her resolve to curtail her social engagements. She fobbed Castalia off with excuses of minor ailments, and when that no longer sufficed, pleaded exhaustion and the need to spend more time with Robbie. Although she felt a lingering sense of guilt at treating Lord Belton so shabbily, she ordered the butler to turn all visitors away. Only when both the marquess and Castalia descended upon her in force did Katherine allow herself to be persuaded to go out for one evening.

She winced at the eager look in Lord Belton's eyes when he saw her enter the music room. He hastened to her side, urging her toward a seat.

Belton leaned toward Katherine while the harpist arranged her music. "You have been far too seldom in company this last week," he gently chastised.

"I have been tired," she explained, grateful that he did not press her too closely. "I find I am unused to the hectic pace of the Season."

"I appreciate your sentiments," he murmured. "I, too, find London can grow wearisome." He gave her a meaningful glance. "I think we would both enjoy a restorative visit to the country."

She nodded briefly, sitting back with relief when the musical program began and he was unable to continue. At this moment, the last thing she wanted was a further opportunity for Belton to press his suit.

"Are you certain you did not wish to accompany us to Lady Worthington's?" Castalia inquired of Katherine as they filed out of the music room an hour later.

"Please do," Belton encouraged.

Katherine felt trapped. To decline now would label her as rude; she could hardly plead overwhelming weariness after venturing out this evening. With the Season at its height, there was a multitude of *ton* parties for Knowlton to choose from. The chances of his attending this particular party were slim when he had so many other sources of entertainment. She nodded in acquiescence, but vowed she would have a long talk with Castalia in the morning.

She was disappointed to find that the Worthington rout had turned into a severe crush even before their arrival. That was another element she found so disturbing about the city—the sheer numbers of people everywhere. She longed for the solitude of a quiet country lane.

"I think half the city is here tonight," Castalia whispered from behind her fan. "That ball in Grosvenor Square must have been a sad affair."

Katherine made a futile attempt to wave cool air over her face with her own fan. "I suppose it is too much to hope that there will be anything left in the refreshment room."

"One can always hope, Lady Robert," Belton said. He took her elbow and carefully pushed their way through the crowded room, leaving Castalia to trade gossip with a friend in the overheated saloon.

The supper room was astonishingly empty; Belton easily appropriated a corner table and chairs, returning swiftly with two overladen plates and glasses of champagne.

"This is much better," he said, saluting her with his glass. "An unexpected oasis of quiet."

Katherine took a sip of her champagne and wrinkled her nose at the tickling bubbles. She had not intended to find herself in such an intimate setting with Belton, and she struggled to find an innocuous topic of conversation. One that would not lead to topics she wished to avoid for the present time.

"How are your library acquisitions coming? Have you purchased any new finds?"

"There is a sale tomorrow I am attending, as a matter of fact."

"Another estate disposition?" She tilted her head in feigned interest.

Belton shook his head. "A private sale, I am afraid. For collectors, so the prices will be high. I may not find anything I even wish to buy, but I thought I would attend just in case."

"Robbie is very much enjoying the copy of *Robinson*

Crusoe you sent him." She flashed him a grateful smile.
"He is struggling now with the choice of whether to join
the cavalry or become an adventurer when he grows older."

"Have you settled on a school for him yet?"

She shook her head. "It is such a difficult decision. Winslow, of course, wishes him to go to Eton, like his father.
But I cannot forget how much Robert disliked the place."
She paused, as if in embarrassment. "I hope you did not
attend Eton."

Belton laughed. "Harrow. So you may malign Eton to
your heart's content."

"I must own that Harrow sounds to be much like Eton.
I am very intrigued with a school in Norfolk. It is small
and features a more varied curriculum." She sighed. "Robbie must choose a career of some sort, and the better his
education, the better he shall do. I detest the idea of his
entering the army, but if that is his choice, unending years
of Latin and Greek will do him little good. Mathematics
and geography will certainly prove more useful."

"Was the school recommended to you?"

She nodded. "The Duke of Hartford sends his son
there—precisely because he hated his years at Eton." The
thought of Hartford caused her mind to drift back to those
easy weeks at Warrenton. When she still had hopes and
dreams.

Standing in a shadowed corner, sipping his champagne,
Knowlton watched Kate and Belton with increasing distress.
She looked entirely too *comfortable* with the viscount. He
winced as she smiled brightly at some comment her partner
made. Entirely too comfortable. They almost looked like a
married couple. The thought caused a wrenching feeling
somewhere in his middle. Knowlton quickly tossed off the
glass of champagne and searched for another.

He had half a mind to saunter over to their table and
pull up a chair. He would like to see the look on Katherine's face if he did. But he had resolved, after their last
disastrous encounter, that he would keep his distance. He
had enough honor left to know she did not wish for a casual
liaison, however much her body might protest to the contrary. She simply was not that kind of woman.

Watching them through narrowed gray eyes, he tried to

objectively evaluate Belton as a partner for her. There was little to criticize. Belton was as solid as they came. A bit boring at times, of a certainty, but he would never be caught making love to an unmarried lady in the library of a friend's house. That alone would do much to commend him to Kate.

Knowlton hoped his contrite note and floral peace offering had mollified her slightly. How could one woman goad him into such a mixture of anger and lust? He began to think there was something seriously amiss with his life. He had offended a woman he genuinely liked, and embarrassed himself in the eyes of one of his closest friends. In short, he had acted like a total fool. Which was entirely unlike him. He was rarely ever rash or foolish; his life had long been one of cold, calculated deliberation. Why was it suddenly becoming so difficult to act in such a manner?

He shrank back further into the shadows as Katherine and Belton left the room. Setting down his now-empty glass, Knowlton followed them back to the crowded main rooms. Knowing there was no point in his remaining, he continued to the door and called for his carriage. Despite the early hour, he gave the order for Upper Brook Street. He was in no mood for company tonight.

Settled at last in his comfortable leather chair, Knowlton stared morosely into the flickering flames of the fire before he tossed back the last of the brandy in his glass. With an unsteady hand he refilled it and took a large swallow.

He wished Katherine had not been there tonight, even though he had gone entirely on the possibility that she would be. But he had thought . . . Just what had he thought? That seeing her with the adoring Belton at her side would free him from the ghost of her presence that haunted him every waking moment and drove the sleep from his brain at night? He uttered a mirthless laugh. More fool he. He had only added months, if not years, onto his torture.

She had looked so exquisite in that clinging blue silk. Cut low over the swell of her breasts, the sleeves barely skimming her bared shoulders, it had made the blood run hot and thick through his veins. God, how he wanted her. He had tried to quench the fire with the body of every willing woman who crossed his path, but that excess had only heightened, not dimmed, his lust. Each unsatisfying

sexual encounter only sharpened his sense of loss and en-
hanced his memory of that last evening at Warrenton. Her
passion would be wasted on Belton.

So what was he to do? Live celibate for the remainder
of his life? Lose himself in more displeasing liaisons? Cavot
and carouse with every piece of muslin he could find until
he had at last exorcised her image from his brain? And
how long would it take? Weeks? Months? Years? The rest
of his blighted life?

She *was* a witch. There could be no other explanation
for the power she held over him. Never had a woman so
filled his mind, pushing all else aside to become the domi-
nant thought during all his waking hours. And unsatisfied
with that achievement, she made his nights a torment.

There had to be a way to free himself from her grip.

Katherine took her seat at the breakfast table, eyeing the
groaning sideboard with distaste. She had eaten far too
much at the Worthington rout last evening, but it had been
easier to eat than to talk with Belton. She reached for a
piece of toast, nibbling on it while the waiting footman
poured her tea. The marquess ignored her presence, his
head buried in the newspaper.

"Well, my dear, when can we expect an interesting
announcement?"

His abrupt question startled Katherine out of her reverie.

"An interesting what?" She directed him a puzzled look.

"Belton. Has he talked to you yet?"

"About what?" she asked casually, although she knew
perfectly well what the marquess meant.

"Good God, girl, are you obtuse? No man pays a lady
that much attention unless he is considering marriage."

"The subject has not come up," Katherine replied
primly.

"And I wager that is more of your doing," said the marquess, laying down his paper with a disgusted snort. "You
are no miss fresh out of the school room; you know how
these things are done. You have to maneuver him into the
right position."

"I have no desire to maneuver Lord Belton into anything," she said obstinately.

"You could not do much better," the marquess mused.

"He has a very good income, a prosperous estate. And he dotes on you."

Katherine had the grace to blush. "Lord Belton is an amiable companion. Nothing more."

"If I thought you were still wearing the willow for my son, it would make sense," the marquess said, his voice rising. "But you ain't, and that's a fact. You are acting like a skittish filly at her first mating. Good God, woman, you're a nearly thirty-year-old widow, with a son to boot. Husbands don't grow on trees for the likes of you."

"I am not looking for a husband," Katherine said, her anger rising. "As I have tried to tell you and Castalia more than once. But you both refuse to listen."

He brushed off her objections with a dismissive wave of his hand. "Of course you want a husband. You need someone who can give young Robbie some guidance."

"I can give Robbie all the guidance he needs." She pressed her lips together tightly to forestall a more heated response.

"The boy needs a man," the marquess roared. "You have been given every opportunity to find one. If you let Belton slip through your fingers, you are a worse fool than I thought." He picked up his newspaper again and retreated behind its printed pages.

Katherine left her half-eaten toast and took her teacup into the library. She was not going to let the marquess goad her into a display of anger.

The marquess, despite his lack of tact, was right. She was acting like a skittish filly. She knew that the slightest word of encouragement would bring a declaration from Belton. Why did she hold back?

It was foolish of her, really. Belton would make an excellent husband. He liked Robbie, and more important, Robbie liked him. He was steady and dependable. She never need worry that he would squander his money on gaming or lightskirts. As his wife, she would have the security she longed for, a house she could call her own. Why, then, was she so reluctant to bring him to the point?

Simply because the sight of him did not take her breath away. The touch of his hand did not send thrills coursing through her body. And she suspected that kissing him would be about as satisfying as kissing a brother.

It was unfair, but she simply could not help comparing her reaction to him with the one she had to Knowlton. And there was simply no comparison. With Knowlton, her pulse raced, breathing became an effort. He had treated her abominably that night at Elizabeth's, and still she found herself melting in his arms. It was a continuing revelation to discover how he could tempt her to throw all her good sense and judgment out the window at the crook of his beckoning finger.

Knowlton did not enjoy his solitary ride through the park that morning. The signs of spring grew more evident each day and hinted of the summer to come. Anyone else would have been cheered by the thought. To Knowlton the idea of summer brought only gloom. He could not think of summer without thinking of Warrenton, and Kate.

"Knowlton! Lord Knowlton!"

He froze at the eager, familiar voice. One more reminder of his damnable folly. "Hello, Robbie."

"I say, Knowlton, it has been ever so long since I saw you last."

"That it has, Robbie." A genuine smile crossed his face. "Still riding Atlas, I see."

Robbie smiled and patted his mount's neck. "He is a good pony. Although Grandfather says I may have a full-size horse this summer."

"Planning on spending the summer with Winslow, are you?" Did that mean Katherine would be there also?

"Mama says we might go to the seashore, but I am not certain we will." He looked glumly at Knowlton. "Aunt Castalia says Mama might have other plans."

Knowlton hastily sucked in his breath. It did not take much effort to guess at Lady Durham's meaning. "I saw your mama just the other night at a party," he said with a forced casualness. "She was with Lord Belton." He watched Robbie carefully to gauge his feelings for his mother's suitor.

"She is with him often." Robbie gave Knowlton a wistful stare.

It was cowardly of him to discuss this with Robbie, but he had to know which way the wind blew. "Do you like Lord Belton?"

"He is nice," said Robbie with a self-conscious smile. "He brings me things a lot. Mostly books. Mama says he collects books. The last one was about a man who is stranded on a desert island all by himself except for a friend he called Friday."

"Robinson Crusoe." Knowlton smiled in remembered pleasure. "And now I wager you wish to go to sea when you are a bit older."

Robbie colored. "Maybe. I still think about the cavalry."

"We never did get you to Astley's last fall, did we?" Knowlton frowned in remembrance. "It was forgotten in all the business after the queen's death."

"Oh, I have been twice this spring. Lord Belton took me once, and Mama and Grandpapa came with me one time."

Knowlton tried to ignore the sharp pain that stabbed through him. How he would have liked to see Robbie's wide eyes at his first glimpse of the delights of Astley's. He would wager a monkey the lad had talked of nothing else for weeks. A deep regret assailed him.

"What else have you been up to these last months?" If Knowlton had been cut out of Robbie's life as effectively as from Katherine's, he could at least hear what he had missed.

"Studying a lot." Robbie grimaced. "I have a tutor now because Mama says I will be going away to school in the fall. Did you go away to school when you were eleven?"

Knowlton remembered those first terror-filled weeks at Eton, when the older students had mercilessly tortured the new ones. Perhaps things were better now. He hoped Robbie would have an easier time. "I was about your age when I went to Eton," he said carefully. "You will make lots of new friends at school."

Robbie shrugged gently. "I hope so. I wish my cousins were older so I could play with them. I miss Sam sometimes."

"Sam is doing well, I hear. I saw him when I was at Warrenton last month. I will tell him you asked after him when I see him next."

"Thank you," Robbie said, smiling.

"Do you think your mama will marry Lord Belton?" The moment the words left his mouth, Knowlton was appalled at his question. But he had to know.

Robbie gave him a curious glance. "I do not know. I

think Grandpapa wants her to. She has not said anything to me. What do you think?"

"I am not privy to your mother's thoughts," Knowlton replied stiffly. He would be the last person on earth to have that news.

"Sometimes I wish we were back at the Rose Cottage," Robbie said quickly. "So I could walk over to Warrenton and visit you."

A sudden impulse seized Knowlton. "Do you still play chess?"

Robbie nodded.

"Then came home with me now. We can have a quick game."

Robbie's eyes lit. "Really?"

"Really." Robbie's enthusiasm bolstered Knowlton's spirits. "You can send the groom back to your grandfather's with the message; I can escort you home later."

"Capital!" the boy exclaimed.

As they swung the horses toward the park exit, Knowlton felt a twinge of regret for all that he had missed and was going to miss. One morning of chess would not count for much over a lifetime.

Chapter Twenty-One

Sweet seducer! blandly smiling;
Charming still, and still beguiling!
Oft I swore to love thee never
Yet I love thee more than ever!
—Thomas Moore, *Song*

*K*atherine looked up in surprise as the butler ushered Belton into the morning room. For a moment she was confused. Had she promised to accompany him somewhere today and forgotten? In the jumbled state her mind was often in these days, it was a distinct possibility.

"I had hoped to find you at home this morning," Belton said.

She let out a relieved breath and flashed him a welcoming smile. "How nice of you to call," she said, setting her sewing aside.

Lord Belton took his seat across from her. Katherine thought he looked oddly uncomfortable today, and the first hints of apprehension teased at her brain.

"Katherine," he began, "you cannot be surprised when I tell you how much I have grown to admire you."

Dread swept over her body. That which she had most feared was happening, and she was beset with panic. What was she going to do? What could she say to him?

"It is always a pleasure to be in your company," she said slowly. How, exactly, did one go about forestalling a proposal? She abruptly stood up and crossed the room to the window, certain that her nervousness was obvious. "The weather looks to be clearing."

He came up behind her. "Katherine, there is no need to be skittish."

She whirled and faced him. "Do you imagine that I am nervous, my lord?"

"It has not escaped my notice that you have been taking great pains of late to avoid being alone in my company. I begin to think I have offended you in some manner."

She uttered a nervous laugh. "Certainly not, my lord. I am sorry if I have given you that impression, for I assure you it was not my intent."

Belton took her hand in his and led her back to the sofa. She sat gingerly on the edge, half-dreading what was to come and half-relieved that it would be out in the open at last.

"Katherine, I find I am no longer able to enjoy a day if I am not able to spend some small part of it in your company."

She forced her gaze to meet his, and the fond emotion that shone in his bright blue eyes pained her. "My lord—"

"Richard."

"Richard." The name sounded strange on her tongue. Could she speak it every day for the rest of her life?

"I think we have spent enough time in each other's company to have a fair estimation of one another's character. There is much to be admired in yours, Katherine. You have grace, and beauty, and serenity."

She stilled the urge to laugh. Serenity. That was one thing she completely lacked. Serenity had fled from her life the day she had met Knowlton.

"You make me sound too much of a paragon," she said lightly. "I fear I could not live up to such standards."

He smiled warmly. "I cannot imagine any such thing," he said, taking her hand again. "I had hoped to invite you to Belton House this spring so you could determine whether you could be happy there." His eyes searched her face. "But I find I am too impatient to wait for such an opportunity. You would do me great honor, Katherine, if you would consent to become my wife."

She dropped her eyes, looking dispassionately at their clasped hands. A proposal. A most honorable one. Castalia and the marquess would be thrilled. Katherine could not put a name to the emotion the offer stirred within her.

As if sensing her hesitation, he sought to further his case. "I cannot pretend to replace Captain Mayfield, either as a husband or as a father to his son. But I know I could be a good guide for your Robbie. And I hope I could be the kind of husband you would wish."

She shut her eyes, feeling the tears welling in them. Why could he not have waited a bit longer, waited until she had her emotions more closely under control? Now she was going to have to say something, and she did not know what her answer would be.

"You honor me with your attention," she said at last, choosing her words with infinite care. "And I cannot say that your offer causes me displeasure. But I do not feel that I can give you an answer immediately."

She looked toward him and smiled pleadingly. "I entertained no intention of seeking another husband when Robbie and I rejoined the family. I felt that the happiness I had enjoyed with Robert was all that one person could expect from a lifetime. To marry again . . . There have been so many changes in my life this past year, I do not know if I am ready for another yet."

She saw the disappointment in his eyes as he sat back.

"I certainly understand your hesitation, Katherine," he said. "I in no way want to make you feel that I am forcing a decision upon you. Perhaps my original plan was best. Later in the spring I could arrange a party at Belton—"

"I cannot expect you to wait so long for an answer," she said, deciding in that moment that she would have to make up her mind soon. "I ask for only a short time to consider your very flattering offer."

"I will await your decision, then," he said in a lighter tone. He brought her hand up and gently brushed his lips against it. "You know that I will hold out every hope that you will find me worthy of your affections."

She wanted to scream at him to stop, to cry out that she was not worthy of his affections at all. That she had given her heart to a callous rake and was almost willing to throw away a good and kind man like Belton because of it. But she remained silent.

Belton rose to his feet. "I will take my leave now, Katherine."

She stood and walked with him to the morning room door. "I thank you again for the honor," she said quietly. "And I promise to give the matter great thought."

He nodded and took his leave.

Katherine collapsed weakly upon the sofa. Dear God, what was she going to do? She laughed bitterly. Last year she had been a near-penniless widow; now she was being offered a life of luxury and ease she could only have dreamed of then.

She tried to school her mind along objective lines. There was no denying that Belton would be a good father for Robbie. They got along well. Belton never talked down to her son, and paid him respectful attention at all times. They dealt well together. And she could not underestimate the importance of Robbie's happiness to her.

It was not any apprehension about Belton's dealings with Robbie that caused her reservations. And she did not hold any concerns about the way Belton would treat her. He was always a perfect gentleman, solicitous, concerned, and willing to do anything to please her. As his wife, she would be worshiped and adored. He would indulge her whims, surprise her perhaps with presents, and be as attentive as she could ever wish.

No, what caused her to pause was the fear that she would be a dismal failure as his wife. Could she truly be content in that role? Or would the ghost of a cynical earl with mocking smile and cool gray eyes always come between them? With Knowlton forever in her heart, would there be room for anything other than warm affection for Belton? He deserved far more.

She wrapped her arms around herself, feeling chilled even in the warm room. Was there any hope of escape from this coil?

Katherine forced her lips into a smile as Robbie entered the room.

"Finished with your studies already?"

He nodded, standing awkwardly, as if considering something in his mind. "Are you going to marry Lord Belton?" he blurted out.

Katherine was taken aback. In all her confusion, she had never once discussed the matter with Robbie. Of course she must speak to him before making her decision. He would be as affected by the matter as she.

"Does that idea displease you?" she asked, carefully watching for his reaction.

He shrugged. "Lord Belton is nice. I just wondered."

"Has someone been talking to you about this?" If the marquess had gone behind her back and hinted to Robbie, she would be furious.

"I saw Lord Knowlton in the park yesterday. He wanted to know."

Just the mention of his name was enough to send her pulses racing. Knowlton's interest puzzled her. But she was certain it meant nothing. It was obvious her relationship with Belton was on everyone's mind.

She reached for Robbie's hand and drew him to the sofa. "We have never talked about the possibility of my remarrying. What do you think about the idea?"

Robbie wrinkled his freckled nose. "It would be all right, I guess. As long as it was someone like Lord Belton or Lord Knowlton. They are fun."

"I do not think it very likely that I would marry Lord Knowlton," she said quickly, the words cutting into her like a knife. "Lord Belton was here this morning, and he does wish to marry me."

"Did you say yes?"

"I did not give him an answer," she explained, relieved that Robbie showed no signs of distress. "I told him I needed some time to consider. I knew that I needed to discuss it with you. I have thought that you two dealt well with each other."

Robbie nodded absently. "If you married him, would we go to live at his house?"

"We would."

"So I would not go to Grandpapa's for the summer?" The disappointment in his voice was clear.

"You could certainly go for a visit," she said. "Lord Belton has a country house of his own, you know, in Dorset. I imagine there are lots of things you could do there."

"And I would still go to school in the fall?"

"Yes."

Robbie stared down at his feet, as if he found them the most fascinating objects. "If you married him, would I have to call him 'Papa'?"

She sensed the anxiety in his question and hugged him close. "Not unless you wished to. Lord Belton knows you remember your papa. You can call him what you wish." Robbie's sigh of relief told her she had mollified his worry.

"Mama?"

"Hmm?"

"Would we ever see Lord Knowlton again if you marry Lord Belton?"

The pain of that thought tore through her. "We might see him in town on occasion," she said slowly.

"I will miss him," Robbie confided. "We played chess at his house yesterday and he said I was getting much better."

"You were at Knowlton's house?" She stared at Robbie in surprise.

"He invited me," Robbie said defensively. "I think he wanted to take me to Astley's, but when I told him I had gone already, he suggested we play chess. It took more than an hour for him to beat me."

"I am pleased your chess is improving," she said quietly. Astley's? How like Knowlton to confound her again. It was nearly impossible to conjure up the picture of him there. She was grateful he had not totally forgotten Robbie. She still felt twinges of guilt at having allowed their friendship to develop so last year.

"Atlas is probably ready now," Robbie hinted.

She pulled him close again. "And ponies must come before mothers, I know." Her voice turned serious. "You are certain you would not mind if I marry Lord Belton?"

"No, Mama," he replied, squirming to be free of her arms.

"Ride carefully," she instructed as he headed for the door.

For a brief moment she wondered at Knowlton's purpose in renewing his acquaintance with Robbie; then she firmly resolved to push all thoughts of him from her mind. She had another man to consider.

But try as she might, she simply could not rid her mind of Knowlton. He had the annoying habit of popping into her thoughts whenever she tried to look favorably upon the idea of marriage to Belton. And she feared that the situation would continue if she agreed to marry Belton.

Knowlton closeted himself in the study at the Upper Brook Street for several days, unwilling to make the effort to go out. The simple act of opening the paper filled him with dread, for he daily anticipated seeing in black and white that which he feared most. Robbie's answers had only confirmed what he had long suspected. Any day now, Katherine would be affianced to Belton and lost to him forever. He had seen the closeness between them at the Worthington rout. It was only a matter of time. Knowlton desperately wanted to be able to wish them well, for he desired Katherine's happiness above all. If Belton could provide it . . .

It took no effort to imagine Katherine in several years, laughing and content with a doting Belton at her side and adoring children at her feet. Knowlton sucked in his breath at the sharp stab of pain that scene evoked.

He groaned in despair as the realization hit him. He loved her. It would be laughable if it were not so horribly true. For so long he had thought himself incapable of that emotion. Yet he knew no other word to describe the hold Katherine had over him, the unbearable yearning and need he had for her. His life had been hollow and empty since the day they had parted, and he knew that he would not be at peace again until she was at his side.

He had to have her. But, oh, the price she demanded. Fear clutched his heart. She wanted a boring, respectable marriage. Could he honestly agree to such a thing?

Marriage would require so much of him. More than he had ever given anyone. Companionship. Dependability. Fidelity. The very words made him cringe. He had demonstrated none of those qualities in his five-and-thirty years. Was there any reason to think he could adopt them now? Could he truly change himself to become the type of man Katherine wanted? Was this newly acknowledged feeling strong enough to carry him through?

He was not even certain he knew exactly what marriage would entail. Was it not laughingly said that every woman changed once the ring was safely on her finger? Or that the thrill quickly faded after the honeymoon period had ended? What would ultimately happen to him and Kate if they joined their lives together?

Somers would know. Somers, who had once been as opposed to marriage as he, could tell him what happened after marriage. Did he now have any regrets over taking Elizabeth as his own? Knowlton abruptly jumped from his chair. He knew Somers had intended to spend only a short time in town. Was he still here? Racing into the hall, Knowlton grabbed his hat and gloves, hastening down the front steps for the short walk to the square. Somers was the one person he could trust to tell him the truth.

"Knowlton, how delightful." Elizabeth held out her hand in greeting.

"You are as lovely as ever, my dear." He smiled, bowing low over her hand, relieved to have found the Wentworths still in town. Elizabeth did look well. Was it true that pregnancy made a woman lovelier?

She laughed. "How well you lie. I know I am horridly huge, and with three more months to go. Somers has already taken to calling me 'the whale.'"

"Shall I call him out for the insult?" Knowlton asked, his eyes twinkling.

"A duel?" Somers asked, strolling into the room. "How exciting. Who is the poor fellow?"

"You," Knowlton replied with a grin. "Elizabeth tells me you have been casting grievous insults at her."

"Nonsense," Somers said, planting a fond kiss on his wife's cheek. "You must have misunderstood. Besides, we are leaving for home on the morrow, so I am not free to indulge your thirst for bloodshed."

"Do I have your leave to withdraw the challenge, my lady?"

"Only if you stay to dine with us tonight," she replied. "For I know it will be ages before we see you again. Babies have such an annoying habit of driving all our friends away."

"Then I shall stay," he promised. He looked to Somers. "I should like to have a word with you, if I may. If your lovely wife will excuse us?"

Elizabeth laughed. "I see even the mention of babies sends you fleeing. Go ahead, leave me here with my book. I shall be content."

Somers nodded toward the door. "We can repair to the study." He gave Elizabeth another kiss and followed Knowlton into the hall.

"You sound filled with mystery," Somers said when they had ensconced themselves in the comfortable leather chairs that flanked the fireplace, glasses of brandy in their hands.

"Elizabeth does look marvelous," Knowlton said, unsure how to gain the information he needed without revealing his thoughts to Somers. "Do all women look so when they are . . . ?"

Somers laughed. "You should have seen her over Christmas, when even the sight of breakfast caused her to turn green. I would waken every morning to the sound of her retching in the washbasin."

His blunt description made even Knowlton feel a bit green. "You did not . . . I mean, it did not bother you?"

"How can I complain when I am the cause of it?" Somers smiled smugly.

"Do you ever regret giving up your freedom?" Knowlton asked bluntly.

Somers eyed him with a guarded expression. "I do not think there is a man alive who has not asked himself that question—particularly after a long night spent in the company of a screaming baby. But an honest answer? No. Never."

"Why?" Knowlton leaned forward, eager for the answer.

Somers smiled enigmatically. "It is Elizabeth, pure and simple. I cannot imagine a life without her." He set down his glass and quickly refilled it. "The night Caro was born filled me with sheer terror. I had thought I was well aware of my feelings for Elizabeth, but that night showed me just how deeply they ran. If anything had happened to her, I honestly do not think I could have gone on."

Knowlton did not realize he was nodding in agreement. Somers noted the action and smiled inwardly. The point of this odd conversation became clearer.

"Is it not frightening to feel so strongly?" Knowlton took a careful sip of his brandy.

"It is terrifying," Somers agreed. "But I would not change it for the world. You cannot know the indescribable joy I feel when I wake each morning and find Elizabeth at my side. I would do anything in my power to make her happy, even if I had to lay down my life for her."

Knowlton pondered this in silence. Somers' words echoed his own thoughts about Katherine, confirming his worst fears. It was love, this strange, unfamiliar feeling that had him in its grip. He did not know whether to laugh or cry at the finality of his knowledge.

"It is funny," Somers said thoughtfully, "for I did not realize for the longest time that I loved her. Oh, I knew I admired her and wanted her in a physical way. But it was not until I realized that her happiness was more important than my own—even if that meant she would be lost to me forever—that I finally understood what love really is."

Knowlton stared morosely into his glass. Could he selflessly let Kate walk out of his life, knowing it was best for her? Was his desperate desire to find some way to possess her an indication that he was still more concerned with his own selfish needs?

Somers eyed his closest friend with curious interest. He well remembered the utter panic he had experienced when he had arranged matters to provide Elizabeth with an independent competence, giving her the option to refuse his offer of marriage. There had been that agony of indecision, knowing he was giving her the very excuse to reject his proposal. That she had accepted sometimes seemed nothing short of a miracle to him. And Knowlton's situation could only be worse. Somers had been no angel, but he had cer-

tainly been more discreet in his behavior than Knowlton.
Katherine Mayfield could harbor no illusions about him.

He began to understand the reasons underlying Knowlton's erratic behavior this spring. Why he had been seen
with a new companion at every turn. He was trying to exor-
cize a woman from his mind. Somers shook his head, a
fleeting smile touching his face. Did Knowlton not know
that course was doomed to failure?

He saw Knowlton pour himself another glass and drain
it nearly as quickly. It looked to be a long afternoon. Somers refilled his own glass, remembering the night he had
walked in on Knowlton and Katherine in the library. She
had looked to be a willing participant in that heated embrace. Yet gossip said she was close to wedding another.
He decided to test his theory.

"I understand everyone is looking to Belton for an interesting announcement." Somers watched Knowlton carefully
and did not miss the whitening of his friend's knuckles on
the glass he held.

"So it is said," Knowlton said curtly, taking another large
swallow of brandy.

"It seems a rather odd match," Somers said with feigned
casualness. "Katherine struck me as a bit too spirited for
a prosy fellow like Belton."

"One can never account for taste."

"I had once thought her taste was excellent. A little adventuresome, perhaps, but pointed in the right direction."

Knowlton pierced him with a withering stare.

Somers grinned. "Of course, I might be mistaken. Perhaps she is in the habit of kissing any number of men behind closed library doors."

Somers was tempted to throw up his hands in a defensive
posture against the glare Knowlton directed at him.

"What I think," Somers said, weighing his words carefully, "is that we have a man who thinks he has newly
discovered he has a heart, yet is terrified to find out for
certain. It is odd, since he has never struck me as a cautious
sort before. Perhaps age is beginning to tell."

"If I thought that there was any hope," Knowlton said
finally, "I might be tempted to speak. But I see no point
in pursuing an impossible quest."

"Are you so sure it is impossible?"

Knowlton laughed sardonically. "What woman in her right mind would have anything to do with me?"

"You do have a point," Somers said, torn between amusement and sympathy. "But do you want to go through the rest of your life never knowing the answer? I suspect you will always be plagued by doubt if you do not speak now. Who knows? Perhaps the sun has touched her brain and she will say yes."

"It is not even her refusal that I fear the most," Knowlton said in a low voice. "It is her acceptance. I know I shall disappoint her. I can never be the man she deserves."

"Should not the choice be hers?"

Knowlton shook his head in despair. "I want to believe it is possible. But if I bring her pain, I will never be able to forgive myself."

"One could argue very effectively that she has certainly seen you at your worst," Somers said. "You have put on a striking demonstration this spring of the very definition of the word 'licentious.' "

"Would to God that I could go back and have it to do all over again," Knowlton moaned, the liquor slightly slurring his speech. "Everything, from the very start."

"You cannot, however, so you may as well stop wallowing in self-pity and decide what you can do now to rectify matters," Somers said bluntly.

"I knew I would get consolation if I came to you," Knowlton retorted.

Somers tossed back his head and laughed. "Is that not what friends are for?" He poured more brandy into their glasses. "Elizabeth will probably not speak to me for a week," he said, beginning to feel the effect himself, "but I think the occasion calls for some serious drinking."

Elizabeth was more than a bit disgusted when Somers and Knowlton finally staggered out of the study at the dinner bell. But she bit down on her lip and did her best to ignore their boisterous display at the dinner table. Besides, if she treated Somers too harshly he would never tell her what had transpired to bring them to such a state. And she had an overwhelming desire to know.

Chapter Twenty-Two

How shall ever one like me
　Win thee back again?

—Shelley, *Song*

*K*nowlton groaned aloud at the bright morning light streaming into his room. He was not certain whether to blame himself or Somers for his sad state.

Despite yesterday's talk with Somers, he was still apprehensive about speaking to Kate of his feelings. Somers had almost convinced him he should make the attempt, but in the harsh light of morning Knowlton was no longer as certain.

He had spoken the truth when he said he feared her acceptance more than her rejection. Because that would put the burden of success squarely on his shoulders. And he could not fail. He himself could live with his failure, for his expectations of himself as a doting husband were low. But other people would be relying upon him, and if he failed them, he was not certain he could ever live with himself again. The hero worship he had often glimpsed in Robbie's eyes frightened him silly. Could he take on the mantle of fatherhood and be a success? He was fond of Robbie, but that was not enough to make him a good father. Lord knew, he did not exactly have a shining example from his own childhood to guide him. The thought of the adoration dimming in the boy's eyes made him wince. He could not bear to see that happen.

And Kate. If he failed her . . . how could he ever live with himself? It was enough to send braver men fleeing in terror. He had disappointed her so many times already.

Breaking his promise not to pursue her while she sheltered under his roof. His abominable tormenting of her at that wretched dinner at Somers's. His blatant flaunting of every Cyprian in the town. If she had only heard half the tales of his recent licentiousness, she was certain to have been filled with disgust. How could he possibly think she would ever seriously entertain the thought of a union with him? The idea was ridiculous.

Yet he knew, somehow, that he had to make the attempt. For his sake, more than hers. He felt that Kate was truly his last hope. If he could not acknowledge and live with his love for her, he would never be granted that chance again. She held out to him a great prize—love, tenderness, compassion, and trust. All the emotions that he had scorned through his five-and-thirty years. All emotions he had not thought a necessary component of a man. Yet he now realized that without them, he was less than a man.

What, in all honesty, could he offer her? He knew she had no care for his title. She had lived too long in the shadow of the power of the Winslow name to hold any affection for that. He knew she would have no qualms about his relationship with Robbie. He could not have been fonder of the boy if he was his own son. But with Robbie's future secured by his grandfather and the rekindled contact with that family, Katherine would not be so needing of a male influence in her son's life.

Of course, he offered financial security. Quite a bit more than that, in fact. Katherine would never want for anything material. He would buy her the moon if he could. But with Winslow's patronage, she would not be perched precariously on the edge of poverty anymore. And Knowlton knew her wants were simple. She was no more averse to pretty things than any woman, but she was neither avaricious nor accumulative. Money would not be a critical point with her.

When all his other advantages had been stripped away, there was really only one thing he could offer her that no one else could—himself. And he feared that was the poorest part of the bargain. One rather cynical earl, with a history that would recommend him only to the boldest lady or the most grasping Cyprian. Certainly not a past that would make Katherine confident of the outcome of any connection.

He would do his best to persuade her that his previous actions *were* all in the past. That he yearned to settle for constancy, for it was the only way he could have her—and be able to live with himself. Would words be enough to convince her of his sincerity when he half-feared his ability to fulfill his pledge? If he had time, he could show her that he intended to follow the new course he had laid out for himself. But with Belton hovering in the wings, Knowlton had no time.

His gut wrenched at the thought that perhaps he was already too late. The bets had not been settled yet at White's, but oftentimes a betrothal remained secret at first. What if Belton had already made the offer—and Katherine had accepted? She would be a fool not to. He could go down on his knees before her, baring his soul, humbling himself, only to find that she was no longer free to accept his suit. That would be the worst torture of all. He would have to speak to her. Today.

Katherine did not look forward to today's outing. She had done everything in her power to forestall Belton from pressing her for a decision. If only she could hold him off a little longer . . . But she suspected that the chances for a secluded *tête-à-tête* would be great today, and once he got her alone, there would be no way to deflect his offer. And it would be difficult to put her answer into words.

It would be cruel of her to refuse him, after she had given him every indication all these long weeks that his suit would be welcome. Yet it was better to cause him pain now than to bind him to a lifetime of torture. He was a wonderful man, kind, generous, caring. But she did not love him. Or at least she did not love him in the way she loved Knowlton. She could not sentence herself and Belton to a lifetime of marriage when her heart and soul were given to another.

She would not mind, terribly, having to say no to him. She had never intended to find herself a husband when she had brought Robbie to London. That had been the plan of the marquess and Castalia. Katherine had allowed herself to be swept up in their enthusiasm. It might have been foolish on her part, but she had not anticipated the harm that would come from it. Now there would be hurt enough for everyone.

She at least would have the satisfaction of knowing that she had done the right thing for Robbie by coming to London. She could be filled with pride as she watched him grow to manhood. There were nieces and nephews for her to dote on. Life as Aunt Katherine would not be unpleasant. Moving from country house to country house, she could stay with each member of the family until her welcome had worn off; then she could move on. For herself, she could keep a small cottage as a retreat when the demands of family grew too strong.

And if she was sentencing herself to a life of unbearable loneliness, well, she was the one who would have to live with it. If there were nights when she cried herself to sleep for what might have been, she would have the satisfaction of knowing that she had not dragged another human into her circle of unhappiness.

She dressed carefully for the trip to Richmond, in a round dress of figured gray silk, with a gray velvet pelisse. As she fingered the ribbons of her leghorn bonnet, Katherine allowed her thoughts to drift again. How content she had been a year ago! If it were not for the advantages to Robbie, she would wish the last year had never transpired. Her mind would be the less unsettled for it.

Lord and Lady Durham soon arrived in the barouche. Frederick waited outside while Castalia came to retrieve Katherine. She was grateful they were meeting Belton at the breakfast, knowing she needed to conserve all her strength for the interview she knew would come.

Despite the title of "breakfast," Lady Gresham's party was close to a luncheon, not starting until half-past eleven. The sun had rallied its feeble spring rays to make the event a success, and tables dotted the south lawn, groaning with the weight of the food upon them. When Katherine and Castalia arrived, guests were already helping themselves to the massive repast.

"One would think some had not eaten for a week," Castalia noted as her husband trailed behind them with the carriage rugs. She jabbed the point of the parasol into a spot of ground she declared to be dry, and her obliging husband spread the rugs around.

Katherine casually glanced about the lawn, wondering if Belton had yet arrived. Now that she had made her decision, she was eager to have it over. She determined to make her refusal as gentle as possible.

Frederick had gone to fill their plates when Belton strolled over to Katherine and Castalia.

"A lovely day for a spring outing," he said, doffing his hat. "And here I see we have two of the most enchanting flowers of the season."

"Sheer flummery," Castalia laughed. "But I will accept it gladly. Do join us. Frederick will be back shortly."

"I thought to ask Lady Robert for a few moments of her company," Belton replied. "The grounds are very lovely this time of year."

Katherine sighed inwardly, knowing the time had arrived. "That would be nice. I should like to stretch my legs after the long drive."

Belton obligingly took her arm and they strolled about the gardens, admiring the view of the Thames and appreciating the riot of color afforded by the spring blooms.

Katherine swallowed hard, trying to decide on a proper method of introducing the subject. But she realized there was no simple away around the matter.

"Lord Belton, I—"

"I asked you to call me Richard."

"I . . . I do not think that would be appropriate." Katherine kept her gaze firmly fixed on the distant vista of the river. "For as honored as I am by your declaration, I feel I must decline your offer of marriage."

"I see."

Katherine dared to glance at him, and she winced at the disappointment she saw in his bright blue eyes. Yet, better a slight disappointment now than the crushing one he would later experience if she had accepted his suit. This way, he would be free to find a woman who could return his affection.

"I am sorry," she said, wanting to make certain he knew that he was not the cause of her refusal. "I wish that I could accept. But I fear that I would make you a very poor wife."

"Am I not a better judge of that?" he asked.

She shook her head. "I am not free to love you as a wife ought," she said quietly.

She saw Belton's startled look.

"I had no inkling there was a rival," he said quietly.

Katherine berated herself for having revealed so much. "It is not that, precisely. It is as I said, I do not feel I would be the right wife for you."

"Should not that decision be mine?"

"No," she replied. "For I know myself better than you do. I am very honored that you think me suitable, my lord, but I fear I am not."

She watched his silent sigh with sadness. In other circumstances, such a proposal would have been most welcome. But it was precisely because she thought so well of him that she could not accept his suit.

"I will regretfully accept your decision, then, Lady Robert," he said, offering her his arm.

In silence they walked back toward the spot where Frederick and Castalia sat, and Belton quickly took his leave. Katherine deliberately ignored Castalia's quizzical expression. She wished she had never consented to come to this breakfast.

Knowlton seethed with frustration as he paced back and forth outside the blacksmith's shop. Why, on this of all days, had his horse decided to throw a shoe? He was half-inclined to unhitch his other mount from the curricle and continue to Richmond on horseback, but the foolishness of that plan struck him at once. It would only be scant minutes before his horse was shod and ready to go on. What did it matter that he had been delayed an hour?

His temper was short from impatience and frustration when he finally arrived at Lady Gresham's. He now had the onerous task of locating Katherine, extricating her from her companions, and attempting to convince her in a very short time that her future should be entwined with his. Only a very small task.

He looked first for Belton. It would be a miracle if he had not escorted her here. Knowlton smiled for the first time that morning. He could only imagine how he was to walk up to Belton and ask leave to speak with Katherine alone. Belton would as lief plant him a facer as allow him a moment with Katherine. Knowlton knew he had not imagined the hostility that came over Belton every time he drew near. But Belton or no, he meant to speak with Katherine. Today.

He spotted them at last, Katherine and the Durhams. He was surprised not to find Belton with them. Kate's new family would have no objections to that man as her husband. Would she be willing to fly in the face of their probable opposition and marry him instead? He was much the poorer bargain.

Knowlton shrugged off these new doubts. He strolled over to the gathering, donning a mask of feigned boredom.

"Ladies. Durham." He sensed Durham's cautious appraisal.

"We have seen so little of you of late, Knowlton," Castalia said with a welcoming smile. "Too busy for old friends?"

"You understand the press of the London Season," he said smoothly. "So many obligations . . . so little time." He turned to Katherine. "I had thought, Lady Robert, in recalling your fondness for gardens, that you might like to examine them with me. Lady Gresham prides herself on her narcissi."

Katherine started to decline, but the pleading look in his eyes changed her mind. She extended her hand and he assisted her to her feet.

"I will bring her back in good time," he assured Castalia.

"You are being so mysterious," Katherine said once they were out of earshot of the others. "What dramatic news do you have to impart?"

"You ascribe more significance to my attitude than is necessary," he said lightly. "I did wish you to see the gardens. They are lovely in the spring." He took her gloved hand and placed it on his arm as they strolled past the end of the house.

The walked along the gravel path for some time in silence. Katherine appreciated the display of spring blooms, but hardly thought it worthy of such a conscious effort on Knowlton's part. What was his true purpose?

Not until they were a far distance from the house did Knowlton speak.

"Is Robbie getting along well with his tutor?" It was an inane remark, but he could think of no other topic to start the conversation.

Katherine looked at him with a puzzled expression. He wished to speak to her of Robbie? "He is. Not so much for the work, but he is excited about the prospect of school in the fall."

"And where shall he go? Eton? Harrow?"

"Neither. I have decided he would do best at the school the Duke of Hartford's son is attending in Norfolk. It is small, without the traditions of Eton or Harrow, but he will receive a much better education there."

Knowlton, remembering his life at Eton, agreed. Her wisdom pleased him.

They soon reached the end of the formal garden. Katherine turned, anticipating the return walk, but Knowlton stopped her with a staying hand.

"I should like to talk for a moment," he said. With each passing minute, his cravat felt as if it were tightening about his neck. Much like a hangman's noose.

Katherine looked at him expectantly. He was behaving very oddly today. Was he still uncomfortable about their last encounter? He had apologized most graciously in his note, but perhaps he wished to do so again in person.

"I understand that congratulations may soon be in order." He would not make a fool of himself if it was too late. He could spare himself that embarrassment at least.

She wrinkled her brow in confusion. "Whatever for?"

"The wagering in the clubs says it is only a matter of days before your betrothal to Belton is announced." He watched her carefully, with mingled fear and hope.

"And where does your money lie?" A flash of anger filled Katherine.

"As a lady I know once said, it is folly to wager on the happiness of other people." He clenched and unclenched his hands nervously.

"I am glad you have developed some sense." Katherine grew impatient to return to her friends, if this was all he had to say. Her emotions were already rubbed raw from the uncomfortable conversation with Belton. It was too difficult to keep herself in check, standing here next to Knowlton.

"You have not answered my question."

"What was the question?" She looked him directly in the eye.

He met her gaze without wavering. "Are you going to marry Belton?"

"No," she replied.

Knowlton felt as if he had been holding his breath for the last five minutes. He expelled the air in his chest in a long outrush. It was not too late. Now, if only he could find the right words . . .

"Katherine," he began slowly, "I hope you can appreciate how difficult this is for me. I have done a great deal of thinking these last weeks. Many nights I lay abed, staring at the ceiling, because I was afraid to go to sleep."

"Afraid?"

"Afraid. Because each night I dream of a beautiful red-haired witch who has cast a spell about me. I struggle and fight against it, but to no avail. She has bound me to her with magic as tightly as any rope."

Suddenly intent on his words, Katherine almost forgot to breathe. "I had not thought there were witches in our modern age."

"Neither did I, or I would have taken greater pains to protect myself." He smiled ruefully. "I am well and truly caught now, and there is no hope for me."

Hardly daring to believe what she was hearing, Katherine took a deep breath. "Perhaps if you spoke with your witch, she would free you from her spell."

"I am not certain I wish her to."

The deep longing she saw in his eyes, the nervous smile that flitted across his lips, sent a strange trembling through her.

Knowlton paused, taking her hands in his and bringing them to his chest, drawing her closer, as if he could transmit his intent to her.

"This is probably the most difficult thing I have ever done in my life." He looked down at their joined hands, then lifted his gaze to hers. "I love you, Kate. I am being driven mad with wanting you. I will not know any peace in this life until I can have you with me again." He paused, his gray eyes reflecting mingled hope and fear. "I know I have little to recommend me as a husband, but I am begging you to marry me."

Katherine could not suppress her stunned surprise. "Marry you?"

"If it is what I must do to have you, well then, I shall do it."

The hope that rose within her fell again. "Hardly an enthusiastic declaration."

"Dammit, Kate." His voice was harsh. "What do you want of me? I have wrestled with this for weeks, arguing with myself, telling myself it would only lead to disaster for both of us. But I have not known a day of peace since you left Warrenton, and I know I will never have another until you agree to be my wife."

Katherine gently freed her hands and stepped back a pace. "I do not wish to cast doubts on the sincerity of your motives, Edward," she said slowly, carefully. "But you were certainly able to put on a very convincing demonstration last fall of a man who scorned the idea of marriage."

"I did. Then." There was an edge of panic in his voice. He had known it would be difficult to persuade Kate of his change, but nothing was going as he had planned. She did not sound the least convinced, and he did not know what new words would convince her.

"I want you," he said. "I . . . I simply cannot imagine life without you, Kate."

She turned away so as not to see the pleading look in his eyes. Damn the man! What was she to do? One part of her wished to fling herself into his arms, accepting his offer joyfully. But she was no longer the impetuous child she had once been. What Knowlton proposed was in direct opposition to all he had said and done since she had first met him. Could one man change so, in such a short space of time?

"Kate?"

The note of raw terror in his voice made her turn. He stood there, hands limply at his sides.

"I am frightened, Kate. I am terrified of what you are doing to me, what I want to do with myself." He closed his eyes as if seeking strength. "Help me. Help me through the fear."

Katherine took a step toward him, reaching out her hand to touch his sleeve.

"I am frightened also," she said softly. "Of what loving you could bring. If I let myself believe, only to discover I was in error, I do not know how I could endure."

He clasped her to him in a crushing hug. "Oh, Kate, I swear I will do everything in my power to make you happy." As quickly as he had grabbed her, he held her away at arm's length. "You have my solemn promise that I will never, ever do anything to hurt you."

Katherine's eyes filled with tears. She wanted so much to believe him. But could she ever be truly certain of his faithfulness? The man whose legendary collection of mistresses was the talk of London? Only a fool would take such a man for a husband.

"I know I have not set much of an example of correct behavior these last few months," he said slowly, evenly, his gray eyes wide with the effort. "It was only a vain search to rid my mind of you." He pulled her to his side again. "You have thoroughly ruined me for any other woman, Kate Mayfield. No matter whom I was with, your face and form always intruded upon my mind until all else became a torture."

He looked down at her, his expression filled with tenderness. "Had I thought there time, I would have reformed myself, to show you how I could behave. And if you should like to put me on trial, I would be more than willing to demonstrate my ability to change. But with Belton so assiduous in his attention, I feared there was not time, and I—"

"Hush," Katherine said, placing a finger against his lips. It was that, then, which decided her. His jealousy of Belton. It explained so much of his abominable behavior—it had all been sheer, jealous anger. She laughed at the joy of it. Knowlton. Jealous. For her.

Her laughter sliced painfully through him and he quickly released her, a hurt expression filling his eyes.

"You were jealous!" she exclaimed, beaming in her joy. "It was pure, simple jealousy."

"Of course I was jealous," he said, puzzled by her reaction. "Watching Belton cozying up to you at every opportunity? It nearly drove me mad."

"And are you certain that it is not madness driving you now?" She searched his face, looking desperately for a final sign of his sincerity.

He leaned down and softly brushed her lips with his. "If it is madness, I welcome it gladly."

She stepped back once again, and he saw the apprehension in her eyes. "Lord knows, you have cause to doubt me, Kate. I do not know what else I can do to convince you. I can only ask for your trust."

"If you so much as touch another woman, I will cut your heart out." Her smile belied her words.

"And I will willingly hold the knife for you," he said, pulling her into his arms once again. "My dearest, darling Kate, say you will."

She smiled up at him, her face lit with a radiant joy. "I think, my Lord Knowlton, that you have yourself a wife."

He stopped any further words with a kiss.

Some minutes later, when he at last released her from his arms, Knowlton slipped his arm around her waist and guided her slowly back to the house.

"It there not something you are forgetting, Lady Knowlton-to-be?"

"What is that, Edward?" How wonderful to speak his name again.

"You have yet to say you love me." His voice was low and husky.

"And are you so certain that I do?" Katherine could not resist the impulse to tease him. She loved him all the more for his newly revealed vulnerability.

He stopped and looked at her in mock despair. "Do not say you are marrying me only for my title!"

"Or your money?" Her mouth curved in a teasing smile.

"Or my body?" He raised an impish brow.

Katherine laughed and wrapped her arms about his neck. "I love you, Edward Beauchamp, foolish as I have often thought that to be. I have loved you for a dreadfully long time, and if you love me half as much as I do you, we will deal together famously."

"Impossible," he said, leaning down for another kiss. "No one could possibly be more filled with love than I." He lifted her in his arms and twirled her in dizzying circles. "Kate, Kate, my lovely Kate," he murmured over and over until they were both breathless and laughing with love and hope.

Allison Lane

"A FORMIDABLE TALENT...
MS. LANE NEVER FAILS TO
DELIVER THE GOODS."
—*ROMANTIC TIMES*

THE NOTORIOUS WIDOW
0-451-20166-3

When a scoundrel tries to tarnish a young widow's reputation, a valiant Earl tries to repair the damage—and mend her broken heart as well...

BIRDS OF A FEATHER
0-451-19825-5

When a plain, bespectacled young woman keeps meeting the handsome Lord Wylie, she feels she is not up to his caliber. A great arbiter of fashion for London society, Lord Wylie was reputed to be more interested in the cut of his clothes than the feelings of others, as the young woman bore witness to. Degraded by him in public, she could nevertheless forget his dashing demeanor. It will take a public scandal, and a private passion, to bring them together...

To order call: 1-800-788-6262